Praise for

SMOKE IN THE SUN

———✳———

"A well-written, lavish conclusion to the dreamlike world created in *Flame in the Mist*."   —*School Library Journal*

"A thrilling finale rife with the perils and secrets within the Heian Castle."   —*USA Today's Happy Ever After*

"Readers who devoured . . . *Flame in the Mist* will not want to miss what's next."   —*Entertainment Weekly*

"With admirable brio, Ahdieh serves up intrigues and counterintrigues, battles and betrayals . . . interludes of heated romance . . . Nuanced female characters drive the action."   —*Kirkus Reviews*

"Ahdieh pulls us right back into her lush world filled with gorgeous prose and captivating plot."   —*BuzzFeed*

"If the first book in this duology (*Flame in the Mist*, 2017) was a slow burn, this conclusion is all action . . . Mariko is a heroine worth following to the thrilling conclusion."   —*Booklist*

ALSO BY
RENÉE AHDIEH

——————

The Beautiful

Flame in the Mist

The Wrath & the Dawn
The Rose & the Dagger

RENÉE AHDIEH

SMOKE IN THE SUN

PENGUIN BOOKS

Penguin Books
An imprint of Penguin Random House LLC, New York

First published in the United States of America by G. P. Putnam's Sons, 2018
Published by Penguin Books, an imprint of Penguin Random House LLC, 2019

Visit us online at penguinrandomhouse.com

THE LIBRARY OF CONGRESS HAS CATALOGED THE G. P. PUTNAM'S SONS EDITION AS FOLLOWS:
Names: Ahdieh, Renée, author.
Title: Smoke in the sun / Renée Ahdieh.
Description: New York, NY : G. P. Putnam's Sons, [2018] | Sequel to: Flame in the mist.
Summary: "Mariko must uncover deception in the imperial court and rescue Ōkami, while
preparing for her nuptials"—Provided by publisher.
Identifiers: LCCN 2018007928 | ISBN 9781524738143 (hardback) |
ISBN 9781524738150 (ebook)
Subjects: | CYAC: Courts and courtiers—Fiction. | Sex role—Fiction. | Brothers
and sisters—Fiction. | Weddings—Fiction. | Samurai—Fiction. | Conduct of
life—Fiction. | Japan—History—Tokugawa period, 1600–1868—Fiction.
Classification: LCC PZ7.1.A328 Smo 2018 | DDC [Fic]—dc23
LC record available at https://lccn.loc.gov/2018007928

Penguin Books ISBN 9781524738167

Printed in the United States of America

Design by Eileen Savage   Text set in Apollo MT Pro

10 9 8 7 6 5 4 3 2 1

For girls around the world:
You inspire me every day.

As swift as the wind

As silent as the forest

As fierce as the fire

As unshakable as the mountain

"Truth is not what you want it to be; it is what it is. And you must bend to its power or live a lie."

—Miyamoto Musashi

A Good Death

———— ✳ ————

S omber clouds waited above, like specters.

Most of the people had donned funereal grey. Their heads were lowered in respect, their voices hushed. Even the smallest of children knew better than to ask why.

This was the honor afforded their recently deceased emperor. The honor of their extreme reverence and their unwavering love. A reverence—a love—the girl did not feel in her heart.

Nevertheless, she kept silent. Appeared to follow suit, though her hands were balled at her sides. She watched from the corner of her eye as the funeral procession wound through the muted streets of Inako. As a light rain began to fall from a dreary silver sky. Her woven sandals soon became wet. The fabric of her plain trousers clutched at her calves.

Her left fist tightened around the rock in her hand.

The drums marching out the processional beat drew closer, their low thunder reverberating in her ears. The reedy melody of the *hichiriki* split through the rising din of the rain.

When the imperial guards posted along the lane turned their gazes toward the crowd, the people bowed with haste, afraid they might be disciplined for any slight, however small. Those in the girl's vicinity bowed lower as the spirit tablet leading the procession shifted into view. Tendrils of smoke from the agarwood incense suffused the air with the scent of burning cedar and warm sandalwood. Etched on the tablet's stone surface were the names of many past emperors—the deceased heavenly sovereigns of the Minamoto clan.

The girl did not bow. She kept her eyes lifted. Locked on the spirit tablet.

If she was caught, it would be tantamount to a death sentence. It would be the height of disrespect—a stain of dis-honor on her family and all those who followed in their footsteps. But honor had never held much weight for her.

Especially not in the face of injustice.

For a final time, the girl clenched her fingers around the rock. Rubbed the sweat from her palm into its roughened surface. Took aim.

And launched it at the spirit tablet.

It struck the center of the grey stone with a sharp *crack*.

A stunned silence descended upon the crowd as those bearing the tablet swayed for a suspended moment. They watched in horror when the tablet crashed to the dirt in several pieces.

A single cry of outrage bled into many. Though there was no love lost between the fallen emperor and the people of the Iwakura ward, this act was an affront to the gods themselves. The samurai guarding the procession reared their horses and charged into the crowd. A collective stammer arose from the people, much like the drone of a beehive on the cusp of exploding. Trembling fingers pointed in all directions, stabbing accusations anywhere and everywhere.

But the girl was already on the move.

She lunged into the shadows behind a small apothecary shop. Her hands shook from the energy pulsing beneath her skin as she yanked a mask above the lower portion of her face. Then the girl grabbed the edge of a pine eave and braced her foot against a stained plaster wall. With lightning precision, she vaulted onto the tiled rooftop.

The shouts from below grew louder.

"There he is."

"That's the one who threw the rock."

"That boy over there!"

The girl almost smiled to herself. But she did not have time for the luxury of emotion. With fleet-footed steps, she raced toward the ridgeline of the roof, then slid down the sloping tile on the other side. The pounding of hooves to her right drove the girl toward the rooftop at her left. She leapt over the yawning space between the two structures and tucked her body into a roll. Even with these cautionary measures, a painful shudder rippled from her heels up her spine.

As she flew across the curved tiles—using the arches of

her feet to grip their damp surface—an arrow hissed by her ear. Like a cascade of water, the girl slid to the roof's edge and dropped into the shadows below.

A quick beat was spent in contemplation. Her chest heaved as she took in one breath. Then two. She needed to get more distance. Blinking back the rain, the girl darted into an alleyway, skirting a discarded cabbage cart in the process.

A sudden rush of footfall rose from her left.

"There he is."

"Over by the alley next to the forge!"

Her heartbeat crashed through her ears as she tore around the corner, the clatter of footsteps drawing closer. There was no place to hide, save for a rain barrel propped against a wall of the dilapidated forge. She would be caught if she lingered for even a moment longer.

Her eyes darting to the four corners of the earth, the girl made a quick decision. As nimble as a cat, she levered her back against a wooden post and kicked upward once, twice. Her body quaking from the effort, she wedged a foot into the crook of a support beam. Then the girl flipped over, pressing her shoulders into the rough straw of the roof's underbelly.

Her sight blurred from fear as a soldier came into view just beneath her. If he looked up, all would be undone. The soldier glanced around before shoving his sandaled foot against the rain barrel. It tumbled aside with a thud, the rain within it joining the mud in a delayed splash. Frustration forced a huff of air past the soldier's lips.

Close by, an unintelligible shout of fury rang out into the sky.

As the soldier's ire grew, the girl squeezed her body tight, the effort straining her core. She was lucky the training she undertook daily had honed her limbs into such lithe lines. Had made her aware of every muscle, every gesture. She held her breath, locking her fingers and feet into place.

The soldier kicked the barrel a final time before racing back into the streets.

After several moments had passed, the girl finally allowed herself to relax. Permitted her body to seek a more comfortable position. She stayed hovering in the shadows until the sounds of tumult melted into the pounding rain. Then—with deliberate care—she reached for the wooden post and let her feet sink into the muck with a muffled thud. The girl straightened, removing the mask from her face.

As she turned to leave, the door leading to the enclosed portion of the forge slid open. Startled by the sound, the girl let the mask fall from her hand into the mud.

Before her stood a woman with greying temples and an unforgiving stare.

Though the girl's features remained expressionless, her heartbeat faltered in her chest.

The woman would be near her mother's age, if the girl had to guess. If she shouted a single word, the girl would be caught. Fear keeping her immobile, the girl stayed silent as the woman inhaled slowly, her eyes narrowing in understanding.

Then she jerked her chin to the left, directing the girl to flee.

Bowing with gratitude, the girl vanished into the rain.

She doubled back countless times as she wove through the rain-slicked streets of the Iwakura ward, ensuring no one could follow her footsteps. When she neared an arched stone bridge—crossing into a grove of snow-white dogwood and pale pink cherry trees—her gait took on a different cadence. Her shoulders dropped, and her neck lengthened. It was automatic, the moment the scent of night-blooming jasmine curled into her nostrils.

Still she did not use any of the main thoroughfares, save for the bridge itself. Concealed beneath a shower of dying petals, she hailed a *jinrikisha* and settled under its worn canvas canopy. Her eyes shuddered closed, and her lips parted as they silently counted each of her breaths.

Ichi.

Ni.

San.

Shi.

Then the girl lifted her chin. With deft motions, she restored her disheveled clothing until nothing appeared amiss. Reformed the topknot at the crown of her head into an elegant coif. Like the gifted quick-change artist she'd been trained to be, the girl transformed from a daring boy into a demure mystery. When she finally arrived at the teahouse gate, she knocked twice, pausing for a beat before rapping her fist five more times in quick succession. A shuffle of feet and a series of whispers emanated from beyond the gate door before it swung open.

Though these servants knew to unlatch the door at this series of knocks, no one was there to meet the girl, as she'd expressly requested. So none of them would ever be forced to lie about having seen her. The girl's misfortunes were not worth the lives of all the young women here, and the cost of asking them to harbor her secrets was far too great.

She made her way across the polished stones of the garden, past the burbling brook and its three miniature waterfalls, into a music of tinkling laughter and lilting *shamisen*. Then she floated by the elegant bonsai garden to walk behind the teahouse itself, toward a smaller structure nearby. Outside an intricately carved sliding door, her trusted maidservant, Kirin, stood waiting, a carafe of clean water in her hands.

Kirin bowed. The girl returned the gesture.

As the girl removed her sandals, the freckled maid-servant pushed open the silk-screened sliding door leading into a chamber flanked by two large *tansu* chests crafted of red cedar and black iron. The girl stepped over the raised threshold and took a seat before a polished silver surface positioned behind rows of dainty cosmetics and glass vials.

She stared at her reflection. At the elegant lines of her face. The ones that concealed her so well within these walls.

"Would you care to have a bath drawn?" Kirin asked.

"Yes, please," the girl replied without looking away.

The maidservant bowed once more. Turned to leave.

"Kirin?" The girl swiveled in place. "Has anything been delivered to the *okiya* in my absence?"

"I'm sorry." Kirin shook her head. "But no messages have come for you today, Yumi-*sama*."

Asano Yumi nodded. Returned her gaze to her mirror.

Her brother, Tsuneoki. would seek her out soon. She was certain of it. Following Ōkami's surrender in the forest three days ago, she and Tsuneoki could no longer afford to remain idle, darting between shadows, leaving whispers in their wake. Nor could they continue to allow their painful past to direct the course of their future. It was true Yumi's elder brother had hurt her. Deeply. With his lies about who he was. With his blind insistence that he alone possessed the answers. That he alone made the choices.

Though his choices left Yumi alone and apart, always.

Years ago, Tsuneoki's negligence had driven Yumi to scale the walls of her perfumed prison and take flight across the curved tiles. Her brother's stubborn conceit had given her wings. And with them, she would fly, anywhere and everywhere.

Absentmindedly, Yumi toyed with the alabaster lid of a jar filled with beeswax and crushed rose petals.

Her brother wore his smiles like she wore these paints. A grinning mask, concealing fury and heartbreak. Their mother used to say they should be careful of the masks they chose to wear. For one day, those masks could become their faces. At this warning, Tsuneoki would often cross his eyes and slide his tongue between his bared teeth, like a snake. Yumi would double over with laughter at the sight. When they were young, her brother had always made her laugh. Always made her believe.

Before the day it all ended, like a flame being doused in the wind.

The lid clattered off the top of the cosmetics jar, startling Yumi from her thoughts. She met her gaze in the mirror. Blinked back the suggestion of tears. Set her jaw.

It was time for the Asano clan to mete out their justice.

A justice ten years in the making.

Yumi thought again of the rock she'd held in her hand. Though the incident had occurred only this morning, it felt like a world away. She recalled the cries of outrage emanating from the crowd. They saw her actions as foolish. But they were afraid, and they'd built their lives upon this fear. It was time to dismantle it from within. Strike it down at its very foundation.

So Yumi had begun with a rock. The sound it had made as it struck the emperor's spirit tablet reverberated through her ears. The first of many battle cries to come.

She could still feel the grit on her palm.

It was time for the Asano clan to restore justice to the Empire of Wa.

Or die trying.

A Mask of Mercy

✳

Outside a ramshackle forge in the Iwakura ward, a patrolling foot soldier came across a black mask half buried in the mud.

Rage clouded his vision. A rage quickly consumed by fear. He'd searched here earlier. The evidence of his efforts—an overturned rain barrel—mocked him as it sank deeper into the mud with each passing moment. If anyone discovered that he'd allowed the boy wearing the mask to escape, the soldier would be punished. Swiftly and surely.

He moved to tuck the mask into his sleeve just as signs of motion caught his eye. A lantern blinked to life behind a dirty rice-paper screen near the back of the forge. The soldier's gaze narrowed. In four steps, he smashed his foot through the fragile wood-and-paper door.

A woman with a small child sat at a table, poring over a scroll of wrinkled parchment. Teaching her son to read. She appeared careworn and overtired, and the young boy kneeling before the low table had eyes that shone like oiled pewter.

Without hesitation, the woman stepped before her son, positioning her body as a shield. She glanced at the muddy mask in the soldier's hand, her downturned eyes widening briefly, but distinctly.

It was not an expression of surprise. But rather one of understanding.

One of recognition.

That moment of clarity made the soldier's next decision for him. It would not do for anyone to discover he had allowed the boy wearing the mask—the traitor who had dared to throw a stone at the emperor's funeral procession—to escape.

With a slash of his sword, the soldier eliminated the cause of his concern. Silenced the woman's voice in a single stroke. As the boy watched his mother crumple lifeless to the packed earth floor, he began to tremble, his pewter eyes pooling with tears.

Uncertainty gripped the soldier for the space of a breath.

No. It would not do for him to take this young life as well. A young life that could one day serve the cause of their divine emperor perhaps even better than he.

So the soldier lifted a finger to his lips. Smiled with benevolence. A mercy that melted away the last remaining traces of guilt. Then he ruffled the boy's hair and flicked the blood from his blade before leaving the way he came.

As he crossed into the deepening darkness beyond the old forge, the soldier raised his chin. The clouds churned above, causing his stomach to knot as if he were in battle. Perhaps it would be wise for him to send someone to check in on the boy at the forge later. Another woman, perhaps. Someone . . .

A frown settled on his face.

No. The boy was not his responsibility. When the soldier had been the boy's age, he had been able to care for himself and his two younger sisters. The boy undoubtedly had family of his own. After all, that forge was not manned by his mother. Imagine! A woman working an anvil. Stoking a bellows. Shaping a sword!

The soldier laughed under his breath. The soft rasp grew louder as the knot in his stomach pulled tight. As a low hum began droning through his eardrums.

His laughter became a cough.

A cough that stole his breath.

The soldier bent at the waist, bracing his palms on his knees. He began to shake as he struggled to take in air. A trembling seized his body until it gripped him at his core. The hum rose through the space around him, keening in his ears.

Forcing him to the ground.

The last thing he remembered was a mask caked in dark mud.

Beside an overturned rain barrel, a fox with yellow eyes watched a foot soldier collapse in the streets of the Iwakura ward and writhe through the mud with a soundless scream.

It grinned slowly. Knowingly. Its sinister task complete. Its dark magic weaving above the earth.

Then it vanished in a twist of smoke.

ᴛall and ᴘroud and ʜapless

———✹———

This was a scene from a story she'd heard before.

A young woman in her rightful place, ensconced at the Golden Castle. Betrothed to the son of the emperor's favorite consort. Bestowing honor on the Hattori name.

The scented water in the wooden *furo* felt the same as it did at home. Like heated silk sliding across her skin. The hands scrubbing at Mariko's arms and shoulders did so in much the same way they'd done at home—without mercy, until her pale skin shone like that of a newborn child, pink and raw and perfect. A servant with permanent lines of judgment marring her brow yanked a comb inlaid with mother-of-pearl through Mariko's hair in much the same way her nursemaid had when she was younger.

It all felt so similar.

But if Mariko could be certain of nothing else now, she could be certain her life would never be the same again.

Under her brother's watchful care, they'd arrived in Inako late last night. To an imperial city cloaked in mourning. To streets teeming with whispers. Today was the funeral of their emperor, who had died suddenly, beneath a veil of suspicion. Upon discovering his body, the empress's wailing was said to have been heard across all seven *maru*. Even beyond the castle's iron-and-gold-plated double gates. She'd screamed murder. Raged at all those nearby, accusing them of treachery. It had taken a flock of maidservants to soothe her and begin ushering her toward her tears.

Toward final whimpers of resignation.

But beneath this hushed intensity seethed something sinister. Last night—when the second pair of gates leading to the castle had creaked closed behind their convoy—the air around Mariko had stilled. The faint breeze blowing past the woven screen of her *norimono* had sighed a final sigh. An owl had blared across the firmament, its cry ringing off the stone walls.

As though in warning.

Here in Inako, Mariko would not be granted a moment's respite. Nor did she wish for one. She would not allow herself anything of the sort.

For deep in the bowels of the same castle, the last in a line of celebrated shōgun awaited his impending doom: the final judgment of the imperial city. And the lies this city wore— lies cloaked in silk and steel—shimmered beneath the surface, ready to take shape. No matter the cost, Mariko would mold them into what they should have been from the start:

The truth.

She bit down hard on nothing. Braced herself for the coming fight. It would be unlike any Ōkami and the Black Clan had prepaired her for in Jukai forest. In this fight, she would not have weapons of wood and metal and smoke at her disposal. She would instead be armed with nothing more than her mind and her own mettle. This would be precisely the kind of fight she'd unknowingly prepared for as a child, when she'd pitted herself against her brother, Kenshin.

In a game of wits against brawn.

Here in Inako, Mariko's armor would not be hardened leather and an ornamented helmet. It would be perfume and powdered skin. She had to persuade Prince Raiden—her betrothed—to trust her. She needed him to cast her as the hapless victim instead of the willing villain.

Though I plan to be a villain in all ways.

If it took everything from Hattori Mariko—even her very life—she would not allow those she loved to fall prey to those set on destroying them. She would learn the truth about who had conspired to kill her that day in the forest. Why they attempted to frame the Black Clan for the deed. And what deeper cause lay beneath their designs.

Even if those at the heart of the matter were the imperial family itself.

Even if her own family might fall into the crosshairs.

The thought sent a chill through her bones, as though the water in the *furo* had suddenly turned to ice.

Kenshin's choice had been made long before he'd marched

into Jukai forest flying their family crest alongside that of the emperor. Even before he'd let soldiers loose arrows around his only sister in a shower of fire and ash. He was a samurai, and a samurai followed the orders of his sovereign, to the death. He did not ask questions.

His pledge was one of unswerving conviction.

But Mariko's time with the Black Clan had taught her the cost of blind faith. She refused to align the Hattori name with that of the shiftless nobles in the imperial city. The same nobles intent on lining their pockets and gaining influence at the expense of the downtrodden. The same people they'd sworn to protect, like the elder woman who cared for the children in the Iwakura ward, who depended upon Ōkami and the Black Clan for support.

Protect.

Mariko drew her knees to her chest, shielding her heart, preventing the worst of her thoughts from taking root.

What if Ōkami is already dead?

She tightened the grip on her knees.

No. He isn't dead. He can't be. They will want to make a show of his death.

And I will be there to protect him when they do.

It was strange to think Mariko possessed the power to protect someone she loved. She'd never known the right words to do so before. Never known how to wield the right weapons. But ingenuity could be a weapon, in all its forms. Her mind could be a sword. Her voice could be an axe.

Her fury could ignite a fire.

Protect.

Mariko would never allow Ōkami—the boy who had stolen her heart in the dead of the night, deep within a forest of rustling trees—to lose all he'd fought to regain. Nor would Mariko allow herself to lose anything she loved. She'd watched from the shadows as Kenshin had permitted soldiers to descend on her in Jukai forest. Felt the pang of her brother's betrayal with each of his questioning glances. She'd bitten her tongue as these same soldiers had forced Ōkami to kneel in the mud and surrender. As they'd taunted and derided him from their lofty perches.

Mariko swallowed, the bitterness coating her throat.

Never again. I will protect you, no matter the cost.

"Look at your nails." The creases across the servant's brow deepened as she spoke, cutting through Mariko's deliberations. Her admonition conjured more memories of Mariko's childhood. "It's as though you've been digging through mud and stone all your life." She *tsk*ed, inspecting Mariko's fingers even further. "Are these the hands of a *lady* or a scullery maid?"

Mariko's sight blurred as she gazed at her scarred knuckles. Another pair of hands took shape in her mind's eye, its calloused fingers intertwined with hers. Laced together. Stronger for it.

Ōkami.

Mariko blinked. Organized the chaos of her thoughts into

something coherent. She bit her lip and widened her eyes. "The Black Clan . . . they made me work for them." Her voice sounded small. Insignificant. Exactly as she intended.

The servant chuffed in response, her expression still dubious. "It will take the work of an enchantress to repair this damage." Her words remained harsh, unmoved by the sight of Mariko's feigned timidity. Strangely—though this woman's rebuke was in no way comforting—it nevertheless warmed Mariko. It brought to mind her mother's quiet, ever-present judgment.

No. Not just that.

The servant reminded her of Yoshi.

At the thought of the grumbling, good-natured cook, Mariko's eyes began to water in earnest.

The servant watched her, an eyebrow peaking into her forehead.

That time, the sight of the older woman's judgment spurred a different reaction.

Anger roiled beneath Mariko's skin. She snatched her hand away and averted her gaze, as though she were afraid. Ashamed. The servant's stern expression lost some of its severity. As though Mariko's embarrassment was an emotion she could understand and accept. When she next took hold of Mariko's hand, her touch was careful. Almost soft.

In the same instant Mariko fought to curb her anger, she paused to take note.

My fear—even when it is feigned—has more weight when it is matched alongside anger.

One of the young women assisting the gruff servant bowed beside the wooden tub before lifting a pile of muddied, fraying clothing into the light. "My lady, may I dispose of these?" Her round face and button nose squinched in disgust.

They were the garments Mariko had worn in Jukai forest, when she'd been disguised as a boy. She'd refused to discard the faded grey *kosode* and trousers, even at Kenshin's behest. They were all she had now. Her eyes widening in what she hoped to be a sorrowful expression, Mariko shook her head. "Please have them washed and stored nearby. Though I long more than anything to forget what happened to me, it is important to keep at least one reminder of the consequences when a wrong turn is taken in life."

The ill-tempered elder servant harrumphed at her words. Another young girl in attendance grasped one of Mariko's hands and began scrubbing beneath her nails with a brush fashioned from horsehair bristles. As she worked, the servant with the round face and button nose poured fine emollients and fresh flower petals across the surface of the steaming water. The colors of the oil shimmered around Mariko like fading rainbows. A petal caught on the inside of her knee. She dipped her leg beneath the water and watched the petal float away.

The image reminded her of what the old man at the watering hole had said the night she'd first met the Black Clan, disguised as a boy. He'd told her she had a great deal of water in her personality. Mariko had been quick to disagree with him. Water was far too fluid and changeable. Her mother had always said Mariko was like earth—stubborn and straight-forward to a fault.

I need to be water now, more than ever.

Mariko wondered what had become of the Black Clan after Ōkami had surrendered to her betrothed. Wondered how Yoshi and Haruki and Ren and all the others had fared following such a dire blow. Only three nights past, they'd learned their leader had been deceiving them for years. He was not in fact the son of Takeda Shingen. The boy they'd followed and called Ranmaru for almost a decade was instead the son of Asano Naganori. He'd assumed the role of Takeda Ranmaru to protect his best friend and make amends for his father's betrayal—a betrayal that had resulted in the destruction of both their families. This boy's real name was Asano Tsuneoki.

They'd all been deceived.

And Mariko's betrothed—Prince Raiden—had left the forest with a prize worthy of laying at his father's burial mound.

The true son of Takeda Shingen, the last shōgun of Wa: Ōkami.

Resentment smoldered hot and fast in Mariko's chest. Guilt coiled through her stomach. She dared to sit in a pool of scented water, allowing her skin and hair to be brushed and polished to perfection while so many of those she cared about suffered untold fates?

She took a steadying breath.

This was necessary. This was the reason she'd asked Kenshin to bring her to Inako. If Mariko intended to act on the plans she'd formulated while journeying from Jukai forest to the imperial city, she had to be in the seat of power. Mariko had to find a way to free Ōkami. She had to convince her betrothed that she was the willing, simpering young woman he surely desired in a bride. Then—once she'd earned a measure of trust—she could find a way to begin feeding information to the outside. To those who fought to change the ways of the imperial city and restore justice to its people.

To topple evil from its vaunted pedestal.

"Stand," the servant demanded in a curt tone.

Respect for an elder—regardless of status—drove Mariko to obey the truculent woman without question. She let the woman lead her to the largest piece of polished silver she'd ever seen in her life. Her eyes widened at the sight of her naked body reflected back at her.

Her time in Jukai forest had changed Mariko on the outside as well. The angles of her face were more pronounced. She was thinner. What had been willowy before was now honed. Muscles she'd not known she'd possessed moved as she moved, like ripples across a pond.

She was stronger now, in more ways than one.

The elderly servant *tsk*ed again. "You're as thin as a reed. No young man will want to caress skin and bones, least of all one like Prince Raiden."

Again the urge to react rose in Mariko's throat. Though she could not really discern the reason for the woman's distain, she suspected the servant believed a girl who lived among bandits did not deserve to marry into the imperial family. Did not merit the attention of a prince. The truth blazed bright within her. She was more than an object of any man's desire. But on this particular score, the servant was right. She did need to eat if she intended to play the part.

Be water.

Mariko smiled through gritted teeth. Let her lips waver as though she were exhausted. Weak. "You're right. Please do whatever you can—whatever magic you possess—to restore me to my past self. To the sort of young woman who might please the prince. I want nothing more than to forget what happened to me." She struggled to stand taller. Fought to look proud.

Though the creases on her features deepened, the servant nodded. "My name is Shizuko. If you do as I say, it is possible we can remedy the effects of this . . . misfortune."

Mariko slid her arms into the proffered silken undergarment. "Make me fit for a prince, Shizuko."

Shizuko sniffed and cleared her throat before directing the other servant girls to come forward. In their arms were bolts of lustrous fabric. Piles of brocade and painted silk, wrapped in sheets of translucent paper. Trays of jade and silver and tortoiseshell hairpieces.

Mariko ran the tip of a finger down the needled point of a silver hairpiece. Recalled one of the last times she had held one in her hand.

The night she'd pierced it through a man's eye for attacking her.

Mariko knew what she needed to do. For the sake of those she held dear, she needed to appear tall and proud.

And hapless.

She spoke in a near whisper, as though her words were nothing but an afterthought. "The imperial family will need me to appear strong, just as they are."

Just as they will need to be.

Because Hattori Mariko had a plan.

And this unwitting woman had already provided her with the first piece of the puzzle.

The Ox and the Rat

———— ✦ ————

Theirs was a complicated relationship.

One built on a bower of hatred, shaped on a foundation of deceit. A relationship rooted in the designs of two young mothers, who'd both raised their sons to share in their mutual enmity, while they'd vied for the attention of a bored sovereign. Yearned for him to bestow his favor upon them.

One mother had played the game well, but she had begun the match with advantages, both seen and unseen. A slender sylph of a woman, she'd captured the heart of the would-be emperor many years ago. A woman with wiles beyond her beauty and magic sliding through her veins. She'd conjured his dreams into reality. Taught him to commune with creatures and collect secrets in the shadows. A woman who'd shown him what it meant to love and be loved. Kanako, who had birthed the emperor's firstborn son, Raiden. Kanako, who had been relegated to second place in his life, despite her dominance in the emperor's heart.

The other woman had been foisted upon the emperor by duty and family. She—with her million-*koku* domain of a dowry—had weighed and preyed upon him, stealing him away from his true love. But he had made her pay for it. For years, the empress Genmei had ruled a lonely roost of tittering minions and nothing more, though she'd been fortuned to bear the crown prince, Roku.

These two women had raised their sons to hate each other.

Yet despite the efforts of their warring mothers, an unlikely kinship had formed between the half brothers.

The spring of his tenth year, Raiden broke a leg when he fell off his horse. While his wound mended, tiny Roku spirited away sweets for him, hidden in his silken kimono sleeve. Then—when Roku caught a perilous illness as a boy of eleven—Raiden sat by his bedside, telling him bawdy stories Roku did not yet understand.

But the younger brother had laughed anyway.

Their mothers had continued whispering in their ears and frowning at their shared smiles, but the two brothers had clasped tight to their bond, forging a lasting friendship. What began as a tentative childhood trust grew more steadfast of late. Yet those who persisted in murmuring at their heels often wondered if the two half brothers had yet to face a true test of their bond.

The test of might versus right.

The ox against the rat. One a creature of industry, the other a creature of ingenuity. Two sides of the same misbegotten coin.

Tonight the two sons of Emperor Minamoto Masaru, stood together in a pool of crackling torchlight, in the lowest reaches of Heian Castle. The taller, elder brother leaned against the stone wall, his burnished armor mirroring bright flame. The smaller, wilier brother paced slowly before a set of stone stairs descending into darkness, his silks pristine and lustrous even in the dimmest reaches of the castle.

"Raiden," the new heavenly sovereign of. Wa said, his back to his brother.

His posture alert, Raiden pushed away from the wall. "My sovereign."

"I know you have questions."

A thoughtful expression crossed the elder brother's face. "Concerns more than questions."

"Ah, but you forget: concerns are for the uncertain." Roku smiled to himself, his back still turned. "And questions for the ill-bred."

Raiden's cool laughter sliced through the stillness. "I suppose I deserved that. Father would be proud to hear you remind me."

"Even if he lacked in many ways, our father always did have a cutting remark at the ready." Roku turned in place and glanced at his elder brother. "But I am not interested in having anyone openly challenge me, brother." His tone was a warning, his features tight.

Raiden crossed his arms, the hardened leather of his breastplate creaking with the motion. "I do not wish to challenge you in the main. I only wish to spare you strife."

"Then cease with being the cause of it." The smooth skin of Roku's forehead creased once. "Our father perished under questionable circumstances, and it is of great importance that we learn who is responsible for his untimely death. Failing to appear strong at this moment—failing to assert my sovereignty over all those who watch like prowling owls—will forever taint my reign. Decisive action is necessary, and I expect you to lead by example, with unwavering obedience." His back straight and his chin proud, Roku shifted toward the stone staircase to begin his descent. A hand moved to stay him. One of the few hands still permitted to touch him with impunity.

"You believe this boy is responsible for Father's death?" Raiden asked.

Roku did not answer. Merely shrugged off his half brother's hand.

"This is beneath you, Roku." Raiden's voice was soft.

The young emperor arched a brow as though in warning.

A smile curved up one side of Raiden's face. "My *sovereign*," he amended, shifting back to bow.

"It is never beneath a true leader to face his enemy." Roku took another step downward, his brother raising a torch to illumine the way. The light danced across the timber-bound stones. "I wish to look upon the face of Takeda Shingen's only son and learn what kind of blood flows through his veins.

What kind of fear lurks behind his eyes." His smile was strangely serene, like ice braced against a howling wind.

Raiden followed closely, his attempts to marshal both his words and his thoughts all too apparent. "If you don't believe him responsible for Father's death, why must you know anything about him? Simply end him and be done with it."

"I never said I believed him innocent, brother. The boy emerged from hiding within days of the emperor's untimely death."

"A coincidence. We drew him out of the forest."

"I do not believe in coincidences." A moment passed in silence before Roku spoke again. "Do you remember the water obelisk Father brought back for us from the west when we were small?"

"The device that reflected the time of day? It broke two days later. We were both punished for it."

"It did not break. I took it apart."

Raiden paused in consideration. "You wished to see how it worked?"

"Perhaps." Roku met his elder brother's gaze. "Or perhaps I wished to know what lay at its core."

"You enjoyed breaking it, then."

"Never something quite so infantile, brother." Roku laughed softly. "I find it easier to control something when it is in pieces. The Black Clan, the son of Takeda Shingen, any enemy who would see our family fail . . . " His voice drifted into nothingness as he took another step down.

Raiden sighed, his frustration winning out. "Takeda Ranmaru is not your enemy. Believe me when I say the lore has bloated the boy's reputation far past reason." His lips curled into a sneer. "He has lived in the forest among drunken peasants for the better part of a decade. He's a thief and a wastrel. Nothing more."

Like a whip from the darkness, Roku's words lashed from his lips. "That wastrel is the son of the man who thwarted our father and defied our family for years. Lord Shingen led the last uprising in our land."

"That does not mean his son will amount to anything. I bested him without even once raising a sword in his direction." The torch in Raiden's right hand flared as a gust of acrid air blew around them.

Undeterred, Roku continued, his smile once more composed. "I've said this before, but your arrogance does not serve you well, brother."

"Your curiosity here will not serve you well either, my sovereign," Raiden said. "Allow me to simply kill him. Let us be done with him, quickly and quietly."

Roku linked his hands behind his back. "Even if he proves innocent, a spectacle should be made of his death."

"Very well, then. We can drown him in Yedo Bay. Upside down, as Father did with Asano Naganori. Or stretch him from the ramparts until his arms split from his sides."

"Eventually," Roku agreed. "But not yet. It does nothing to merely chop down a weed. One must tear it out by the roots." He closed his eyes as though the motion would clear his mind. Lend clarity to his thoughts. "This was the mistake our father made. He did not wish to unearth the seed of Takeda Shingen's discord. He did not take the time to reduce his enemy to pieces, and it resulted in his death." His eyes flashed open as a shadow fell across his face, like storm clouds gathering over a lake. "I will be a better emperor than our father. I will find every last one of these weeds and tear them out by their very roots." He spoke the last softly, in a voice tinged with menace.

When Raiden replied, it was with great care. "Perhaps you are right, my sovereign. No one can deny that the Takeda family has been a problem, ever since Lord Shingen questioned our father's designs for the empire." He inhaled through his nostrils. "But perhaps if we learn to control his son—or even sway him to our side—it could be possible to do what our father failed to do, and unite our land."

Roku considered his brother as though he were considering a foolish child. One for whom he held fond feelings. "Unite our land?" His features hardened for an instant, a caustic laugh bursting from his lips. "I know where my strengths lie. Do you?"

"My strengths are in serving and protecting my sovereign." A cold light sparked in Raiden's eyes. "And enacting vengeance on those who seek to destroy us."

"If you wish to protect me, brother, you must learn how to exert control over those around you." Roku took an apprising breath. "Vengeance will come in time. Control is what I seek. Fear will be my weapon."

Understanding settled onto Raiden's face. "You wish to control Takeda Ranmaru through fear."

Roku nodded. "First we must give him reason to fear—not about something as simple as death. Something deeper. And that task begins with the mind. If I wish for the people of Wa to respect me without question, this must be my course of action."

Raiden paused in thought. "You are concerned your people will not respect you? They will, because you are their heavenly sovereign. It is their duty and your right."

"No, brother." Roku shook his head. "Respect is not a thing granted. It is a thing earned." With that, he quickened his stride over the last few stone steps and glided to a halt. Allowing time for his eyes to adjust, he began murmuring to a wall of darkness before him.

Like a ghost, a man emerged from the reaches beyond. Between his skeletal hands rested a small wooden trunk, bound in bars of dull iron. At first glance, the iron seemed to be marred by rust, but the hint of something far more sinister pervaded the air, like the scent of copper left too long in the rain. The man bowed, his cowl falling lower across a forehead peppered with burn marks. Without a word, Roku motioned for the hooded man to follow him.

Raiden lingered, his features caught in turmoil. He glanced about at the darkness before him, then turned toward the remaining light at his back, his gaze catching on signs of motion near the top of the stairs.

The flowing figure of his mother passed beneath a haze of torch fire. She stopped when she saw him, her head tilted to one side, her unbound hair an inky waterfall over one shoulder. Without a word, she bent the wisps of smoke from the nearby torch between her palms, rolling her fingers in a slow circle. Shapes began to form at her command. They solidified in the firelight and came to life as she blew a soft stream of air their way, sending them wafting toward her son.

A wily vermin being crushed beneath the hooves of a massive ox.

Raiden frowned at his mother. When he was younger, his mother's magic had entranced him. With it, she'd brought stories to life in ways other boys could only dream of. Her magic had granted him solace from the judgment of others at court. It had been a reason for the nobles to show him a measure of respect, despite the circumstances of his birth.

This fear of his mother's magic had been a form of control, for magic was a rarity. And magic like that of his mother? Rarer still. Granted once in a generation, by the spirits of a world lost for countless lifetimes.

It was a magic he did not possess. A magic Raiden had once tried to understand, only to discover he never could, for he was not meant to wield it.

He had not been blessed with talent.

Irritation passed across his features. He'd been right to

rebuff his mother's counsel. After only a moment of hesitation, Raiden followed in his emperor's footsteps, his back turned from the magic that had saved him as a child.

Kanako watched her only son disappear into the darkness below. A deep pang unfurled behind her heart. It writhed through her chest and nestled in her stomach, a slithering eel lurking in the reeds, ever present.

She'd known her warrior son would not falter in his allegiance to his sovereign, but she had tested him anyway. Just to see how he would respond. To see if he might change his mind. Raiden was at that particular stage in life in which he wished for all, thought he knew all, and expected to live forever. On occasion, it prompted unforeseen outcomes.

But time had taught Kanako that what was expected rarely came to pass. Death always collected its due. The only thing that remained steadfastly true was power. The power you had. The power you gave.

The power you concealed.

Raiden's loyalty to his younger brother ran as the river Kamo through the center of the imperial city, cutting the land in two. Perhaps Kanako and her son would stand on opposing banks from time to time, but when the plans she had carefully been laying for years finally came to pass, he would be standing beside her, without question.

It was true Raiden loved his brother with an admirable kind of ferocity. But Kanako was his mother, and she had lost much to give him all. Taken much from many, even their very minds and thoughts and hearts.

She would not see him waste it, especially not on a sniveling rat dressed in yellow silk.

With a sigh, Kanako turned in a circle, the edges of her kimono taking to the air, swallowing her like withering petals until she vanished, leaving behind nothing but a trace of her perfume.

possessed by the wind and sky

---✳︎---

It was a night for magic. A night swirling with mystery, an unknowable energy pulsing in its depths.

A promise and a threat.

It had begun earlier, as the scent of metal and moss had collected in the air. The summer storm that had followed had livened all it touched, forming a lushness that lingered long after the sun graced the clouds.

The promise.

Following the first smattering of rain, lightning had cracked across the sky. Thunder had growled from the distant mountains.

The threat.

The fortress of Akechi Takamori stood stalwart against the storm, as it had for five generations past, in unflinching service to the Minamoto clan. After all, a dusting of rain was nothing compared to the monsoons that were sure to come in the future months. Tonight, the thunder and lightning felt strangely at odds with the indifference of the rain. As though the threat levied by the clouds had been halfheartedly carried out.

As the rain collected—its patter becoming one with the echoes of chirping insects and burrowing creatures—a new sound rustled through the trees on the edge of the Akechi domain.

From the deepest reaches of shadow, figures began crawling forth. Their angles and contours seemed fashioned from night itself. Each of their footsteps pressed against the earth as though choreographed by an unseen hand. Tales of old would have cast them as demons crawling from the forest, summoned beneath a darkening sky. These stories had been lost over time, just as the ancient magic became rarer with each passing season. Now only those born into the skill and those willing to risk their very lives to acquire it lived to breathe truth into them.

But these were not demons of the forest, come to life. Save for one, they were men. At least forty of them. Masked and dressed in black, an air of urgency propelled them through the darkness to the very foundations of their enemy's lair. They crouched low to the ground and made their way across the gently flowing creek bed just beyond the stacked stone walls of the Akechi fortress, stopping in unison beneath a rise of shadows. The unseen hand split the group of men in two, without a word. One half crouched lower, gliding single file toward the reeds near the rear gate, their synchrony perfect, their strides an unbroken ripple. If the night breeze were to fall to its death without warning, the only sounds that would be heard would be the stretching of climbing rope, the whisper of blades being drawn.

The short breaths of anticipation.

The second group of men moved toward the wall on the opposite side of the compound. They pressed their backs against the stacked stone as their leader—the lone demon of their ranks—studied the grooves above: the notches worn into the surface, the space between the mortarless stones. Then the masked demon made a call like a starling, his signal rising crisp and clear into the night. It was something he'd learned from his father, Asano Naganori. This ability to sound a call above detection.

From the ring of tall shadows at the edge of the forest beyond, an expert bowman took aim, his black leather *kosode* and shining eyes framing his motions. The first arrow sailed through the darkness, whistling as it neared its mark. Its steel tip embedded between the stacked stones an arm's reach above their heads.

Asano Tsuneoki took hold of the arrow. Checked his weight. Then levered upward in a graceful stroke. Before his other hand even made it to the next hold, a second arrow sailed through the night, just above the first. The arrows continued flying toward the wall as he swung his way toward the battlements above, each of his movements unhurried and precise, aided by the strength of the demon that thrashed through his veins. The same demon that—when left unchecked under the

37

light of the moon—rose to the surface in the form of an other-worldly creature: half wolf, half bear.

Once he reached the top, Tsuneoki breathed deep and waited, staving off the desire to crow in triumph. Their task had only just begun. Though the Black Clan had already cast two of the emperor's loyal subjects from their lands in only four days, this particular stronghold would provide a bastion for his men. A place for them to regroup and strategize in safety, for however long it might last.

Moreover, Tsuneoki wanted this fortress. After all, Akechi Takamori had been the first daimyō to turn his back on Tsuneoki's father a decade ago. The first to set fire to the Asano stronghold and watch with glee as it burned.

Now—after ten long years—Asano Tsuneoki would take back a measure of what his family had lost. Beneath him, a spark of flint striking stone flashed through the darkness. An arrowhead dipped in pitch caught flame, multiplying into many tongues of fire, forming an even row below.

In unison, the men of the Black Clan nocked their fiery arrows, then loosed them all at once. The flaming arrows reached skyward—suspended for an eerie instant—before looping over the wall and striking the thatched roofs on the other side.

In the moment it took to blink, the straw caught flame. Hoarse voices and sleep-laden shouts began emanating from within the Akechi courtyard. An eerie wail unfurled into the darkness, like that of an animal caught in an iron trap, watching its life slowly bleed from its limb. Most of the men ringing the perimeter waited. Two more figures clad in black began scaling the wall, using the same embedded arrows to brace their weight.

As the fire grew fast and bright, the wailing within intensified, its sound caterwauling into a midnight-blue sky. Unnerved, the second group of men hovering in the reeds near the rear gate stilled, the hairs on the backs of their necks standing on end.

Atop the battlements, Tsuneoki signaled to those below as he watched Akechi servants with jars and pails begin shambling toward the gate. Soon enough, the iron bars were lifted by the unsuspecting people within, and the entrance creaked open. Men and women began lurching toward the water. Triumphant in the success of their plan, the members of the Black Clan waiting nearby took to their feet, anticipation unfolding between them.

Before more than a single step could be taken, they halted in their tracks, their triumph muddied by a sense of alarm.

The caterwauling rose in pitch until it became a screeching buzz. A drone. It took flight in their ears, causing several of the men to clamp their hands to the sides of their heads. Wordlessly, the people who'd stumbled past the gates began filling their pots and pitchers. A figure on horseback galloped past them, cracking a whip in its wake.

Concerned by the mounting strangeness, Tsuneoki removed a loop of sturdy rope from its place at his left hip. After securing it to the battlements, he slid toward the ground of the Akechi courtyard, the rope smoking between his sandaled feet. The instant he relinquished hold of the cord, he tore his *katana* from its scabbard and began searching for signs of soldiers. Finding none, Tsuneoki grabbed the shoulder of a young woman tripping toward the blaze with a cracked pitcher in hand. She whirled in place, the blacks of her eyes twitching. Her mouth hung open as though in a silent scream.

Tsuneoki gasped. Nearly stumbled back. The girl's head blurred as it shook. Moved in all directions like a broken doll, unhinged at its neck. She began vibrating into solid motion. Her face appeared contorted in horrific pain, yet she said nothing. Did nothing, save attempt to shake his grip from off her shoulder.

The beat of Tsuneoki's heart rose in his ears. Began chiming in a low hum. A shudder rolled through his chest, that same peculiar trembling taking root in him as well. Again he searched for soldiers, for samurai, for anyone who might be able to offer an explanation for the sickness plaguing this domain.

These people were not whole. Something had clamped down on their minds and taken hold of their thoughts, its grasp unrelenting and merciless. Tsuneoki whistled for his men, this time his cry like that of a water bird, his fear sharpening the sound.

Flee. He signaled his men. *Flee this place, at once*.

As soon as he relinquished his hold on the young woman's arm, the buzzing in his ears began dying down. But still the trembling of his body did not cease. In a flash,

Tsuneoki turned his gaze to the moon, deep breaths rocking through his chest in an attempt to dispel the shuddering. With utmost control, he asked the night sky to do his bidding. It descended upon him in a rush. A cool shock of moonlight glowed through his veins. He began turning, shifting, an ice-cold fire rippling beneath his skin, his fingertips burning into tendrils of dark smoke, the demon taking shape.

A howl passed his lips, growing more feral with each passing moment. A further warning to all those who followed his orders. *Get away, while you still can.* He threw his head back—leaning into the cry—and then moved forward, his black bear's claws landing soundlessly in the soft earth.

As soon as Tsuneoki opened the eyes of the beast he'd channeled for nearly a decade, the twitching figures around him began moving his way. He heard his men shouting beyond the wall, heard them call for Ren, who appeared to be defying his orders, as always. His animalian sight—now unencumbered by darkness—took in the lurching forms around him as they began closing in on him. Backlit by a white moon, Tsuneoki finally caught sight of what he'd sought earlier. A figure on horseback paused in the middle of the winding dirt lane to his right, watching the scene unfold as though it were part of a play.

The rider's features were masked by a horned helmet, but Tsuneoki recognized the unmistakable outline of a samurai. As the warrior cantered his way, the insignia of the Hattori clan—two arrows facing opposite directions—became clear.

Beside the lone samurai's feet strolled a ghostly fox, with yellow eyes much like Tsuneoki's own. Beastly and unnerving. Otherworldly. A creature of magic. A creature that had sold some part of itself to gain this ability, just as Tsuneoki had. Just as Ōkami had, on a dark night many years ago, revenge feeding their choices like dried brush to a flame.

The fox loped closer, the grin on its impish face widening. Without warning, its thoughts invaded Tsuneoki's mind, shot across the distance with clear intent, its voice rasping and indistinct.

Run, nightbeast. While you still can.

No. Tsuneoki bared his own fangs, giving his wordless reply teeth.

Run or stay and watch as I turn your men into creatures of my bidding. As I steal from you all your thoughts, your hopes, your dreams. Until you are nothing but a husk drifting about at my whim.

Tsuneoki widened his stance, driving his heavy paws into the ground, anchoring himself to the earth. Preparing for combat. The fox stopped gliding toward him. Glittering white smoke—a preternatural mist—began swirling around its feet.

Don't be a fool, it said.

Tsuneoki threw back his head and let loose a mournful bay. A howl meant to drive his men back to the forest. A howl demanding them to flee. Demanding Ren to listen and obey, for once.

The fox's grin broadened as it quirked its head. *We are both creatures possessed by wind and sky. Honor me, and I shall honor you. Defy me, and I shall drive you—and yours—to utter ruin.*

In the shadows, the samurai on horseback continued watching. Waiting. Tsuneoki began his charge, his claws spreading into a dark fog. The fox responded in kind, the wisps of shimmering white haze spinning in lazy eddies.

Two billowing clouds of smoke—one light and one dark—clashed together in the middle of the winding dirt lane, their figures trailing mists of magic, their bodies slamming into one another with a force that cracked through the night air. The fox was smaller, but faster. Its first gash was just below Tsuneoki's snout, clearly aimed for his neck—a wound meant to kill rather than incapacitate. In response, Tsuneoki feigned a yelp, limping back, luring the grinning fox closer. Then he pounced, slashing into the creature with a sideswipe of his front paw, catching just below one of its front legs. The fox cried out, then locked its yellow eyes upon him. The color in their centers caught flame. A sinister sneer curled the edges of its black lips. It twisted, the smoke around it dark now instead of light.

Before Tsuneoki could devise a plan, something ripped through his side. A flash of heat tore beneath his ribs, clamoring for his heart, its nails sharp, its bite remorseless. The clawing heat grasped for his mind, twisting and unraveling whatever it managed to uncover. It sank its fangs, trying to force him under its control, but Tsuneoki fought back. Pressed the demon's magic away from the brink, the effort causing his sight to blur.

With a snarl, the fox wreaked a new kind of havoc as its retribution, stealing from Tsuneoki his most treasured memories, his most secret desires.

What began as a bear's roar of pain faded to the cry of a young man.

Tsuneoki landed against the damp earth with a thud, no longer a creature of magic. The wound across his torso—a slash of bleeding fire—flowed into the ground. The fiery touch of the fox burned through his skull.

Foolish, foolish boy. The fox *tsk*ed as it floated in a circle around him. It stopped to inspect its own wound. Licked the blood from it with complete leisure.

Yumi is her name? It smiled serenely. *When I find her, your sister will pay for this.*

Marked for Life

※

The emperor and his elder brother moved through the bowels of the imperial palace—a place where only the lowliest of servants trudged alongside scuttling creatures and reeking refuse. Deep in the shadows beneath a trifling excuse for a window were two single cells barred by iron doors, braced by wooden rafters. Each cell possessed a grate for waste and a floor covered in rotting straw. Nothing more.

It was a small and spare space, but the Golden Castle did not have need of a prison beyond this. Those with the gall to offer insult to the emperor or any of his liege lords were faced with one of two punishments: death or banishment, with death culminating in any number of colorful ways: being dragged through the streets by the throat, hung upside down and drowned, stretched from the ramparts, thrown into a venomous snake pit, or—if luck was at all on the offender's side—being simply beheaded.

And those who were banished?

They were marked for life.

Roku and Raiden made their way to the cell in the far corner, with four imperial guards at their flank, and the scarred man dressed in shadowy robes still in tow, bearing the iron trunk stained with dried blood.

Crouched against the stone wall sat an unassuming figure. A tangle of dark hair shrouded his features. His black *kosode* was coated in ash and blood and grime. The shifting moonlight above threw the maze of rafters into sharp relief, cutting angles across the floor beside his feet.

"Takeda Ranmaru," Roku began in a soft voice. "It is a great honor to finally meet you."

Ōkami did not move. Failed to acknowledge the greeting with even a glance.

"On your knees, you filth," Raiden said, his fingers twitching above the white snakeskin *samegawa* of his *katana*. "Bow before your emperor."

Save for a small smile, Ōkami remained seated amid the filthy straw, stretching his legs before him as though he were blissfully unaffected by Raiden's threat.

Roku grinned slowly. "A rather pitiful show of defiance."

Still no sign of a response.

At that, Raiden nodded, silently ordering one of the imperial guards to unlock the cell.

The emperor raised a hand to stop them, his head canted to one side. "Words of kindness do not seem to move you,"

Roku mused. "And my brother has already opted for intimidation. I've lowered myself to base insults, all in the span of only a few moments. What is left?"

Ōkami glanced at the hooded figure hovering to one side. Studied the dark trunk clasped between the man's bony hands, and the hungry sneer of his cracked lips. "Threats." His response was pronounced in a cool, unhurried fashion. Though appearing at ease, his body remained carved from stone, like a somnolent mountain.

"This is true," Roku agreed. "Would threats work?"

"Pain," Ōkami continued, his gaze never once falling from the trunk.

Roku's smile was fierce, almost as though he relished the prospect. "Would that work? If I threatened you with pain, would you cooperate?"

Ōkami remained unconcerned. Raiden nodded again toward the imperial guards, and the lock on the cell door unlatched with an ominous series of clicks.

Roku sighed. "It troubles me that we cannot share a meeting of minds even on this very simple matter, Lord Ranmaru."

A grin coiled up one side of Ōkami's face, accentuating a diagonal scar through his lips. "My mind exists on a mountain. Yours exists in a field. Should the mountain kneel before the field?" He bared his white teeth in a dark smile, then nodded to the straw before him. "Or will the field crawl to me?"

"You traitorous swine." Stepping into the cell, Raiden

47

freed his blade from its *saya* with a rasp. "You will address your heavenly sovereign with respect." His words were as sharp as a reaping scythe, his weapon raised with murderous intent.

At that, Ōkami looked up. The moonlight sifting through the slatted window above bent as though it were reaching for him. But he remained just beyond its grasp, the scar through his lips turning silver.

"So soon," he murmured.

Raiden blinked. "What?"

"I've learned your weakness so soon, Prince Raiden."

His eyes narrowing, Raiden drew back his blade and struck the stone wall a hairsbreadth from Ōkami's head, and a shower of golden sparks descended around them.

"Brother . . ." Roku said quietly. "Patience."

"You yearn for respect, even in a world designed to offer it to you, without question," Ōkami continued, his black stare unflinching. "But maybe it was withheld by someone as a child. Or perhaps you predictably despise your fate?" He lowered his voice. "Firstborn, yet destined for nothing."

Just as Raiden drew back his sword a second time, Roku raised his hand to silence them both. "And what is your weakness, Lord Ranmaru?" the emperor asked his prisoner.

As expected, Ōkami did not answer.

"Very well, then." Roku inhaled, ever the picture of patience. "Will you answer my questions if I call you Ōkami instead? I've heard you prefer it. I'm willing to grant you that boon."

48

Ōkami lifted his chin. Leaned his head against the wall, his unbound hair falling from his bruised face as he met the emperor's gaze. "You wish to know my weakness? Interesting that you would ask for it so openly. Perhaps you are not what I thought you would be." He unfolded his palms, holding them at either side of his body, as though he concealed nothing. "Or perhaps that is exactly what you wish for me to think."

Roku smiled again, and the expression crinkled the corners of his eyes, marring an otherwise smooth countenance. "Perhaps you are wrong about one thing and right about another. Only through honest discourse will we know."

Ōkami laughed drily. "You may ask whatever you wish, But I do not owe you a response." Easing forward, he raised a knee to rest an elbow upon it, his chains clanking.

"Integrity," Roku began.

Almost imperceptibly, Ōkami's eyes narrowed.

Roku continued. "Courage and benevolence."

Though he did not lower his *katana*, Raiden sent a quizzical glance his younger brother's way.

"Respect, honesty, honor." Roku paused. "Loyalty."

Ōkami shifted, the dirty straw beneath him rustling with his chains.

The puzzlement emanating from all sides seemed to imbue the young emperor with strength, as though he enjoyed playing the role of a mystery. He stood taller, his gaze focused. "You are the son of a famous samurai. Which tenet of *bushidō* is your weakness?" Roku took five paces to one side of the cell before retracing his steps as though he were on an afternoon

49

stroll. "Which of your many failings gives you fear in the dead of night?"

Ōkami did not answer.

"A thousand apologies." Roku clasped his hands behind his back, his remark failing to sound the least bit apologetic. "Ōkami. The Honshō Wolf. The Dog of Jukai Forest," the emperor said in a soft tone, the jibe nevertheless sharp. "With a kennel of filthy bitches at his back."

The shadows in Ōkami's face hollowed further as his lips pressed into a frown—the first sign that the emperor's words had any lasting effect on him.

"Very well, then," Roku continued. "*Ōkami* . . . I will trade my weakness for yours. I will tell you what it is I fear most, in exchange for you doing the same."

After a moment of silence, an amused snort followed. "I think not."

"You refuse to barter with your enemy?" Roku offered him yet another close-lipped smile.

"No. I refuse to barter with you."

The emperor stopped his pacing and turned in place to meet the eyes of his prisoner. "I've heard many say your father was the same kind of willful man. It cost him his life, though it gained him nothing. My father often remarked that Lord Shingen was the greatest of all fools. One who thought principle was of more value than action."

"Insulting my father will not provoke a response from me, nor will trading smiles as though we are old friends. I expected better of you, Minamoto Roku." Ōkami returned the same thin smile, irony curling its edges. "Why don't you just kill me? That's what your father would do. That's all that men of your ilk know how to do when faced with a challenge." He crossed his arms. "Kill me and be done with it." His tone turned mocking. "Then you can rule the Empire of Wa unchecked, like a true leader. Is that not your dream, Roku-*chan*? To remain an unchecked child for all time?"

A roar of fury flew from Raiden's lips at the insult to his younger brother. To his *emperor*. Raiden balled his armored fingers into a fist and levied a backhanded blow to Ōkami that sent the latter reeling into the greying straw.

As his elder brother kicked their prisoner in the chest, Roku waited patiently, an odd look of bemusement settling onto his features.

His face seething with hatred, Raiden continued raining blows on Ōkami until Roku lifted a hand, directing his brother to cease. Ōkami spat blood into the straw and took in a wheezing breath before pushing back onto his heels. He coughed to clear his throat. Then he paused to stare up at the emperor, the signs of lingering humor at odds with his broken, bloodied face. "It appears insults do have an effect on your brother. How predictable."

"Insults are indeed a base form of intimidation," Roku replied, not seeming to care about the slight tossed his brother's way in the process. "I agree they are the least effective in situations like this. But it is not often that I encounter a foe of a similar mind." He gestured for the shadowy man holding the trunk to step forward. "And since we agree on these matters, there's no need to waste time on such baser means of intimidation."

Ōkami did not balk. "I am not afraid of pain."

The smile that spread across the emperor's face began with an unnerving kind of sweetness. It widened into something wicked, tinging the air with an oddly saccharine scent. "But I am not talking about your pain, Ōkami."

For a moment, he was met once more with silence. Then Ōkami leaned forward, his voice dropping to a whisper. "You have nothing to gain from harming any of the men unfortunate enough to call me friend."

"I will be the judge of that." Roku resumed his pacing. "Any man unfortunate enough to call you friend would also be unfortunate enough to possess vital information."

"What information?" Ōkami laughed cuttingly. "Do you wish to know upon which rock I lay my head in the forest? Or perhaps it is important for you to learn how I prefer my tea."

"Or maybe I wish to know how you enjoy your meals," Roku said. "I've heard your cook was quite excellent—a relic of your father's household, was he not? A shame I could not meet him. I've been searching for loyal servants. But, alas, I've heard this particular servant will be of service to no one." A deliberate pause. "Ever again."

This time, the silence that took shape around them was different. Weightier, a low hum gathering in the air. "It would not have made a difference if he were here," Ōkami said, his words dangerous in their control. "Yoshi would not have said anything to you."

Roku lifted a finger to emphasize his point. "That may be true. But I am remiss. There is no need to resurrect dead cooks. We have in our possession—at this very moment—someone who could answer all these questions and more. Someone far more . . . pliant."

"Ah, of course." Ōkami lowered his head, letting his hair veil his features once more. "The feckless daughter of Hattori Kano. This should prove amusing."

Roku glanced his brother's way. "Brother," he began, "your bride lived alongside all these men, no?"

His expression souring, Raiden sheathed his blade. "My bride? I have no intention of taking that dirty sparrow to wi—"

"Nonsense." The emperor whirled in place, the hem of his lustrous silk robe dragging through the grime. "We cannot go back on our word. Nor can we ignore the last wishes of our esteemed father."

Raiden inhaled with distaste. "Even if the goods have been sullied beyond repair?"

Though he snorted in amusement, the chains near Ōkami's fists clanked softly.

"Hattori Mariko has sworn her loyalty to you and to our family, has she not?" Roku continued.

Raiden nodded, his features still dubious.

"Then," Roku said as he locked eyes on his prisoner, "your union must go forward with all haste."

"My sovereign," Raiden replied, "perhaps we could—"

"I will not be challenged on this, brother. By anyone." His nostrils flaring, Roku spoke over him, his reedy voice almost grating in its force. "There is only one way to know for certain if Lady Mariko retained her honor in Jukai forest." A gleam alighted his gaze as he watched Ōkami's obsidian eyes flash. "Take her as your wife. And if she is indeed sullied—if she has lied to us—her punishment will be the slow death of a traitor." He waited to see how his words hung in the air. Then the emperor met the stony face of his prisoner. "And the Dog of Jukai Forest will be there to bear witness to it."

The Ashes of Loyalty

— ✴ —

E scape.

And regicide.

They were notions Ōkami had not entertained in a long while. While he received the newest blows dealt by Prince Raiden, he wondered to himself at the irony of it all.

That he would have come here. Willingly. Accepted this abuse. Willingly.

Any given night on the journey to Inako, Ōkami could have escaped. Could still have escaped, if his chains had been but an arm's length longer.

For many years, such a thing as escape had not been a cause of concern for him, because he'd always believed he would never surrender to anyone. The deal he'd made with a demon of darkness had ensured that no one could take him prisoner, so long as the night sky touched his skin. His power to move with the wind—faster than a flash of lightning—

enabled him to vanish like a shadow in the sun, even in the direst of situations.

After witnessing his father's grisly death as a child, Ōkami had sworn to the heavens that he would die before allowing any man to possess that kind of power over him. The power to murder without consequence. The power to separate a man from all he loved and rob a young boy of all he'd ever known in one fell swoop.

This boyhood vow had been the reason Ōkami had made his deal with a demon during the winter of his tenth year. He'd taken the demon's blade of strange black rock and sworn his oath. Considered it well worth the cost to his well-being and to his future.

Though he'd risked both not once, but twice in recent days. All for the sake of love. For love, Ōkami could very well lose everything.

As for regicide? There had been a time—not long after the death of his father and the loss of his family's fortune—that Ōkami had contemplated murdering Minamoto Masaru and being the cause of the imperial family's downfall. Even now—with a fond bitterness—he recalled longing for the day when he would be strong enough to destroy those who had laid siege to his world.

But it had all been childish folly, this idea of revenge. The musings of an angry boy, bereft of purpose. After all, what kind of purpose did retribution provide? It was the kind that destroyed its bearer in a ceaseless cycle of hatred.

Not long after his father's death—when Ōkami had been

faced with the cold, with death, with hunger, with the echoes of ridicule—he had drawn away from such notions and instead opted for the comfort of self-preservation. At least then he would not be the reason anyone bound to him perished for the sake of revenge.

Yet here he was now, pondering the possibility of escape. Dreaming of running a white-hot blade through the heart of this fatuous emperor. Watching his blood flow through the grate meant for waste. Laughing to himself as the life dripped from Roku's body.

Knowing all to be hopeless endeavors.

Each time Raiden's fist connected with his skin, Ōkami felt his body brace itself, though his mind knew better; it knew nothing could spare him the inevitable rush of pain. Soon each blow melted into the next, until a steady thrum of anguish coursed through his chest, his limbs, his stomach. Until his head rang dully as though a gong chimed within.

Then the beating ceased as abruptly as it had begun.

It seemed odd that they had yet to question him. He thought at the very least they would wish to know if the Black Clan was responsible for the death of the emperor. About what these men did and why they did it. Who comprised its membership. What designs they might have with respect to the future of the empire.

Yet they had asked him nothing of import, save for what it was he truly feared.

Which . . . gave him pause.

Ōkami rolled onto his back and let the sounds of their

speech fade as though he were submerged beneath water. Tried his best to ignore the invective in each of the words, regardless of who spoke them. Raiden wore his hate like armor, and a part of Ōkami preferred it that way. The elder brother possessed a naked, unsophisticated kind of hatred, easily seen and easily understood. Easily dismantled. The kind of hatred Ōkami had faced as a young man, with none but his father's trusty samurai, Yoshi, and his best friend, Tsuneoki, at his side.

Roku did not wear his hatred on the surface. He masked it with cheerful grins and unnerving calm, as though he were trying to cajole or entice his victims into submission. It was a dangerous kind of hatred, because it was hard to sense how deep its roots lay. The more Roku spoke, the more his poison seeped through Ōkami's skin, setting his teeth on edge.

Raiden's hatred was easy to ignore. Roku's was a winding lane beckoning Ōkami forward, into a thorny underbrush.

Ōkami's face throbbed. Every breath he took strained the muscles in his chest. One eye was swollen shut. Nevertheless he stared up at the beam of moonlight. That single stroke of luminous white, cascading from the narrow window above. His body reached for it instinctively. Sought its solace. Its strength. The light of the night sky could be his savior, just as it had been his demon for so long.

His bare foot stretched its way, almost as though it were held in a trance. A cloud passed over the moon, shrouding his savior in further darkness.

So close. Yet so far.

Too far to be of any service.

The hateful words flowing around Ōkami continued to wend through his chest, wrapping around his heart. He would not give anyone the satisfaction of seeing him lowered to despair. Though his face pulsed and his chest ached, he would never let a single tear trek down his face. He would not give anyone—least of all these foolish boys playing at being men—the satisfaction.

The last time tears had flowed down Ōkami's face had been the day his father had died, eight years ago. He had not cried once since then, not even to himself.

Ōkami resisted the urge to shout. To rage against the dying light and strike back at the pain winding through his body. It was not the pain of the repeated beatings. It was the pain of his fear. That cold, dark fear Ōkami had ignored for so long. The possibility that—no matter how hard he had fought to avoid it—there were people who'd managed to gain control over him, in their own way.

Not these young fools standing before him with their glittering weapons and radiant silks. These fools for whom power had only ever been absolute. No. Never them.

But the people Ōkami loved. The people whose laughter had wormed its way into his soul. They were the ones who inspired his loyalty, no matter the reason or the cost. It was something Yoshi had always said, when Ōkami had questioned why the wizened samurai had wasted years of his life in service to a young *rōnin*, fixing eggs for a spoiled little boy.

Loving someone is to lose control, Yoshi had said with a fond smile. *And I promised to love you always, as I loved Shingen-sama, my loyal brother in arms.*

Yoshi. His father's faithful samurai and confidant, who had been by their sides following the disappearance of Takeda Shingen's wife in a storm at sea. The man who had sheltered Ōkami as a lost, lonely boy. The man who had kept him safe, even when Ōkami had wished him away.

And Tsuneoki. His dearest friend. A boy racked with the guilt of his father's betrayal. One that had resulted in the death of Takeda Shingen, by his own hand. Ōkami had wished Tsuneoki away, too, when they were younger. Asano Naganori's son had been a constant reminder of what Ōkami had lost. But Tsuneoki had never once faltered in his loyalty. Even when Ōkami had agreed to grant a dangerous demon a foothold in the mortal world in order to gain his power, his oldest friend had followed suit soon after, without hesitation. He'd taken a blade of black rock and made his own blood oath with a nightbeast. Just as he had when Ōkami had opted for a rootless existence, living nowhere and everywhere.

Where you lead, I follow, Tsuneoki had said. *I am not afraid of the unknown. If you can do it, so can I.*

And Mariko.

Hattori Mariko was the worst offender. She'd given Ōkami a reason to wish for things he'd never dreamed of having. To put everything at risk, just for a moment together beneath a blanket of mist, watching the way the water slid down her skin. He'd cursed her for it, time and again. That first long night he'd lain awake in captivity, he'd turned his eyes toward the stars, knowing he could escape if he tried, and knowing what might become of Mariko—and his men—should he even attempt to do so.

He'd cursed her then, too. Even though his every waking dream had been about her. Even when the scent of passing orange blossoms had made him smile.

Ōkami knew this treacherous would-be emperor wished to use his supposed weaknesses against him. He'd expected Roku to do as much. To tarnish everything Ōkami loved with this poison, then use his fear in an attempt to control him.

He'd been prepared for this.

Nevertheless, it did not dull the sharpness of the sniveling emperor's words, nor the barbed statements of his watchdog brother, to have it put to practice.

The light was still too far.

Ōkami's chains were too short. Too heavy.

And that girl. That ridiculous girl, who pursed her lips in thought and wore her intellect like a mark of honor. Who—despite a world that conspired against her—was far more ingenious than any of the men Ōkami had ever known.

He would not risk Mariko.

Not for every night sky in the world. Not even for a single star.

"It should not take much to sway the heart of a simple girl." Roku's venom bled into Ōkami's mind the moment he surfaced for air. "Women are fickle creatures, willing to smile at any listening ear. The only woman a man can trust is the woman who gave birth to him, and even then, I would advise caution at all times." His brow furrowed for a moment, then smoothed with the dawning of another smile.

It was the smile that gave Roku away. In it, Ōkami caught a glimpse of annoyance. Save for his mother, it was likely that women had been dismissive of Roku for most of his short life. Ōkami could well see how the young ladies of the imperial court had looked upon the crown prince. Smaller and less fearsome than his handsome elder brother. Second choice in all things, save the one he did not earn—his birthright.

This was Roku's twisted truth.

"It is possible Lady Mariko harbored fond feelings for you," Roku continued.

"Only after you surrendered did she step forward. Or perhaps it wasn't you that drove her from the safety of the shadows. Was her heart moved by the son of Asano Naganori? My father mentioned that Naganori had a way with women."

Ridiculous. In all respects. Yet it burned to hear this boy say it.

Ōkami began laughing. He started softly, then let his laughter rise into a low rumble. When he glanced at the emperor, his laughter died on his swollen lips, a new realization rendering his truth in starker colors. It startled him. Sobered him.

For it was like looking in a mirror.

"Is this the best you can do, Minamoto Roku?" Ōkami stood suddenly, his pulse hurtling through his veins. "You must be very afraid. Your weakness is courage, is it not?" He moved the single step forward his bindings would allow him.

"Is that what you're afraid of? To be betrayed, as your father was before you?" Ōkami's voice reverberated against the iron bars. "Do you fear you might die as he did?" He paused, letting his words fade to a whisper. "Or maybe you're afraid I might break free of these chains and finish what my father started." For emphasis, he yanked on the metal links binding his wrists and feet, the sounds clanging through the dark.

As expected, the boorish watchdog at the emperor's side brandished his *katana* once more, his features contorted with anger.

"There it is," Roku said softly. "It was worth letting you into my mind if it meant giving me a chance to peer into yours."

Ōkami lifted his chin, his eyes wide as he cursed the far-off light.

"Loyalty," Roku said.

The blood drained slowly from Ōkami's face, collecting behind his heart, his pulse drumming in his ears. He stilled further.

It appeared Roku had glimpsed the same truth Ōkami had.

For fear was the greatest of equalizers, save for death itself.

The emperor spoke once more. "So fitting. I should have seen it from the start. Your father died for his lack of loyalty. Of course it would be your burden now." Satisfaction passed over his vulpine features.

Ōkami cursed himself in the same breath he cursed his tormentors.

"Now that we are at last on equal footing, shall we begin?" Roku gestured behind him, beckoning to the figure in the shadows.

Stumbling at the entrance of the cell, the strange thin man made his way toward Ōkami, the wooden box clasped tightly before him. When Raiden and the four imperial guards moved to restrain Ōkami against the wall, Ōkami responded instinctively. The reaction of a boy who'd sworn never to appear weak—never to show his fear—no matter the cost. Who'd promised the heavens he would not lose himself to a lesser man, as his father had.

Ōkami shoved into Raiden's chest with his shoulder, then slammed his forehead into the prince's face. Raiden grunted in pain as he recoiled, then took hold of Ōkami's throat, the hardened leather of his gauntlet digging into Ōkami's skin. His teeth bared in fury, the prince smashed Ōkami's face twice against the stone wall. An imperial guard landed a well-timed blow in the center of Ōkami's chest. Another to his gut. With a gasp, Ōkami doubled over and spat a mouthful of blood in the filthy straw, his ears ringing and his vision swimming. Blood trickled past the tip of his nose from a wound splitting across his brow.

"Enough!" Roku's reedy voice spiked into the rafters. For an instant, Ōkami thought the emperor might succumb to the rage simmering beneath the surface. Then Roku sighed, long and loudly. "Brother, you—and your cursed temper—have ruined my plans for our prisoner's punishment."

His fingers still wrapped around Ōkami's throat, Raiden

glanced over his shoulder toward his younger brother, his eyebrows raised in question.

"His forehead is cracked and bleeding." Roku inhaled, his eyes closing for a moment, steeling himself once more. "His face is a mess."

Only a breath passed before Ōkami understood the emperor's meaning. Realized what lay in the skeletal man's iron-bound trunk.

Insult. Upon injury.

Gritting his teeth, he marshaled his fury. Silenced his fears.

Ōkami would need all his wits about him for what was to come.

"I . . . apologize, my sovereign." Raiden's hesitation offered Ōkami the barest glimpse into the prince's mind, past all the rage and spite. Something about the emperor's actions troubled his elder brother. But Raiden's reluctance flickered once, then vanished with renewed resolve. He relinquished his hold on Ōkami's neck the same instant the imperial guards tightened theirs. "What would you have me do?" Stepping back, Raiden bowed, again the emperor's loyal watchdog.

"We must think beyond tradition now. Beyond what is expected." Roku shifted closer, his nostrils flaring as he studied Ōkami's face. "I want him to see it, to feel it—to witness his truth—for the rest of his life, however short that may be." A spark of inspiration lighted his gaze. "Place the mark on the side of his neck."

Ōkami closed his eyes as the chains around his ankles

were yanked from under him. Resentment coursed beneath his skin as he struck the stone floor, bile churning through his throat. It was followed by bitter amusement. Cold irony. Always irony. He had but to choose which feeling to wear tonight. His eyes opening—locking on the willful light beyond his grasp—Ōkami settled on the darkest kind of humor. As a child bereft of his family, Ōkami's humor had often been the only thing keeping him sane.

The mark was meant for the forehead. Thieves and petty criminals were branded thus. Black symbols inked their crimes onto their brows, making it impossible to shed the stain of their folly. It was just as well. Ōkami *was* a thief, after all. And if this was to be the first of the new emperor's forays into torture, it was a decidedly less gruesome one than Ōkami had expected.

The scarred man unlocked his box. In it was a series of small, needled blades. He lifted two jars into the nearby beam of moonlight. The first was filled with the expected black ink. The second? A sinister grin took hold of the man's features, stretching the spray of burn scars peppering his skin. The second vial contained a thick silver substance that glowed as he swirled it. He dipped one of his needled blades in the luminescent liquid, and the edge of the blade sizzled like fish scales above a fire, distorting the space around it.

Acid. The mark would be fused to Ōkami's skin with acid.

Twisted and unnecessary. Meant to elicit pain and nothing more.

Pressing his filthy sandal down on Ōkami's brow, Raiden shoved Ōkami's face into the straw.

Ōkami inhaled. He'd fought once. It had given the emperor satisfaction to see him struggle. To witness him being beaten into submission. Metering his breaths, Ōkami glanced upward to gaze upon the placid face of the emperor. He refused to give Roku that satisfaction ever again.

The next time Ōkami fought before this weasel of a sovereign, it would end in rivers of royal blood.

"What do you wish for most at this moment, Takeda Ranmaru?" Roku asked, his tone blithe.

Ōkami wished for many things, but he refused to give the emperor any further power over him. He stayed silent, his eyes gleaming like daggers.

"You wish for vengeance, do you not, phoenix?" Raiden said softly, as he increased the pressure of his foot against Ōkami's face. "To rise from the ashes?"

Roku smiled as he spoke, his voice barely above a whisper.

"First you must burn."

Traps of spun silk

Mariko kept her head bowed, her eyes lowered. She followed in the footsteps of the servant Shizuko, each of her split-toed *tabi* susurrating across the polished wooden hallways of Heian Castle.

It felt strange to once again don the garments of a young woman. Though Mariko had lived as a boy in Jukai forest for only a few weeks, her instincts had changed even in that short time. As she shuffled down these vaunted corridors, Mariko wished to raise her head and take unabashed stock of her surroundings. To commit every detail to memory, for she did not know when even the most insignificant one might be of use.

Instead she forced herself to settle back into the steps of the dance she'd performed most of her life.

Head bowed. Eyes lowered. Voice a whisper not even the wind could catch.

As she and Shizuko turned another corner, two young servants took their places at her flank. Mariko glanced over one shoulder, and the small pieces of silver and jade dangling from her hairpiece tinkled across her forehead in a merry chime. She used the motion to lift her gaze surreptitiously, taking in the silk-covered walls and the elegant screens of the sliding doors—some opened to allow for a breeze and some latched shut, in no particular order—as well as the delicate paper lanterns covered with cranes and roaring tigers and serpentine fish.

As her eyes returned to the floor, Mariko once again focused on the almost rhythmic motion of her footsteps. They glided in a schooled fashion, each heel in line with the other. Her kimono rippled like waves on either side of her split-toed socks. Mariko's gaze drifted over the gleaming hem of the pale *tatsumura* silk.

The long sleeves of her *furisode* were covered with an intricate array of tiny flowers—camellias, violets, orange blossoms, and sakura—each individually sewn onto the garment by hand. Linking all the flowers were painted vines shadowed by veins of liquid gold. Tiny birds flitted from blossom to blossom across the entire expanse of the watered silk. This kimono was Mariko's armor at court: the most ornate armor she had ever worn in her entire life. It had been brought from the imperial family's personal store of garments, as a way to honor her status. When the kimono had been unveiled in her chamber earlier this afternoon, the wide eyes and muted gasps of those around Mariko had not escaped her notice.

She was being brought before someone important. That was all Mariko knew.

Perhaps her betrothed. Or perhaps even the emperor himself.

She took a deep breath. Strange how her fortunes could turn so much in the matter of a few short days. Mariko had arrived in Inako two nights ago, in the filthy *kosode* of a warrior returning from battle. Now she was dressed as an empress and being led through the Golden Castle for an audience with a member of the imperial court.

If Mariko had any desire to find humor in her situation, no doubt her task would be an easy one. The sort Ren would scoff at, and Ranmaru—no, Tsuneoki—would tease her for afterward. But the desire to laugh had been set aflame in Jukai forest, managing to burn to ash on her tongue in less than a week.

Mariko focused instead on preparing herself for what was to come.

Will I be questioned? Doubted? Made to answer for someone else's crimes?

There was no way to be certain this was not a trap, after all. If she'd learned anything about the imperial court, she'd learned it was a place of secrets and deceit.

And with such things came the possibility of anything at all.

As Mariko's small assemblage of women made their way into another corridor, the ceilings above them vaulted higher, and the carved screens along either side became even more ornate. Beneath her silken *tabi*, the floors squeaked loudly as though they were ancient and in need of repair. Mariko had heard tell of these floors. The sounds they made were reminiscent of the *uguisu*'s cry; thus, they were called nightingale floors. The wooden surfaces had been constructed to prevent anyone—friend or foe—from traversing across them without being heard. The fact that Mariko walked over them now meant she was entering a part of Heian Castle that was undoubtedly under heavy guard.

Beneath the layers of her kimono and its many underrobes, Mariko's knees began to shake. She curled her toes as she walked, forcing her legs to remain strong. This dance would be a difficult one, and Mariko needed all her emotions in check to perform it well. Despite the efforts of her parents and numerous tutors, she had never been the kind of girl who could enter a room and feel at ease. Mariko had always preferred the company of her own mind to the witless prattle of those in the nobility.

Her thoughts drifted to Yumi. The *maiko* had been one of the few exceptions to that rule. Asano Tsuneoki's younger sister possessed a formidable intellect and a gift for understanding what men wanted, besides the obvious. Though Mariko had spent only a few short days in her company, she'd come to believe that Yumi knew what men wanted even before they themselves did.

I would give every gold ryō *in my dowry for a chance to learn the art of poised conversation from Asano Yumi.*

Mariko was so consumed with her thoughts that she all

but stumbled at the next sight that greeted her. Her throat caught on a slew of questions, the loudest ones threatening to barrel forth at any instant:

What have they done with Ōkami? Is he . . . dead?

She was not foolish enough to think she would ever receive an answer. Especially not from him. Not from this boy who gazed on her with such mistrust.

Standing at the entrance to one of the corridors branching off the main thoroughfare stood a silent figure, waiting for them to pass. His features were solemn, his posture rigid. His dark silk *hakama* was crisp and unwrinkled. He was a young man for whom such things appeared as natural and unstudied as herons in flight. Only his eyes were at odds with his demeanor—a shadow Mariko could not place darkened their depths.

Kenshin.

Her brother. Her twin.

The blood crept up her neck, heating her skin. Mariko stopped her fists from clenching, then let her gaze rest on her brother in what she hoped was an expression of affection.

Be water. Move with the current.

He watched her. Carefully. Even from this short distance, Mariko knew her twin well enough to see that he did not believe a single word she said. It cut at something deep within Mariko's chest. Threatened to sever a bond that had existed between them since their birth. The night they'd left Jukai forest, he'd studied her with the same look, as though he were gazing upon a riddle he could not solve. Though the Dragon of

Kai said very little, it was clear Kenshin questioned every move Mariko made, both in the past and in the present. Wondered if duplicity lay at its root. Each time she locked eyes with her brother, Mariko beheld mistrust and uncertainty.

Two things that had never crossed their paths before.

She wondered what he saw when he looked at her. She'd wager it was something different, yet the same. Something tinged in pain.

"Mariko," Kenshin began softly.

Her retinue paused before him. Shizuko and the servants at their flank bowed low. After all, Hattori Kenshin was the Dragon of Kai—one of the most famed warriors in the entire empire. The son of an honored daimyō. A samurai held in high esteem amongst the members of the imperial court.

Mariko coaxed herself to smile. Forced her eyes to mean it.

"Did you . . . rest well these last two nights?" Kenshin asked.

"Very well." She nodded. "It's the first restful sleep I've had in weeks."

Yet another lie.

She'd already lost count of how many she'd told him.

"I'm glad to hear it. You look . . . better. More like yourself." The Dragon of Kai chose his words carefully, as though he were picking fruit from a tree. It was just like him to behave in such a manner. Exacting to a fault.

But Kenshin's principles would not serve him well today. His unspoken questions hung in the air like spiderwebs, waiting to catch their victim unawares. And Mariko knew it best to avoid any traps of spun silk, at all cost. Her voice needed to match her face. She let her shoulders fall in relaxation. Made her neck lengthen as though she were confident.

I am speaking to my brother, as I have done for nearly every day of my life. Nothing more.

She smiled at him, allowing her mind drift to memories of a fonder time. An easier life. One in which the truth of her family's wealth and privilege still remained shamefully beyond her notice. "I have not had a chance to thank you properly—for saving me."

It was not a lie, in a manner of speaking. He'd brought her to Inako, as Mariko had wished, and she did feel a sense of gratitude for it.

Kenshin nodded, his eyes narrowing at the corners. "You would do the same for me."

"Of course." Mariko breathed deeply. "But—now that I've had a moment to recover—there are matters I wish to discuss with you."

He nodded again. "I'm . . . glad to hear it. I, too, have things I—I wish to tell you." Kenshin winced as though he were in pain. A part of Mariko wanted to press him for details, but it seemed odd to expect frankness from him when she herself would not give it. "When you've had a chance to recuperate fully, let us make time to speak with each other," he finished.

"I would like nothing more than that," she said. "After all that has happened, it will be a comfort to speak with someone I love and respect, rather than listen to idle men who prey

74

on the efforts of those above their station." Mariko continued smiling as she spoke, in a sad attempt to dispel the awkwardness. "I appreciate your patience with me, Kenshin."

Her brother nodded, then glanced once more at the silken collar of her kimono. As he took in the long sleeves laden with intricate embroidery, his eyes grew wide. Even a warrior with little understanding of women's clothing knew it to be a kimono without parallel. "Are you meeting with Prince Raiden?"

Her smile faltered. "I . . . have not yet been informed as to where it is I am going."

Mariko watched her brother stop himself from reacting in plain view of the servants surrounding them. Servants who were likely in place to report anything suspicious. Again this attempt to deny his instincts—however poorly—was so unlike Hattori Kenshin. It was the kind of behavior that had undoubtedly been learned during his short tenure in the imperial city.

Kenshin took a step forward, one hand resting on the hilt of his *wakizashi*. Mariko could not tell if he wished to protect her or if he wished to offer her a warning. His lips remained poised between sound and speech. Then Kenshin stepped back, nodding to himself in decision. "Be a tribute to our family, Mariko." His words were echoes of their father's final admonition, that fateful morning she had left on her journey for Inako.

They only strengthened her resolve.

She would earn herself a place of trust in the imperial

court. Forge alliances wherever possible. Undermine the cause of the emperor at all turns.

And do whatever it took to free Ōkami, the boy she loved.

Never mind that it sounded foolish—like the dreams of a small child with ambitions far beyond her ken.

Everything in life began with an idea.

Shizuko bowed beside Mariko and Kenshin, offering an end to the odd silence that had settled between them. Her sudden deference did not seem in keeping with the servant's demeanor for the last two days. "I beg pardon for the intrusion, my lord, but we must proceed on our path toward the empress's pavilion."

Kenshin glanced at the servant as though he'd only just noticed her presence. "The empress?"

"Yes, my lord." Shizuko turned toward Mariko, a frown tugging at her lips.

"I've been instructed to bring Lady Hattori to the Lotus Pavilion. The empress would like to see her now."

Gilded Petals and Dripping Wounds

—— ✦ ——

As they neared a set of sliding doors adorned with carved lotus blossoms, Shizuko slowed, Mariko still trailing in the servant's wake. The guards standing on either side moved apart to let them pass. Mariko crossed the threshold and bowed low, her feet resting just beyond the raised wooden sill. Her forehead touched the newly woven tatami mats, their fresh scent curling into her nose, clean and piney and inviting.

When she and Shizuko took to their feet once more at the far end of a vast receiving room, something caught her eye, and a new realization settled upon Mariko. One she'd managed to miss for the last two days, consumed as she was with her own worries. Shizuko had proven beyond capable and efficient, if somewhat thorny. Just this morning, Mariko had wondered why the older woman—with seniority over many of the other servants—had been relegated to assist with the bastard prince's bride, rather than serve in a more venerated position within the imperial family's personal retinue. It was only when Mariko watched Shizuko struggle to her feet that she understood the reason. The grimace and the momentary imbalance gave her away.

Shizuko had an injury to her neck—perhaps even to her spine—that gave her movements an impermissible flaw, likely beyond her control. A servant in the imperial court could not distract from anything. They needed to move about like flitting shadows, and shadows did not sport their flaws before the emperor.

Anger coiled through Mariko's throat, making it difficult to swallow. She chastised herself for not noticing Shizuko's condition earlier. Wondered what could have been the cause. How could Mariko ever attempt to champion those less fortunate—to claim to care for someone besides herself—while mired in her own concerns? If Mariko wished to see beyond her own experience, it was clear from this misstep that she was doing an abysmal job of it.

In that moment, a sense of awareness descended on her. The kind that crept over Mariko with surprising frequency of late. It had first struck her when she'd witnessed the family partake of their meager evening meal on her father's land, the night the Black Clan raided the Hattori granary. That night, she watched a small child don the mantle of a much older soul. There—hovering in the darkness, with Ōkami by her side—Mariko realized that every person she'd ever met, from the smallest of children to the most notorious of thieves, had a life as intricate and significant as that of an emperor or a samurai or an elegant lady of the court. Not once in her seventeen years had she heard a member of the nobility discuss this. Those who served them had been born beneath unlucky stars and could never share the same sky, no matter how hard they might wish for it.

"Men cannot change their stars, just as cats cannot change their stripes," her father had often said with a shrewd smile.

The remembrance caught in her chest, its bitterness clawing at her tongue.

She looked to the right as one of the young servants—the same girl with the round face and button nose from the day before—rearranged Mariko's skirts. While the girl worked to ensure that her mistress appeared nothing less than perfect, Mariko studied her face, taking note of the small scars along her jaw, likely from a childhood illness.

"What is your name?" Mariko whispered to the girl, her lips barely moving as she spoke. They were too far away for those at the opposite end of the chamber to overhear their exchange. Nevertheless Shizuko startled beside her, proceeding to chuff with irritation.

Color mottled the young servant's skin. "Isa."

"Thank you, Isa." Mariko committed the name to memory. Then she lifted her gaze to take in the sight of a long receiving room with a low ceiling constructed of polished acacia wood. The walls were papered in thin silk, adorned with elegantly gilded paintings—scenes from spring gardens, replete with flowers and arched bridges framed in the amber glow of an afternoon sun. Fresh tatami mats arranged in a perfect grid lined the floor, which was warmed from beneath by slow-burning charcoal braziers.

Young women knelt on either side of the space, their garments fanning about them becomingly. They were likely courtiers or daughters of the empire's most important families. The women murmured among themselves at the sight of Mariko, their beautiful kimono rustling as they struggled to seek better vantage points. If Mariko were to squint, the chamber before her would greatly resemble its own elegant garden, its blossoms swaying in a dainty breeze—splashes of pink and purple and pale green petals dyed to resemble jade, arranged as though every color had been chosen in an effort to bring to life the artwork gilding the walls.

At the opposite end of the chamber sat an elegant woman on a silk cushion positioned before a low throne, with a wooden back lacquered to look as though the teak wood gleamed from within.

Mariko did not meet the eyes of the stately figure awaiting her arrival. After gliding to the foot of the slightly raised platform, she knelt with great care, slipping the front of her kimono beneath her shins to keep the delicate material from wrinkling. The brush of the silk across the tatami mats was like the whisper of a sword being drawn.

She bowed once more, careful to avert her gaze until addressed.

"Hattori Mariko." The empress spoke in a high-pitched tone, almost girlish in its lilt. "Welcome to the Lotus Pavilion."

Inhaling through her nose, Mariko lifted her gaze.

Her Imperial Majesty Yamoto Genmei, Empress of Wa, rose to her feet in a seamless motion, a warm smile spreading across her features. She appeared small and delicate, swathed in a peach kimono. But her presence was nevertheless commanding, especially for a woman who had just lost her husband. Mariko had first thought she might find the empress in mourning, but it did not appear to be the case. She seemed determined and at ease in her station. Perhaps it was because within the same breath, the empress had lost her husband and also gained a son in the seat of power.

It appeared that fear and sadness did not suit the occasion.

Mariko concealed her surprise at the unabashed kindness in the empress's expression. After all, Mariko was betrothed to the son of the previous emperor's beloved consort, and everyone in the land had heard the rumors of the empress's distaste on the matter.

"It is an honor to meet you, my lady." Mariko lent her voice the delicate melody of a songbird, just as she remembered Yumi doing in the presence of those the *maiko* had wished to impress.

"And it is my honor to meet the future wife of Prince Raiden." The empress motioned with her hand to an empty space beside her. "Will you join me for refreshments?"

Mariko was led onto the low platform, a silken cushion positioned to the empress's left. With Shizuko's assistance, Mariko knelt upon the cushion as two small tables were brought forth. An array of food was placed upon each tray: rounds of colorful *daifuku* encircled by edible flowers in an inviting arrangement, a bowl of iced persimmons garnished with gold flakes, *azuki* beans covered in sugar, and tiny squares of pastel steam cakes. To one side sat a flawless white egg in a porcelain dish, still ensconced in its shell.

The sight almost brought a smile to Mariko's face.

I wonder what the empress would do if I were to remove the shell as Yoshi taught me to do it.

In silence, similar trays were brought forth for all the ladies present. All the while, Mariko kept her eyes lowered, letting her gaze flit about the space covertly, trying her best to appear demure and at ease all at once.

An impossible feat.

Soft laughter danced around the room.

"You are quite a little doe, are you not?" the empress said with another warm smile.

Uncertainty took shape within Mariko. She had never been gifted at the art of conversation. Was the empress's comment a compliment or a criticism? Or worse, was it a criticism veiled as a compliment? How best should she respond? Hand-wringing did not seem to be an adequate reply, nor did outright churlishness.

This was why Mariko had floundered around other women, especially girls her own age.

"If it pleases my lady, I am happy to be a doe." Mariko bowed her head.

The empress laughed. "And if it displeases me?"

Mariko hesitated. She looked to the left, as though

she were seeking assistance. Many of the other young women gazed upon her with pointed interest, even as they took dainty sips of their tea. And offered nothing by way of help. Several of them even tittered behind their hands.

Mariko took in a steadying breath. "If it displeases the empress, I am happy not to be a doe."

Another ripple of amusement passed the empress's lips. "How did you ever live for so long amidst a group of hea-thenish men, with such pristine manners? It appears you are relatively unscathed after your ordeal"—she paused to sip her tea—"or are appearances as deceiving as they all say?"

Mariko squeezed her eyes shut, steeling herself. Then she met the empress's gaze, willing her countenance to appear earnest. Trustworthy. "They did not touch me," she said firmly. "Their leader forbade it. I believe he meant to barter with my father to return me unscathed for a higher profit."

"How very fortunate for you." The empress quirked her head, the motion causing the jewels in her hair to flash as though in warning. "And rather fortunate for Prince Raiden as well."

It appeared the rumors being passed through the nobility were correct. The empress did not have fond feelings for the son of her husband's consort. Mariko knew the correct thing to do in this case would be to remain quiet and offer little in the way of opinion. It would not do for her to speak ill of her betrothed in an attempt to ingratiate herself to the empress. Were Mariko's mother present, she would have urged her daughter to comport herself as all the other young ladies did at court—with nods and smiles and murmurs of agreement.

Mariko tried to smile. The empress did not return the gesture. Any suggestion of kindness on her features had vanished.

What does she want? What is she trying to do?

As though she could hear Mariko's thoughts, the empress answered. "I'm sure you are curious as to why I asked to see you even before you were brought before my son. The emperor is keen to meet you, of course. He has great affection for his brother." Her jewels flashed once more, like bladed mirrors.

Mariko lifted a small porcelain cup to her lips and pretended to swallow her tea. The rim of the cup was painted in liquid gold, the contents within it perfectly brewed. The scent alone told her so. Her heart thudded in her chest with such force that it caused her hand to tremble and the tea to slosh from brim to brim.

What does she want with me?

"Has Prince Raiden been attuned to your needs?" the empress asked, as though she were inquiring about the weather.

Startled by the question, Mariko flinched, jostling the tiny cup against her lips, the pale liquid inside burning her tongue. She put down the cup with great care, her mind sifting through all the possible answers she could offer. The possible questions to follow. All the endless possibilities, in all directions.

Stop it, at once. Do not permit yourself to be rendered a fool.

Unless that is the most advantageous course.

"Prince Raiden has had much to contend with over these last few days, following the skirmish with the bandits in Jukai forest," Mariko said softly. "But, yes, he was very kind on our journey here."

The empress laughed as she had not laughed before. When the sound of her amusement filled the space, the women on all sides laughed in turn, but none with as much vigor as the empress.

"Prince Raiden? Kind?" The empress laughed again. "My, he must have been charmed by the sight of you, even though you were covered in several weeks' worth of mud."

Her sarcasm was not a thing to be missed. Buried beneath it—alongside the naked spark of cruelty—Mariko sensed something much darker. It was clear the empress disliked Prince Raiden. But simply attempting to cause him strife by tormenting his future wife seemed . . . unsophisticated. All too predictable.

Perhaps she's trying to learn whether or not I am happy to be marrying Prince Raiden. And, in turn, learn whether or not I can be of use to her, whatever her agenda might be.

Mariko thought quickly.

Though she'd eschewed the notion only a moment ago, Mariko decided it was best to appear foolish when it came to this particular matter. Foolish girls were easy to dismiss, and women like the empress enjoyed doing so almost as much as many of the men Mariko knew. She swallowed and held her breath, biting down on her cheek near to the point of drawing blood. She allowed the strain to become evident, hoping they would mistake her discomfort for embarrassment.

It rang true, even to her. For there would have been a time—not so long ago—that Mariko would have felt nothing but sheer terror at the thought of being embarrassed in a roomful of whispering silk.

That time had not passed. It had merely changed. What would have once been shame had morphed into anger and calculation.

Where there was anger, there was no room for shame.

Mariko bowed, her eyes locking on a piece of unraveling straw from the tatami mat near her left knee. "I am grateful to Prince Raiden." She spoke to the floor. "If he found something about me pleasing—despite my dirty appearance—I am fortunate for it. He rescued me from a fate I would not wish on my worst enemy. If he only ever glances my way in passing, I will be happy."

"Happy?" The empress paused. Her expression turned sinister. "And are you *happy* with the fortunes your life has granted you?"

Mariko blinked. "I—"

"You do not know what it means to be happy," the empress said. "Happiness is not a thing to be found here in the imperial court. We take moments of pleasure. Collect them and keep them tight in our chests. And we hope they are enough to fill whatever holes our truths leave behind."

Mariko lifted her gaze to meet the empress. The same voice

that had been filled with a careful balance of benevolence and scorn had changed further as she spoke. Grown higher-pitched and almost shaky. For a moment, Mariko thought the empress might be on the verge of losing hold on her emotions and showing everyone present her true self.

The moment passed as quickly as it came, and the empress's features leveled once more. She gestured to one side, and a servant scurried from the shadows to place another silken cushion in the center of the room, between the lines of attentive courtiers. Mariko wondered if she would be asked to sit upon it now. To be dissected by the women around her for all her many failings. It was like a childhood nightmare. One in which Mariko had been stripped bare, her every flaw exposed for all the world to see.

Murmurs began rippling through the room. Several of the young women leaned forward as though they were hungry panthers, awaiting their turn to pounce.

In the back of the room, the sliding doors rasped open, and sounds of commotion unfurled into the air. Caught between two imperial guards, a young woman in a simple white kimono struggled in vain to free herself. Her arms were linked behind her back, and her face was stained by tears.

The murmuring grew louder as the guards dragged the girl forward. With a sob of protest, she was forced to her knees upon the silken cushion. Her unbound hair caught in one of the guard's gauntlets. After he wrenched it free, the long dark strands wound about the girl's neck in a snarl.

Pity formed a tight knot in Mariko's throat. Were the

girl properly attired and not in the throes of despair, Mariko wagered she would be quite striking, with such lovely skin and a large set of eyes.

Confusion warmed through Mariko, causing the knot to tighten further.

What are they going to do to her?

"Hirata Suke," the empress began.

The young woman's head fell forward in a strangled moan. "Y-yes, my lady." She sniffed as she placed her forehead on the tatami mats in a pitiful bow.

"You stand accused of cavorting in the gardens with a man beneath your station."

Another sob.

"Is this true?" the empress asked in an amiable tone, as though she were asking after the girl's family.

"I—I was only smiling in his direction, and we—"

"Before you refute the charges, know that three of the ladies now present saw you with the boy and are willing to say as much to the emperor."

Suke glanced around for a moment—her features in a panic—willing someone to come to her defense. Several of the other girls near her age averted their gazes or sipped their tea as though Suke's future were not on trial before their very eyes. When she realized she was utterly alone, Suke sobbed once more.

"You are to be joined in union with the son of Lord Toranaga, no?" the empress continued.

Suke did not reply.

The empress's lips gathered. "Answer me at once, or we will leave you for the men to punish as they see fit."

"Yes, my lady." Suke bowed. "I am to wed Lord Toranaga's eldest son at the end of the summer."

Her expression stern, the empress unfurled to her feet in a rustle of silk. "So you are to be wed to one man, yet you shamelessly cavort with another, mere weeks before your union?"

Suke's eyes flitted around the room once more, but this time she did not seek an ally. Her lower lip trembled in betrayal as she struggled to find the sources of her misfortune. "Yes, my lady."

One girl—whose heart-shaped face had paled—coughed to clear her throat, then looked away again.

"You shameful piece of filth," the empress said to Suke. "I should tell the emperor what you have done and ruin the entire Hirata line in the process. You stain the reputation of the imperial court with your wantonness." The lines deepened across the empress's forehead as she spoke. As she stared down at Suke, the moment stretched thin. Thinner than a strand of hair about to snap. Then the empress's face smoothed all at once in an unnerving fashion. "But I am forgiving, am I not?" Her voice became gentle and lyrical once more. Almost pleasant.

"Yes, you are, my lady." Suke bent her forehead to the floor in yet another humbling obeisance.

The empress's tone turned quiet. "I could tell my son, the emperor, what you have done, and your future—the future of your entire family—would be ruined."

Even from this distance, Mariko saw Suke's eyes shimmer with unshed tears. "Yes, my lady."

"Is it not better this way?" the empress asked. "For you to admit your guilt and take your punishment safely among your own?"

Suke squeezed her eyes shut. Let the tears fall as she took in a shuddering breath. "Yes, my lady."

Satisfaction passed across the empress's features. She glanced about the room. "Once the justice of the Lotus Pavilion has prevailed, we will speak of this matter no longer. Absolute mercy is our just reward." Her admonition echoed throughout the space—a warning to all the other ladies present.

Anticipation writhed throughout the space. Its menace pulsed to all four corners.

The empress waited, a single brow arched.

Suke lifted her chin and rolled her shoulders back. "I admit to behaving licentiously with a soldier on the outskirts of the imperial gardens. I am undeserving of my lady's mercy, but I beg for her pardon, and I swear on my family's name that I will never be so untoward again."

"Our mercy is granted." The empress all but beamed at the trembling young woman. "You may begin," she added almost absentmindedly.

Confusion once again took shape in Mariko's chest. Suke's

shoulders sagged forward, and it was impossible for Mariko to tell whether it was from relief or defeat.

Another moment of utter stillness passed before a single egg soared across the room and shattered against Suke's head. Though she clearly knew to expect it, the girl cried out in surprise and raised both her hands to defend herself, then immediately put them back in her lap. Another egg pelted toward her from the opposite side, the bright orange center sliding down the front of Suke's white kimono. The women began to laugh amongst themselves.

All at once, eggs flew across the room at Suke, shattering over her lovely skin and silken garments. A well-aimed one struck her cheek hard, and a small trickle of blood flowed down one side of her face like a twisted tear.

Soon all the eggs had been launched.

Save one.

The empress looked at Mariko purposely, her attention drifting to the egg Mariko thought she'd concealed in her palm.

A rush of indignation passed through her body.

Why am I being asked to participate in this kind of cruel sport? It is not my place.

She did not know this girl. And Mariko could not stomach doing something humiliating to someone else. Especially a girl she suspected to be innocent of the charges. Another tense moment passed before Mariko realized exactly why she had been asked to see the empress today. This display was to be her introduction into the empress's fold. Into the inner workings of the imperial court.

This sad display of power over an innocent young woman.

But Mariko did not have the time to contemplate the reasons why she'd been brought here. It came down to a simple decision for her.

She could act from her heart. Or from her head.

Her heart—a compass directed by emotion—pointed her toward the wrongness of the action. How it would eat away at her later if she did such a thing and caused another young woman pain.

Her mind told her what would happen if she failed the very first of the empress's tests. She would lose an opportunity to gain footing in the imperial court, and the tasks she wished to accomplish would be forced beyond reach. Mariko glanced once more at Suke. At the silent tears the girl spilled as bits of egg dripped down her hair and clothing.

I . . . can't do this to her.

But the empress's eyebrows drew together. Her lips pursed. Her stare was a thousand daggers, each aimed Mariko's way.

This was not about punishment. Though it was meant to be seen as an attempt to keep the morals of the young women at court in line, it came across as anything but. Pelting a girl into submission—even with something as harmless as an egg—was a rather strange show of power.

Despite the warnings of her mind, everything in Mariko's heart rebelled against it.

This strange show of power.

The empress continued to stare at Mariko. In response, Mariko weighed the egg in her hand. Let it roll across her palm. Considered throwing it at the empress in defiance.

But now was not a moment for dreams.

"Do you feel as though I am unjust?" the empress asked coolly.

Mariko gazed up at the dowager empress's face. When Yamoto Genmei had been younger, she must have been a beautiful woman. But time and pain and pettiness had withered her features into something unseemly, from the inside out. For the empress, every young woman she met was like the servant Isa—someone beneath her, meant for her to trample upon whenever she saw fit.

It probably began like this. With a simple choice.

Inhaling through her nose to allay her disgust, Mariko lobbed the egg hard at the pitiful girl, who dripped with enough food to feed a family for several weeks, letting it waste onto the freshly woven tatami mats. The egg landed at her knee with a splat, a pitiful finale to a sickening show.

Guilt spiked in Mariko's stomach when Suke looked up at her, a mixture of embarrassment and gratitude passing across her features. Mariko swallowed.

She is . . . grateful?

"I was a silly little fool just like you, once," the empress said to Mariko, her head canted to one side. "I thought myself principled and that my principles would carry me through my life, especially in the most difficult of times, when life did not turn out as I had dreamed." The empress smirked to hide a sudden flash of pain. "Principles are well and good when you are young and life is at your feet, Lady Mariko. Perhaps you see me as cruel, but I am saving this girl from experiencing far more ruin in this way. And making all these young women present realize a harsh truth: men are allowed to wander in their desires." She sniffed. "Women who wander risk their very lives."

Mariko dropped her gaze, settling once more on the piece of unraveling straw near her knee. Back at her father's province, she had known people like the empress. Women and men who took perverse pleasure in exacting unnecessary revenge on others. Even Ren had been guilty of similar behavior. But the empress was a strange variation of this. She believed herself better because she enacted cruelty to prevent something worse from happening.

Sparing girls public spite by encouraging it in closed settings.

Perhaps the empress was not at all like the people Mariko had known back home.

She was worse.

"Time teaches us all that we need to be better than men. But only by a thread." The empress rose. "Cling to that thread. You will need it." She gestured for one of the young attendants in the wings. "You will see my son now." The empress smiled at Mariko's kimono. Then shook her head in an approximation of regret.

"What a shame. That one was a favorite of mine, many years ago."

Gleaming Darkly

———— ✳ ————

Mariko's hands shook. As the attendants slid open the doors, she gripped her kimono sleeves without a care for rumpling the delicate fabric. Her eyes averted, she bowed one last time to the empress, who remained on her throne, a serene smile upon her face.

Beyond the sliding doors stood Kenshin, as though Mariko's torment was meant to be unceasing. If possible, her brother appeared even wearier than before. He looked at her face. At the frown tugging her lips and the lines creasing her brow. Then he cleared his throat, his gaze piercing, offering his sister silent advice.

In an instant, Mariko controlled her features.

Kenshin motioned for her to follow him. They turned to the left of the chamber, instead of the path to the right, which would have returned Mariko to the rooms she'd occupied since her arrival in Inako. As they walked, Mariko noted how many paces it took to move from one structure to another.

They exited the Lotus Pavilion and made their way toward a set of ornate sliding doors leading to the central courtyard. The men standing guard just outside were in simple *hakama*, each of their two swords slung through silk cords around their hips. Samurai, who would unsheathe their weapons only in dire circumstances, and never in front of the emperor, for death was the punishment if anyone dared to brandish a blade in his presence.

Forty-nine paces.

They waited while sandals were brought before them, Kenshin's the simple *geta* of a samurai, and Mariko's gleaming darkly of lacquered wood. Beyond the reaches of the castle, the sun had begun its descent below the horizon, its light caramelizing all it touched.

Mariko followed Kenshin across the center courtyard toward another wing of Heian Castle, one that rose from the main edifice of seven gabled roofs. The scent of the orange blossoms mingled with the *yuzu* trees, and the blend of sweet and sour citrus floated past Mariko, beckoning her toward the woods beyond. Strange how the forest had never transfixed her before, yet now called to her whenever its jagged shadows came into view.

As they strolled beneath a covered walkway—her wooden *zori* crunching over small white stones—Kenshin slowed.

Sixty-two paces.

"Do not react," he said. "Not to what I'm saying, and not to what you are about to see."

Though her first instinct was to ask questions, Mariko tamped down the desire.

Be water.

"They are trying to see how you will behave," he continued. "If I've learned anything about the Minamoto family in my short time at Heian Castle, I've realized they are always testing you. React in a way that shows you care about the son of Takeda Shingen, and it will be used against you both."

At the mention of Ōkami and the confirmation that he still lived, Mariko faltered in her steps, the rhythm of her motions broken.

"Am I wrong, then?" Kenshin asked quietly.

Mariko stood taller. She wanted so badly to tell him the truth. To tell him all that lurked in her heart, all that spun through her mind. To freely share with her brother every thought, every fear, every dream, just as she had when they were children. But she could not. Not until she understood why he no longer trusted her. Why he'd not once thought to ask before passing judgment.

Why he'd failed to come to her aid and averted his gaze from her wordless pleas.

"You're wrong," Mariko said, her tone curt.

Kenshin glanced over his shoulder at her, his eyes narrowing. "I don't think I mistook the emotion on your face when Takeda Ranmaru revealed his identity in Jukai forest."

Laughter trilled from Mariko's lips—an attempt to bring levity to the situation. "Now you are adept at reading emotion?" she teased. "I am glad for you, especially on behalf of Amaya."

To her surprise, Kenshin flinched as though she'd struck him. "Do not speak her name to me ever again, Mariko." His voice was low. Laden with feeling. Not at all the kind of response she had expected.

At a loss, Mariko said nothing.

They continued toward the central structure of Heian Castle, removing their sandals before entering the wooden hallways. Here, everywhere they stepped they were met with the shrill creaking of the drafty nightingale floors. But they did not walk in the direction of the emperor's receiving room. Instead Kenshin led her down a side corridor, past a series of shuttered doors, toward a darkened expanse with a set of aging stairs cut into its center.

Thirty-seven paces.

Once they descended and Mariko peered down the dimly lit pathway, another layer of the castle came into view. It seemed as though this hidden structure had been constructed from the earth itself. A warren of tunnels branched into low-ceilinged rooms, upon which the seat of the imperial city rested. As the lore suggested, Heian Castle was indeed built in an odd fashion, with a sense of magic loitering in every shadow. It had been designed centuries ago by a famed mathematician, aided by the power of a reclusive enchantress.

But even knowing these things did not prepare Mariko

for what she now beheld. Most fortresses she'd encountered in the past did not possess a mysterious structure beneath them. Reinforced on all sides by stone and immense timber beams, this place was meant for something secret. Perhaps even illicit. Seemingly crafted without design, it was impossible to determine where the passages began or ended.

In silence, the two siblings wove through this dank underbelly of the castle. Mariko shivered, the warmth of the sun lost in this underground lair.

When the light began to wane, Kenshin paused to reach for one of the torches anchored to the wall. Before they moved toward the second set of stairs—these carved from solid stone rather than timber—he turned to her.

"Show them nothing," her brother said quietly.

Mariko did not know if he spoke to her or to himself. The wet smell wafting from below almost drew a shudder. As they descended, her eyes locked on her brother's shoulders. On the unwrinkled expanse of his *kosode* and the comforting weight of the swords at his sides. Ever since they were children, Hattori Kenshin had always embodied the perfect ideal of a samurai.

In these creaking halls—taking in this poisonous air—Mariko wished that she, too, had the weight of a weapon at her side.

As the silence between them grew heavier, an onslaught of questions caught in her throat. Mariko wanted so much to confide in her twin. But the way Kenshin disdained her these last few days—the way he'd treated her like a thing beyond his consideration—remained in the forefront of her mind.

She thought he would at least give her a chance to explain. But he was not the same brother Mariko had left behind. Something had changed in Kenshin, and she wondered whether it had anything to do with the mention of Amaya's name.

They moved past a stack of used charcoal near the last step, and the hem of Mariko's kimono slipped through a patch of murky water, dripping from a large stone channel above. She gasped as the icy wetness soaked through her *tabi* onto her feet.

In that moment, Mariko recalled the empress's parting words about the priceless garment.

Where am I being taken? Am I being led to my death?

No, her own brother would never be party to that. But the memory of how he'd stood by as Minamoto Raiden threatened her . . . that memory could not be ignored, no matter how much she wished it. No matter how many excuses she wanted to grant her brother, Kenshin had done nothing, save watch the spectacle unfold.

Just as he continued to do after arriving in Inako.

The clang of metal against stone ricocheted in the darkness, startling her into awareness. A lone torch flickered through the gloom ahead. She shifted her eyes to the floor, her hands and feet turning to ice even as the blood flashed hot through her body. She kept her gaze averted until a vaguely familiar groan echoed through the darkness before them. Its echo haunted her, almost halting her steps, making her fear to look upon its source in unfettered light.

She breathed deeply before recoiling against the smell. It was not just the expected rot and ruin of a space bereft of sun. The closer Mariko and Kenshin came toward the flickering torch, the stronger the scent of singed flesh permeated the air.

They burned Ōkami.

Mariko fought to maintain her composure. When the light of the torch crackled nearby, her vision distorted. She forced herself to look away. Forced herself to remain silent and accept the cold glare of truth.

A huddled heap lay against a wall of darkness before her. Iron bars separated her from the broken young man lying within. The metallic scent of blood filled Mariko's nostrils, making her gaze swim.

They'd burned him. Beaten him. Bled him. And for what?

Ōkami had already surrendered. Not once on their journey had he put up a fight.

Which meant that pure suffering had been the goal.

Fury and humiliation warred within her. Calling upon all the strength Mariko could muster, she forced herself to tuck both emotions away, deep behind her heart, where no one could find them.

No matter what they have done to Ōkami, I will look upon him without fear.

"Kenshin-*sama* . . . it is good to have you once more in the imperial city." When the emperor spoke, Mariko took a moment to form a memory. At first glance, much about

Minamoto Roku appeared uninteresting. His skin was inordinately pale, his features forgettable, especially as he stood alongside his taller, far more commanding brother. The grandest thing about Roku was his garments. They were made from a costly silk of burnished gold.

On second glance, however, there was definitely something more to be found beneath the surface. Though he was deep in a dank pit, far beneath the splendor of the world above, Roku spoke as though he were in the midst of a comfortable gathering between friends. A lighthearted affair, perhaps in a flowering garden, rather than a meeting in this gloomy underworld.

In contrast, his elder brother did not appear at ease. Not in the slightest. Prince Raiden reminded Mariko of a caged beast.

At least he *has the grace to appear unnerved by these circumstances.*

Mariko desperately wished to learn more about Ōkami's condition, but she refrained from glancing his way. She did not trust herself to remain coolheaded. Not yet.

The emperor continued addressing Kenshin in the same unhurried manner. "I have no doubt you will enjoy your stay here even more than before. I've already composed a message to our favorite teahouse in Hanami; you'll recall it from that unfortunate incident several weeks ago. As a reward for your success in apprehending this criminal and rescuing my brother's betrothed, please be my guest there tomorrow night." A crisp nod punctuated his directive.

Kenshin bowed, ever the ideal samurai honoring the wishes of his sovereign.

"You may return to your rooms now, Kenshin-*sama*," the emperor finished.

Though Mariko knew something had broken between her and Kenshin, her heart lurched in her chest at the thought of her brother leaving, as though his presence had provided her with a last bastion. A final buffer between Mariko and imminent doom. After passing to one side of Prince Raiden, Kenshin paused to glance back at her, and the torchlight flashed across his eyes. Their darkened centers delivered Mariko a final reminder:

Show them nothing.

In silence, her brother took his leave. Once his steps had faded into the murkiness beyond, the emperor shifted her way. "Lady Mariko." He canted his head as he regarded her. "The adage must be true. Even in war, flowers will bloom."

Despite the disgust rising in her throat, Mariko bowed even lower than her brother had. "It is an honor to be in your presence, my sovereign."

Another choice made. Another part of myself lost.

But honor would not gain her a footing in the imperial court. Nor would it spare those she held dear.

"It is unfortunate that it had to be under such circumstances." Minamoto Roku smiled at her. As with his mother, the young emperor's expression almost surprised her with its show of kindness. Had she not spent most of the afternoon in the presence of the dowager empress, Mariko might have been fooled.

But no member of this family would ever fool her again, even for a moment.

Mariko bit down hard on nothing before standing taller. She struggled to keep her voice even. "I, too, am deeply saddened about the circumstances surrounding my arrival in the imperial city. But my sadness has been eclipsed by gratitude. I am thankful to be here now, my sovereign, and doubly thankful to have been rescued by my brother and my betrothed."

The emperor stepped closer. Too close. He stood barely taller than she, his gaze nearly level with hers. Roku's eyes drifted across her face, as though he were taking note of every feature, every flaw. "I'm sure you are wondering why I asked to meet you here, in the bowels of the Golden Castle. It is because I wished for you to witness how we punish those who dare to challenge us. And especially how we punish foolish young men who dare to touch another man's bride." He glanced toward the cell at his back, his expression imbued with meaning.

Heat flared across Mariko's cheeks as he spoke. Knowing she owed it to Ōkami—and to herself—Mariko followed the emperor's gaze and took in the dreaded sight of the boy who'd become a source of strength for her, even in a short time. The boy who carried her heart with him, wherever he went.

This boy, who was her magic.

Covered in blood and grime, the son of the last shōgun

lay in a pile of filthy straw. His chest rose and fell with each of his heavy breaths. A faint wheeze whistled from the back of his throat. One side of his face had swelled to the point of being unrecognizable. He remained silent and still as they spoke around him, causing Mariko's heart to ache with worry.

Nevertheless, she kept her features locked. Immobile.

"Are you gratified to see the sight?" Roku asked. Again he tilted his head to one side, and the gesture reminded Mariko so much of his mother.

She forced herself not to wince. "Gratified, my sovereign?"

He continued studying her, searching for chinks in her armor. "Did this traitor not steal you from your rightful place and force you to work like a beast of burden for him?"

As with the dowager empress, Mariko suspected that Roku did not simply wish to hear the correct reply. He wished to unravel his own truths, concealed beneath the things people said—the things they felt in the darkest reaches of their hearts. Because of this, Mariko realized it was possible to err by agreeing with him immediately and offering the right response. True ladies of the nobility did not condone violence, at least not outwardly. She remembered the day she'd first laid eyes on Ōkami, when they were children. The day his father died. She'd seen the blood on the stones. The pain in his eyes. Her nursemaid scolded her for looking upon it all without batting an eye.

Ladies were supposed to look away, and Mariko refused

to do so, even as a child. But if she channeled outrage now, it would come across as disingenuous. *A strong affirmation often masks a denial.* It was something her father used to say.

Mariko weighed the words on her tongue before speaking them. "I am never gratified to see the suffering of any creature, my sovereign. Even thieving cowards." Still refusing to look away from the evidence of Ōkami's silent suffering, she threaded her fingers and pinched at the meat of her palm. With utmost focus, she latched on to the pain. Let it radiate through her, so it reached her face from a place of truth.

So it masked the rising fury.

Roku stood tall, his eyes unflinchingly upon hers. She envied the emperor's ability to hold his features in complete control, without the use of any diversions. It was a skill she lacked.

I would rather be as I am. Because this boy lacks any evidence of a soul.

Her nails dug into her palm even farther. She swallowed in an attempt to look unnerved. "But I *am* gratified to see my future family best our enemy," Mariko finished in a clear tone.

At this, the chains binding Ōkami jangled. Her eyes going wide, Mariko watched him struggle to sit upright, strangely grateful to know he still retained some of his faculties. To know that a part of him still lived. As his face shifted into a pool of torchlight, her nails nearly drew blood.

Please let my sorrow be masked by my pain.

The beating had been worse than she first thought. Now

Mariko could make out a terrible, glistening wound on his neck, just below the right side of his jaw.

Ōkami stared straight at her, even through an eye swollen shut.

Then—to the surprise of all present, save Mariko—he began laughing. He coughed around the sound as he leaned closer to the torchlight. The flickering flames rendered his broken face into a mass of moving shadows. "You brought the useless girl with you. I hope it was worth getting her dressed like an empress to see this," he rasped with amusement.

Ōkami had said something similar to Mariko before. Called her useless when she'd felt most vulnerable. It had stung then, laden as it was with truth. But Mariko knew he said it now for a reason. She could see the glint of something in his gaze—a strength of will the sons of Minamoto Masaru had not even begun to break. And Mariko knew Ōkami was trying—even as he lay broken and bleeding against a filthy mound of straw—to offer her comfort by hearkening back to their time together.

To spare her from his suffering, even in the smallest of measures.

Mariko swallowed slowly, letting her vision blur. Shoring up her reserve.

At Raiden's behest, the lock of the cell was unlatched by a waiting soldier. Ōkami raised himself on an elbow, and the emperor's brother stepped inside to level a vicious kick at his midsection. Mariko bit her tongue to keep from crying out at the muffled thud.

"You dare to address a lady in such a manner?" Raiden spat on Ōkami before kicking him again.

Mariko's teeth ground together. It took every bit of her remaining willpower to stay motionless. Down to the marrow of her bones, she despised Raiden. Briefly she considered the satisfaction she would feel at shoving a blade through his stomach.

One day, I will make sure he pays for every wound he inflicts.

But she could not contemplate these thoughts now. The darkness needed to invade her. A cool wash of ice needed to flow through her veins. She needed this detachment. Needed to make sure she felt everything in a single instant and then nothing at all in the next breath.

As he watched her inhale, Roku stepped closer. Close enough to touch. The smell of fine silk and the hint of camellia oil radiated from his skin as he placed a sympathetic hand on her shoulder, startling her. Roku smiled. "Don't worry, Hattori Mariko. We've made certain the son of Takeda Shingen won't forget his place, not even for an instant. For the remainder of his short life, he will not be able to escape the tarnish of his treachery." With a wave of his hand, he beckoned toward his brother.

Raiden moved the torch closer to Ōkami's face.

In the dim reaches of the firelight, Mariko saw the wound below his jaw, etched into his skin in jagged strokes.

At first glance, something about it looked amiss. But when Mariko tilted her head, she realized what they'd done. The two characters meaning "loyalty" had been inked into Ōkami's neck, but they'd been placed backward. A mark of mockery and shame. One undoubtedly meant to burn the memory of Takeda Shingen's treachery into his son's flesh.

As though it had not been there already.

Mariko's first desire was to react with rage. She wanted to knock the emperor's hand off her shoulder and sear the smile off his face.

It was a child's desire. An exercise in futility.

Roku was a cruel boy playing a cruel game. It was clear the empire's newest sovereign was a shrewd young man, but it was also evident that his cruelty rivaled his intelligence. The Emperor of Wa enjoyed toying with people to see how they would react. And Mariko refused to be any man's toy.

It was time to show she had a spine. There was a possibility doing so would prove foolish; it was a gamble to allow anyone to see past her armor. But Mariko had assembled her own suspicions in the short time she'd stood calmly beside Roku. As he'd searched for what lay buried behind her heart, Mariko had done the same with him.

If Roku still watched over his prisoner's cell long after his punishment had been doled out—if the emperor had chosen to keep Ōkami alive past the point when wisdom would have dictated otherwise—Mariko wagered it was not merely for the sport of it.

Something about Ōkami had wriggled beneath Roku's

smiles. The Emperor of Wa was not done causing the son of Takeda Shingen pain. Which meant he relished lording his power over others.

Mariko began with a low bow. She let the blood collect in her head so that when she stood once more, her face appeared flushed in what she hoped was a becoming fashion. "I beg your forgiveness, my sovereign. I do not mean to be impertinent, but I am still uncertain as to why I have been brought here." Her nails continued digging into her palms. "It's true this boy took me prisoner. He and his men forced me to work for them until my hands bled. But I am not gladdened to be reminded of this, nor am I the kind of woman who would enjoy seeing cruelty befall any living creature." Mariko's voice dropped to a hush. "Have I been brought here as a test of loyalty?" she asked outright, not caring that indignation seeped into her tone.

Roku peered at her, his gaze taking in her every move. "And if you were?"

She nodded once, biding her time. "I would understand why, my sovereign. But it would still cause me pain to hear it."

"Why is that?"

"Because my loyalty—the loyalty of the Hattori clan—was never once put to question until I was stolen from my family against my will." Mariko focused her attention on the floor, feigning humility as her speech turned tremulous. "Again I beg pardon for my frankness, but I have had a trying time recently." She swallowed hard, as though she were warding away tears, her breath wobbling past her lips. "Is it wrong for me to believe I have suffered enough, my sovereign?"

Roku linked his hands behind him. "Then you do not wish Takeda Ranmaru to perish for his crimes?"

It was a delicate balance—the two sides of this game—for it was evident the emperor did not see the truth as she did. As Kenshin had warned, this was a test. If Mariko were simply to say she wished Ōkami dead, the emperor would continue toying with them. An easy answer would not lead to an easy outcome, not with a boy like Minamoto Roku.

Be water.

Warmth pooled in one of Mariko's palms. Her nails had drawn blood. She let the pain radiate to her eyes and imbued grief into her expression. "Please do not think me ungrateful, my sovereign, but I would never wish to bring about a man's death, no matter how deserved it might be." A single tear welled in her left eye as she lied without so much as a care to the Emperor of Wa. Her heavenly sovereign.

It was an artful attempt at persuasion, especially when contrasted with her pitiable efforts earlier. Alas, Mariko's attempt to convey sorrow did not appear to move Roku in the slightest. He said nothing as his eyes constricted, suspicion tugging at his lips.

Like the pounding of an approaching stampede, Mariko's heartbeat rose in her ears.

Even with my best efforts, I've failed to convince him. Of anything.

Just as she thought her cause utterly lost, a figure shifted nearby. Mariko's betrothed moved toward her from his place beside Ōkami's cell, his torch still wavering in his grasp. "It is not the sight of suffering or death that should thrill you. It is the sight of our sovereign's justice." Prince Raiden's thick eyebrows gathered. His eyes raked over her, not in appreciation but in consideration. As he caught sight of her tears, the tension in his arms seemed to abate. "I imagine the idea of torture must be disturbing to you, nonetheless, as a woman." Though Raiden's manner oozed of superiority, his expression looked tinged with something . . . strange. Something unexpectedly earnest. Something Mariko had yet to encounter within these walls.

Compassion? From this *brutish boy?*

The very idea made Mariko feel as though insects were scuttling across her skin.

When Raiden drew even closer, his body curved protectively around her, as though he were a cocoon and she a wingless creature caught in a trance. Mariko stepped away out of habit, twisting to meet his gaze. When Raiden realized what he had done—that he'd instinctively moved to protect her— furrows formed on either side of his mouth.

In that moment, Mariko knew it was more important than ever for her to begin channeling every skill of Asano Yumi she could espouse. Even then it would likely never be enough. A certain amount of confidence was needed to navigate the waters of artful seduction. Mariko was confident she did not possess it.

These worries fraying at her resolve, Mariko forced herself to keep her thoughts at bay. Gazing up at the stern and unforgiving countenance of Raiden, she brought to mind a different face. One of a boy in black with scarred lips and a sly smile. A boy who understood pain in a way these fools could not even begin to fathom. The same boy who undoubtedly watched her from his cell, in calculating silence.

"Please, my lord," Mariko said to Prince Raiden, her words measured and clear. "I wish never to see the son of Takeda Shingen ever again. He stole me away from my family. Away from my future. Away from . . . *you*," she breathed without a sound. A fat tear trickled down her cheek. Mariko lowered her lashes, her body tingling with awareness.

It's too much. It won't work.

No matter how hard I try, I will never be Yumi.

The doubts crept into her throat. The blood began to well in her palm, threatening to catch notice, even in the darkness.

She remained still, her breath bated.

To her shock, a large hand took hold of Mariko's elbow. Though it was a warrior's roughened palm, its touch felt awkwardly gentle, as though it were unaccustomed to offering comfort. "I will see to it that you are returned to your chambers at once." Raiden spoke gruffly.

When Mariko opened her eyes once more, she caught sight of the emperor in silent conversation with his elder brother. If Roku was surprised or displeased at this turn of events, he did not show it. The two sons of Minamoto Masaru held each other's gazes for a moment before the emperor nodded once in dismissal.

Her betrothed bowed in deference to his younger brother. The next instant, Raiden directed Mariko's elbow forward, away from the blood and the ruin.

Every part of her wanted to turn back, one last time. To offer Ōkami a measure of solace. At least the same strength and solidarity he'd given her. The son of the last shōgun remained quiet throughout these exchanges, but Mariko felt the weight of his gaze. Heard the strain of his thoughts. And she wished more than anything that she could share in them.

But Mariko did not so much as look over a shoulder. She knew better than to let either the emperor or his elder brother suspect her sentiments for even an instant. Instead Mariko permitted Raiden to lead her back toward the stairs. The recent ordeal had caused her shoulders to tremble, but she did not prevent them from shivering as she would have normally done, for she'd learned much in the last exchange she witnessed between the two brothers.

Signs of her fragility moved Prince Raiden, even when nothing else did.

Even when it had the exact opposite effect on the emperor.

Mariko intended to take every advantage of this, especially if it meant seeding enmity between the brothers. When she and Raiden started ascending the stairs, she pretended to stumble as though she'd missed a step. Her bloodied palm braced her fall, and she pressed her skin into the rough timber beam along the wall. With a soft cry, she inhaled abruptly. A whiff of the discarded charcoal used to heat the braziers floated into her nostrils, and the crystallized dust swirled down her throat, its flakes causing her to cough.

Raiden caught her against his side. "Are you injured?"

Her expression rueful, Mariko lifted her bloodied palm into the light. "I'm not badly hurt, my lord. Just clumsy." She smiled a hesitant smile, lingering to gnaw on her lower lip. "Thank you . . . for being there to catch me, my lord."

Raiden let his eyes run the length of her. He paused on the soiled hem of her kimono. On her trembling hair ornaments. On her bloody hand and tearstained face.

Then made a decision.

"You're welcome, Mariko."

secrets of a ʙamboo sea

———— ✳ ————

Whenever Tsuneoki had time to himself, he liked to reflect upon life. To consider the many decisions— both good and bad—that had led him to where he was now, strolling alone through a forest of bamboo, with nothing but sparkles of sunlight to guide his way.

As a boy, it had been easy for him to make rash decisions. Youth was a powerful excuse for folly. After Asano Naganori betrayed Takeda Shingen—accusing him of moving against the emperor—a chasm formed between factions of the nobility. In the chaos following, Tsuneoki lost his best friend. Then—a mere month later—he lost his own father. Alone and afraid, he swore to do whatever it took to earn Ōkami's trust again.

And Tsuneoki had done anything and everything. Even sold his own soul.

Not long after the death of Takeda Shingen, Tsuneoki's

father was executed for treason as well. Tsuneoki fled his family to follow after Ōkami, leaving his mother and younger sister in the care of others. It seemed so simple at first, to disappear with his best friend on another adventure, as they'd often done before. To forget everything, especially his sorrowful mother and his wailing sister.

But they were so hungry on their own. Cold. Ōkami was lost. Tsuneoki was desolate. Against Yoshi's advice, they met with a bedraggled wielder of magic, who brokered a deal for the boys in the winter of their tenth year.

With the aid of blood oaths and a black-stoned dagger, Tsuneoki and Ōkami gave their futures to demons of the forest—his to a nightbeast, and Ōkami's to a shapeless demon of wind and fire. Tsuneoki learned to control his beast before it wrought havoc on everything it encountered. Ōkami's demon was harder to control, but these demons of old relished the chance to once again take shape and be more than spirits sighing in the night.

The two boys swore to never betray their demons.

To follow the light of the moon.

To never have children of their own, for the demons would always be their masters. These decisions had been easy for boys barely ten years of age. Simple things to barter for the power to move about without fear.

But now?

Tsuneoki pushed aside the bright green shoots in his path. Paused to catch his breath before continuing his trudge through the sea of swaying bamboo. He'd long harbored the hope that one day Ōkami would return to his rightful place. Begin to care about things of significance again. Tsuneoki started the Black Clan—this band of wayward *rōnin*, set on offering hope to those in need of it—with a mind to inspire his best friend to greatness. But Ōkami built a wall around himself, preventing him from feeling anything of significance, be it pain or joy or sorrow.

Nothing Tsuneoki did or said managed to breach that wall, not once in years.

Until the arrival of Hattori Mariko.

A sharp pang seared through Tsuneoki's side. The injury inflicted by the ghostly fox had just started to mend, and its memory was still sharp, the creature's claws raking over his insides, even as he slept.

He could not shake the sense of disquiet that had lingered in him ever since the Black Clan attempted to take Akechi fortress. The dark magic he'd felt there reminded him so much of that fateful night eight years ago, when he and Ōkami met with a sorcerer clothed in tattered garments, beneath the light of a sickle moon.

That same sense of disquiet had descended over him then, as it did now.

He shook it off with a turn of his shoulders. Tsuneoki moved forward. The bamboo stalks bent at his will, his body rolling across their smooth surfaces. When he listened closely, a hushed melody seemed to sigh from their hollow centers, spilling secrets to the birds above. Soon he found himself winding down a narrow path, hidden deep in the woods.

He paused again to take stock of his surroundings.

Following the attack that had taken place in Jukai forest the week prior, the Black Clan abandoned their former encampment; it was no longer an option for obvious reasons. The battle against the imperial forces cost them many good fighters, each with families and lives and dreams of their own. Upon learning of these losses, several of the fallen warriors' relatives elected to take their places and bear weapons against those in the imperial city. Word had spread across the nearby provinces. Friends and family members rode through the night, intent on joining the ranks of the Black Clan. They'd answered the call to action—the call to justice— being painted on stone walls and aging fences, hearkening to the not-so-distant past. Nodding to a symbol that combined the crest of the Asano clan with that of the Takeda.

The events in the forest had been an awakening for them all.

With the capture of the only living son of Takeda Shingen, the nobles loyal to the Minamoto clan attacked the last vestiges of the old ways. It was true that both Takeda Shingen and Asano Naganori mounted an uprising and were executed for treason as a result, but before that, they were heroes. Warriors of legend, upholding a sense of honor that had defined their ranks for centuries.

Over the last few days—despite all the odds—Tsuneoki had witnessed his numbers swell. Families who were no longer content to watch the fruits of their labor fill the coffers of their overlords had sent their sons to the Black Clan. Their brothers. Their fathers. Their nephews.

In less than a fortnight, they'd become too many for any one village to conceal.

Two days ago, Tsuneoki and his men took refuge in an unexplored domain, set against the mist-covered mountains. This maze of bamboo was known as the Ghost's Gambit, famed for the unfortunate wanderers who had lost their way and were now believed to haunt its twisted paths. Tsuneoki's men decided not to fight against this sea of bamboo, but to work with it. In doing so, they devised a unique kind of refuge.

Tsuneoki listened to the chiming of the wind as it flowed through the hollow bamboo stalks. A soft melody coiled around him, its ghostly fingers a whispered caress. It was the kind of song one heard if one knew how to listen. Soon he found the spot he'd been looking for. Not a clearing, but a narrow stream blanketed by a haze of fog. At first glance, nothing around him stirred, save for the rustling wind and the burbling water. Everywhere he looked, all he saw were long branches creaking in a liquid sway.

Then figures materialized from behind the stalks.

The Black Clan had built their homes in these trees. They used the bamboo as a means to conceal themselves. By collecting and weaving the sturdiest fronds through the treetops, they created platforms upon which structures had begun to take shape, floating in the canopy above. A wandering traveler would see nothing along the forest floor, save for the swirling mist.

Ren shifted from behind a curtain of stalks, a typically sullen look pulled across his features. One moment he was not there, the next he was in full view, the bamboo undulating in his wake. A boy no older than fourteen trailed at his heels—Yorishige, the nephew of Yoshi, who had traveled far to avenge the death of his eldest uncle.

After sliding down a sturdy rope, Haruki, the Black Clan's metalsmith, crouched near the stream to wash the sweat from his shining face. "Is it true, then?"

Tsuneoki nodded. "My riders tell me the domains of the Yoshida clan and the Sugiura clan and the Yokokawa clan have fallen the same way as the Akechi. Not a single soldier is anywhere to be found; they've all fled or disappeared. It appears their minds have been swallowed by a dark magic."

"All of the clans you named are fiercely loyal to the emperor," Haruki mused further.

Yorishige nodded as he cracked his knuckles. "For at least three generations, they've reaped the rewards of serving the Minamoto family."

Ren cleared his throat, tugging on the sling still wrapped around his injured arm. "It would be too fitting to think they are finally getting their just rewards. Someone—or thing—is out to control them. What do you think the wielder of this evil magic means to accomplish by doing so?"

"Perhaps it intends to cut the supply lines and dismantle support for the new emperor," Tsuneoki said with a wry grin.

Ren spat in the misted earth by his feet. "A fine idea. It's a shame we had it first."

"The facts would indicate otherwise," Haruki said with a peaceful smile.

Yorishige laughed softly, and the sound reminded Tsuneoki so much of Yoshi that it cut through his chest.

Ren glared at the boy and the good-natured metalsmith. "These cursed demons are stealing our ideas, and you two have the nerve to be droll about it?" he grumbled as he stooped near the creek bed, sneering through a grimace of pain. "It must be Raiden's witch mother."

Tsuneoki frowned. "Perhaps." Uncertainty lingered in his voice as he recalled the figure of the samurai that night within the walls of the Akechi fortress. The Hattori crest had been emblazoned on his armor. But—as he had for several days— Tsuneoki continued to hold that information close. At least until he learned more about it.

Any fool could wear a crest if it served his purpose.

"What could the witch want or hope to achieve by attacking these domains?" Haruki asked, ignoring Ren's mockery. Though he appeared serene—as though his mind floated among the clouds—Haruki's attention remained firmly rooted to the earth. As always, the metalsmith possessed an uncanny ability to notice anything and everything. Not just the things any man could see, but the things concealed from sight and buried deep. "Her own family holds the seat of power right now," the metalsmith continued. "Why would she lay siege to those who are loyal to the Minamoto clan?"

"It's not her family." Yorishige cracked his knuckles once more.

His left eye twitching, Ren glanced sidelong at the boy. "Just her son." His features gathered with distaste. "That witch probably wants what any mother in her situation would want—her son to be emperor, rather than the little ingrate currently sitting on the Chrysanthemum Throne."

Haruki sighed. "She's mad if she thinks the people of Wa will depose their rightful ruler and put a bastard in his stead."

"Stranger things have happened." Tsuneoki watched the flowing stream as it tripped around a nearby bend.

With another sigh, Haruki swiped the dripping water from his brow. "Since our plan to overtake strongholds loyal to the emperor has been enacted by others, what is the next course of action, my lord?"

"As you learned only a few days ago, I am not your lord, Haruki, nor did I ever wish to be," Tsuneoki said. "There is no need between any of us for those kinds of formalities. What we need to do instead is continue gathering our forces in secret and start expanding on these efforts. It is more important now than ever that we take advantage of the shift in power within the imperial city. And the chaos accompanying it."

Haruki nodded. "You intend to mount a rescue for Ōkami and Mariko, then?"

"No. Not yet."

Surprise rippled across the metalsmith's face, then vanished in the next breath. Yorishige opened his mouth to reply before reconsidering, one fist wrapped by the other.

Tsuneoki inhaled through his nose, trying his best to quash his uncertainty on this matter. A true leader revealed weakness from a place of strength, when the tides were on his side. "I worry what might happen if this dark magic spreads to other domains and takes hold of the people there. If the Minamoto clan does not intend to protect even those loyal to it, we cannot expect them to do anything for anyone else."

"Good riddance to all those idiots anyway," Ren said with a burst of cold laughter. "Good riddance to any fool daft enough to swear allegiance to that sickly pretender. The Takeda clan should be the one protecting the people, as it did before, for a thousand years. I say we storm Heian Castle and reinstall Ōkami to his rightful place as shōgun. Anyone who disagrees can be swallowed by this plague of dark magic."

At this, Haruki turned toward Ren to face the shorter, stockier boy head-on. "You should not wish harm on those unable to defend themselves." Creases of concern marred the glistening skin of his forehead.

Yorishige offered a sage nod while gnawing on his lower lip.

"May the spirits forgive me for daring to wish ill on those *who tried to kill us*," Ren retorted without missing a beat. "I think you of all people should be in agreement with me, Haruki, especially after what they did to you as a—"

"Ren," Tsuneoki said in a warning tone.

Irritation flared across Ren's face as his eyes shot to skies. "Forgive me for being unfair to your new favorite, my lord

Ranma—, I mean, *Tsuneoki*." He sneered.

Despite the pointedness of Ren's gibe, Tsuneoki did not respond immediately. He resumed his earlier train of thought, his attention drifting toward the swaying bamboo, as though he sought answers in its ghostly song. "It might not be a bad idea to capitalize on the undercurrent of fear flowing through the villages near the seized domains. I think now is the time to rally the people there. As much as I am loath to admit it, fear can be a strong motivation for action. If the emperor cannot protect his people, why should his people continue to serve him?" Wincing through the motions, he crouched near the stream, using a twig to draw in the earth.

The Empire of Wa had been formed from a chain of islands. The legend said that a mystical sword dipped into the sea, dragging fire and earth from its depths. The isles rose to the surface in the wake of its blade. Tsuneoki outlined the largest one. Then he scored four marks on it, for the four corners of the mainland. He connected them at the center to form a cross, then turned toward Haruki. "We should begin spreading the word that we are mounting an opposition against the Minamoto clan."

Ren snorted. "How will we go about doing that? Ravens or starlings? Perhaps sea serpents?"

"No. I thought to use the golden crane of your dearly departed soul," Tsuneoki gibed back. "Tell our riders to use arrows and mulberry paper."

Again Ren laughed, the sound coarse in its amusement. "I can write the letters. We can seal it with that hideous symbol—the one that combined the crests of the Takeda and the Asano clans. No one will suspect who might be behind it. Come one and all! Join our band of traitorous brothers here in this godforsaken part of the Ghost's Gambit." He shrugged. "Hope you can find your way here without dying."

"Brother, you are too much." Yorishige smothered a grin.

Ren harrumphed. "I'm not your brother, you grain of rice."

Haruki glanced away to conceal a grin at the same time Tsuneoki laughed outright. "Ren, you should be sure to clench your teeth," Tsuneoki said.

Ren turned in their direction, a suspicious light catching in his gaze. "Why?"

"So they don't rattle in your skull when I hit you." As he spoke, Tsuneoki lobbed a small rock at Ren's bound arm. In his attempt to avoid being struck, Ren fell headfirst into the muddy embankment. He swore as the sling around his arm caught, tripping him farther. A litany of curses flew from his mud-covered mouth. When Yorishige moved to help him, Ren hurled a fistful of muck in the boy's direction.

Laughing to himself, Haruki shifted beside Tsuneoki, who continued studying the drawings etched into the fragrant loam. "Then we are not even going to attempt to rescue him?" He did not need to say whom. The name was always present, on the edge of every conversation they shared.

"If I know Mariko, she is halfway done composing a plan far better than any I could devise," Tsuneoki said.

A thoughtful expression settled on Haruki's features. "There was a time when you would have been concerned with nothing else, save sparing Ōkami. It would have consumed you. Driven you mad in a way that makes it difficult to see the dangers lying in your path."

Surprise flashed over Tsuneoki's face at Haruki's frankness.

Haruki continued. "I did not mean it as a criticism. Your devotion to those you love is the reason why so many of us have followed you for so long without question." He selected a twig from several collecting at the edge of the creek bed. "I only meant that it is sometimes difficult to see the future when you are so focused on the past."

"It would be suicide to try to storm the castle. It's enclosed on all sides by seven enchanted *maru*." Tsuneoki cleared his throat. "I won't ask that of anyone."

"But the Black Clan would follow you if you asked. I would follow you." Haruki reached for another twig and ran it through the mud to fashion a phoenix, with feathers of fire flowing from its wings and tail. Then he scribbled through them with a line of curving mountains, from which he began to shape the image of a sea serpent.

As he watched Haruki work, Tsuneoki studied the metalsmith's tranquil features. Features that—as always—hid a mind in constant turmoil. It was a trait they all shared, these warriors of the Black Clan: this roving, unceasing mind. It was something Tsuneoki had noticed in Mariko, the day he'd first encountered her, when he'd followed her in the form of a nightbeast. A trait that had especially bonded them all. Each member of the Black Clan had a past shaped by turbulence and haunted by specters, both dark and light. Haruki's past was not one he often shared, but they'd all seen the vicious scars coiling up his shoulders. They'd all heard his screams in the middle of the night, when sleep had been more of a curse than a blessing. Both Ōkami and Tsuneoki had long held Haruki's counsel close. Despite a childhood colored by violence, the metalsmith possessed an excellent mind and a carefree demeanor, unshackled by so many of the demons young men like Ren carried with them wherever they went.

But Haruki had never spoken so frankly about Tsuneoki's devotion to Ōkami before. As though the metalsmith could see the truth at its core. Had always seen it.

Discomfort coiling through his stomach, Tsuneoki glanced at the four corners he'd drawn in the earth nearby, joined at the center. At the sea serpent Haruki had fashioned beside it. A childhood memory began to form in his mind. Not of the Takeda lands nor of the lands Tsuneoki's father had controlled. They weren't an option anyway, as the emperor had seized them many years ago. But a different idea began to take shape, as though it were being conjured from the ashes of the past.

Ōkami's mother was the daughter of a powerful warlord. Her family's crest had been a sea serpent, guarding a trove of diamonds.

Her land had been along the coast, not far from the imperial city.

If Tsuneoki remembered correctly, the lands in question had been deserted for years. Ōkami's mother had disappeared in a summer storm during his third year. A lover of the sea and all its secrets, she'd scorned the advice of the fishermen, and ridden out beyond the bay, only to be taken by a giant wave. Not long after her death, her parents had perished of a mysterious illness, born of the briny air. Following this wealth of misfortune, their lands had been abandoned, branded as cursed.

Tsuneoki drew four diamonds to represent the four corners of the empire. He encircled them with the tail of a watchful serpent. Then he stood, ready to take action. Ready to do whatever it took to spare the son of Takeda Shingen any more strife and give his dearest friend back the legacy that had been stolen from him.

To restore the Takeda family's good name.

All for the boy Tsuneoki loved most of his life, in secret. In his own whispered song.

"Tsuneoki," Haruki said.

Pausing mid-step, Tsuneoki turned back to look at the metalsmith, still crouched near the stream.

"Even if you didn't ask me," Haruki said without looking his way. "I would follow you anywhere."

The song of the Nightingale

———✴———

Sleep continued to evade Mariko, as it had for each of the three nights she'd been in Inako. Each time her mind would settle, another thought would wind through it, spiraling downward, taking hold of her heart. Her emotions roiled within her. Fury, pain, bitterness, uncertainty, each of them churning in a ceaseless cycle.

When the scars inked into Ōkami's skin first came into view, she'd wanted to strike out at something and inflict wounds to match on her betrothed's face. But the words of her brother had stopped her—had chided her silent—for though Kenshin had failed to be a source of comfort in the last few days, his earlier warnings continued to echo through her mind. A semblance of direction, in a world gone horribly awry.

Say nothing. Do nothing. Do not react.

Mariko had coaxed her expression into one of dismay. As

she'd taken on the mantle of a victim in need of comfort, she channeled her rage. Molded it into something she could control. Moved it with the newest current. Even a mild-mannered young woman would react to the sight of brutality. It had been a stroke of luck that her tears and her trembling had caused Prince Raiden to spare her from any more of the emperor's mind games. Once Raiden left her outside her chamber doors, she stood there in stunned silence, her eyes wide, like a rabbit caught in a darkening brush, uncertain how to proceed. As soon as she granted herself a moment's peace, Mariko's chest began to hollow with pain and regret.

Not once had she looked upon Ōkami with any sympathy or offered him anything of value—no information, no key to unlock his bindings, no reassurances of solidarity. None of the things her mind and heart would starve to possess, were she to share in his predicament.

Mariko had offered him nothing. Not even the smallest gesture of comfort or encouragement. Not even a single smile.

Her pain grew sharper when she recalled the glint of his warmth, hidden beneath his mocking exterior. Even though Ōkami had undoubtedly spent the last few hours in tortuous agony, he'd grinned up at her, a sly look that—at first glance—appeared taunting.

But it had given Mariko strength.

The useless girl.

It had given her the drive she needed to take action.

Hours later—beneath a glossy coverlet—Mariko waited until the sounds of motion outside her door steadied to a trickle. She made certain to note how often the guards patrolled past her chamber. Then Mariko knocked back the ridiculous blanket of padded silk and rose to her feet in a single motion. She slipped her toes in a new pair of soft *tabi*, then crept her way toward a *tansu* chest of fragrant pine, positioned against the far wall of her chamber.

There—folded in a neat stack—lay the clothes she'd worn when she first arrived in Inako. A loose *kosode* and a pair of faded trousers. They'd been washed and put aside, as she'd directed her servants to do earlier.

Her heart pounding in her chest and her ears on alert for any sounds of movement, she changed into the roughspun linen, its color a drab grey. It had once been black, but time and wear had lightened it. It was one of several that had been begrudgingly passed down to Mariko from Ren. Once she finished dressing, she gathered the items she'd hidden earlier and tucked them in a bundle within her *kosode*, strapping them securely to her side.

Ever vigilant, Mariko slid open the silk-screened entrance to her chamber and made her way into the corridors, careful to stay to the shadows. The dark edges along each hallway provided a place of safety, and she moved between the flickering lanterns, counting each of her steps, all while holding her breath tight in her chest. With great care, she followed the same path she'd taken earlier, out into the courtyard, across the tiny white pebbled walkways, her stockinged feet soundless as she glided through the night.

For a beat, she waited in the shade of a flowering orange tree, its scent soothing her rampaging nerves, until the patrolling guards on the outside of the gabled structure passed just in front of her. Then—in watchful silence—she made her way through one of the unlatched sliding doors and into Heian Castle itself.

Now was the true test.

The nightingale floors.

Mariko crouched on the wide sill just inside the main corridor, knowing full well that any misstep would alert all those on patrol outside to the presence of an intruder. She tested one foot on the wooden surface. The suggestion of a creak sighed beneath her toes the instant she put her weight on it.

I could crawl.

But that would be foolish. The more places her body made contact with the polished wooden beams, the more likely they would be to make noise, and crawling on her hands and knees created four points of pressure, rather than the two of her feet.

How do I make myself smaller?

Mariko paused in consideration. She thought back to a winter several years ago, when she and Kenshin had been children playing on the outskirts of their family's domain. Kenshin wondered how far he could travel across the surface of the frozen lake before it gave way. The ice began to crack around Kenshin's feet, and her brother responded by immediately lying flat against it, so that his weight was spread evenly on the frozen surface.

She wondered if she could do something similar here. Mariko bent and placed her wrist on the floor until her hand was spread flat across it.

Only the slightest hint of a complaint could be heard beneath the floorboards. Her pulse flowing with the steady rhythm of a drum, Mariko moved her other hand alongside the first.

Now she was stretched across the floor, her toes still resting on the edge of the thick stone sill and both hands spread in front of her as though she were about to take flight.

What do I do with my feet?

On instinct, she shifted her right foot forward, balancing her body on her three remaining appendages. Then she placed her foot on top of her hand, spreading it from her toes to her heel slowly and evenly, compensating for any additional noise around her by shifting her stance.

When the nightingale floor bore her weight without any loud protests, Mariko almost crowed aloud, only to have her triumph abruptly silenced. The creaking sound of an approaching guard emanated outside the hallway to her right. Mariko stayed hovering above the floorboards, her limbs starting to tremble from the strain of remaining still.

Once the footsteps faded into the distance, Mariko resumed her crablike scuttle across the nightingale floor, rolling her hands and balancing on her toes, all the while anticipating any sounds of protest from below. The faintest whisper continued emanating from beneath her, that same odd creaking sound, muted by her watchful efforts.

After she passed over the central corridor, she broke away and followed the path she'd trod earlier, in the shadows along each wall.

Her lips counted out her steps, and her heart thundered in her chest as she made her way past the stone walls bound in aged oak timbers to the darkness of Heian Castle's underbelly. Again she stayed to the walls, aiming toward the narrow slit of window cut high into the wall to the far left. It sent a strip of moonlight downward, just near the entrance to Ōkami's cell.

Ōkami stirred as she neared, his chains grazing the wall. "Well, I can't say I'm surprised he sent an assassin in the—"

"Be quiet!" Mariko said in a low rasp.

A moment of shocked silence passed.

"Mariko." The sound of his voice changed in a single word. Her name. There had not been many occasions for Ōkami to use it, for he'd not learned of it until recently. And each time Mariko heard him say it, a warmth enveloped her for an instant, like the falling of a cloak around her shoulders on a chilly autumn night. For just a moment, it made her feel like one of those silly lovesick fools she'd disdained for most of her life.

Enough.

Now was not the time or place for Mariko to enjoy

hearing anyone's name on anyone's lips. Without stopping to even acknowledge Ōkami, she removed the parcel she'd stuffed inside her *kosode*, her heart hammering for a different reason.

"What are you—"

"Follow directions for once in your life, and keep silent while I work," she admonished. Guilt rippled through her when she realized how harsh she must sound, especially to someone who'd been tortured and mistreated by soldiers for days on end. Without pausing in her task, Mariko tossed a wrapped steam cake through the bars, in Ōkami's direction. Then she took hold of the large iron lock securing the metal gate. After only a moment's consideration, she uncapped a small vial and poured a thin stream of oil inside the lock, turning it on all sides before dripping any excess liquid onto the dirty straw at her feet.

Mariko felt his eyes on her as a soft rumble of laughter passed from his lips.

Of course Ōkami knew what she was trying to do without her needing to say a word.

"Be quiet, please," she repeated through her teeth. Her hands shaking under his watchful gaze, Mariko lifted the wax taper she'd pilfered from her chamber into the moonlight emanating from the small window above. She struggled to light the wick, her fingers trembling spitefully. She tried once. Twice.

Finally, it caught.

Even through the darkness, the weight of Ōkami's

attention fell heavy upon her. Though he remained silent, his unspoken question hung heavy in the darkness.

Mariko sighed. "I'm fine. Nothing horrible has happened to me yet. I've managed to eat well, and I've slept far longer than permissible beneath a blanket of padded silk."

"Are my thoughts so loud that you can hear them?" His amusement filled the space.

"They're debilitating. Now keep silent." Pursing her lips, Mariko shifted the lit taper slowly on its side, until the flame bent into the wax. It began to drip. Without a word, she inserted the thin metal bar of the tortoiseshell hairpiece she'd filched from Shizuko's tray into the lock itself. The melted wax trickled around the bar, and Mariko rotated the lock in careful quarter-turns, coating its insides. She paused until the cooling wax pushed past the entrance of the keyhole, then kept steady, waiting for it to harden and lose its translucent quality.

Just as she began to see the light at the end of the path, the sound of approaching footsteps ricocheted from the stairs behind her.

Panic drove her to meet Ōkami's gaze, his eyes like two black diamonds buried deep in the shadows. While Mariko pinched out the lit taper, he gestured with those flashing eyes toward the far wall. A moment later, she found herself pressed against the cold sludge as it oozed through the thin fabric of her garments. Many-legged creatures scuttled in all directions along the wall behind her, their tiny limbs like wet feathers brushing across her outstretched fingertips. She did not cringe away from the darkness and the creatures it brought. Welcomed it for the cloak it provided.

The footsteps grew louder. The light of a torch wavered into view.

Mariko held her breath tightly in her throat, wishing once more for the weight of a weapon at her side. Wishing for anything that could be used in her defense, beyond an endless store of lies.

With nothing but her wits within reach, Mariko waited to see what hand Fate would deal her tonight.

if

---✳---

A torchlight angled toward them, glancing the way of Ōkami's cell. Its tongue of fire leapt across the walls, pitching shadows at the slightest suggestion. It paused for a moment, a stone's throw from where Mariko stood, her body flattened against the muck. She willed herself smaller, her eyes squeezed shut, her nails digging into the slime.

When the torch's bearer found what he sought—the emperor's prisoner, still ensconced in his prison—the light returned the way it had come. After a period of perilous silence, Mariko crouched back to her position beside the lock, inhaling through her nose to settle the strain of keeping her body still.

The wax she'd poured within the lock had hardened to a pale yellow. Gingerly she began prying the thin metal of the tortoiseshell hairpiece from the tumblers. The oil she'd used to coat the inside of the lock helped loosen the wax, and the entire mass broke free after Mariko wiggled it back and forth, easing it from its position.

What she removed resembled a twig with many miss-hapen branches springing from its end. She knew somewhere beneath this contorted lump was the form of a key. Mariko studied it, turning it this way and that, her fingers still shaking from the recent ordeal. Breathing deeply, she mopped the sweat from her brow with the back of her sleeve.

Now came the difficult part: fashioning a working key from this convoluted mold.

"This is dangerous." Ōkami's words were so soft, Mariko first thought she'd imagined them.

"Don't talk."

"I don't want you risking yourself for me," he continued, his voice unhurried. "Not anymore."

"I'm not risking myself for you," Mariko retorted. "I'm here for *me*. Because I still have things I wish to accomplish with my life." She refocused her attention on the misshapen mass. Slowly began chiseling away twisted fragments of wax, using a lacquered chopstick she'd pilfered from her evening meal. "It turns out my wishes have something to do with you."

A moment passed in stillness. "I don't have any wishes, Mariko," he said gently. "I haven't had the luxury of dreams for many years."

"Liar." Her brow furrowing in concentration, Mariko broke away another piece of hardened wax.

"I'm not lying."

"Then what are you doing here? Why did you allow

yourself to be captured?" she asked in a hollow whisper, her exasperation mounting. "Why do you persist in provoking them? Do you hope they break every one of your bones a million times over?" Her ire grew with each question, but Mariko could sense Ōkami smiling as she continued chipping away at the hardened wax.

"Are we in a lovers' quarrel?" He laughed. "I've missed sparring with you, in words and in . . . other ways."

Her fingers tightened around her work as warmth blossomed in her neck. "Stop acting like a fool." Mariko gritted her teeth. "It's not going to work with me. Stop pretending nothing matters, when I know that to be far from the truth."

Ōkami did not reply immediately. "I guess you know all my secrets now." Though amusement tinged his tone, Mariko caught the spark of something else beneath it. Something limned in fire.

Anger.

He is not the only one with a reason to be angry.

"Clearly I don't know all your secrets." Mariko let the sound of indignation mask her pain. "Or have you already forgotten how you concealed your identity from me for weeks?" A flash of recent memories caused her sight to swim. "Even after we'd shared more than I've shared with anyone else?". She swallowed. "Even after I'd given you my heart?"

Ōkami said nothing for a time. The pain renewed in her chest, spreading like blood through water, but she refused to fill the silence first. Refused to ask the question that had been burning on her tongue since that fateful night in the forest.

"You can ask me, Mariko," he said finally. "From you, there is nothing I wish to hide. Not anymore."

Mariko inhaled. "Why did you lie to me about who you were?"

"It was enough that Tsuneoki and Yoshi knew. In truth, I would have preferred it if no one did."

"That's not an answer."

He frowned. "I didn't want anyone to think they owed me allegiance or apology."

"So you lied to everyone from a misguided sense of nobility?" She blinked. "Allow me to congratulate you, Lord Ranmaru, for you are now the noblest of fools. And now your life may be forfeit."

Ōkami's eyes glinted as he shifted forward. "My life is always at risk."

"I see," Mariko replied. "So why bother trying to preserve it for anyone, least of all for yourself?"

"I'm glad you're finally seeing things clearly, Lady Mariko."

Her brow furrowed. "Don't mock my pain."

"My apologies. I'd say I was only taking the bait, but my foolish nobility dictates I behave otherwise." His words were measured, refusing to engage her in any meaningful way. Refusing to offer the slightest apology. With a yawn, Ōkami leaned into the wall at his back, as though he were bored and in need of rest.

It was what he always did. What he'd always done since the day in the clearing when Mariko had first met him. As soon as Ōkami was ever forced to answer anything of substance, he found a way to worm out of it with a dash of humor or a turn of apathy. Like a coin being tossed through the air.

Tonight his apathy enraged Mariko beyond measure. It grated on her even more than his usual condescension. She'd managed to keep the worst of her fears at bay for much of the night, but now they threatened to return, their claws scraping near her heart.

"After all your family lost, I don't understand how you can continue to be so indifferent. Are you feigning it?" Mariko demanded. "Or have you been feigning apathy for so long that you no longer know the difference? Do you even know what it means to truly feel?" The words left her in a sudden rush, her anger mounting beyond her control. With a muted cry, she threw the empty vial of camellia oil against the iron bars, the glass shattering on contact. The exploding shards rang out a twisted melody as they struck the metal, the song clamoring through the darkness, threatening to draw the notice of anyone listening above. A gasp of fear escaped Mariko's lips. A worry that her anger at him would be their undoing.

They waited like statues until silence once more engulfed the space.

When Ōkami spoke, his voice was soft. Apologetic. "That was . . . dramatic." He sighed. "But I suppose I am to blame for that." All trace of sarcasm had vanished. "I have no excuse for provoking you, especially when you came to help me."

"No." Mariko shook her head, her right hand trembling as she brushed a tendril of hair behind one ear. "My behavior is mine and mine alone. You are not to blame. I let my anger take hold, and anger is a temperamental beast."

"As always, you are the wisest man I know, Sanada Takeo," Ōkami said gently.

"Ha!" Mariko resumed her work with the lock. "When I next see Yoshi, I will be sure to tell him you said that."

Ōkami did not respond immediately. "I can think of nothing I'd want Yoshi to hear more." He cleared a strange rasp from his throat. "Though he would likely agree with you, especially after all that has transpired."

Another small piece of wax fell from Mariko's hands. "I still don't understand why you allowed Prince Raiden's men to put you in chains. Why didn't you simply turn into smoke and kill them that night in the forest?"

"I could have done that, it's true." Another beat of quiet passed as Ōkami pressed farther into the shadows, all but concealing his face from view. "But I could not take the risk of what might have followed."

Mariko's focus remained fixed on the makeshift key. "That we might have won?"

"No." He paused. "That I might have lost . . . everything."

"Noble fool," she grumbled.

"We do what we must." Ōkami leaned forward. "It's my turn to ask a question. What are you doing here, Mariko?"

Startled by the question, Mariko almost dropped the lacquered chopstick. "Isn't it obvious? I'm here to rescue you."

"You volunteered to come to Inako—to marry a heap

of steaming dung like Prince Raiden—simply to set me free?"

Mariko chewed on the inside of her cheek. "Do you not wish to be set free?" Her forehead creased. "To fight alongside your men to restore justice to our land?"

"Justice to our land?" Ōkami laughed. "You've been spending too much time around Tsuneoki."

"Stop making jokes. They're inappropriate at a time like this. They won't do anything to dispel your anger."

"I disagree." Ōkami sat up, wincing through the motions. "And I'm not angry. Just bitter." He paused in contemplation. Took a deep breath. "I watched Yoshi die, Mariko."

A sudden hush settled around them as Mariko stilled in her work, her hands dropping into her lap. It was as though something had reached into her chest and wrapped her heart in a burning vise. The feeling grew until it reached her eyes. All the burdens of the last few days seemed to descend on her in a rush, as though a dam had been broken, the water fighting furiously to regain its lost ground.

Tears began rolling down her cheeks in steady streams. Tears she had once considered a sign of weakness, but Mariko knew—in this moment—that Yoshi would have encouraged her to shed them. Encouraged her to be true to herself, no matter the cost.

It had taken her losing everything she knew to finally understand. Feeling pain and sorrow was not at all a sign of weakness.

It was a sign of love.

As he watched her cry, Ōkami let his head rest against the wall, his fists clenching at his sides until his knuckles turned white. As though he could take hold of his pain and leash it tightly to him. He said nothing for a time, and the space around them fell silent, like Death itself had come to roost.

Mariko concentrated on the sound of his breathing. Despite the worrisome whistle emanating from his throat, she let its rhythm lull her into a feeling of calm. The last time she'd listened to Ōkami breathe was the night he came to her tent in Jukai forest, after she'd been welcomed as a member of the Black Clan. The first girl to join the ranks of their brotherhood. Ōkami fell asleep beside her, his bare skin pressed to hers, and Mariko kept still, not wanting to disturb him.

Not wanting the magic to end.

It had been the last time she'd felt as though all would be well. As though hope were a sunrise, burning brightly along her horizon.

If her family would let her be.

If Mariko could have stayed there, free to blaze her own path in life.

If Ōkami would be by her side. Always.

If.

If.

Understanding flared within her, like a moon emerging from behind a bank of clouds. This must have been what Ōkami dreamed of. The same thing that kept him from

chasing after his birthright. The need to be at peace, surrounded by those he trusted.

Safe.

When was the last time Mariko had felt safe before that
night?

I can't remember.

"After I lost my mother to the sea, I spent a great deal of
time with Tsuneoki's family," Ōkami began in a calm voice.
"My father's position often took him away from our province,
so it was better for me to remain among friends. Better for us
all. When we were small, I would often find myself fighting to
defend Tsuneoki. Even though he is taller than I am now, he
was small for most of our childhood and a bit odd, not unlike
you." He smiled to himself. "One day during the winter of
our fifth year, I slipped and fell while chasing after a boy
who'd been trounced by Tsuneoki in a game of Go. The boy
had taken his loss out on Tsuneoki's face, which was unfortunate, since Tsuneoki's appearance has always been his only
asset." His grin widened, and Mariko found herself smiling
with him, despite all.

Ōkami continued. "When I fell, I landed in a patch of melt-
ing snow. It splashed everywhere, and my nursemaid had to
drag me indoors before I became sick from the cold. The boy
and his friends laughed like it was all a great joke. Later that
night, Yoshi found me crying outside. It was one of the last
times I remember crying. When I tried to hide it—because
I'd been taught that a young man, especially the son of a

fearsome shōgun, did not cry—he said, 'Little lord, don't stop yourself from feeling. That is what it means to truly live.'" Ōkami fell silent, lost in remembrance, his eyes hinting at something deeper. Richer. Truer.

"That . . . sounds like something Yoshi would say," Mariko said as she wiped the tears from her chin.

Ōkami laughed. "It's very irritating, isn't it? He was always so irritating."

The sound of his amusement lessened the grip around her heart. "Irritating in that perfectly Yoshi way." She chewed at her cheek. "Did he suffer?"

"A little. But I stayed with him until it was over."

"That must have been difficult to watch. It was kind of you to do that."

He laughed again, the sound strained. "Uncharacteristically unselfish, no?"

Mariko frowned. "You are many things, some of them quite troubling. But I think you pretend to be selfish and unkind so no one expects better of you. In truth, I think you are extraordinarily kind at heart. And loyal to a fault."

At her words, a shadow fell across his features. "Then we really do need to get to know each other better," Ōkami said. "On that score, I feel congratulations are in order." Something glinted in his gaze, like the edge of a blade being sharpened on a whetstone. "It appears your betrothed is well on his way to falling hopelessly in love with you. Well done on that account."

It took Mariko a breath to see the truth beneath his words. "Are you jealous?"

A pause. "Only a fool would not be."

"That's ridiculous. Jealousy is for boorish people. Are you a boor?"

"Of course I am. And of course I would be jealous. That steaming heap of refuse doesn't have to sleep in a barred cell. He can gaze at the moonlight whenever he wishes," he muttered.

"It's a shame the moon has eyes for another." With a secretive smile, Mariko used the chopstick to pry away a final piece of hardened wax. She lifted the makeshift key into the light to check it a final time before placing it into the lock. As it engaged the tumblers, she turned it gently. Something began to shift inside, the metal components creaking, giving way.

It's going to work.

The next instant, bits of wax fell apart around her hands as the metal from the tortoiseshell pin twisted free. Mariko sat there, allowing herself to go numb, the last traces of joy fading from her chest like a flame sputtering in the darkness. Her shoulders sagged forward, the despair gripping her stomach from the inside.

"It was a good idea," Ōkami said gently. "For a useless girl."

With a muffled shout, Mariko grabbed the broken pieces of wax and threw them past the bars, toward his head. She sat back on her heels, her body wilting from defeat. They both waited until her frustration began to fade. Then Ōkami's features turned serious. He shifted forward, his chains scraping along the stone. "Thank you."

"For what?"

"For defying all the odds to try to rescue a selfish thief who lied to you at every turn. You are the least useless warrior I've ever met, Lady Mariko. Never forget that."

The hairs on her neck stood on end.

He's trying to say good-bye.

Mariko refused to allow it. "This is far from over, Lord Ranmaru." Her eyes darted around, as though she could find an answer in the chilly darkness. "What is stopping you from turning into smoke and disappearing? Is it me? Are you so worried about my safety that you would continue subjecting yourself to this barbarism?"

Ōkami frowned. "No. The light of the moon needs to touch my skin in order for the magic to work." He inhaled, as though he wished to steel himself for the next admission. "The demon I serve is cleaved from darkness. In order to wield its power, I had to swear several oaths, the first being that I cannot call upon it if I am beyond the light of the moon. If I even attempt it, I might lose control entirely."

"What?" Fear caused Mariko's voice to splinter. "What other oaths did you swear to a *demon of darkness*? Why would you do such a thing?"

"I was a boy of ten when it happened." Ōkami's expression turned somber. "And you've known what I am since the night we first met—self-serving at every turn. The sort of boy who risks his well-being in order to wield dark power. Who permits his best friend to assume his identity and all the perils that come with it." He shuttered his gaze. "You shouldn't concern yourself with me anymore, Mariko. It's a mistake."

Anger ignited in her chest. "If you didn't want me concerning myself with you, perhaps you should have considered that before—"

"I did not mean you made a mistake in caring about me. I meant that you have far more pressing concerns." Ōkami took in another deep breath. "Today the emperor informed me that your marriage to his clod of a brother will take place in the coming days." His words became clipped as he spoke, as though he were trying to marshal his fury. And failing miserably.

Mariko blinked, her mouth hanging ajar. "So soon." She shook off the sense of foreboding that began sinking its claws into her. "I don't think Raiden is of the same mind." Her voice turned resolute. "He barely spent a moment in my company on the journey here, and it's clear he only tolerates my presence as a courtesy."

"It doesn't matter. Pushing your marriage forward is a way to test your loyalty and drive me to ruin, all at once." Ōkami kept still. "Though I believe Roku remains uncertain of our connection, I fear he will soon realize the truth." His laughter was cold, its echo hollow. "Our deepest truths are usually the hardest to conceal."

Though it was inopportune and inappropriate, that same mixture of pleasure and pain gripped Mariko again, as though a balm had been applied to a wound. It burned and soothed all at once. She leaned her forehead against the cold iron bars without thinking. Simply wishing she could be closer to him.

Perhaps this was what it meant to feel love. To be together and apart in the same instant.

Be water.

Mariko nodded as though a spirit had whispered to her through the seeping stone walls. "You once told me I was water," she said to Ōkami. "It is something I think about a great deal when I'm left alone with my thoughts. Water shifts and flows with its surroundings, but I've realized something else. Still waters turn foul over time. Even if I am uncertain of the destination, I must keep moving. You must keep moving, before you rot from the inside out. Do not give up."

Ōkami did not respond immediately. "If you are water, I am fire. Fire destroys all that it touches. I will not destroy the people I love. Not anymore."

"That's the excuse of a weak man. You owe those who love you a great deal more than that. I'm not leaving here until you tell me what we should do—until we come up with a plan, together." Mariko filled her words with all the conviction she could muster. "Though you've never wished to be a leader, it's time for you to be more. To be better and stronger and wiser than this."

Ōkami kept silent as he studied her through the iron bars of his cell. "I would never presume to tell you what to do, Mariko. I can only tell you what I want."

"What do you want, then?"

He crossed his arms, then wiped his chin, the wound from his head oozing a fresh trail of blood down his face. Despite his injuries, his battered features managed to look circumspect. "I want you to get as far away from the city as possible, perhaps meet a nice young man—whom I would find deeply flawed—and build a life apart from this world and its poison." Though Ōkami spoke in an almost teasing fashion, Mariko recognized the truth hidden beneath the sarcasm.

"That's unfortunate," she replied in an equally sarcastic tone. "Since it's clear I don't like nice young men, I'm afraid I can't help you with any of that. What else do you want?"

Ōkami pressed his hands to the earth and pushed himself to standing, each of his motions a struggle, every movement marred by pain. Mariko took to her feet with him, as though she were offering him a shoulder to lean on. A hand to hold. The support she had not been able to give him earlier today.

They stood across from each other—bars of iron and blood and darkness separating them—yet Mariko felt his presence as though he stood beside her, his fingers curled around hers, a cloak falling across her shoulders.

"I want to tell you I love you, without chains around my feet," Ōkami said. "Without reservations."

Mariko nodded, unable to speak.

He continued. "I want to hold you as I say it. Beneath an open sky."

She inhaled carefully, her heart thrumming in her chest. "Why?"

"You look like you need to be held."

"Because I'm a girl?"

"No." He smiled as he struggled to keep his body straight, every motion visibly taxing. "Sometimes we just need to be held." It sounded soft, each word like a caress.

She swallowed, the ache in her chest spreading to her fingertips. "Unfortunately for us both, I can't help you with that. Anything else?" Mariko reached for one of the bars to steady herself.

"I want to touch you," Ōkami said softly. Shockingly. The moonlight slipped behind a fleece of clouds, the darkness deepening around them.

"Ōkami, I—"

"I want to run my hands across your skin and listen to you sigh."

Though she could no longer see past the bars, a fire burst to life in her core. This was not appropriate. Now was not the time for him to say such things, let alone for her to listen. "Stop it." Mariko gripped the iron tightly. "I can't think of a worse time and place for you to say something like that to me."

"We do what we must." He repeated his earlier words.

The clouds passed, and the white light of the moon streamed through the window once more, as though it had always been watching over them. Merely turned an eye for an instant.

Flustered by the flurry of emotions warring within her, Mariko began gathering her things. "I'll work tonight to devise a different plan for helping you escape." She stopped, her mind moving faster than her lips. "How cold does it get down here?"

"Cold enough."

"Have you ever seen any signs of ice?"

Ōkami shook his head. "You don't need to—"

"Stop talking unless you have something worthwhile to say."

He laughed under his breath.

Mariko smiled to herself, then tightened the cord around her waist before collecting her things to leave.

"Mariko."

Again the way Ōkami said her name rippled down her body—the hot chased by the cold—from the nape of her neck toward her toes. She both hated and loved it all at once, this blending of extremes. "What now?"

"I want one more thing.".

She turned his way. Waited.

The chains behind Ōkami clanged together as he took a single step forward, grimacing the entire time. "Come here."

Under normal circumstances, Mariko would have rebuffed such orders, especially coming from him. But it did not sound like a directive now. It sounded like a plea. As Mariko drew closer, he took another step toward her, his chains losing the last of their slack. Ōkami moved as far as his bindings would allow, until his hands were balled into raised fists.

The closer he came toward that single stripe of moonlight, Mariko could see more evidence of all they had done to him. Every cut. Every bruise. Every burn.

The ink seared into his skin.

Loyalty.

Her heart pounded at the way Ōkami looked at her, the way he studied her . . .

As though he might forget the lines of her face.

Mariko took hold of the bars in both hands, gripping them forcefully, her fingers turning bloodless. "What do you want, Ōkami?"

His lips curled upward. "That metal pin."

Ever the Hero, Ever the Villain

---✶---

His father used to say that a man could be a leader or a follower.

But never both.

In moments like these, Kenshin understood the comfort of taking orders, rather than of being the one to give them. Leaders needed to know what lay around the next bend, even when moving through uncharted territory. A follower need only concern himself with each of his steps. Each of his breaths. He could move forward, oblivious to the path ahead. Trusting in those left to make the decisions.

If Kenshin was only a follower for the rest of his life, then perhaps he could remain as he was now. Comfortable. Adrift in the waters of a summer sea.

Drunk.

Hattori Kenshin had lost track of time. The feeling was a supremely blissful one. He assumed several hours had passed since the elegant *jinrikisha* had delivered him to the front of the finest teahouse in Hanami. Several hours since the silk screens had slid closed and his first drink had been poured. Now Kenshin found himself lounging on a lustrous cushion, listening to the distant chiming of music, the occasional splashing of a drink. The titters of feminine laughter.

He let his head fall back and his eyes drift closed for an instant. When he opened them again, his vision swam in a slow circle before it focused, seeking something on which to ground itself. Kenshin gazed about. At his feet were fresh tatami mats, bordered in deep purple brocade. Above him swung lanterns carved with creatures from a mystical sea. Their shadows danced along the walls suggestively, the blue flames within glowing bright. When he took in a deep breath, the sweet scents of jasmine and white musk rose into his head, wiping his thoughts clean with their fresh, heady perfume.

Making him forget.

Everything about this place was designed to make a man forget. To let him believe—even for just an evening—that he was all he'd ever hoped he could be. Everything his father had dreamed. That his life was one of possibility, instead of disappointment.

Slurring through a spate of laughter, Kenshin took hold of a small porcelain cup. A delicate hand to his right poured another measure of warm sake. Without even a glance in the beautiful *geiko*'s direction, Kenshin knocked back the drink, its warmth blossoming through his chest, lulling him into a stupor.

The sounds of laughter and merriment faded to a dull roar as Kenshin continued to drink. He sank into the roll of cushioned silk to his right, leaning his weight upon it and closing his eyes once more. He enjoyed the sensation of depriving himself of sight. All his other senses became brighter in response. He let the sounds around him grow until they filled his ears with their cacophony, the scents hanging in the night air bringing to mind carefree days in his past. Enticing him to forget.

A cold hand clawed into his chest, wrapping his heart in a vise, ceasing its soothing beat for an instant.

Kenshin could never forget.

Amaya was gone.

The only young woman he'd ever loved—ever shared anything of meaning with—had perished in a blaze before his eyes, while he'd stood by and watched, unscathed.

Ever the hero. Ever the villain.

Hattori Kenshin—the Dragon of Kai—had failed Muramasa Amaya in every imaginable way. When he'd been given the chance to stand tall, he denied his feelings for her. Then he indulged them in secret to their mutual detriment, when he'd known their dreams for a shared life could amount to nothing. They'd been caught together on an early spring morning. Even now, he remembered it so clearly. Kenshin thought to bring Amaya the first signs of life he found just beyond his family's land—a handful of tiny white blossoms. In return, she cooked *fukinoto* for him—the first plant to push through the frost and reach for the sun.

Even apart, they'd shared the same thought. The same wish for each other.

He still remembered how the strange little vegetable tasted on his tongue. Bitter, yet full of life and promise.

After discovering them together, Kenshin's mother had quietly demanded that her son stop seeing Amaya. Though the girl was the daughter of a famed artisan, she did not possess the dowry or status the Hattori clan required to wed their only son and advance their position. At least his mother had shown some regret for her son's resulting pain, though she was quick to silence any desire to coddle it. His father had been . . . even less kind about the matter, though he didn't order his son to stop seeing the daughter of his renowned sword maker, Muramasa Sengo.

Interestingly, it was his father's attitude that finally drove Kenshin to put an end to his relationship with Amaya. Even now—while he lounged in the most expensive teahouse in Inako, filled to the brink with its finest sake—Kenshin felt his father's words sear through his mind with the freshness of dried kindling.

Dally with her, if you wish. But promise her nothing. There are ways to get what you want from young women, without being burdened by the weight of expectation. If you do this well, you may even be allowed to continue seeing her once we secure an advantageous union for you. I have done much for Muramasa Sengo and his daughter. We've given them a home here, a place for him to further hone his craft in comfort. Sengo-sama will turn a blind eye if we wish him to do so. Of that I have no doubt.

The horror Kenshin had felt at his father's callous disregard for Amaya's future was all the motivation he'd needed to cease things with her. He cared for Amaya too much to allow any man—even his own father—to look upon her with such disdain. And Kenshin loved her too much to even hint at the idea that she could be his mistress.

Amaya was worth so much more than that.

Kenshin put out his hand for another measure of sake. The warm liquid no longer burned his throat. His limbs were heavy, though he felt more unburdened with every sip he took. As though nothing of import remained. As though he owed no one allegiance or expectation. The idea itself was so freeing. Even if it was only for this night, he needed a drop of hope amid a sea of joylessness.

He tried to paste a smile to his face. Thought to see if it was possible at all. The expression felt foreign to him in a way he'd never known. After all, such a gesture was meant to be offered without consideration. But pain gave the simplest actions meaning. What had been effortless was now more difficult than it had ever been before. This morning, it had taken far more strength than was permissible for Kenshin to rouse himself from his sleeping pallet. In a fit of rage, he'd smashed an oil lantern against the silk screens of the sliding doors near his chamber. The oil had dripped down the silk, forming an eerily beautiful pattern on the wall, like the branches of a broken tree, trying to take root.

Beauty from ruin.

He cursed Amaya for being who she was. For taking his

reason to hope away in one simple, selfless action. Kenshin inhaled deeply, letting his eyes return to the ceiling of the teahouse. Even the wooden rafters were etched with rows of intricate carvings. When he looked closer, he realized each timber told its own story. He followed one until he caught sight of a row of carved cranes soaring from one rafter to the next.

A story that ended in death. Golden cranes were meant to depict the flight of departing souls. Kenshin imagined that the crane bearing Amaya's soul blazed the path of flight for those in its wake.

Even when he shifted his gaze beyond his reality—tried to forget—Kenshin was unable to escape the cold truth of her absence.

He was alone. Utterly.

The noise around him died down in a sudden hush, but Kenshin kept his eyes trained on the ceiling, allowing the sensation of the silk against his skin to steady his thoughts. Softly strummed shamisen music flowed from the far corner, its timbre poignant, its melody sad. A murmur of male approval began to take shape.

Kenshin let his gaze drift down from the ceiling. His vision spun for a moment before locking on the figure of a new *geiko* posed near the entrance, in preparation for a dance. Her face was half covered by a lacquered fan, but her eyes caught his attention. Large and perfectly bright, their centers glinted with mischievousness before sloping down at their edges. Kenshin locked eyes with her, and he saw a flash of something in their dark grey depths, there one second and gone the next. As though they'd borne witness to their own share of pain. Even if Kenshin saw nothing but her eyes, he would find the girl arresting. He did not even care to look elsewhere, so entranced was he by the story buried in their shining depths.

She held his attention with nothing else. Rapt, as though he'd been ensorcelled.

The *geiko* moved her fan in a graceful arc and turned in a single smooth circle. The back of her neck was long and pale, carved from smoothest alabaster. The faint luster of crushed pearls gleamed on her skin in the light emanating from the lanterns above.

Kenshin sat up, awareness flashing over him, making him feel all too alive. Alive in a way he had not felt for long days and endless nights.

The *geiko* lowered her chin and glanced over one shoulder, a half smile wending up her face. The sort of smile Kenshin knew to be false.

For a true smile did not involve thought or effort.

Nevertheless he found himself leaning forward. Bending toward her like a willow caught in the wind. The *geiko* anchored her eyes on him as she began her dance.

Even if she behaved in a similar fashion with every man in the room, Kenshin did not care.

He had to know her. Had to speak with her. Had to learn if her sadness mirrored his own.

The *geiko* whirled one fan around her right index finger

and fluttered the fan in her left hand through the air as though it were buoyed upon gently rolling waves.

Kenshin knew better than to allow himself to be mesmerized by a young woman who specialized in such things. For most of her life, he was certain she'd practiced the art of the dance until her fingers blistered and her ankles swelled. She undoubtedly knew poetry, knew how to sing like a songbird, knew how to laugh with a mind to beguile, and knew how to smile until a man would give anything to know her secrets.

And yet that glimpse of pain Kenshin had seen in her downturned eyes. The story in the simplest of her movements.

It was as though no one else existed at all.

He closed his eyes. A memory of Amaya flitted through his mind, burning through his vision. Her earnestness. Her love. Her trust.

Kenshin cursed her once more. She'd left him alone. Ashamed.

Angry.

He opened his eyes, and the *geiko* smiled at him as she finished her dance. She swept the train of her luminous kimono behind her with a delicate motion, allowing him to catch sight of her small feet, encased in the white silk of her *tabi*. Then she shuffled his way, ignoring all else around her.

She bowed low, the dainty ornaments in her hair tinkling and flashing together like magic. With a stern look at the young woman still waiting by his side, the *geiko* exchanged places with his former attendant in a flurry of flying silk. Kenshin breathed deep as she leaned his way.

Orchids and honey. Escape and abandon.

"May I serve you, my lord?" she said softly.

There are ways to get what you want from young women, without being burdened by the weight of expectation.

His father's words echoing in his ears, Kenshin nodded, his mouth dry. "I am"—he cleared his throat—"Hattori Ken—"

"The Dragon of Kai," she replied. "I know who you are." A true smile touched her perfect rosebud lips. "My name is Yumi, my lord. How may I serve you?"

the sword of truth

---✶---

What am I doing here?

Mariko struggled to answer this question last night, when Ōkami had posed it to her beside his cell. At first, she thought the obvious response was to rescue him. But it had seemed incongruous in that instant. Especially because she failed to do so only a breath before.

She'd not considered the possibility of failure. Nowhere in her plans had she thought she would be unable to find a way to save Ōkami, somehow. Ever since she was a child, it had been Mariko's long-held belief that there was always a solution, so long as there existed a spirit. In truth, she'd hoped to free Ōkami from his cell soon after arriving in Inako, so as to thwart any possible attempt on his life.

How silly she'd been.

Hattori Mariko had known she was coming to a city built on secrets and lies, and she'd believed her time dressed as a boy, sleeping beneath the trees like a wood sprite, had taught her everything she needed to know to fight whatever enemy wandered into her path. As though such a thing could be taught at all. Not once had she considered whether or not she possessed the tools needed to take on such a task.

Once again, Mariko was a silly girl, just as she'd been before, when she'd thought to disguise herself in a dead man's clothing and triumph against seasoned warriors in the process. She was arrogant in her intelligence. As though the greatness of her mind had granted her leave to act without thought.

At least Mariko had not arrived completely empty-handed and addlepated. She'd worked to devise a plan while they'd journeyed to Inako, the winding roads jostling her about in her makeshift *norimono*. The litter had been a twisted nod to the first time she trekked to the imperial city as a bride, less than one month prior. From its shadowy confines, Mariko had laid out a strategy. By day, she would convince the imperial family of her harmlessness, until they'd all but dismissed her as useless. By night, she would learn where they'd imprisoned Ōkami, even if she had to search every corner of the castle herself. From there, she would use whatever means were at hand to help him, whether she had to lie, cheat, steal, or kill. She would do what needed to be done to set him free and learn why someone had gone to such lengths to frame him for her murder several weeks ago.

Mariko had begun pilfering items as soon as she'd arrived to her rooms. First the metal hairpin from the elderly servant Shizuko. Then the camellia oil from her nightly regimen.

Then the taper and the chopstick. Following these insignificant thefts—the kinds of thefts that should go largely unnoticed by her countless attendants—Mariko made plans to take note of all the many paths across the castle grounds. A task that filled her with strength, for she found the solution to her biggest quandary even before beginning her search.

The fools had led her straight to Ōkami's cell.

But her ingenious plan to pry open the locks proved disastrous. She'd watched, helpless, as it crumbled to pieces before her very eyes. While traveling to the imperial city, Mariko considered many ways to help Ōkami escape his bindings. She devised a mental list. But even the simplest undertakings had been hampered by both her lack of opportunity and her station as Prince Raiden's presumed bride. By the watchful eyes that followed her wherever she went. As a lady of the imperial court, she owned nothing and controlled even less. Were she to ask for a bar of soft iron and a smelting tool, Mariko knew well the questions that would likely follow.

Of course she'd considered the possibility of picking the lock. But she'd quickly dismissed that idea the moment she'd taken a closer look at it, even in the darkness. Ōkami had shared the same initial thought. He'd asked for the metal pin to try his hand at prying open his chains, but Mariko knew that to be equally impossible, if they at all resembled the lock securing the iron bars of his cell. That tumbler had at least three working mechanisms within it. He would need a source of bright light and more than one piece of metal—perhaps even three—to make any headway.

But it would occupy his time. Perhaps instill in him a measure of hope.

These realizations alone had driven Mariko to do something her better self cautioned against: masking the harshest truths to spare a loved one even a moment of pain, just as Ōkami had done by making her laugh.

But humor was not the only thing they both needed now.

Hope was the thing.

And Mariko needed both humor and hope more than ever. She'd been so concerned with following through on one course of action that she'd all but ignored the rest.

Her betrothed asked to see her. Finally. On her third day at court.

An array of thoughts and feelings flashed through her mind at the request. Disgust and fury were the most primal. Then the realization that Mariko could not rely on such emotions in the tense moments that were sure to follow. Anger was indeed a temperamental beast—a dragon that threatened to burn all in its path—and she could not afford to let it drive Raiden away or spark any sense of suspicion.

Mariko needed Prince Raiden to trust her enough to grant her permission to travel into the city. She had to meet with Asano Yumi so that the *maiko* could establish contact between Mariko and any surviving members of the Black Clan.

Tsuneoki needed to know that Ōkami was still alive.

That his circumstances could change at any moment.

That the emperor was the quiet, devious sort, who appeared to lean toward violent means to justify his ends. That his mother, the dowager empress, was deeply concerned with appearances. And that his brother, Prince Raiden, harbored the beginnings of doubt.

Any and all of these facts could be used to the Black Clan's advantage, especially if they meant to punish those responsible for destroying their home. For murdering Yoshi. For taking Ōkami captive.

If Prince Raiden did not trust Mariko or failed to see her as an ally, she would no longer be in a position to help her brothers in the Black Clan. Nor would she ever be granted the freedom to roam the imperial city at her discretion.

So Mariko had done what any decent emissary would do.

She'd donned another disguise. Become the fox cloaked in lambskin. With her smiling eyes and shy laughter, Mariko rallied Shizuko to her cause, then called the maidservant Isa to her side. Together they selected—from the countless stores of garments at Mariko's disposal—a kimono far less extravagant than the one she'd worn the day prior. In truth, it was far less in some ways, and far more in others. The collar hung lower down her back, exposing more of her bare neck. This was a deliberate choice. Through Isa's connections, Mariko had managed to glean several things of import.

Green was Prince Raiden's favorite color. The green of the finest jade. He disdained most cosmetics on the ladies of court, save for a hint of color on the lips. And he enjoyed gazing at the back of a beautiful young woman's neck. So Mariko waited now in a receiving chamber, her cheeks pale and her lips stained, wearing garments meant to entice a boy she despised.

She considered the space, searching for sources of possible conversation. As Mariko had expected, the walls of Prince Raiden's receiving chamber were lined with polished weaponry, some of them housed in ornate display stands, others resting on honed stone pedestals.

The sounds of voices and movement gathered just beyond the doors. Mariko arranged the folds of her layered underrobes and gripped her sleeves to allay her nerves. A moment later, the screens behind her slid open.

A pause followed. One that grew around its void, until discomfort settled in its place. Though she was curious, Mariko elected not to turn immediately. When she did, she moved with deliberation, letting her eyes fall half lidded in the same way Yumi had gazed upon Ōkami that night at the teahouse. The motion felt foreign to her. Forced in a sinister fashion. But she was here to play a part, and she would play it to the best of her ability.

She bowed toward her betrothed, letting the blood rush to her head. Letting her breaths deepen until her pulse settled beneath her skin. When Mariko straightened once more, she found Prince Raiden standing just inside the shuttered doors, his expression thoughtful.

"You look . . . different," he began. Though he appeared

daunting and confident—with his broad shoulders and richly appointed *hakama*—his speech came across as strangely uncertain.

Mariko let her smile waver. "I feel more like myself."

"It's amazing what a proper bath and well-trained servants can do." His grin turned arrogant.

Irritation flared behind Mariko's heart. As she'd first suspected, Prince Raiden was proving to be precisely the spiteful, judgmental young man she'd first believed him to be. "We are in agreement on that, my lord." She inclined her head sweetly, remembering her wish to endear herself to him.

He cleared his throat and looped his thumbs through the thick silk cord at his waist. Where his half brother, Roku, appeared like a snake—with his cutting eyes and insidious grin—Raiden most resembled an osprey, its wings hovering as it scoured the sea for signs of its prey. Lofty and above reproach. Mariko remembered a time—not so long ago—when she'd listened to her maidservant Chiyo gossip about how handsome Prince Raiden was and what a wonderful husband he would be.

How wrong she was.

As though he could sense the tenor of her thoughts, Raiden frowned. "I am . . . not good at this."

Surprised by this admission of weakness, Mariko responded without thinking. "We are in agreement on that score as well, my lord." Dismay settled on her skin. She gritted her teeth against it and tried her best to appear steely. Above reproach, just as Raiden was. As though she'd meant to say it just that way and had no intention of apologizing. With seasoned warriors, it was best to meet strength with strength. Ren had been the one to teach her this lesson, with his snide comments and well-aimed pebbles.

Raiden's eyes widened. "Are you teasing me?"

The dismay wound through her stomach. "No. I mean yes, my lord. I mean . . ." Mariko trailed off, frustration taking root in her core.

I am awful at this.

"You're not good at this either." Raiden smiled with pompous satisfaction, but Mariko caught a hint of humor in his eyes.

She remained silent.

"I'm sure you know why it is I've asked to meet with you." He did not grant her a chance to reply, so certain was he of his position. "The emperor wishes for us to wed in the coming week."

Her heart leapt into her throat. She nodded to buy herself a moment to think.

"I can't say that I know what to do or say at present, given the unconventional circumstances," Raiden continued, his elbows crooked at his sides and his feet widespread. Ren sometimes did this same thing: occupied more space than necessary. It was the tactic of a boy with something to prove. But again, Mariko caught the glimmer of hesitancy.

The prince continued. "This situation has proven to be

somewhat difficult. My . . . interactions with women outside my family have been brief. I don't know how to speak my mind to you on this matter without causing offense."

Given Raiden's status, none of these things were appropriate to say to his betrothed. But Mariko appreciated his honesty. At least he didn't try to hide his thoughts.

When she still did not respond, Raiden pressed on. "Since I don't know where to begin, I'll start with the first thing that comes to mind. What do you want to do, Lady Mariko?" he asked. "Do you wish to be my bride?"

Again he took her off guard. Not once in the entire time her family had been in negotiations with the imperial family had anyone thought to ask Mariko what it was she wanted.

Strange that it would be Prince Raiden to first pose the question. Instead of answering, Mariko turned to pace the room and grant herself leave to consider this unforeseen turn of events. In silence, she studied the collection of weapons adorning the walls. Some blades had been sheathed in their ornate *saya*, then placed on lacquered wooden stands. The crests of vanquished clans adorned many of the scabbards. In some cases, the designs had been worked into the gleaming handles themselves. Mariko caught sight of dried blood wedged in the elaborate etchings of an ivory *tsuba*. She stopped to consider what story this weapon told. What lives had been taken with every swing of its blade. What sorrows it had wrought.

As she turned to face Raiden again, a particular weapon

caught her eye on a pedestal in a darkened corner, discarded from the rest.

Its blade was white. Almost luminescent. There appeared to be a bar of curved gold through its center, around which an almost alabaster stone had formed. The *katana* was not housed in its *shirasaya*, which lay to one side, a firebird etched into its ivory hilt. Its handguard was fashioned from alternating tongues of fire and phoenix feathers, all inlaid with gold. It was a thing of supreme beauty. A blade meant to be seen and studied. Yet strangely it had not been placed in the center of the room, where it would undoubtedly be the talk of any gathering.

Even though it had been cast off in the shadows, Mariko recognized the weapon the moment she laid eyes on it.

"It's the Takeda sword," Raiden said as he moved to stand beside her. "It's called the Fūrinkazan. A weapon forged by the spirits from a bolt of lightning after it struck the sand dunes by the Sendai river over a thousand years ago."

Mariko shifted closer to the blade. Farther away from the prince. "If it is truly a thousand years old, it is in remarkable condition," she murmured.

"Bewitched blades do not rust, nor do they have any need of sharpening."

She took note of the inscription etched where the alabaster blade met the golden *tsuba*. "As swift as the wind, as silent as the forest, as fierce as the fire, as unshakable as the mountain."

"The Takeda motto." Raiden frowned, and the gesture carved lines around his mouth. "This blade interests you." His nostrils flared.

"Of course it does," she replied in an airy tone. "It is unique, and I am fascinated by unusual things. Are you not, my lord?"

He did not reply.

"May I ask what made it glow that night?" Mariko sent a tentative smile his way.

Irritation took further hold of his features. "It glowed because it was in the presence of the Takeda heir, no matter how unworthy he might be. The lore says when the blade is wielded by a warrior possessing a pure heart, it will become a weapon unlike any other. Stronger than any other." He waved his hand in a dismissive fashion. "Throughout history, only men of the Takeda clan have proven worthy, but I doubt any son of Takeda Shingen's line could possess those traits in truth." Every word he spoke oozed with disdain.

He's wrong. The Fūrinkazan burned for Ōkami.

In that instant, Mariko realized why the blade had been cast to the side instead of being granted a position of honor in Raiden's receiving chamber. The blade had responded to a thief in the forest. But it had not responded to him. Which meant that he—the great Prince Raiden, firstborn son of the heavenly sovereign—was not a warrior with a pure heart. He was not good enough.

He doubts his worth.

With this newfound realization, Mariko chose to employ

Raiden's own tactic against him. Instead of asking a question, she made a statement. "You detest Takeda Ranmaru—not just for what his father did—but for something else."

Raiden snorted. "It doesn't matter what I think of that traitorous coward. He is to be executed soon. I am pressuring my brother to put an end to this farce and send him to meet his father, at long last." A shadow fell across his face. "May they meet in the fire where traitors dwell."

Mariko's vision swam. She gripped the edge of the stone pedestal housing the Takeda sword. A strange sensation took shape in her stomach, akin to being sick.

I pressed him too far.

"It doesn't matter." Raiden paused. "As its master's vanquisher, this sword belongs to me now. Everything that once belonged to Takeda Ranmaru belongs to me now. My father set aside the Takeda lands for my inheritance, years ago." He stepped away as he spoke, dismissing the now trivial item of the sword. His expression turned morose. "Though it may not matter what happens with it, if this mysterious plague continues to wreak its havoc."

"Plague?" Mariko's eyes narrowed. "Is something amiss beyond the city, my lord?"

Raiden considered her before replying. "A foul wind has settled on several provinces east of Inako. Entire villages have succumbed to the illness. Those who still cling to life have lost control of their minds, mumbling and trembling as though they are fevered."

Mariko's hand barely muffled her gasp. "My lord, if you

would permit me to—"

"It should not concern you. Your family's lands are far removed from the source of the disease." Raiden drew himself up to his full height. "And you are under my protection while here in Inako."

"I would not only be concerned for the welfare of my family, my lord. If any people of Wa are suffering, it is a cause for my concern."

Raiden blanched. "Of course. I only meant that you need not worry. Others will worry on your behalf. Those with the skills to handle these kinds of difficult situations."

His pompous dismissal of both her and her abilities grated on Mariko's nerves. "Which lands have been affected by the plague, my lord?"

"The Yoshida and the Sugiura lands. The Yokokawa clan. The Akechi lands."

She paused in consideration. "They are your family's loyal bannermen."

Raiden nodded.

The wheels in Mariko's mind continued to turn in careful circles. "Have imperial troops been deployed to help? Have the people residing on these lands been quarantined to prevent the plague from spreading? Have healers been sent to study the nature of the affliction and isolate its cause?"

A grimace touched the edges of Raiden's features, there and gone in the blink of an eye. "It is true there is much to be done. I am certain the emperor will send along help as soon as he has settled the most pressing matters of the imperial city." He spoke the words with a conviction that belied his actual sentiments, for his eyes told a far different tale. They flitted from side to side, searching the rafters above for a shade of truth.

A cold mixture of fury and fear raked across Mariko's skin. Fury at the emperor's dismissiveness. Fear at Prince Raiden's unquestioning support. Their foolishness was undoubtedly costing a great many lives. She grasped the edge of the stone pedestal even harder and stared at the Fūrinkazan, willing it to grant her focus. Willing it to prevent the words collecting in her throat from pouring into the air.

As her vision locked on the center of the alabaster sword, the faintest light seemed to spark in its golden core. Mariko stifled a gasp, then stepped back.

It was gone, just as quickly as it had come.

"I do not wish to discuss this matter further," Raiden said from behind her, his voice filled with conceit. Mariko turned to face him, and he moved closer, his arms akimbo and his legs spread once again. "We have other matters to discuss. You have yet to tell me what it is you want regarding our union."

Mariko gazed up at him, schooling her features blank. The entire time they'd spoken with each other, Raiden's back had been to the door of his receiving chamber, as though he alone controlled who entered and who left. Ōkami would have scorned the prince for keeping his flank open to a surprise attack. Tsuneoki would never have allowed an enemy to approach him unawares. Fear made both of them stronger. Smarter. It would make Mariko stronger and smarter, as well.

"I want whatever it is you desire, my lord." She bowed.

Raiden snorted. "You've been raised to say the right things. But I'm not interested in what you should say. I'm interested in how you feel."

Mariko found herself once more at a loss.

"Don't mistake my curiosity for consideration," he continued. "I do not believe I want this marriage to take place, and if you are against it, that may serve my purpose."

"Why do you not wish for this union to take place?"

"Though I find you less . . . troubling than before, I still don't trust you."

Mariko took a chance. His honesty had unseated her, and she hoped her own forthrightness would win her similar consideration. She met his stony gaze without flinching. "I don't trust you either, Prince Raiden."

He stood still, his eyes narrowing, his fists dropping to his sides. His knuckles were bloodied from when he'd beaten Ōkami. The prince's face was one many young women might find pleasing, but all Mariko saw on it were the scars he'd incurred in battle, the ones he'd gained inflicting pain on others. The lives he'd undoubtedly taken, without feeling or remorse.

The only thing that gave her pause was the fact that Prince Raiden did not at all resemble a simpering member of the nobility. He'd bloodied his own hands. Raged with his own fists. And he wore his scars just as he wore his victories—proudly. Even if everything he represented was deplorable, Minamoto Raiden at least did not lie on silken cushions and leave the fighting to others.

"Why don't you trust me?" Raiden asked. His tone was cautious—as though he loathed having to ask her this question. "Your brother trusts me. Do you doubt the judgment of your own flesh and blood?"

Mariko thought quickly. She turned in place and began pacing in a circle around the receiving chamber, glancing at the weapons lined along the wall like the severed heads of conquered foes. "It is not that I doubt Kenshin or any member of my family. But I came to the imperial city glad to be your wife." She glanced over her shoulder at him and chewed at her lower lip. The motion drew Raiden's eyes to her mouth. "I . . . have not been met with the same sentiment, though I have only ever been faithful to my vow. I did not realize you were against our union, especially since you'd already agreed to it."

"Would you be against our union if you learned that I'd resided among young women for the past few weeks, as the only man?"

"I would not doubt your word, my lord." Though a flash of fury passed over her vision, Mariko inclined her head and smiled.

Raiden nodded slowly. "You have spirit. More spirit than I would have thought at first glance."

"Thank you."

"But you have not answered my first question. Do you wish to marry me? If not, I will release you without question. If you're worried about what this will do to your reputation, I will take matters into my own hands." His grin was one of supreme arrogance. "Fear of my wrath is an extremely good reason for your detractors to keep silent."

Such bluster.

Mariko's responding laughter was shaky. Not knowing how else to reply, she let the nervousness take hold, as though she'd been moved by his declaration, instead of mildly sickened. She knew the next words she spoke would decide her fate.

If she told Prince Raiden she no longer wished to marry him, he would free her.

How strange to hear this, when—not so long ago—it had been her greatest hope. Mariko had dreamed of this exact scenario the night before she left her home for the imperial city. Of a world in which she was allowed to remain where she pleased, unburdened by the responsibility of marriage, free to invent to her heart's content.

It had been the vain wish of a silly young woman, absent purpose.

If Raiden freed her, Mariko would be sent back to her family. Even with his reassurances, her parents would view his rejection as a stain on the Hattori name. Fortunately, that worry no longer held the same sway over Mariko as it had before. Far more pressing matters had taken its place.

If she left her post in the imperial city, Mariko would be unable to give the Black Clan any more aid from within the castle walls. And she would never be able to save Ōkami, especially if Raiden's earlier threat came to pass.

But if Mariko married Prince Raiden . . .

She would have nothing she wanted. And everything she needed. A trusted position in the imperial court. In the imperial family itself. She'd earn a position next to the seat of power, and from it help to bring about the downfall of the cursed Minamoto clan and its inept young emperor.

Perhaps this was why Mariko had come to Inako. Not merely to spare the life of the boy she loved. But to be something more, just as she'd asked of Ōkami. To do something more.

Ōkami did not want to lead. He'd indicated as much to her on several occasions.

And Mariko did not yet know if she could. If this world would allow it.

All she did know was that she could not permit Roku to retain his power. If Prince Raiden's revelations were true, the new emperor had already shirked his responsibilities to his most loyal bannermen, with disastrous results. A plague spreading across his land should not be second to planning his brother's wedding or torturing a prisoner.

It would have been different if Mariko thought Roku could become a better ruler than his father. One who cared for the plight of others. But she'd already caught sight of the fearful glances exchanged by the servants attending the mercurial new emperor. Stopped to offer comfort to Isa after finding the maidservant weeping in a corner when the girl thought no one was watching.

As Mariko strolled slowly from weapon to weapon, she connected the reason for the young woman's sadness. Isa's family served the Sugiura clan. Perhaps they'd succumbed to the plague already.

The emperor was not even caring for those loyal to him. His brother, Raiden, was no better. A dog digging for bones in a graveyard.

She could weather this storm if she had to. All her life, Mariko had been trained to be exactly this kind of woman and nothing more. Her eyes fell on the Takeda sword nearby. It seemed to warm at her gaze, a spark catching in its center, the white skin of its *shirasaya* glinting like a mirror.

A trick of the light. Nothing more.

It was impossible that the sword would respond to her. She'd come to Inako to lie, steal, cheat, and kill. A bewitched blade would know her for what she was the moment it came in contact with her.

Impossible.

Despite this truth, Mariko wanted to be worthy of the Fūrinkazan. A warrior with a pure heart, no matter her devious intentions.

Raiden studied her, his features tight. Waiting.

If Mariko agreed to this marriage, she would have to be this boy's wife. She would have to laugh with him. Share a bed with him. Share his secrets.

Be water.

In silence, she closed the distance between her and Prince Raiden. Reached for his hand, her grasp tentative. At the touch of his skin to hers, every part of her body screamed in silent horror. Ached for rebellion.

We do what we must.

Mariko laced her fingers through his. She swallowed slowly and stepped into his space. The space of a warrior, who stiffened immediately at her intrusion. Seeking to disarm him further, Mariko shifted her fingers to his jaw in a tentative touch. His brow furrowed. He glared down at her, the center of his eyes still unsure. Mariko wet her lips with the tip of her tongue. The trick worked again. Raiden's eyes flashed toward her mouth, his grip on her hand tightening.

Then he made a decision, as he often did, without any warning.

When Raiden kissed her, Mariko did not expect it, even though she'd baited him for precisely this purpose. He was not gentle or tender. Not at all like the first boy she'd ever kissed, that afternoon in the hayloft. And he was *nothing* like Ōkami.

Ōkami only took what was offered freely and without reservations.

Raiden did not care to ask. Did not think to ask.

His lips were possessive. The feeling of his mouth moving against hers crawled up Mariko's spine in a way that made her almost flinch.

But Raiden's kiss was a reflection of him. Of the kind

of boy he was, and the kind of man he would be. Her first lover was shy. Ōkami studied. Purposeful. A boy who enjoyed playing a game for the sole purpose of getting caught.

Raiden did not play games with anyone. He pressed a large hand on the small of her back and drew her against him to deepen the kiss. Mariko returned his affection automatically. Turned off any hint of emotion, her eyes wide. When the prince released her, she took in a shaky breath. Then Mariko lowered her head. Peered up at the prince through a fringe of dark lashes.

If she was to agree to this union, she intended to walk away with the things she wanted.

Protect.

"It would be my honor to marry you, my lord Raiden." Mariko inhaled with care. "But I have two requests."

A life unchosen

———— ✳ ————

Yumi rode through the rapidly fading dusk, her rough-spun cloak flying about her like the wings of a bat. The piece of folded *washi* paper pressed to her chest felt as though it were burning a hole straight to her heart.

Tsuneoki had not answered her pleas to retrieve her from the *okiya*. To bring his sister into the fold and make her a member of the Black Clan. He'd allowed Hattori Mariko to join their ranks.

Why not Yumi?

She was far more practiced with a blade than the daughter of Hattori Kano. The blood of Asano Naganori ran through Yumi's veins, the desire for revenge glowing steadily in her soul.

Still her brother denied her the satisfaction.

Anger rippled down Yumi's throat. She hunched over

her chestnut horse and urged the stallion faster. There wasn't much time. There was never enough time.

Tsuneoki had gladly taken all the information Yumi passed his way. Her brother had cheerfully replied to anything he considered worthy of further investigation. Praised her on gathering news concerning the nobles and their countless machinations.

Yumi had been passing along this information to her brother for the better part of the last two years. Her unique position as a *maiko* of repute in the grandest teahouse in Hanami afforded her a vantage point from which to see the inner workings of the imperial court in a way others could only dream.

But it was long past time for Yumi to select a benefactor. She'd been an apprentice *geiko* for far too long. A *maiko* rarely waited in the wings for two years, especially one of her caliber. There had been countless requests for her companionship. If she were to select from any of these extremely wealthy, high-placed noblemen, Yumi would not want for anything in life. She would no longer have to work in the teahouse, entertaining inane drunks with no security to offer beyond vague promises of wealth. She wouldn't have to practice the shamisen until her fingers bled and dance each night before a roomful of idle men, all for the chance to be crowned the greatest *geiko* in the city.

But if she made her choice and selected a benefactor, Yumi would never be anything more than a mistress. Though her position as a *maiko* gave her the chance to learn and experience much of a life denied to most women, this was not a life she would have chosen for herself.

She had her brother to thank for this, as well.

Hot tears streamed down her face, carried away by the wind as she urged her stallion even faster. They entered Jukai forest, and branches tore at her cloak. A leaf scraped across her cheek.

It did not matter.

None of it mattered.

Her brother was too concerned for Yumi's safety. Concerned to the point of forbidding her from experiencing anything of worth. But Tsuneoki did not know how often Yumi defied his wishes. He did not know how often his younger sister prowled the rooftops of the imperial city. How skilled she'd become at throwing daggers.

He knew so little of her. Cared to know so little.

And it made her furious.

Yumi rode to the clearing that once housed her brother's favorite watering hole. It had been abandoned after the elderly man who ran the establishment had been murdered by the Dragon of Kai, according to an anonymous note left at her *okiya*, he'd been cut down where he stood, along with his two grandchildren. The boy, Moritake, had been friends with Yumi when they were children. His sister had trailed behind them while they played, ever a loving nuisance.

They'd all been killed in cold blood by Kenshin.

It was not an accident that Yumi had set her sights on the

Dragon of Kai. A boy so different from his sister, yet so similar. Both were prideful. Both were stubbornly certain of their own correctness, even in the face of their many failings.

At least Mariko was willing to learn. She possessed a mind like a trap. Kenshin did not wish to know anything. His mind was a void, yawning and deep.

Yumi slid off her horse before the beast came to a full stop. She took off running, past the fringe of maple trees, through the field of overgrown grass surrounding the abandoned lean-to. She came to a skidding halt beside the flowing branches of an aging willow that had always offered those who wandered by a measure of shade.

Her breath flew past her lips in shallow gasps. The anger returned, tearing away the last of her sanity. Yumi knew she shouldn't do this. Tsuneoki had forbidden her from initiating any unnecessary contact with him. He claimed the risk to her safety far too great. There were channels in place for her to communicate with those outside the imperial city. What Yumi planned to do next was not one of them.

Her brother always thought he knew best.

Yumi bit down hard on nothing until her jaw ached. Then she tore the creased paper from her *haori*, her gaze fixed. Determined. She'd not waited for the missive to dry before folding it. Her handwriting had smudged, a stark contrast from the measured, elegant script Tsuneoki had come to expect from her.

Asano Yumi did not care. She'd had enough of being told

where to go and what to do, by a boy with only a single summer more to his name.

Yumi yanked a hairpin from the twist at the crown of her head. A ring of hair tumbled down her back. She studied the note still in her grasp. The symbol of a starling stared back at her. Years ago, Yumi had chosen it to represent herself. A simple bird that did not evoke fear on its own, for it was small and rather annoying.

But a flock of starlings?

They could decimate everything in sight. Destroy entire crops. Lay siege to a domain's livelihood in the span of a single day, if they worked together.

Using her hairpin, Yumi stabbed the piece of *washi* to the willow tree. Stepped back with satisfaction. Maybe Tsuneoki did not see her as strong enough to fight alongside the men of the Black Clan.

But he would see how wrong he was very soon.

The suggestion of a smile taking shape, Yumi mounted her horse and raced back through the trees, ignoring the way the branches almost unseated her as she tore past them.

Tsuneoki would scold her if he knew the entirety of her plan. Would rage and yell and lecture. But Yumi did not always tell her brother everything. And she'd learned only today that the newly instated Emperor of Wa would be in a very specific place, at a very specific time in the coming week.

Asano Yumi intended to be there as well.

the masked troupe

—✦—

Murmurs followed her wherever she went. Mariko moved through the crowd toward her seat, her head held high. Demonstrating a fearlessness she did not feel in her heart.

She'd come to the city's theater district with a purpose today.

Keeping her gaze focused on the path before her—and nowhere else—Mariko took her place on a silken cushion in a shadowed corner, far removed from the common folk who jostled for a better look at Prince Raiden's bride. They muttered behind their hands as they waved their painted fans. Wondering. Whispering.

The murmurs died down with the first flash of fire. When the clash of a wool-covered baton against a drum bounded through the space, the people positioned on the low benches began cheering. The sound and fire represented the thunder and lightning at the start of the play. A play that showcased how their brilliant former emperor had rooted out the traitors from his court and punished them for their duplicity.

The crowd cheered as the first masked member of the theater troupe took to the stage, the monkey fur around his mask trembling with each of his exaggerated steps. He crowed like a buffoon, his speech a singsong celebration of simple achievements, such as managing to clean his own backside and not stab a servant for brewing the wrong kind of tea. This fool of an actor was meant to represent Takeda Shingen, who—if the play were to be held as true—was nothing more than a pompous oaf who bungled his plan to overthrow the great Minamoto Masaru.

As the crowd's laughter lilted into a sky set aflame, another equally ridiculous man in a grinning mask lurched to the first actor's side to portray the role of Asano Naganori. A gaggle of swooning young women trailed in his footsteps, their lips puckered, their hands clasped, as he bombarded the audience with tales of his numerous sexual exploits, including his discovery that bigger breasts were better. In fact, bigger *everything* was better.

The fool and his flock of honking geese.

Ōkami's father and Tsuneoki's father were being rendered as bumbling louts to entertain the masses and eradicate any trace of their greater deeds. Mariko watched and pointed and laughed with them all. She tittered behind her lacquered fan, until she'd lost the attention of those in attendance, who undoubtedly found the spectacle onstage far more captivating.

She'd chosen this particular play for many reasons. No

one would question her request to see it, for it would seem odd to prevent her from watching a tale lauding the achievements of her future husband's family. Following Minamoto Masaru's death, it was only natural that there would be many performances depicting his heroism. His brilliance. His ingenuity, even in the face of such reckless traitors.

But this particular play?

It was a long one. Far longer than usual. It would hold its audience's attention well past nightfall.

As the story continued—as the rapt masses became absorbed in the tale of treachery unfolding before them—Mariko slid farther into the darkness along the edges of the outdoor pavilion. She eased to standing, then lingered on the fringes, carefully fading into the deepest shadow beside the walls of screened *shoji*. As she moved, she slid the tinkling ornaments from her hair. Pulled a thin bundle of dark silk from her kimono sleeve. Then—when Takeda Shingen and Asano Naganori's duplicity was unmasked onstage to sounds of sheer loathing—Mariko let the shouts and the jeering and the pounding of the drums conceal her departure.

Her heart hammering in a steady thrum, she wrapped her shoulders in silk the color of night. The silver flashes and thunderous roars of the performance reached their pinnacles, and Mariko shouldered past the gap between two *shoji*, angling for the small alley nearby.

"My lady?"

A voice rang out from her right.

Mariko stopped short, a wash of panic unfurling across her skin.

Isa.

Struggling to paste a smile onto her face, Mariko turned to meet the confused gaze of the young maidservant. Isa took in Mariko's unmistakable attempt to conceal her appearance, however haphazardly.

The girl did not need to ask any questions.

Mariko's shoulders sagged. Isa would tell whomever she reported to that Prince Raiden's bride had attempted to flee into Inako without warning. The guards posted near the entrance of the theater pavilion would escort her back to Heian Castle, where she'd be forced to face her betrothed.

And explain herself to the emperor.

"Please," Mariko said softly. She took a step, then stopped, not knowing what to say or do. If she should say anything at all.

Isa's chest rose and fell. The puzzlement remained on her features, her forehead creased with concern. "Why?" she whispered.

Mariko shook her head. "Please, Isa-*chan*," she entreated once more. "I'll return before the play is finished. No one would need to know."

Isa's eyes darted to Mariko's face. Back over her shoulder. Then toward the entrance where imperial guards awaited their return. She took another deep breath. It was as though Mariko could see Isa's heart and mind at war with each other. Her loyalty should be to their emperor. Just as Mariko's should be.

The same emperor who had turned a blind eye toward a plague as it ravaged Isa's home province.

Mariko watched the maidservant make her choice.

The lines across Isa's brow vanished. Without a word, she bowed low and went back toward the performance.

Mariko did not stop to think. She raced into the alley, pulling the silk tightly around her shoulders. In less time than it took to flutter her fingers, she was hidden beneath the canopy of a *jinrikisha*, being whisked into the winding roads just beyond the theater district.

Gratitude coursed through her veins. Isa had bought her this chance. And Mariko had no intention of wasting it on this play of lies and puffery. Her marriage would occur in a few short days. Acquiescing to it had granted her a single night to wander the city of Inako without a full retinue in tow.

Mariko needed to move quickly.

Without a moment's hesitation, she told the driver of the *jinrikisha* where to go.

The moment Yumi saw Mariko, her reaction was to chastise the girl for coming to her *okiya* unannounced. The daughter of Hattori Kano must be ignorant to her brother's recent comings and goings, and the Dragon of Kai would likely arrive at the teahouse next door at any moment.

If he saw her . . .

In the same breath, Yumi realized that Mariko had come

alone. An impossible feat for any lady of the court. Suspicion flooding her mind, she shoved the girl into a shaded alcove, then pressed her through a set of sliding doors to a private room cloistered in the shadow of a birch tree.

"Whatever reason drove you to come to Hanami, I sincerely hope it to be a good one," Yumi began in a hushed voice.

To her credit, Hattori Mariko did not waste time on unnecessary chatter. "Have you received word from your brother?"

Yumi pursed her lips at the younger girl. A part of her could not ignore the annoyance she felt whenever she considered Lady Mariko. After all, this was the girl her brother had allowed into the Black Clan. The girl who'd won the heart of Ōkami. For the last few days, Yumi had soothed her bruised ego with the possibility that this alone was the reason Tsuneoki had allowed Mariko into the ranks of their brotherhood. For Ōkami's sake. No part of Yumi wanted to believe that Mariko deserved her brother's admiration, much less that of the Honshō Wolf.

When Yumi was a child, she'd adored the son of Takeda Shingen. Even gone so far as to insist they would marry one day, despite his loud protestations. Age and circumstance had disavowed her of the notion. She now considered Ōkami more of a brother than her own flesh and blood, but it did not stop her from wondering what this earnest-eyed waif possessed that she did not.

"I do wish you would exercise more caution, Lady Mariko," Yumi said, even as she continued pressing the girl's back into the wall. Restraining her. "This city thrives on gossip, and information of this sort—that Prince Raiden's bride was seen in Hanami—would undo most young women."

An exasperated sigh passed Mariko's lips. "I don't have time for caution or silly traditions. Please answer my question. Why has Tsuneoki not attempted to make contact with me? Does he have any plans to mount a rescue effort for Ōkami?"

"Keep your voice down." Yumi chastised her with a sharp glare. "I don't know if he plans to mount a rescue yet. There have been some . . . developments along the eastern edges of the empire, and they've been a hindrance to passing and receiving information."

"You're speaking of the plague." Mariko nodded, her tone hovering just above a whisper. "I do not have many details, but I do know that it has also been a source of consternation between the emperor and his elder brother."

Unable to withhold her appreciation for the girl's resourcefulness, Yumi tilted her head in thought. "Interesting."

"Can you find a way to deliver Ōkami out of the city, if I manage to get him to you?"

The girl was relentless, and it made Yumi's begrudging admiration for her grow. "That might prove to be difficult," she said drily. "It would not be an easy feat to leave the city with Takeda Shingen's son and Prince Raiden's betrothed in tow."

"I will not be going with you. It will just be Ōkami. But these details are unimportant right now. Do you have a way to get word to your brother and see if he can assist?"

This time, it was impossible for Yumi to hide her surprise at Hattori Mariko's revelation. "You do not intend to go with Ōkami, Lady Mariko?"

"My name is simply Mariko," she said. "Please call me that and dispense with all these ridiculous formalities." She bit at her lip while seeming to struggle for the best way to lend her thoughts a voice. "I would like nothing more than to leave this place behind, but I do not think it is possible, and"—Mariko sucked in a breath—"I believe I can serve the Black Clan better if I remain at Heian Castle. They will need a listening ear at court if they ever intend to prevail over the Minamoto clan, and I can easily provide that as Prince Raiden's wife."

Yumi nodded, impressed by her logic. Hattori Kenshin's sister was not the same girl who'd been left to convalesce in the *okiya*, broken and burned after the disastrous raid on the Hattori granary. Thus far, Yumi had thought Mariko simply possessed a mind for invention. Not an eye for strategy.

"My brother will not leave you behind." Yumi sighed. "And Ōkami will never permit it."

"It is not something for him to permit." Mariko spoke with conviction. "It is my choice. I'm counting on you to help me with it, Yumi-*san*. You know it is the best course of action for me to stay at court. I will only slow their escape, there-fore . . ." She glanced at Yumi sidelong, an unspoken request hanging in the air.

"You wish for me to lie." It was not a question.

"I wish for you to help me by holding these details close at hand, only for a short while."

"You wish for much." Though Yumi wore a steely expression as she said the words, she began to relax for the first time since she'd set eyes on the girl today.

They'd spent time in each other's company before. Yumi had cared for Mariko while the girl had healed from her injuries. Though Yumi had kept Mariko hidden and fed, she had not spent much time actually speaking with her.

It was quite simple: Yumi had not trusted her. And why should she? Ōkami had been livid when he'd brought the girl to the *okiya*. Mariko had concealed her identity from him, putting them all at risk.

Any esteem Yumi had felt for her had been relegated to the simple fact that Mariko had won over the heart of Ōkami. Another impossible feat. Up until now, Yumi had seen little to recommend a true friendship between them. Yumi held her secrets close to her heart, and Mariko was direct in her pursuits. Far more direct than Yumi thought wise.

Though it pained her to admit it, Yumi realized her reticence to befriend Mariko might stem from jealousy. It bothered her immensely to know that. She had far better things to do with her time than be jealous of another girl.

The two young women knelt in the center of the small chamber of Yumi's living quarters, regarding each other in silence. Her trusted maidservant, Kirin, slid open the doors, and an elegant courtyard framing a serpentine stream flashed into view. The calming sounds of the winding water granted Yumi a moment of serenity in a world of madness. Her sense of peace renewed, Yumi smiled as Kirin shuffled back to the sliding doors, leaving a tray of steam cakes and other refreshments behind.

Yumi and Mariko drank their tea. From beneath her eyelashes, Yumi studied Hattori Kenshin's sister, trying to glean more of her personality.

Now that Yumi had spent two nights in Kenshin's company, she could say without reservation that Mariko did not resemble her brother at all, in manner or in speech. There was a beautiful urgency to everything she did. An earnestness that both warmed Yumi and cautioned her in the same instant. In contrast, Kenshin seemed determined to punish himself for every breath he took. Nothing seemed urgent to the Dragon of Kai, save for escape.

For the first time, Yumi understood what Ōkami saw in Mariko. Unfaltering resolve. Ōkami had always been steadfast in his lack of principles. One could even suggest it was an honor-bound struggle for him. He cared about little and loved almost nothing. Yumi understood why. He'd lost everything, just as she had. In recent years, Ōkami provided her with a foil for Tsuneoki. She'd knowingly used her affection for him to inflict hurt on her brother.

To make him feel the pain of her rejection as she had felt the pain of his.

Yumi set down her porcelain cup and let her shoulders fall

in relaxation. "Mariko, we've spent most of our time together speaking about the men we are unlucky to know, but I wish to learn something of you. Why are you doing this?"

Dismay flashed across Mariko's face. "What do you mean?"

"You don't have to be involved in these matters. You could simply live your life. Get married if you wish to marry, go home if you wish to go home. You are not in a situation where your life depends on whether or not we can depose Minamoto Roku. In fact—given your family's longstanding support of the Minamoto clan—it might be more problematic for you than helpful to assist us."

A breath passed in stunned stillness. Yumi watched Mariko's features shift from astonishment to guilt to calculation. She appreciated the girl for not trying to play a game of words simply to impress. It shed further light on her character.

"I've not spoken about this with anyone before," Mariko said. "No one in my family's province could have been trusted with it, even my personal attendant—a girl who died trying to save me that day in the forest, when my caravan was overrun by bandits. I've been listening to the words of men all my life. I've done what I was told to do for seventeen years. Before I infiltrated the Black Clan, do you know the last time I felt in control of my own life? The last time I felt alive?"

Yumi waited.

"It was not long after my parents formalized the match with Prince Raiden," Mariko said. "When I wished to do something bold that only I would know, that only I would understand. I seduced a young man in a hay loft, with the intention of losing my maidenhead to him purely out of spite."

Yumi's eyes went wide.

Mariko continued. "But that wasn't the only reason. I did it for myself; so that I would not feel like a piece of chattel traded at the whim of men. So that I would know at least one part of myself I gave of my own will."

Yumi kept silent.

Toying with the rim of her cup, Mariko averted her gaze. "I learned something else that afternoon, though it would take me an unforgivable amount of time to realize it fully. I learned how unaware I was of life outside my experience. I used that poor boy like a thing to be discarded, never once considering what might happen to him." Something caught in her throat, a shimmer welling in her dark eyes. "Do you know the most important time I realized my own ignorance?

Yumi shook her head.

"It was that night you and I first met, at the teahouse next door. When I watched you dance wearing a mask meant to entice, and I was so jealous of you. Even more jealous when I saw you doff the mask for Ōkami. I knew at that moment how much you cared for each other. I realized then that every person has a story to tell. And for every person, that story is the most important one. Since the day I first saw you, that feeling has stayed with me." Her eyes locked on Yumi, her expression wholly without guile. "I never want to be the kind of person who uses others solely for her own gain again."

In silence, Yumi moved to her dressing table. Her chest

felt strangely tense, though her soul felt lighter than she could recall it being for a long time. She twisted the lid off a jar of white paint, then dipped a dampened sea sponge in its center. With careful patting motions, she covered her face and neck until they were coated in a thin layer resembling the palest cream. Then she picked up a charred piece of paulownia wood, holding its edge to a flame until it began to smolder. Yumi felt Mariko's gaze on her as she used the ashes to darken her eyebrows.

"What do you see when you look at me, Mariko?" Yumi asked while she painted careful lines above her eyelashes with a three-haired brush.

"A *maiko*. A smart, lovely young woman."

"Anything more?"

"I see mystery and sadness. Anger. Not necessarily because you were born a woman"—Mariko smiled in obvious remembrance of what Yumi had said not too long ago—"but more because you have always been treated as less than what you are."

"Those feelings are to be expected," Yumi said. "Young women do not find their way to an *okiya* from a place of hope. Whatever mystery you sense is the work of my trade." She put down the smoldering paulownia wood. "In truth, I hate the idea of mystery, and if I could, I would say whatever I wanted and do whatever I wished every day of my life."

Mariko's grin widened. "We should create a world for women like us. It would be a thing to see."

"I intend to do just that," Yumi said. She loosened her *obi* from around her waist, then untied her kimono to hang it from a wooden display rack with great care. After she crossed to the back of the room, she removed two sets of nondescript garments from a fragrant *tansu* chest.

Garments made for a boy.

"Will you join me?" Yumi asked. She let her smile widen slowly until it took on an air of mischief. It was a look Yumi hid from most people. One of unbridled happiness, absent any calculation.

After the initial shock, delight warmed across Mariko's face. "It would be my honor to join you."

Her openness endeared Mariko to Yumi even further, for the younger girl did not ask where it was they were going. What it was Yumi wished them to do.

Hattori Mariko trusted Asano Yumi.

Later tonight there would be time for Mariko to share any more information she might have obtained at Heian Castle. For Yumi to agree to pass along Mariko's revelations to Tsuneoki. For Yumi to continue playing Mariko's brother for a fool.

But for now?

They would be two girls racing across the rooftops of Inako, with freedom coiling through their hair and their shadows fading into the dusk.

Together.

more Than love
✦

You won't believe what she did next." Mariko leaned forward conspiratorially as she continued working in near darkness. "That same man who yelled at the melon vendor tried to filch Dragon's Beard candy from a little boy. Yumi was incensed, so she stole a *chamber pot* and emptied it on his head." She snickered while tying the last little vial to the loop on the end of the string. "He screamed as though he were being murdered. We had to leap over two nearby rooftops so he wouldn't catch us. I almost fell, but I haven't laughed so hard in forever."

Grinning, Ōkami took hold of the other end of the string, sliding the vial past the iron bars of his cell, over the strip of moonlight, and into his waiting hand.

"If only her brother had been able to see that," he said.

Mariko met his gaze, her eyes wide. "Would he be mad?

Should I not have told you? I was trying to share something lighthearted."

"No, I asked you to tell me what you did today." Ōkami's laughter was quiet and warm. "I just didn't realize you'd clambered onto the city's rooftops to terrorize the populace with Asano Yumi."

Mariko gnawed at her lower lip. "I wouldn't want to get her in trouble with Tsuneoki. I . . . really like Yumi."

"Since I'm currently in chains awaiting execution, her brother likely won't find out anytime soon. But in the event my circumstances change . . ." Though his face still appeared bruised and battered, Ōkami's grin turned sly. "I can't make any promises about staying silent. If you wish to offer me a bribe, I would not protest."

"That's not the least bit amusing." Mariko cut her gaze. "Only you would jest about dying."

"I think it's appropriate, following a story about a man being drenched in someone else's waste." The chains by his feet jangled as Ōkami braced his elbows on his knees. "The best jokes end with shit or death."

At that, Mariko laughed again. The same kind of laughter she'd shared with Yumi earlier that evening. It had been the first time in a long while that she'd allowed herself the luxury. Indeed there had been a moment just yesterday when she'd wondered if she would ever laugh at anything again.

Upon returning to the castle grounds, the first thing she'd wanted to do was tell Ōkami what had happened. To laugh with him about it. Sometimes it frightened Mariko how much he had come to matter to her.

"Is the lock cold yet?" she asked softly, so Ōkami would not detect the emotion in her voice.

Ōkami reached down into the small hole beside his foot. The sound of shifting metal coiled into the night air. He sighed. "Not yet."

Mariko exhaled with frustration.

It's taking too long.

The night prior, Mariko had brought a pilfered spoon to Ōkami. She'd instructed him to find a soft space in the earthen floor near his legs. To dig a small but deep hole, large enough to fit the lock securing his chains.

Her idea had been to weaken the metal by exposing it to the kind of cold that never saw the sun. The kind that froze into the earth and never thawed, even during summer. In her chamber, she'd crushed remnants of charcoal she'd collected from beneath the castle. After storing the powder in two empty cosmetic vials, she'd brought them to Ōkami, thinking to pour them into the lock and spark a controlled burst of fire within the mechanism. Hoping it would give way.

"I wish it weren't so warm outside," she said. "If the lock doesn't frost over, it may not work."

"I would not be disappointed in you if it failed, Mariko." Ōkami's voice was thick. "You astound me at every turn."

Mariko glanced around for a way to change the subject. Her eyes settled on the stream of moonlight cascading from the narrow window cut high above. It made her long to be bathed beneath its cool glow, fast asleep in Ōkami's arms.

"The moon is beautiful, isn't it?" she said.

"I imagine the moon would be a thing of beauty on a night like this. But I prefer what I'm looking at now." His eyes remained focused on Mariko as he spoke.

Ōkami had been right when he'd said Mariko eschewed most sentiments. But this was a feeling she could not ignore. A vital feeling, like a hand being burned when held too close to a flame. "You likely say that to all the girls who rescue you," she mumbled.

He did not smile. "They are a candle in the sunlight compared to you."

Mariko blinked, embarrassment blossoming beneath her skin.

Ōkami rested his head against the wall and looked up, intensifying the shadows on his face. "Actually you are nothing like sunlight. You're something else entirely. A well at dusk. That's where you exist for me. In that place where it's still and dark and deep."

A different kind of discomfort washed over her. A mixture of pleasure and pain. She did not find it unsettling, though the sensation was not what she'd imagined it would be. The stories from her childhood had made love seem poetic and grand and tragic all at once, not this odd blending of opposites.

Loss had taught her yet another lesson. Real love was more than a moment. It was everything that happened after. Chaos in one instant, simplicity in the next. Everything and nothing in the space of a simple breath.

It was clarity, sharp and numbing, like a winter's morning.

When Mariko said nothing, Ōkami laughed. "Don't let your mind escape you."

"I—" She cleared her throat, searching for the right words.

"You don't have to say anything, Mariko. I already know."

It galled her to realize how well Ōkami had come to know her in such a short period of time. But Mariko would have it no other way. A part of her knew she should tell Ōkami how she felt. To admit it aloud, so that it could never be ignored or denied. But Mariko stayed silent. Mere words felt hugely inadequate. And she wouldn't have the right words anyway. Not now.

"It's getting late," Ōkami said. "You should return to your chamber."

"I don't . . . wish to leave."

"And I don't want you to go, but the longer you stay, the more you risk your safety."

I should tell him I love him. What if I never see him again?

Mariko gritted her teeth. She would not tell him how she felt from a place of fear. Though she'd learned to embrace it—to make fear serve her instead of control her—Mariko knew better than to let it dictate something so precious.

"I'll return tomorrow night with some firestones." Her voice rasped with all she could not say. "If that doesn't work, I'll devise another way." Already her mind began working through possible options.

"Sleep well, Lady Mariko. You are loved. It isn't enough, but it's all I have."

Mariko gathered her things, her brow furrowed, her thoughts a jumble. Wordlessly she counted the paces toward the stairs leading up from the castle's underbelly. Despite her best efforts, regret had already begun to take root in her chest, as though she'd failed yet again. In all respects.

No. I will not let these fears rule me. I have better things to do with my time.

Ōkami was right. Love was not enough. It wasn't enough to convince Ōkami to cast aside his doubts and fight. And it wasn't the reason Mariko had offered to come to Inako. They both needed more than love. More than their heart's desires. They needed a way to bring about action.

And Mariko did not have that answer. Not yet.

Hattori Mariko slipped soundlessly through the courtyard, her path lit by the light of a sickle moon. As she paused between the painted posts supporting the covered walkways, white pebbles crunched underfoot several paces behind her.

Someone was following her.

Panic caught in her throat. She dropped into a crouch, stealing a moment to collect herself. If this person had not called for the guards or accosted her outright, then he—or she—was trying to obtain information on Mariko's whereabouts. Perhaps they did not yet know her identity.

But that seemed unlikely.

Mariko knew if she dallied, the intruder would only

become more emboldened. It was possible this person did not have much experience tracking or remaining beyond notice. Failing to conceal the sound of movement was a very basic error.

From her crouched position, Mariko tied a mask around the lower portion of her face, then tucked her body into a roll. She reoriented herself behind a row of manicured hedges near a grove of yuzu trees, their sweet citrus scent wafting through the cool night air. She waited once more. Closed her eyes. Let her ears catch any signs of motion.

Nothing.

Mariko scuttled in the shadow of the hedgerow framing the grove. The muscles in her stomach knitted together from the strain of staying low to the ground. When the hedgerow came to an end, she paused once more. Still she could hear nothing in her wake.

Her chest began to relax.

Then the faintest smell of sake curled into her nostrils.

Crunch.

She tore from the bushes toward a ceremonial gatepost bordering a stream. Like a whip through the darkness, Mariko raced into the deepest shadow she could find. Behind her, she heard someone—a man—grunt and stumble, striking the soft earth.

A shout rang out, followed by several more. Lanterns flashed in Mariko's periphery. Without thought, she slid down the bank of the small stream and tucked into a hollow beneath a small arched bridge.

She waited there, trembling uncontrollably as soldiers apprehended the man trailing her. As their shouts melted into muffled conversation. Words she could not discern from the babbling water.

Mariko waited nearly an hour, until the eastern sky began to lighten along its edges, her eyes wide, her fingers in fists. Then she crawled from her hiding place and back toward her room to vomit in an empty chamber pot.

A Pliant Mind

There were many layers to life. Especially a life like her own.

It was trite to say that not everything was as it seemed. But that fundamental understanding had become a necessary part of life. Time had taught Kanako that even the silliest thought—the most insignificant revelation—often held a deeper meaning.

One that could be used to her advantage, if she was given the opportunity.

She'd learned it first as a child. Rare was it for a poor village to raise a young girl with threads of magic running through her veins. The elders had said it happened once in a generation. Usually magic like this only manifested among the nobility—in those whose bloodlines had remained untainted. Kanako's magic had not been very strong at first. It had been so slight that her parents had not even thought to send her away to the imperial city to study with a true illusionist. It had begun with an ability to talk to animals and glean their thoughts.

When Kanako had grown older, she'd followed a yellow-eyed fox into the forest on a misty spring morning. Beneath a tree with blackened branches, the fox had revealed to her that it was a demon of the wood. It had told her how serving this demon would make her magic stronger. How it would enable Kanako to do not just one small thing, but many larger, greater things. Perhaps something large enough to catch the attention of those in power. With this stronger magic, maybe she could find her way to the school in Inako after all.

No matter that magic had a price. That great magic had an ever greater price.

The things Kanako had lost to the fox demon had gained her far more. It had been a small price to pay, to know that any pain she endured, she endured for a purpose. Any secrets she kept, she kept with this in mind. After all, her magic was of a finite nature. It would weaken with Kanako the more she used it.

This was the mantra by which she lived: the greater the magic, the greater the price.

Recently she'd found herself losing time. Her mind would turn blank for the space of several breaths. Thankfully no one around her had noticed. Nor had they noticed how much longer it took for her to heal from any wounds. The injury inflicted upon her by Asano Tsuneoki that night at the Akechi stronghold still pained her greatly.

But it was a trifling consideration. These costs had gained her a place in the imperial castle. The heart of sovereign. The son she held so dear.

And it was for this son that she did everything.

Channeling the shape of her fox demon, Kanako concealed herself behind a thorny rosebush, biding her time. She waited in the shadows of the enchanted *maru*—the place she'd conjured to conceal the evidence of her darkest deeds. A place she went to for a breath of calm. Her pulse was slow and steady, her breaths carefully metered, her paws anchored to the earth. Her eyes glowed through the darkness as they sought her mark. She knew he would be returning from Hanami soon, for she'd watched and listened for this precise opportunity.

Hattori Kenshin had disappeared to a teahouse in Hanami for the past several nights. As luck would have it, not once had he elected to take an escort or ask for the company of others.

He would be alone.

Kanako had set her sights on him weeks ago, as she'd worked to ensure her son's ascension to emperor. In this instance, she felt it only fitting; Lord Kenshin was the elder brother of Raiden's future wife. Of course he would have a reason to assassinate the current ruler. If he did, his sister would be the wife of the next emperor. His family would rise in station.

In the aftermath, this would make sense to those searching for it. The Dragon of Kai had murdered Minamoto Roku for being an obstacle to his sister becoming empress.

And a silly empress she would be. Kanako sneered to herself as she recalled Hattori Mariko and her pitiable attempts to deceive those in power. Kanako had watched for signs of a threat. When she saw the young woman with the doe eyes round the corner that first day, she'd observed nothing but an earnest child with a desperate wish: to be *more*. It was this earnestness that had caused Kanako to dismiss her outright. The main difference between Lady Mariko and her twin brother was that the latter had a pliant mind. The former possessed one locked tight under her control.

Useless to Kanako.

Months ago, she'd put this plan into motion. She'd thought to have Mariko murdered on the way to marry her son. With great care, Kanako had planted the seeds of this desire into the mind of her lover, the emperor, until he, too, believed it to be the best course of action. They would blame the Black Clan for the girl's murder. It would unite the nobles against the last vestiges of insurrection. After Mariko's death—the murder of an innocent young daughter of an esteemed daimyō—there would be no objections about sending soldiers into the forest to root out the sons of Takeda Shingen and Asano Naganori. To give her warrior son the chance he needed to prove how much more suited he was to the role of emperor, rather than his infantile younger brother. All the while Kanako had concealed a darker plan beneath this simple one. The plan to secretly blame the girl's murder on the empress and the crown prince. To once and for all sever any ties of loyalty between her son and his younger brother.

And then Hattori Mariko had survived.

Inconvenient, to say the least. But Kanako had been quick to formulate a new way to ensure Raiden's path as the next emperor of Wa. It was not as simple as using magic to orchestrate a death, for it could not seem in any way as though Kanako had shaped these outcomes.

She needed to appear untouchable, at all times.

When Kenshin staggered into sight—his garments muddy from an apparent stumble—Kanako moved from the shadows into his path. Quirked her head at him, letting a ghostly mist take shape around her, glistening of moonlit magic.

Kenshin stopped in his tracks. Teetered to one side, recognition catching his notice. He shook his head as though to clear his thoughts. Kanako smiled at him, her black lips curling upward, beckoning him closer. She knew he would identify her as the fox from his memory, just as she'd intended.

It had been so easy that time in the forest, beside the watering hole. So easy to infiltrate his trusting mind and test its bounds for her purpose. Lord Kenshin was the kind of young man who'd lived a life without question. What he saw was what he believed; what he heard became his truth; what he felt became fact.

Simpleminded fool.

In a way, he resembled the late emperor as a young man. When Kanako and Masaru first met as children, it had been his malleable mind that had drawn her to him. He'd been entranced by her magic, enthralled by her beauty.

At the thought of him now, storm clouds darkened Kanako's view.

He'd loved her. And she'd loved him, in her own way.

But Death always collected its due.

Now it was time to use her skills of persuasion once again. As Kanako could conjure shapes from nothingness, she would conjure outcomes from ideas. She smiled once more at Kenshin. He stepped toward her, his motions clouded by drink. Her long tail swishing through the air, she loped before him and gazed upward expectantly.

"What do you want?" Kenshin murmured, his words slurring.

She winked at him, then glided toward the vine-covered entrance of the enchanted *maru*. As she drew closer, the plants near her paws curled toward her. Kanako whispered to them, and they began changing their colors, the glittering mist coiling around their waxen leaves.

She glanced over her shoulder.

Hattori Kenshin watched her, mesmerized, just as the emperor had been many years before.

But he didn't trust her. Not anymore. In his suffering, doubt had begun to take root. Doubt in himself. Doubt in others. It was clear he did not trust her as he had that day in the forest, when Kanako had first taken hold of his mind. When she'd found the rage he'd kept locked away and used it as kindling to serve her designs. It had been so easy for Kanako to infiltrate his thoughts then.

He'd wanted to kill the old man that day in the clearing, for defying him. He'd wanted to slash his swords across the girl, who'd tried to defend her grandfather, and the boy, who'd attacked him in a fit of rage. Kanako had simply made it easier for him. She'd removed the obstacles he'd placed before his own desires.

Just as she intended to do now.

She resumed the slow infiltration of his mind. He continued pushing back at her intrusion. Kanako gritted her teeth, the wound in her side burning bright. The pain momentarily blinded her, but she felt Hattori Kenshin's resistance fade with her efforts.

His features slackened. The light dulled from his eyes. He followed Kanako past the entrance of the enchanted *maru* into a world bereft of color. Tones of silver and black washed across Kanako's vision. Along the boundary, the edges of the garden flashed as though every leaf were a tiny mirror. As though the world around them was constructed of nothing but mirrors.

With a furtive smile, she led her prey toward the flowering oak tree, its massive trunk wide and its branches rustling in an imaginary wind. She waited for his drink-addled mind to see past the first glance. To question the trick of the eyes and the blurring of the senses that so many failed to notice in this realm of magic.

Making them vulnerable.

For there—buried upright in the trunk of a mighty tree— slept a lovely young woman. One half of her face was terribly scarred, but she lay wrapped in the bark of the white oak, a soft haze of silver light around her. She looked like a resting spirit, enchanted from starlight.

Kanako watched his handsome face as he recognized the girl within.

"Amaya," he whispered. Kenshin shook his head as though it could not be possible. As though he'd finally learned not to trust everything he saw.

Inconvenient that he would choose now to doubt his own eyesight.

Hattori Kenshin took a slow step closer to the tree. His right hand rose from his side, his fingers stretching toward Muramasa Amaya's cheek. Shock took hold of Kenshin's features as truth settled on him. With both hands, he reached for the bark encasing her, as though he meant to rip its cocoon from around Amaya's body.

The cloud of light surrounding the sleeping girl flared, burning his fingers. The pain startled him into full awareness.

Kanako could have warned him, but she knew the best trials were the ones by fire. He would know now that he would need to suffer in order to free Muramasa Amaya from her oaken prison. This was necessary to drive him to do her bidding.

Then—as the shock began to wane—a figure stepped from behind the tree.

Kanako smiled to herself and let the rest of her plan fall into place, without having to utter a single word.

The sake had addled his mind.

Or he'd struck his head and was now in the midst of a frenzied dream.

Those were the only two possible explanations for what Kenshin saw now.

This had been a night of impossibility, from beginning to end. Yumi—the *maiko* who captured his attention the past three nights—had been late to arrive at the teahouse. His frustration at her absence caused him to drink even more than usual and leave before he had a chance to lose his sorrows in her lovely grey eyes.

Upon his return to the castle, he'd thought to seek out his sister. To speak with her frankly and close the distance that had continued to develop between them.

Only to find Mariko's chamber empty.

His suspicions had grown, despite his drink-addled mind. Kenshin made his way to the only place he felt certain his younger sister would venture in the dead of night: the cell of Takeda Ranmaru.

When he watched a lean figure clad in the clothing of a boy climb from the castle's underbelly into the light, Kenshin had known it was Mariko. He followed her, uncertain of how best to confront her for her lies. For her treachery.

Only when he stumbled as he chased her—drawing the attention of patrolling imperial guards—could he make a decision. He should have sent the soldiers after Mariko.

Should have forced her to admit her deception and accept her punishment.

But he'd made a spectacle of himself instead, granting Mariko a chance to conceal herself and escape. Kenshin—a samurai of the highest order—betrayed his sovereign to aid his traitorous younger sister. Still he did not know why he had done it.

He needed another drink. He needed to forget.

So Kenshin had followed the ghostly fox into a world between worlds. One limned in a delicate fog, with all its colors leached from sight. There—in the center of an immense silver tree trunk—rested the unmistakable face of Muramasa Amaya, the only girl he'd ever loved.

As his muddled mind latched on to her burned features, the images in his periphery had begun to spin. The leaves began turning in place like tiny mirrors throwing white light in all directions, as though he were in the center of a giant diamond caught in the rays of the sun.

The tree had burned him when Kenshin tried to rescue her, though it did not appear that Amaya was suffering. She looked as though she were asleep—merely blanketed by the rough bark of the ancient oak.

And now, his eyesight tricked him again.

Just like with Amaya, Kenshin had thought the man standing before him had perished. Kenshin had been certain of it.

"My lord," the figure said in a low voice. Nobutada—his father's most trusted samurai—bowed without hesitation.

Kenshin did not know if it was wise to speak. "I—thought you died in Jukai forest."

"No, my lord. I am not dead." Nobutada glanced sidelong as though he was certain an eavesdropper lurked in the nearby branches, or perhaps waited in the neatly trimmed hedge of mirrored leaves. "I know you have many questions."

Kenshin could not find the right words. His mind was too far gone—a persistent ache pounding in its center—the sake poured for him in Hanami continuing to fog his senses. "How—" he tried.

"There is no time for me to explain, my lord."

"Help me, Nobutada-*sama*," Kenshin began again, his voice coarse in its urgency. "I don't know what foul play is afoot here, but we must free Amaya from this tree."

"That is what I wish for us to discuss, my lord."

"Speak quickly." Kenshin closed the space between them, his temples hammering in time with his racing heart. "Then help me free her."

Nobutada shook his head. "I'm afraid there is no way to free Muramasa Amaya, my lord. I have been trapped here, too, at the behest of the former emperor."

"Am I trapped here, as well?" Kenshin backed away, the desire for self-preservation evident.

"No, my lord. You were not brought here as a prisoner. You entered this place of your own will, so you are free to leave."

"Amaya was brought here as a prisoner?" Anger clouded Hattori Kenshin's face.

Nobutada looked about, discomfort settling into his expression. "I cannot be certain."

Kenshin pressed his palms into his eyes, as though it would force the drink from his head. Raking his fingers through his disheveled topknot, he gazed once more in disbelief at the very much alive samurai who'd been sent to keep his sister safe on her journey to Inako. "I thought you were dead. Tell me how you came to be here, Nobutada-*sama*. What is this place? And what must we do to free you both?"

Nobutada kept silent, his expression grim.

"Is the late emperor responsible for this as well?" Kenshin's voice was a dangerous whisper.

"It is treason for me to speak of these things."

Fury overcoming him at Nobutada's reticence, Kenshin took hold of the wizened samurai's collar. "Was it Minamoto Masaru?"

Wincing, Nobutada nodded once. He inhaled through his nostrils. "It was our former emperor, my lord."

Kenshin's fist tightened around his collar, his bloodshot eyes wide with rage.

His father's best samurai put his hands in the air—palms facing out—in a gesture of peace. "The former emperor took me prisoner after he sent a band of thieves to murder your sister."

A beat passed in silence. As Kenshin studied Nobutada for signs of artifice, he released his hold on the samurai. Forced his rage to die down to mere embers. "Why would he agree to Mariko's marriage if he only wished to kill her?"

"I believe he wished to forge this connection with your father, and then thought better of it. Perhaps a better offer of marriage was already in the works." Nobutada sighed with defeat. "There is no way to know for certain. But I do know he did not want his son to wed Lady Mariko."

Kenshin nodded, his longstanding suspicions confirmed. He crossed his arms in an effort to stand straight, his feet still unsteady. "What must we do?"

"The key lies with . . . the new emperor." Hesitancy marred the samurai's words.

"I don't understand what you—"

Nobutada interrupted Kenshin, his tone urgent. "He cannot be allowed to live, my lord. Not after what his father did to the Hattori clan. Not after what he plans to do now. He is neglecting his people. Tales of suffering are sprouting from the east. The people of Wa are being tormented by a plague, and the son of Minamoto Masaru has done nothing to address it."

The world around Kenshin started to spin. "You are suggesting we commit treason. That I break every oath I have ever taken."

"My lord, the emperor and his son have trapped me as their prisoner. They prevented me from saving Lady Mariko that day in Jukai forest. It is likely they have stolen away the daughter of Muramasa Sengo, for her to exist in this half world, to live a half life in slumber, buried in the center of an enchanted tree."

Kenshin's eyes locked on the sleeping form of Amaya. Was it possible the emperor took her as a means of controlling him? To offer further insult to his family? Kenshin could not fathom attempting to kill the new emperor. No matter how much he might wish Roku's death, Kenshin was a samurai who served at the grace of his sovereign. "I cannot forsake my oath to the emperor."

"I understand your hesitation, my lord," Nobutada said. "But if he and his father have committed such atrocities, perhaps it is time for their family to pay the ultimate price."

Kenshin's eyes narrowed. "If you've been trapped here since the attack on Mariko's convoy, how is it you know what Minamoto Roku has failed to do?"

"The fox comes to visit, once in a while." Nobutada inclined his head toward the animal sitting placidly beside him, as though it were his pet. "As a creature of magic, it is allowed in this colorless half world. A world the emperor used to conceal the worst of his atrocities. The fox took pity on me and brought me food. Often it brought me the information I sought, as well. Scraps of correspondence and the like."

Though the ache in his head continued to grow, Kenshin glanced down at the fox. Something about its wily smile unnerved him, as though it were supremely pleased by this recent turn of events. But this same fox had helped Kenshin before, that wretched day in the clearing when he'd lost memories. The fox had led him to safety before anyone could see the terrible atrocities he had committed.

"I have sworn an oath to serve Minamoto Roku. It does not matter what his father did. I must remain steadfast in my loyalty," Kenshin said. *Bushidō* dictated nothing else.

"And if I told you Minamoto Roku was responsible for the death of his father—that we serve a family of liars and murderers—where would your loyalties lie then?"

Kenshin said nothing, his eyes betraying his heart. He turned his back, tormented by a flood of thoughts and feelings.

"Do not look away from what you know to be true, my lord," Nobutada said.

"How do I know you are not the one who killed the emperor?" Kenshin asked. "You disappeared on the day my sister most needed you. How do I know where *your* allegiances lie, Nobutada-*sama*?"

The elder samurai drew himself to his full height. "If you do not trust me after all my years of service to your family, my lord, then I am truly dead already."

Frustrated by the tenor of their conversation, Kanako decided to step forward. She'd tried to press Kenshin to do her bidding—gentle nudges on his thoughts—but his mind was stronger than before. Far less pliant. His renewed resolve irritated her greatly. The sight of his trapped beloved should have made his mind even more open to infiltration. Not less. He should be willing to do whatever it took to free Muramasa

Amaya, without question. Perhaps Nobutada's assertions had not worn Kenshin down as she'd hoped. Perhaps they'd only made him more resilient.

It was time for Kanako to take direct action.

She let her mind fade into nothingness, then barreled into Kenshin's thoughts without warning. As she searched for the best way to wrest control, she paused to take in the full tumult there.

So many sources of discord. So many sources of heartache.

Kanako latched onto the thing causing him the most pain. Now was the time to use the memory of the girl he loved. Of Amaya, trapped within the enchanted oak.

"The demons of the forest wish for a reckoning, Lord Kenshin," she whispered into his thoughts, her voice an indistinct growl. "Bring the spirit of the silver oak the head of the new emperor, and it will relinquish the girl you love from its grasp."

Kenshin's mind twitched. It pushed back with far more force than it ever had before. Frustratingly strange. Kanako surged on, taking root in his weaknesses, turning the spark of discord into a flame. She let the rising plume cloud the rest of his mind, like smoke in the sun.

With a groan, Kenshin gave in, his eyes turning white, his mouth hanging open in a soundless scream.

When he returned to himself, Kenshin did not appear to be addled by drink any longer. He looked focused and aware. Without a word, he turned on a heel and left the colorless *maru*, blood trickling from his eyes.

Once the Dragon of Kai left this world between worlds, Kanako let her magic glimmer over her fox body. It flowed through her, like the tremors of an earthquake beneath the soil. She uncoiled to her feet in a ripple of grace, letting her long hair stream behind her in a silken cloak.

She glanced at Nobutada. She'd known for days that the wearied samurai was losing his sense of conviction. The lies he was forced to tell the son of his daimyō had taxed him. The grief in his eyes was apparent. Kanako moved closer to the wizened samurai. His shoulders fell in her presence.

"You are troubled by what must be done," she said in a soothing voice.

"After the death of the former emperor, I am not certain why I am still here. What purpose am I meant to serve now, my lady? Why do I remain here when our sovereign has passed into the next world? How am I to serve his sons by spreading these lies?"

Kanako inclined her head sympathetically. "You are meant to serve my family. To serve the new emperor, as well as my son. That is your vow. Your way, as a warrior."

The samurai's features lost a measure of their severity. Then they began to wilt even more. Until the edges of his lips were downturned in defeat.

Kanako took in a steadying breath. Her resulting smile was one of peace.

"I wish to thank you, Nobutada-*sama*," she began.

He nodded once, the resignation plain on his face. As though he'd known for far too long that he'd been played for a fool.

She continued. "I know how difficult it was for you to turn your loyalties away from your daimyō in service to your emperor, but the circumstances could not be avoided. We must continue to do all that is possible to defend the empire and the family at the heart of it. Especially after our last emperor was murdered in his own garden—within the walls of his own castle—we know there is no one who can be trusted. And this includes your lord, Hattori Kano."

Again the samurai nodded.

But Kanako knew too well that her words were no longer taking root. His mind was no longer the malleable thing she'd first sought out with her powers. The strength of her magic had faded rapidly of late, and she'd had to expend far more of it on Hattori Kenshin than she first thought.

Kanako leveled her gaze. "I apologize, Nobutada-*sama*. For this and for so much else."

Even before the words left Kanako's lips, she pushed her magic outward in a blunt blow to his chest. He gasped as the air left his throat, and his body flew back, tossed about like a sack of rice.

This was inelegant, but necessary.

Kanako needed pliant minds. Minds lacking conviction. Lacking focus. Minds like that of the last emperor. Like those of the Akechi clan and the Yoshida clan. It was true that the lord of the Sugiura clan had been more difficult to contain, but even he fell in the end. She needed a mind like Kenshin's the day in the clearing beside the watering hole. When he'd killed for her without question.

Nobutada could no longer be trusted.

It took too much of Kanako's power to turn a resistant mind. Made it difficult to do anything else. Made her weak. This was the second such mind she'd been forced to turn tonight. But Kanako could safely stay in this colorless world until her strength was restored. She did not wish to kill Nobutada. Not yet. It would be a loss to them all if the empire no longer had such a fine warrior serving its cause.

So she used all of her remaining strength to take apart Nobutada's mind. To dismantle every last form of resistance found within. The claws of her fox form drove into his chest, tearing through his heart, raking over his mind. It was not as difficult as it had been with Asano Tsuneoki that night at the Akechi fortress. The boy had his own power. And it had forced her out before she could wrest firm control. But she'd still found something of use there, buried beneath his convictions.

Men with convictions bored her most of all.

Kanako tore through Nobutada's mind until there was nothing left. Then she reached back into herself, seeking her center, returning to her human form.

She could not stand at first. She fell to her knees, gasping for air.

A part of her worried she spread herself too thin. Those long nights overtaking so many minds in the eastern reaches of the empire had taken a heavy toll. The tiny mirrors along the hedge of the colorless world began to shimmer as though a gust of wind had raked across their surfaces. As they shimmered, they took to the air, their shapes like that of otherworldly butterflies. They blossomed and burst into hollowed husks of human beings. Like shadow selves.

All around her, Kanako saw the true souls of the minds she'd stolen from the people of Wa. The ones in constant agony, as they awaited an unforeseen fate. Kanako struggled to her feet, her sight lost as she gulped for breath. She fought for something to grasp. Something with which to pull herself up.

She'd spent years of her life quietly absorbing ridicule. Quietly enduring mistreatment by the ladies of court who followed that hag of an empress like ducklings across a pond. She said nothing as they demeaned her. Done nothing, save nurture her hate in cold silence.

But Kanako had witnessed what the empress Yamoto Genmei had done that night beside the moon-viewing pavilion. How she'd murdered the emperor to secure her own position and that of the crown prince. Kanako would continue splitting what remained of her power—until it was whittled down to nothing—if it meant she could destroy that woman and do away with Genmei's power-hungry son.

If it meant Kanako could see her beautiful Raiden sit on

the Chrysanthemum Throne, there was no cost too high to pay.

Nobutada stood, his eyes wild, and his mouth ajar. If he could make sounds at all, Kanako knew they would be sounds of terror. Of loss. She waited while his true soul rose from his body, turned into a silver butterfly, and settled itself in the hedge, its wings a twinkling mirror of dark and light.

A Broken Smile

---✶---

Mariko stood in a circle of pastel flowers, smiling as the ladies of the court fawned over her. Whispered about her upcoming nuptials. Wondered aloud at how lucky she was to be joining the ranks of the imperial family.

"I've heard that Prince Raiden is the best rider in the *yabusame*," one girl began as she strolled past a flowering hedge in the most vibrant part of the imperial gardens.

Another laughed. "And the most handsome."

"I care not a whit for his looks," a third young woman announced. "He is wealthy and strong, which are all the things that matter to me in a husband."

They spoke just softly enough to maintain a semblance of decorum.

Just loudly enough to be heard.

They continued their prattle until its discordant melody became a drone. Mariko forced their words to blur together.

She desperately wished to leave them behind and wander through the gardens on her own, so that she might at least have a moment of peace to herself. Ever since the announcement of her marriage celebration to Prince Raiden—which would take place in only two short days—she'd been beleaguered by questions and exclamations.

An elder lady of the court had been the first to excuse the impropriety of holding a marriage not long after the death of their last sovereign. "It is true it might be too soon, but the festivities will be a way to move our city past mourning."

The other ladies of court had replied with solemn nods, as though this were a fact of true import. Mariko almost snorted at this. She had yet to witness mourning of any kind since arriving in Inako. As she suspected from the onset, the former emperor was far from revered among the nobility. They may have feared him, but they had not worshipped him as they were meant to do.

The idea of it. Worshipping a man as a god.

What would it look like to truly worship anything?

As Mariko glanced about for a way to excuse herself from the gathering, her eye caught on a familiar face, staring off into the distance beside an arrangement of spiraling gardenias.

Hirata Suke. The young girl who had been pelted by eggs the day after Mariko's arrival. It had been a week since the events of that afternoon, but Mariko had not seen Suke since then, though she'd searched for her. As Mariko made her inquiries, she'd recalled her father speaking of the Hirata clan in passing, and it had not been in a favorable tone.

Hirata Suke's father had often questioned the actions of Minamoto Masaru. The Hirata clan had been one of the last to turn away its loyalties from the former shōgun, Takeda Shingen.

Unsurprisingly, these facts motivated Mariko all the more to seek out Suke.

Slowly—so as not to draw attention—Mariko made her way to the girl's side. Suke lowered her head and looked away, as though she wished for Mariko to pass her by. Leave her be.

"We have not yet had a chance to meet formally," Mariko began with a smile.

Suke returned the smile, albeit awkwardly. "It is a pleasure to be seen in your company, Lady Mariko. Congratulations on your forthcoming union. I wish an auspicious occasion for you and a bright future for your children."

Perfectly delivered. Yet Suke's voice sounded hollow. That hint of dejection pushed Mariko to delve deeper.

Letting a cheeky light enter her gaze, Mariko smiled. "Do you wish an auspicious occasion for Prince Raiden as well?" It was a dangerous question, to be sure. But Mariko did not have the luxury of being indirect. If Suke reacted badly, Mariko could simply make a jest of it all and walk away.

Suke lifted her eyes with a touch of surprise. She said nothing in response. Her lips gathered in the suggestion of a pout. As though she were forcing them to keep still.

A twinge cut through Mariko. Though she'd given Suke an opportunity to reassure Mariko of her loyalties either way, the girl had instead chosen to say nothing at all. Her question had surprised Suke, but then it was clear—by the shadows under her eyes—that lies did not become her.

Unwilling to admit defeat, Mariko took a step closer. Dropped the amusement from her tone. "It was unfair of me to put you in an uncomfortable situation with my question."

Though her eyes widened at the edges, Suke remained silent.

"I wanted to"—Mariko paused—"apologize for what I did the other day, in the dowager empress's receiving room. For . . . participating in that spectacle."

Mistrust clouded Suke's expression. "There is no need for you to apologize, my lady. I was in the wrong. It is I who should humbly beg your forgiveness."

Mariko took a tentative step closer. Almost too close. It felt as though they were grazing the surface of the truth. "There is no need to apologize to me either. I've been in the wrong since I arrived here, especially when compared to others."

"We must distance ourselves from comparison." Suke dipped her head in a bow. "That is the only way to be truly free."

"Those are wise words."

Suke tucked a tendril of loose hair behind an ear. "They've given me a great deal of strength these last few days. In a world built on comparison, it has been very freeing to see all those around me in this new light."

"I could not agree with you more," Mariko said, meeting her gaze straight on.

Suke finally smiled, and the gesture caused the edges of her eyes to crinkle in a becoming fashion. The small scar on her cheek from the eggshells had nearly healed. Mariko indicated for Suke to walk with her, and the two girls commenced with their stroll, though Suke maintained a wary distance.

As they stopped to admire a cloud of colorful butterflies, three girls walking together in the opposite direction bowed to Mariko, then sniffed at Suke with disdain. Mariko recognized one of them from that day in the Lotus Pavilion; this girl had been troubled to see misfortune fall upon Suke. She'd averted her gaze and her cheeks had grown pink with discomfort.

Despite their dismissal, Suke bowed at them, a graceful smile on her face. After they passed, she murmured, "We were childhood friends. I used to roam these halls with those girls at my side. And now?" She exhaled slowly. "I am dung beneath their sandals."

Mariko kept silent in consideration. "I admire you for having the strength to continue treating them with respect after their betrayal." She glanced at Suke sidelong. "I wish you could teach me how not to care. How to stay resilient in the face of all this . . . foolery."

"It is not my own resilience, my lady," Suke said. "I've had a great deal of guidance these last few days from someone who should not have reached a hand out to me. Especially after all those times I participated in shunning her from court."

Mariko stopped walking to meet Suke's gaze. "Is there a lady of court I have not met?"

Suke nodded, a hint of humor in her reply. "Your future husband's mother."

Mariko kept her features steady, though a curious drumming caught in her chest. Following her conversation with Raiden, Mariko had wondered when she might have a chance to encounter the late emperor's consort. As could be expected, the enchantress had been absent from any court event attended by the dowager empress. Raiden had assured her that his mother had little interest in court.

Mariko grinned brightly. "I have not had a chance to meet her. But I would welcome the opportunity."

"I'd be honored to take you to her," Suke replied with a bow. "Perhaps later this evening?"

"That would be wonderful. Thank you for the introduction. I'm not sure when—or if—any of the other ladies of the court would offer Prince Raiden's mother or myself the same courtesy." Mariko's smile widened. "So what should we do until then?"

Surprise flashed across Suke's features. "We?" She blinked.

Mariko leaned closer. "Have you ever played Go?"

Prince Raiden's mother was not at all what Mariko had expected her to be. She'd expected a woman of great beauty, bedecked in sumptuous silk. A woman who did not shy away from flaunting the proof of her good fortune. Instead she found an enchantress dressed in simple dove-grey linen, without a hint of jewels or opulence anywhere to be found. Not even a single bar of tortoiseshell through her hair.

They met beneath a darkened sky, beside a pavilion set under the rising moon. Raiden's mother stood barefoot by the water's edge, her hair hanging down her back.

Free.

She glanced over at Mariko and smiled. Her expression was not kind. Nor did it appear contrived. It was strong. Clear. Guileless. Which gave Mariko pause. A woman like this— perhaps the greatest enchantress of her generation—did not rise to her station without being shrewd. Without being a gifted reader of minds.

Mariko stepped beside her. Turned to face her. Studied her as she studied Mariko, without even the slightest hint of pretense. Raiden's mother was still a beauty. Age had not lined her appearance as it had others. She looked clever. Watchful.

Before Mariko spoke, she caught herself silently hoping to resemble this woman when she was of a similar age. She stopped herself, caution demanding her to stay vigilant. Raiden's mother had not survived decades at court without a great deal of resourcefulness.

"I'm sorry it has taken me so long to meet with you, Mariko-*chan*," she began. "Forgive a mother for being cool to the woman who will steal her son away in a few short days."

Mariko bowed. "There is nothing to forgive, my lady."

Raiden's mother laughed. "I am no lady of this court."

"But you are my lord's mother, and I offer you the greatest respect I have to give."

"Kano-*sama* should be quite proud of you. You are a credit to your father's name."

Mariko dipped her head once more. "I am undeserving of your praise."

"I disagree." She lifted her hands to direct a gliding black swan toward the bank, its feathers glistening in the moonlight. "I think it extraordinary that you managed to survive an attempt on your life, at such a young age. Then managed to stave off your doom while living among murderers and thieves."

As with the empress, Mariko knew she was being tested, but in a different manner. It troubled her to realize she could not sense the intent. "I did very little, my lady. The stars were with me."

"Of course." The enchantress's voice turned circumspect, almost as though she were beginning to lose interest.

They watched the black swan swim to a stop. Lower its head, as if in a bow. Then take its leave.

"My son will not be an easy husband."

Mariko did not respond.

Raiden's mother continued. "I've not raised him to be agreeable. I've raised him to fight. To be beyond reproach. It has been the only way for me to ensure his safety. My greatest desire has been to raise a son not even the heavens could find fault with."

Mariko's eyes widened.

In that respect, she has failed. Utterly.

The shrewd woman turned to face Mariko once again, her gaze direct. "I am not delusional. I know Raiden has his faults." Her features hardened. "He is still young and in need of guidance. Unfortunately he no longer has time to listen to the word of his mother." A smile touched her lips as she gazed over the waters of the gently flowing pond. "Sometimes men do not realize the power a woman can possess. That many things begin and end with you. What I wish for Raiden is that you will be as direct as I was with him. That you will not allow his faults to overshadow his greater self."

Greater self?

Mariko maintained a solemn expression. She nodded slowly, as though she'd been given sage advice. After all, this was what she'd been raised to be: a doting wife and a loving mother. Were these things her greatest wish, it would indeed be a gift to have her husband's mother offer her such guidance.

"Impressive." The light of the moon twinkled in the enchantress's eyes. "You are more than what I thought you would be." She did not appear to be lying.

"I am thankful for your wisdom, my lady. And for the compliment."

"It wasn't a compliment, Lady Mariko. It was a word of caution." Raiden's mother reached for Mariko's hand. The woman's touch startled her, for it was unusual among the nobility to cross into another's space in such a manner.

The enchantress's hand was cool, her touch soft. Mariko felt a soothing warmth flow from her fingers into her arm, as though she were being lulled to sleep. She wanted to yank her hand away. Fought the urge, for it would be the height of disrespect.

Her body squirmed. Her mind remained still.

Raiden's mother took in a careful breath. "Do not lose hold on your many strengths, my daughter. I did not know until today how much of a boon you could be to my son. And I am thankful for it." The enchantress bowed low. Kissed Mariko's hand.

Then disappeared from the riverbank in a whirl of linen.

A sleeping Dragon

———✶———

Two days.

Two days were all Mariko had left to free Ōkami from his cell and help him escape the imperial city. Once she was married to Prince Raiden, she could not spend her nights experimenting with charcoal crystal behind her *tansu* chest or disappearing beneath the castle to pass an hour in the company of a traitor.

In two days, her nights would be spent with her new husband.

And Ōkami would be free, or he would be dead.

These were not thoughts Mariko cared to dwell upon.

Urgency driving her every deed, she collected more of the crystallized scrapings she'd stolen from beneath Heian Castle. The dark grey flakes smelled of metal and soot. But she knew as well as any how they could be highly flammable when touched by heat in just the right way.

Mariko took the small porcelain bowl she'd pilfered from her evening meal. She added whatever she could find to the charcoal flakes and tested the mixture. First she used nightingale dung. Then she stirred in salt crystals. Ground the shavings down to a powder.

Still they did not produce enough heat to spark.

What she wouldn't give for one of the pale purple flowers that hung above the hot springs near the Black Clan's encampment.

A memory flashed through her mind. Pinked her cheeks.

Those hot springs had proven dangerous on more than one occasion. For more than one reason. The memories they conjured were moments of brightness for her. The touch of her hand to Ōkami's bare chest. The brush of his fingertips down her spine.

The feel of his lips upon hers.

To me, you are magic.

A sadness weighed down on her like an anchor in the sea. Mariko quickly shoved it aside before it could find purchase. There was no need to dwell on the past. If she wanted the boy she loved to have any kind of a future, she needed to remain cold. Detached. Her purpose was not to simply be any man's bride. If she could not have the boy she wanted—the life she wanted—she would forge her own path.

She would be more.

Mariko decided to separate the lighter crystals from the darkened dregs. She poured water into the small ceramic bowl, then placed it above a taper, suspending its brim between two lacquered chopsticks. In silence, she let the water rise to a low boil above the candle, then deposited the charcoal crystals inside, careful to watch the water level so that nothing burned.

After the liquid had boiled away, she was left with crystals resembling the kind of rock salt used to keep horses from dehydrating on long journeys. Mariko took a single crystal and balanced it on the edge of a cosmetics brush. Using the firestones she'd pilfered from a shrine to the late emperor, she lit the crystal. It sparked hot, crisping the end of the brush.

A grin began to form on her lips. Mariko proceeded to boil the remaining charcoal flecks until a small amount of refined crystal formed a pile on top of a piece of *washi* paper. But would it be enough heat to break the chains binding Ōkami? How many crystals would be needed to destroy the tumblers? It was key for a bright flash of fire to combat the brisk cold of the hole Ōkami had dug in his cell. That combination of extremes should weaken the metal.

There is only one way to know for certain.

With that, Mariko gathered everything in a bundle and slipped out into the night.

She moved between the shadows of Heian Castle, her steps measured. Despite the alarming incident from the night prior, Mariko had yet to encounter a guard. Perhaps that fact made her bold.

Perhaps it made her foolish.

Mariko glided down the stairs into the warren of underground tunnels, her skin tingling with awareness. Tonight a greater sense of importance dictated her every move. Time was not on her side. She made her way down the narrow corridor—counting each of her steps—toward the widening cavern before the two barred cells.

As she stepped from the shadows near the foot of the stairs, sounds of movement caught her attention. The rumble of male voices. Her pulse leapt in her throat, and fear began churning through her veins.

Someone was beside Ōkami's cell.

Just as silently as she'd come, Mariko turned back, with a mind to retrace her steps. Then—at the top of the stairs above—another torchlight blazed into view. If she did not hide immediately, she would be trapped.

Breathe. This is exactly why I sought to learn all I could about this place.

She closed her eyes and prepared to count her paces. Eight steps to the left. Three steps into a corner encased by darkness, where she could crouch unseen. It would be simple to keep track of where she moved. From the beginning, Mariko had known that—if she was going to help Ōkami escape—she would need to move about freely without carrying a source of light that could catch unwanted attention.

As she began to turn left by the stack of discarded charcoal, a hand shot from the shadows and gripped her by the arm, thrusting her into the inky space beneath the stairs.

She almost squealed. Then immediately fought back. Her fists connected with a broad male chest. A man who smelled suspiciously of sake. It did not matter. Mariko leveled a kick at her assailant's shins, then twisted her wrist in an attempt to break free. She angled her elbow—the hardest part of her body—and positioned it to slam in his face.

Grunting, the man grabbed her by the shoulder and yanked her arm behind her back. Mariko refused to cry out at first. But he applied more pressure, until she relented with a gasp.

They both froze beneath the stairs until the man with the torch—the one who'd caught Mariko's attention mere moments before—descended, the dust of his heavy footsteps powdering their hair. His gait was hefty, his movements purposeful. Undoubtedly a soldier. The man paused at the bottom of the staircase and then proceeded down the corridor toward Ōkami's cell. As soon as he was out of earshot, Mariko attempted to break free again. Her assailant tightened his grip, almost to the point of pain.

"How dare you?" Mariko whispered, her voice sounding tinny and ineffectual.

Her assailant shoved her forward, relinquishing his hold on her arms. "How dare I?" He spat the last word.

Kenshin.

Mariko whirled in place. "You're following me? Were you following me last night, too?"

"You're fortunate I did," Kenshin rasped back. "If I hadn't, you would have been caught. An imperial patrol was only steps away from finding you. I'm following you now to make sure nothing else happens to you."

She pushed him. He did not budge. Kenshin always held himself like a stone. "Why?" Mariko demanded. "Why would you . . . help me?"

"Because you're as big a fool as Father always said you were." Her brother spoke in hushed tones, each of his words sharp. "And because . . . I can't bear to lose you."

Elevated voices emanated from the darkness beyond, near Ōkami's cell. Kenshin stared at her, his eyes glittering with feeling. They remained silent. Not even a breath could be heard between them, but her brother's anguish felt alive, as though it had taken on its own form. They waited until the voices in the distance dropped, becoming indistinguishable once more. Until sounds of a skirmish wound through the space.

They were beating Ōkami again. Simply for sport.

Mariko closed her eyes, taking note of every blow. Shuddering as though they'd been delivered to her. Now that her brother had discovered her truth, she no longer needed to conceal her feelings. When Ōkami finally cried out, Mariko turned in place to hide a rush of hot tears, knowing that the sound of his suffering likely saved them from being discovered. Again Ōkami helped her, even when he did not know it.

"You're going to be caught," Kenshin said softly.

Mariko composed herself, brushing away her brimming tears. "No, I'm not."

"Takeda Ranmaru could be killed at any moment. He's

been beaten enough to die, but still he clings stubbornly to life. The boy could be executed tomorrow." Kenshin paused. "Why risk yourself for him?"

"He won't be executed tomorrow," Mariko said, facing Kenshin. "He'll be executed after my wedding."

Her brother's eyes went wide. "What?"

"I told Raiden I didn't want a spectacle to be made of his death. I didn't want his followers making him a martyr to their cause. So I asked Raiden to instead end his life quietly on the evening of our wedding day, when the attention of the public would be absorbed in more joyous festivities." Mariko glared through the darkness, trying not to flinch at the unending blows. "Ōkami will be spared until then."

"And then what do you intend to do?"

Mariko did not respond.

Kenshin continued. "Why are you here? Why have you come here for the past few nights, if not to see him?"

Again no response.

At that, Kenshin gripped Mariko by the wrist. Grim acceptance lined his features. When he grasped the hanging fabric of her sleeve, his touch turned rough.

"If you're going to dress as a man, be prepared to be treated as one." Kenshin pushed her into the rough stone wall at her back as he searched her sleeves, like he would a thief's. When he found nothing, he patted Mariko's sides until he found the pouch she'd concealed in her *kosode*.

Her cheeks aflame with indignation, Mariko reacted without thought. The blow she leveled at her brother's face caught him by surprise. He stumbled back, his eyes wide.

"If you wanted to know if I had hidden something, you should have asked." Mariko ripped the small pouch from beneath her *kosode* and dropped it at Kenshin's feet. She fought to conceal the despair clawing at her stomach, knowing how desperately Ōkami needed to escape, and how difficult it would be to remake the crystals and pilfer another set of firestones.

Anger blazed across Kenshin's face. For an instant, Mariko thought he might strike back at her, but his expression turned cool and distant, just as it had every other time they'd spoken since arriving in Inako. "Return to your room, Mariko."

Rage mingled with her despair. The tears threatened to fall in earnest. "There is a special place in Yomi for those who fail their families."

"And there is a special place in Yomi for those who lie to theirs."

Mariko kept silent, her chin quivering.

Her brother's features turned forbidding. "Don't return to this part of the castle. There is nothing for you here. You risk your life with this behavior, and I won't save you again. You don't deserve to be saved. What you've done rejects everything you've been raised to be. It is an insult to our family. Would you have us—our mother, our father—all perish for your childish notion of love?" Kenshin asked in a harsh whisper.

Just as he finished speaking, the blows and the taunting echoing from beyond the corridor ceased as abruptly as they had begun. Mariko and Kenshin stared at each other, one imploring through the silence, the other fighting through her tears.

Mariko's fists balled at her sides. "I would rather die for love than stand by and watch my love perish."

At that, Kenshin raised a hand to strike her. Mariko did not flinch. He caught himself just before his hand connected with his sister's face. Shaking, he pulled back. Detached. Nothing could mar the coolness of his affect. It was as though Kenshin had been carved from an ancient tree. "I will make sure guards are posted outside your chamber from now on."

Lines of anguish collected around Mariko's features. Hot tears coursed down her cheeks as she spun away from her brother. Away from this last—most precious—chance.

Kenshin waited until Mariko was out of sight.

He stood in the shadows and let the stabbing pain inside him fade with each of his breaths. Amaya's smile beckoned to him. Her laughter echoed in his ears, his failure searing through his memories. Mariko did not know what had happened to Amaya. She'd been ignorant of what Kenshin had done. What he'd failed to do. And still it was as though it were written in black ink across his forehead.

In silence, Kenshin unwrapped the package Mariko had hidden away to deliver to the son of Takeda Shingen. The boy she loved. Kenshin had thought it might contain a key, or maybe some form of nourishment. It would be all but impossible for Mariko to pilfer a key, since the only two keys in existence belonged to the emperor and his elder brother. But if anyone could purloin an item not meant for her use, it would be Mariko.

Inside the pouch he discovered pale grey crystals, not unlike the kind collected from the salt flats. He'd come across something similar in a faraway desert by the Sendai river when his family had traveled there years ago. Beside these crystals was a small piece of waxen paper and two firestones.

Whatever device Mariko had invented with the intention of helping Takeda Ranmaru, it was sure to be elaborate and ingenious. Kenshin tucked the small package into the sleeve of his *kosode* and moved through the pathway beneath Heian Castle toward the prisoner in his cell.

Kenshin knew from his conversations with the emperor that Roku would visit Ranmaru each night and reopen all manner of wounds. Tonight the emperor had come later than usual to inflict his particular brand of torture. It was cruel and unbecoming behavior for a heavenly sovereign, but the Dragon of Kai had realized almost as soon as he arrived to the imperial city that the new emperor was not a man of honor, but rather one of duplicity.

This boy Kenshin was bound to serve.

At this thought, a sigh seemed to emanate from behind him. The gust of air that followed was icy. It touched the back of his neck before sliding down his spine in a cold caress. The voice carried on it was a garbled one, but a thought settled at the back of his skull. A thought of blood and death. Kenshin shook it off with a toss of his head, the troubling feeling still scraping at his skin. He moved forward in time to hear the sound of fists against flesh resume.

Pleased to see Kenshin join in this nightly ritual, the emperor nodded at him appreciatively.

To his credit, the son of Takeda Shingen had stopped crying out. In truth, Kenshin suspected he might not live to Mariko's wedding day, despite her attempts to spare him. While the emperor continued taunting his prisoner, Kenshin waited to one side with an air of nonchalance. The smell of blood saturated the space with salt and copper.

Kenshin remained unaffected as he watched the son of the last shōgun take his punishment. Wondered what kind of boy existed beneath that battered shell. There was defiance there. Strength. These were surely the reasons the emperor could not bear to leave Takeda Ranmaru be. What was it Mariko had called him?

Ōkami. The wolf.

Wolves were pack animals. They smelled blood from leagues away. Tracked it for days, even through snow and through sleet. Fought to defend their own without hesitation or remorse.

And they did not leave a member of their pack behind.

When the emperor had had his fill of bloodshed, he ordered his guards to stand down. The soldiers locked Ranmaru's cell behind them and left after bowing to Kenshin, who lingered behind. As Roku took his leave, he paused, an eyebrow arched in question. "You wish to remain here, Kenshin-*sama*?"

"I wish to enact my own punishment on this boy for what he did to my sister." Kenshin bowed low. "If you would grant me permission, my sovereign."

Roku's expression remained unreadable. "By all means." He led his soldiers down the corridor toward the stairs, a pleasant smile on his face. As though he were a child recently gifted with a sweet treat.

Kenshin moved closer to the barred cell. Over his shoulder he heard the sound of returning footsteps. Though the emperor had given the impression of trust, Roku had sent one of his soldiers to keep watch over Kenshin. Which meant the emperor did not wish for him to be alone with the prisoner, despite all that Kenshin had done to demonstrate his loyalty. Despite the way he'd threatened his sister. Even if he meant to protect Mariko by doing so, it did not erase his pain when he thought of her words.

I would rather die for love than stand by and watch my love perish.

Kenshin listened to the wheeze of Takeda Ranmaru's breath. The struggle as he tried to right himself and no longer choke on the blood dripping from his nose and mouth. "I hear you are to be my sister's wedding gift."

Takeda Ranmaru coughed. It sounded suspiciously like laughter.

"Don't try to escape," Kenshin continued, his tone hollow.

"Don't fight back. If you attempt to harm any member of my family ever again, I will flay you alive and wear your skin as a cloak."

The guard settled to one side as Kenshin bent to pick up a small stone resting between his feet. He tossed it through the bars, striking the boy's shoulder. Then he picked up another one. Perhaps it was dishonorable to behave in such a fashion. But Kenshin's pain eclipsed his sense of propriety. He lobbed another small stone at the broken young man inside the cell. "I am grateful you will no longer be a torment to my family."

"As am I." Takeda Ranmaru coughed again. "I wish to be rid of the cursed Hattori clan as soon as possible."

Kenshin pitched another stone. It ricocheted off the wall near Ranmaru's head. "And we wish to be rid of you." He crouched even lower and threw the small pouch he'd taken from Mariko through the doors. It struck the boy's thigh.

The son of Takeda Shingen had the good grace to flinch, though a flash of recognition passed across his face. He lifted his eyes to meet those of Kenshin.

Then he nodded once.

Kenshin took to his feet, his fists at his sides. "I wish you to disappear from our lives, Takeda Ranmaru. Forever."

The shrine of the sun Goddess

———✸———

It was Mariko's wedding day.

She'd been prepared for it only a few weeks ago. Perhaps prepared was the wrong word. She'd been resigned to it. But her union to the son of Minamoto Masaru was not a cause for concern anymore. It fell in the shadow cast by a far greater goal.

Mariko would rescue Ōkami today, even if it meant she had to marry a snake, kiss a spider, and burn a golden castle to the ground to do it. She waited with her attendants in a low-ceilinged room, her head bowed, her eyes affixed on the polished wood floor.

Suke watched her carefully, anticipating her every need, as only the best courtier could do. Following their conversation in the imperial gardens and a rather spirited game of Go, Mariko had requested for Suke to be the first official member of her circle at court.

"Is there anything you desire, my lady?" Suke asked.

"A way to turn back time."

Suke smothered a smile. "And if that is not possible?"

"A way to speed it forward, so that I may know what the future might bring." Mariko lifted her chin, and the heavy ornaments adorning her hair—styled in the classic coif of a bride—tugged at the mass of artificial strands near her crown. She grimaced, then sent a smile Suke's way. "Are the other ladies of court still cold to you?" Mariko dropped her voice as she glanced to one side of the chamber, toward the group of girls to which Suke had once belonged. Mariko had learned that this trio contained the most desirable young ladies of the imperial court. Women with wealthy fathers, exorbitant dowries, and judgmental notions.

Suke eyed them sidelong. "Not cold. Simply indifferent."

"So much for their absolute mercy." Mariko coughed through her laughter, the dryness in her throat catching her unawares.

Another grin ghosted across Suke's lips. "Would you care for some water, my lady?"

"Yes, thank you."

Suke slipped past the maidservant Isa. She took hold of a square of soft linen and held the cloth to the rim before placing the cup against Mariko's lips, for the long sleeves of Mariko's formal bridal kimono were far too heavy to lift without assistance. It was known as a *jūni-hitoe*—a twelve-layered garment. A mountain of multicolored silk, beginning with a snow-white underrobe and ending with a rich purple coat that reminded Mariko of plums in springtime. Each hue had its own elaborate name. When all twelve layers were assembled, the garment's colors comprised a poem. At her collar and along her sleeves, the tiers of fabric resembled a rainbow. The garment was ridiculously heavy, though it did look beautiful, in that way of outlandishly expensive things. Every kimono Mariko had ever worn before paled in comparison, and she'd been fortunate to don some spectacular garments in her short life.

When Mariko caught signs of dismay on Isa's face, she stopped short. "What is it?"

Isa balked for an instant, as though she dared not offer any criticism.

"If something is amiss, don't be afraid to tell me. As I've been informed many a time in the last few days, all eyes will be upon me." Mariko smiled comfortingly.

"Yes, my lady." Isa bowed. "The rose-petal stain on your lips has bled down your chin."

Mariko turned to Suke. "Do I look a mess?"

Suke's nose wrinkled in appraisal. "You look like the most beautiful demon bride I have ever beheld."

Mariko laughed outright, then turned to Isa for assistance. The girl's stature was smaller than Mariko's, as was often the case. For most of her life, Mariko had found herself among the tallest girls of her acquaintance. With the added bulk of her *jūni-hitoe*, she was sure to look like a colorful demon set on devouring everything within reach.

When Mariko angled her head to help Isa reapply the

260

rose-petal stain on her lips, her intricate headdress slid to one side, almost jerking her neck in an unnatural fashion. Mariko refrained from letting loose a chorus of Ren's choicest curse words.

"Why won't this monstrosity stay on straight?" Mariko grumbled.

"My lady?" Isa began. "Perhaps . . ."

Mariko waited for her to continue.

Isa swallowed before speaking. "I believe it is a result of your hair's length. Usually a bride's hair is quite a bit longer than yours, and it helps to hold all the necessary ornaments in place. We tried to use a piece of tufted brocade to bolster the style, but I am certain it is quite uncomfortable."

Mariko sighed to herself and closed her eyes. She knew this was the way of it. This was how it was done. How a girl marrying into the imperial family comported herself.

For a moment, Mariko allowed herself to dream of what a wedding would look like if *she* were to dictate its terms, instead of having them dictated to her. She'd never been like Chiyo, her maidservant at home, who'd often fantasized aloud about the colors she would wear or the way the sky would look on the day of her wedding. But just this once, Mariko allowed herself the luxury.

She kept her eyes closed, as though she were composing herself.

In her dreams, her wedding would be during the fall, in a pavilion at the end of a tree-lined lane. Though many believed spring to be the loveliest time of year—with its pale pink cherry blossoms tumbling like silken snow—Mariko always preferred the way the trees looked in fall. Deep red leaves that resembled bleeding stars. Alongside them, there would be ginkgo trees, bursting with golden yellow fronds. If a breeze were to brush through their branches, the leaves would flutter like tiny fans.

Mariko breathed deep.

At the end of a lane strewn with red and gold leaves, there would be a boy with scarred lips and a sly smile. He would be dressed in black, his hair flowing into his face. He would watch her as she walked toward him, his eyes for no other.

Ōkami.

Together they would step inside the simple wooden pavilion at the end of the lane, secluded from any wandering eyes. Even though tradition dictated that others be present— a chief ritualist to run the ceremony, a chamberlain wearing a centuries-old weapon, a court lady, and an unwed priestess as a symbol of purity—that would not be the case for Mariko and Ōkami. They would exchange symbolic sips of sake to declare their union, and no one else would be there, save for the swaying trees and the whispering wind.

How would I look?

Her kimono would be simple, but of the finest silk.

And her hair?

"I wish you could just wear it unbound and loose," Suke said, interrupting Mariko's reverie. "At least then you'd be able to hold your head high and move about without having your neck twist in such unnatural angles."

Like Raiden's mother.

Mariko's eyes flashed open. She glanced toward her maid-servant. "Isa, will you please request that Lady Kanako join me for a moment?" Satisfaction warmed across her skin. If Mariko wished to buck tradition, she would need an ally. And something told her that her future husband's mother—a woman who'd made it a point to sneer at tradition—would be the best person to assist in this endeavor.

Mariko's body had been purified from head to toe, in preparation for the steps she would take in her next life.

It was time for her mind to make a statement of its own.

Mariko began her ceremonial walk, pacing slowly through the ornamental forest toward the shrine to the sun goddess, her head bowed, her fingers trembling in her rainbow sleeves. The sky above was grey. No rain had fallen yet, but the setting sun seemed determined to remain hidden. As though it did not condone what was about to take place.

The blood rushed through Mariko's veins. Her nerves wound tightly in her chest. Any moment now, those in attendance would notice her small act of defiance.

Not a single soul said a word, but Mariko sensed the tenor change in the air when they caught sight of her unbound, unornamented hair. She eyed the attendants lining the pebbled footpath and the nobles watching and waiting behind them. For an instant, she locked gazes with her brother.

Kenshin's features were somber, as though he were present at the commemoration of a death, rather than the uniting of two powerful clans and the rising tide of his family, of whom he alone represented. The wedding had been planned too quickly for their parents to make the journey.

Mariko watched Kenshin struggle to conceal his frown. Around him, those of the nobility looked away, discomfort rippling through the crowd. The sight imbued Mariko with strength. She lifted her head—again flouting tradition—her gait fearless, despite the immense height of the lacquered *zori* on her feet. Though she appeared at peace, her mind spun in constant turmoil. Calculating. Considering. Wondering if the Black Clan had received the messages she'd passed through Yumi. Wondering if the rudimentary map she'd sketched had made its way to Tsuneoki's hands.

Ignoring all else around her, Mariko centered her thoughts on Ōkami. If her plan failed today—if those she trusted did not take advantage of the distraction her wedding provided— Ōkami would die tonight. He would take with him so many of their hopes and dreams.

Yumi's dream for revenge on those who had destroyed her life.

Tsuneoki's hope that his friend would become more than the Honshō Wolf.

Mariko's dream for a world with a place for her in it. Not as someone's daughter. Not as someone's wife. But as a woman who made her own choices. Lived without fear. Even if it meant being married to Prince Raiden, Mariko wanted to live in that world. A world in which the boy she loved still lived. A world in which she could bring about lasting change.

Her hope blazed bright at the thought, despite the fear lurking in her heart. The final strides she took toward the shrine were not shrouded in darkness. It did not matter that the sun refused to shine. Mariko was not beholden to its light.

When she mounted the steps, she was surprised to discover only the participants of the ceremony present, as well as the emperor and Raiden's mother. The dowager empress was not there. Neither was any member of her retinue. Mariko removed her shining black sandals, and a light rain began to fall, misting everything it touched. A good omen.

Heads turned once more to watch Prince Raiden make his entrance, dressed in a *sokutai* dyed in the brilliant hues of a setting sun. The elaborate *kanmuri* on his head was fashioned of black silk. His features looked chiseled from stone. Upon his arrival, the prince was presented with a sacred sprig.

Mariko drowned out the sound of the emperor offering them his grace and protection. Of Raiden pledging his unending loyalty. She instead gazed upon the solemn figure of his mother, watching them closely. When their eyes met, Kanako smiled, the ends of her hair lifting in a passing breeze. Though Mariko still did not trust her fully, she felt a strange sense of solidarity with her. As though they fought alongside each other, bearing the same standard. It comforted Mariko. When she'd requested assistance with her hair—in tossing aside decorum—Raiden's mother had offered nothing but enthusiasm, almost to the point of amusement.

The emperor witnessed the occasion with a small smile pasted on his face. When the chief ritualist moved to finalize the union, Mariko hid her shock at the glimmer of emotion that passed across Roku's features. It was clear these feelings were reserved for his elder brother. A bolt of lightning could strike Mariko down where she stood, and the emperor would simply go about his day. But he genuinely cared for Raiden. Odd how such a cold and calculating young man could harbor true affection for his elder brother, especially one raised to be his enemy.

As the ceremonial cup of sake was passed his way, Raiden looked down at Mariko, his brow furrowed. Uncertain. A pang of indecision unfurled in her chest. It had been a mistake for her to imagine this moment with Ōkami. The ache that settled in her throat refused to fade. Raiden touched his lips to the rim of the cup, his gaze locked on Mariko's face. She wondered what kind of thoughts he might be hiding behind his eyes. What worries or regrets he might be concealing.

Why he had even agreed to marry her.

He passed the sake her way. It was the final symbol of their union, this shared cup between a husband and his wife. Mariko gritted her teeth and brought it to her lips. Their marriage would be a small price to pay if it paved the way to greater opportunities. If it allowed her larger plans to fall into place.

Before Mariko could take a sip, the screams began.

The first arrow struck the emperor in the shoulder, clearly intended for his heart.

Without a moment's hesitation, Raiden shoved Mariko to the ground, the cup of sake rolling across the polished wood floor. He growled at her to keep still before leaping to his brother's aid.

A second arrow shot from a higher angle grazed Prince Raiden's arm before all the guards had managed to surround them. Kanako shouted in fury, her hands twisting through the air, calling for a fog to settle around the pavilion.

Mariko's heart pounded against the wooden floor, the wind struck from her chest, her breaths coming in shallow gasps. Before she could regain control of her body, she was lifted to her feet and cocooned in the center of armed samurai, each with their hands on their weapons, the emperor being whisked from sight beneath a canopy of shields.

Shouts of servants echoed nearby. Mariko could see nothing but molded armor, white smoke, and flashes of silk. They crossed into another room before she was shoved in a darkened corner, three samurai guarding her path.

"Where is Kenshin?" she gasped.

They did not turn to look at her once.

Fear gripped her from within. She did not know if her brother was safe. And now that Mariko was under watch, she could not make contact with those outside to ascertain whether Ōkami had been rescued. This assassination attempt would ensure that every entrance and exit to the castle grounds was heavily guarded, every samurai on high alert.

If Ōkami had not already managed to escape, it would be all but impossible now.

She'd failed him. Just like with the waxen key. Like the night with the firestones, when Kenshin had caught her. There had been so many times Mariko had tried to rescue Ōkami and failed. Why had she even come here?

For more than a week, Mariko had fought to stave off an onslaught of tears. Tears of pain and fear and desperation. The only times she'd permitted herself to cry openly and without reservation had been strategic. If her tears did not serve an immediate purpose, Mariko had considered them a waste.

Now—huddled in a corner, with samurai shielding her from prying eyes—Mariko cried in earnest, watching her tears fall on the many layers of her wedding kimono. Watching them seep through the twelve layers, like blood.

something barely human

---❋---

He'd been unable to channel his demon, even after the moon had emerged from behind the clouds. Though Ōkami had managed to free himself using the firestones Mariko's brother had tossed his way, it had not made a difference. His body was too far broken. The moon had tried to imbue him with strength. Had tried to heal him. Its light had fought to find him through the darkness.

But it had not been enough.

"I need to be outside." He groaned, his head lolling to one side.

When Tsuneoki first caught sight of Ōkami lying beneath the slip of moonlight, he'd stopped short. Even Ren had kept silent, his eyes bulging from his skull. The third member of their party—a boy whose features reminded Ōkami greatly of Yoshi—could not look away even as he heaved an iron axe against the lock of the cell.

"I'll destroy all of them," Tsuneoki ground out. "Every bit of pain they inflicted will be met, ten times over."

Ōkami struggled to sit up. He would not be able to walk without support. At least four of his toes had been broken. The instant he put weight on his left foot, a searing pain shot up his thigh.

He would never be able to move about like this.

"Just get me outside," he repeated, biting down to keep from crying out. "Into the light."

The boy who resembled Yoshi braced Ōkami against his side. Ren took hold of Ōkami's other arm, and the two young men began dragging him from his cell. Dirty water dripped from the conduits above. As they hurried through the blue darkness, Tsuneoki guided them with surefooted steps, even absent a source of light. Ōkami found this strange, as he was certain his friend had never been here before.

His unspoken question was answered when Ōkami realized Tsuneoki was counting his steps. Only Mariko could have found a way to give the Black Clan this advantage. He smiled to himself as another shock of pain rippled across his body. Ren had inadvertently jostled his side.

"Sorry, sorry, sorry," Ren mumbled.

"Keep at it." Ōkami tried to jest through the pain. "A few of my ribs aren't broken yet."

The boy resembling Yoshi laughed awkwardly, though he loosened his grip on Ōkami, as though he were handling a frail creature at risk of shattering at any moment. "I am Yorishige, my lord. It is an honor to—"

"Save your deference for the deserving, Yorishige-*san*,"
Ōkami muttered.

Tsuneoki held up a hand to halt their steps. Even through
the thick stone walls, Ōkami sensed a strange hush descend
on them, like the calm before a summer storm.

Ren gripped Ōkami tightly, urging him forward.

The collective roar that emanated from above was one of
shock. Not of celebration. Stampeding footsteps shook the
very walls of the castle.

"Something's wrong," Tsuneoki whispered. They
crouched in the shadows while he paused to note where they
were in relation to the map in his hand. "Thirty-two paces
forward, turn left, move for twenty-four paces, enter a low-
ceilinged hallway with the distinct scent of burned charcoal.
Proceed," he whispered.

Ōkami knew his friend said this aloud to edify them all.
If they backtracked or were forced to split apart, they would
need to know how to return to the same place. To resume the
same path.

Leaning his weight on Ren's shoulder, Ōkami lifted his
head, forcing his swollen eye to stay open. "If something is
wrong, we need to—"

"Before you say another word, know that we are not stopping to rescue Mariko," Tsuneoki said.

Ōkami braced himself against a sudden wash of fury. "If
you think we are leaving her in this castle to—"

"It was not my decision."

It took Ōkami only a moment to understand. Then he laughed softly. Bitterly. "Of course it wasn't."

"We told her we could find a way to get her out safely, my lord," Yorishige said. "But Lady Mariko . . ." He trailed off.

Ren harrumphed. "She declined, like the little half-wit she is."

Though anger flared near Ōkami's heart, pride swelled alongside it. Hattori Mariko had never been one to choose the easy path. Nor did she make decisions from a place of fear. Her courage made him stand taller, despite the task set before them now.

The task set before Mariko, as the new bride of Prince Raiden.

Tsuneoki studied his friend. "You're worried about her marrying that foul boy."

Ōkami said nothing for a time. "Mariko is more than capable of caring for herself. I know she will always make the best decision she can, given the circumstances." His features hardened, causing him to grimace. "But if Minamoto Raiden touches her against her will, no one will be able to save him. Not even the sun goddess herself."

Ren's eyes narrowed to slits. "If he hurts Mariko, we'll make him wish he were dead, several times over."

Tsuneoki said nothing, though his eyes indicated his agreement. They waited in silence for a beat. Then Tsuneoki consulted his map once more. Directed them down another corridor, toward a low-ceilinged tunnel, slick with mold and lichen. Ōkami nearly lost consciousness from the pain of forcing his shattered body to move. Finally they stopped beside the entrance to a large drain. Stinking water flowed past their feet, picking up speed as it turned a bend.

"There are not many reasons for this kind of unrest within the walls of Heian Castle," Tsuneoki said. "If it's what I think it is, soldiers will be watching every entrance and exit now. We'll wait until the tumult dies down, then make our escape."

Ren sniffed with distaste. "Right alongside their waste."

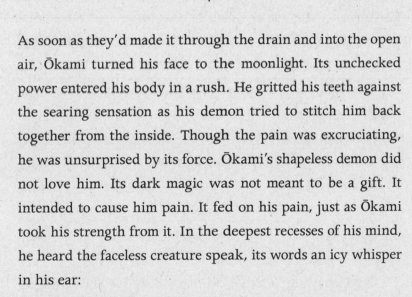

As soon as they'd made it through the drain and into the open air, Ōkami turned his face to the moonlight. Its unchecked power entered his body in a rush. He gritted his teeth against the searing sensation as his demon tried to stitch him back together from the inside. Though the pain was excruciating, he was unsurprised by its force. Ōkami's shapeless demon did not love him. Its dark magic was not meant to be a gift. It intended to cause him pain. It fed on his pain, just as Ōkami took his strength from it. In the deepest recesses of his mind, he heard the faceless creature speak, its words an icy whisper in his ear:

This will cost you.

Ōkami knew it would. Had always known it would. And he would give it, until there was nothing left to give. To this demon, he was eternally loyal. The hum of magic curled through his ears, and Ōkami attempted to take flight in a burst of dark smoke. He turned his eyes to the moon again.

It failed him. Again.

A wave of pain tore through his chest. He cried out, a curse barreling from his bleeding lips. If Ōkami's demon betrayed him now, all their lives would be at risk.

His friends—his family—would die for it.

And Mariko . . .

"He's too weak," Ren said, panic underscoring his words. "It's not working." The boy's typically cruel demeanor was nowhere to be found. Tsuneoki helped brace Ōkami while Yorishige moved ahead to scout the landscape. Vegetation grew high on the hillside just to the right of the drain, concealing them from view.

Tsuneoki said, "Then we'll carry him out of the city."

"No." Ōkami spat the blood and salt from his mouth. "You'll be caught."

"You think we didn't consider that before coming here?" Tsuneoki shot back.

Ōkami almost smiled. "I've missed you, you bastard." He slumped against Ren, the pain turning his sight black for an instant.

"Stop acting like a child," Ren demanded. "Stand up straight. Fight." His words reminded Ōkami of Mariko and her countless admonishments. She wanted him to be more. They all wanted Ōkami to be more.

Ōkami let his head loll again, his eyes drifting closed.

Why did they not realize their words fell on deaf ears? What would it take for them to understand he was not worth such faith? Ōkami wished he could return to his cell. Wished he could continue receiving the blows he'd deserved for a decade. He flinched as he recalled a particularly vicious kick to the head that had sent stars across his vision.

Even his father's sword had gleamed with promise when Ōkami had drawn near. Despite all the evidence to the contrary, that ridiculous blade believed in him, if the lore were to be held as true. It was supposed to recognize the pure heart of a warrior. There was nothing pure about Ōkami, even if the blood of Takeda Shingen flowed through his veins. Ōkami did not want the responsibility. What had his father's pure heart earned him in the end?

A chance to die in front of his only son.

Ōkami opened his eyes and glared at the night sky. He let the hum rise once more in his throat, the vibrations ripple over his broken bones. He bit his tongue until more blood pooled in his mouth. His body was too damaged. The demon had turned its back on him. Ōkami's knees started to give. He wanted to sleep. To lose consciousness and fade into nothingness.

Tsuneoki grabbed him by the collar. "Takeda Ranmaru, don't you dare—"

An arrow hissed through the vegetation, a hairsbreadth from Tsuneoki's head. Yorishige burst through the curtain of vines concealing them, his features horror-struck, just as a second arrow rasped from the darkness at his back. It struck Yorishige spearing clear through his chest, killing him instantly. He toppled to the ground like a doll, his mouth hung open in dismay.

"Get to the clearing!" Tsuneoki said before fading into the darkness. Disappearing from sight.

"There are more men beside the drain," a voice cried out from beyond the vines. "They tried to murder our emperor. Show them no mercy!" The roar of gathering soldiers—their armor clanging through the air like warning bells—grew with each passing moment.

"Go with Tsuneoki," Ōkami said to Ren, his eyes locked on Yorishige's motionless form.

Ren leaned Ōkami against the drain, then whipped his hooked swords from his back and assumed a fighting stance.

"Leave me," Ōkami said. "Get out of here, you fool!"

"Not a chance, my lord," Ren shot back under his breath before dissolving into the shadows on the other side of the drain.

Again Ōkami glowered at the moonlit sky, a wave of pain swelling across his body. An arrow whistled past his shoulder, nicking the skin of his arm. Another rebounded off the drain. Though it had taken Ōkami off guard to watch his friend vanish at the first sign of a threat, at least Tsuneoki had known better than to stay. Ōkami was grateful for his friend's pragmatism. The men of the Black Clan would need their leader. Soldiers crashed through the vines, their weapons raised, their shining blades catching the stars above.

As the light of the moon continued burning through him—trying in vain to stitch his broken bones back together—Ōkami used the sturdy stone of the drain to keep his body upright. He struggled to breathe. Fought to find focus so that he might defend himself. As the soldiers came toward him—weapons in hand, arrows pointed at his heart—a figure advanced through the darkness, a pair of hooked swords linked as they slashed through the air.

An arm was severed from the soldier bearing down on Ōkami. Howling in pain, the man fell into the tall grass, blood spurting through the sky in a wicked arc. The other soldiers turned to meet this new foe. Arrows rained down around them without a shred of mercy.

Ren charged. He fought—a blade in either hand—his eyes glowing with rage. An animalistic growl emanated from behind him. A growl Ōkami would recognize anywhere. Before the soldiers could blink, a nightbeast leapt into the fray, snarling as it ripped an axe from a soldier's grasp, taking a hand with it.

Tsuneoki had turned to his demon for assistance.

Ōkami could not remember a time in his life when he'd felt more useless. More of a burden than anything else. He'd fought for a life devoid of this feeling. A life in which no one needed to rely upon him.

He'd enjoyed living without this burden. Without these responsibilities.

Yet he stood here, watching as two of his dearest friends fought to keep him safe. Risked their lives for his own.

A yelp cut through the din of clashing metal, and Ōkami saw Tsuneoki limp away on three of his four legs. He'd been wounded. Or a past injury had been aggravated. Ren continued fending off the onslaught of soldiers that poured from the hillside beyond. Everywhere he spun his blades, blood spurted in their wake. His eyes were alight with fury. He turned into the path of the blade that caught him. It speared him clean through his stomach, cutting upward at the last instant. One moment Ren wore a look of triumph, the next of confusion.

"*Uesama*?" he mouthed to Ōkami.

It was what his father's men had called Takeda Shingen. Their shōgun.

Ōkami's features twisted at the sight. He yanked the metal pin Mariko had given him from his shirtsleeve and lurched into the fight. Narrowly dodging the swing of a *katana* in his path, Ōkami stabbed the pin into the neck of the nearest soldier, then tore the screaming man's weapon from his grasp.

Hatred flowed through his veins.

More of the people Ōkami loved were dying because of him. Even when he'd fought for so long to prevent it. He grasped the hilt of the blade in both hands. The stars above him seemed to sway. Searing pain rippled across his body.

He saw Ren fall to the ground, his eyes frozen open in shock, as though—even in death—he still could not believe he'd been beaten. His body struck the earth slowly, as though time had stilled. First his knees, then his torso, then his head. Ōkami felt each of the jolts as though they were punches to his gut.

Here one moment, gone the next. In the stories, all the heroes had time for farewells. In truth, Ren had time for nothing.

Everything around Ōkami ground to a halt. It was as though he were viewing these events from above, as a detached observer, witnessing the end of a foolish boy who should have known better.

His rage was clarity. His rage was strength. His rage moved him to action.

Ōkami still had broken bones. He still felt each of the agonizing twinges and aches of his protesting body.

It no longer mattered.

He grabbed hold of another weapon. A smaller sword, so that he held one in each hand. It had been years since he'd fought with blades. His fingers trembled from the weight, but Ōkami swung both swords in unforgiving arcs. Shouts of agony rained down around him. Though his body was shattered, the weapons felt natural in his hands, like extensions of himself. Of his pain. Of his heartbreak.

He faltered as he moved forward. Lost his center for a moment. A sword slashed past his side, the edge of the blade nicking his skin. Glancing off his ribs.

That soldier lost his head in a single blow.

Then Ōkami reached Ren. Before he could grant himself a

chance to think, he locked eyes with the moon and yelled the guttural yell of something barely human. Then he dissolved into a dark smoke that spiraled into the night sky, the echoes of an otherworldly scream trailing in its wake.

When Ōkami landed in the clearing, he dropped Ren's lifeless body. Then he took a single breath before collapsing to the ground.

severed limbs and broken ties

———✳———

Hours later, in a darkened corner of the castle grounds, the imperial guards found a boy trying to conceal a bow and arrow deep in a servant's well. He panicked when he saw the samurai racing toward him. In his panic, the boy nearly threw himself into the well along with the weapons.

He could not have been more than twelve years of age.

When the boy was brought before Raiden, tears streamed down his cheeks. He was not even old enough to have a single hair on his chin. The first thing he asked for was his grandmother. A soldier cuffed him across the side of the head for his insolence.

It would not be the last time the boy was struck.

Raiden clenched his right fist. The ache from his injured arm radiated into his side. He let the pain wash over his body, reminding him of how closely he'd strolled beside Death.

How closely his emperor—his younger brother—had been to meeting his end.

He intended to punish the boy. Extract whatever information he could, and then separate the boy's head from his body with a single swipe of a sword.

Alas, that was not his brother's plan.

Mariko remained kneeling on her chamber floor for hours before Isa slid open the doors. The maidservant bowed at the threshold and set down a tray of food. Then the samurai guarding Mariko permitted her brother to enter. To speak with her, alone.

Though he appeared stern, haggardness lined Kenshin's features, as though he had not slept for an age. Mariko's fingers shook with relief at seeing her brother unharmed. "Is the emperor badly wounded?"

"No." He stayed beside the door, declining to meet her gaze.

Mariko swallowed. "Is Raiden?"

"No."

He sounds . . . disappointed.

Unsure of what to say, Mariko bided her time. "I—"

"Once the commotion dies down, I intend to leave Inako and return home."

Though she was surprised to hear this, Mariko kept it to herself.

After a moment of stony silence, Kenshin continued, still refusing to look her in the eye. "Now that your marriage ceremony has concluded, I intend to seek the whereabouts of—"

"What happened to Amaya, Kenshin?"

Her brother stopped short. His weariness grew even more apparent. "I asked you before not to—"

"No." Mariko's words were a tattered whisper. "I've kept silent. I've done this dance of lies so many times I fear I no longer know what's true. I've hidden my thoughts and feelings from you in ways I never believed I would." She tried to stand and failed, the heavy silks of her layered garments making it impossible to take to her feet without assistance. "Why are you treating me as though I am a criminal, Kenshin?"

He crossed the room in two long strides, towering over her. "You think I'm the only one among us who has acted unfairly?" Kenshin's breath shook with rage. "Not once—not a single time after the battle in Jukai forest—have you looked at me without duplicity in your eyes."

"If I deceived you, it was only because you left me with no choice," Mariko cried. "You never once thought to ask me what happened after my convoy was overrun. The moment I emerged from the forest, you treated me with nothing but cold disdain." She took a halting breath. "You let Raiden and his men fire arrows at me. You didn't care if I was hurt, so long as you stood on the winning side."

"What should I have done? What *could* I have done?" A look of abject pain crossed Kenshin's face. "What choice did you leave me? You were fighting alongside traitors."

She forced her back straight and lifted her chin. "I was not allied with them. I was their prisoner." The fingers folded in her lap trembled.

"More lies, little sister," he said in a dangerous whisper, his expression turning to ice. "I saw your hands. The mud you used to make it seem as though you were being held captive. It coated the sprays of blood from battle. Why would you have smeared mud on your body if not to conceal the proof that you fought alongside them?" Each word was a small cut made with a newly honed dagger. Kenshin continued looming over her, his fists curling and uncurling at his sides. As though he wished to strike something and watch it shatter in his shadow. No trace of the brother Mariko had known and loved all her life remained. He was a warrior intimidating his quarry. A samurai intent in his purpose. The threat of violence tinged the air like a blade shining in the sun.

For the first time in her life, Mariko felt afraid of her brother. The feeling stole her breath, like claws tightening around her neck. "How could you possibly have known any of that before you let Raiden's men try to murder me?"

Kenshin's nostrils flared. "I am the Dragon of Kai. Do you think I would not know when a mere girl tried to deceive me?" His gaze darkened as though clouds had settled across his vision.

At the sight, Mariko tamped down the urge to strike out at him. To silence him where he stood. Horror followed the thought.

Mariko wanted to cause her brother physical harm.

This was Kenshin. Her twin. Her family. No matter how much they differed—how at odds they were in both attitude and agenda—she'd never wished to truly hurt him even once in seventeen years.

A muscle ticked in Kenshin's neck. With visible effort, he battled against the rage teeming like an unchecked demon beneath his skin. "Do you think I had a say in what happened that night in Jukai forest? The instant I put our men in formation behind Prince Raiden, I knew I had lost all control." He dropped his voice. "You are not foolish enough to believe I could have stopped them. And this is not about what happened that night. No words can excuse what we did to each other. You are just as much to blame as I am." He drew closer, his toes grazing the edge of her silken hem. That same desire to strike out at him—to spare herself from being cornered by a bigger, stronger foe—caused Mariko's fingers to ball into fists.

He is my brother.

This would always be their truth. Just as it would always be their truth if they crossed an irrevocable line right now. If Kenshin tried to hit her. If Mariko moved to attack him. It would be an action that could never be undone. There were ways for her to disarm her brother, even now. To allay his fears with falsehoods. At the mere thought, lies began collecting on the tip of her tongue.

But Mariko had lied to him for so long. It wearied her, these stories she spun like yarn to everyone around her. Just once she wanted to tell Kenshin the truth. To put an end to this dance of fury and deception. It was a risk, but her brother had kept her most precious secret in the last few days.

Perhaps it was time to trust him with more.

"Stop it, Kenshin." Mariko decided to begin with a small truth. "You're frightening me."

He stood straight at her words, his face suddenly stricken. Kenshin took a step back, then stopped, his movements awkward. Then he held out a hand to help Mariko to her feet. She briefly considered rebuffing it, but gripped his palm until she stood before him, face-to-face.

"No more lies," Kenshin said, his voice weary. "If you want me to be truthful with you, then you must do the same with me, Mariko."

She nodded.

"Why did you turn your back on your family to fight alongside these traitors?" Kenshin asked.

Mariko hesitated for a breath. "Because I believe in their cause."

"Their cause?" He scoffed.

"Don't you see, Kenshin? We are like well-clothed leeches, with all our fine silks and elegant fans. We do nothing for the people who work our lands."

"How can you say that?" Kenshin asked. "Father feeds and clothes and—"

"Our father is among the worst offenders. Have you ever gone into our rice fields and looked into the eyes of those who work the soil, day after day, with only a pittance to show for it?"

"Of course I have. We played in those fields when we were children."

"No, Kenshin." Mariko shook her head. "Not with the eyes of a child. And not just a passing glance. Have you ever looked at any of them and seen an equal? Seen someone who struggles and lives and breathes and loves just as you do?" She reached for his hand, her voice barely audible. "Can you tell me even one of their names?"

He did not take the hand she offered. Instead Kenshin stayed silent, his gaze searching.

"You can't," Mariko continued, stepping back. Giving her brother the space he needed to think. "I still cannot call a single one of them by name. It's not enough for us to pretend to be better than they are. Because we are not. We cheat and kill, lie and steal to get what we want. And we don't care who we hurt to get it."

"On that point, we agree," Kenshin said softly. "Because you are still lying to me, little sister. Still hurting me. You fight alongside the Black Clan because you are in love with the son of Takeda Shingen."

Mariko blinked. Kenshin wasn't wrong. But it wasn't that simple. It had never been that simple. For an instant, Mariko thought of spinning another lie to spare herself any more of Kenshin's judgment. But why did it matter?

Mariko was married to another. And she no longer wished to deny her heart its truth. Her eyes clear and her heart full, she stared up at her brother. "His name is Ōkami."

"No," Kenshin replied. "His name is Takeda Ranmaru, and he is the son of a traitor."

Mariko nodded once. "Then I am in love with the son of a

traitor." She took a step closer, daring her brother to challenge her. "Tell me, Hattori Kenshin. What do you love? What do you fight for?" Another step. "Do you fight for Amaya?" She stopped directly in front of him. "I hope you do. Especially since you failed to fight for her when it mattered most."

Kenshin's hand flashed toward Mariko before she could move away. It struck her cheek in a crack that reverberated through the room. Blindsided by her brother's blow—by the irrevocable choice he'd made for both of them—Mariko reeled to the floor, her fingers covering her cheek. Tears streamed down her face from the shock.

Kenshin's eyes were wide, his skin paler than freshly fallen snow. "Mariko—"

"Don't apologize." She struggled to sit straight.

He knelt before her as he would kneel before his lord, his head bowed, his eyes averted. Her brother reached for her hand. "Please forgive—"

Mariko snatched her fingers away. Took in a steadying breath. "Look at me."

Kenshin waited a moment, struggling to maintain control. Then met her eyes.

"When I asked about her before, you lashed out at me with words. Today it came to blows. What happened to Amaya?"

"She"—Kenshin shuddered before he spoke, his eyes darting about as though he were searching for a handhold on a cliff—"was lost. In a fire. Father and I watched while she tried to save our people. There was an explosion in our granary, and . . . it collapsed before I could save her."

Mariko took both his hands in her own. Squeezed them tightly. "I'm sorry, Kenshin. Sorrier than you will ever know," she said, her features laden with grief. "Travel safely home. Do not write to me. Do not make inquiries about me. I do not wish to see you ever again."

The instant he laid eyes on it, Kenshin upended the low table in the center of his room. All the beautiful food—the sea cucumber and grated yam, the turnip dumplings and brightly colored radishes, an entire copper pot of crackling rice with spring onions and pufferfish—crashed to the floor, staining the tatami mats in brilliant hues.

He watched as servants rushed into the darkened room, their eyes averted, whispers of apology falling from their lips. They hurried to clean up his mess. To hide the proof of his hideous temper.

And they apologized to him as they did it.

Disgust clawed at Kenshin's throat. He crouched to help a servant collect the shattered pieces of a porcelain bowl. Startled by his sudden attention, the girl nearly fell over.

"Please forgive me, my lord," she murmured, her voice shaking.

Kenshin met her gaze. "Do not apologize. This is my fault, not yours."

Fear washed across her features. As though the girl suspected Kenshin of playing games. Of testing her. The look of terror in her eyes was exactly like the one Mariko had shown him only moments before.

Kenshin glanced around the room. Some of the faces he vaguely recognized, as they were servants who'd been attending to him ever since he'd arrived to the imperial city. All of those present were afraid of him.

He did not know a single one of their names.

"Go." Kenshin cleared his throat. "Please take your leave. I will clean this myself."

The servants paused, uncertain. Then—under the direction of the most senior among them—they quietly exited the room. Kenshin sat with the mess he'd made. The waste of expensive food and the heap of broken dishes carefully sculpted by the hands of a master artisan.

His sister despised him. And the girl he loved—

Kenshin furrowed his brow.

He did not know why he'd been unable to tell Mariko that Amaya had died. He'd said she was lost. As he attempted to share the story with his sister, his memories turned foggy. Strange images of Amaya's face, carved into the center of a tree, had taken shape instead. Dreams of fluttering silver leaves and a world without color.

Kenshin pressed the heels of his hands into his eyes.

He'd lost time again today. Just as he had the day by the watering hole, when he'd woken to find his hands stained with the blood of three slaughtered innocents. He had no memory of killing them, but the evidence had been irrefutable. He'd lost his honor, just as he'd lost his mind. Then a few days ago, when he'd returned from Hanami to catch his sister sneaking back to her chambers, it had happened again. After he'd been waylaid by the imperial soldiers, Kenshin remembered drunkenly following a smiling fox through the gardens.

He recalled nothing after that.

Today—as he'd moved to take position during his sister's wedding—he'd lost consciousness again. A strange heaviness had settled behind his eyes, dulling his senses. The last image he recollected was Mariko beginning her long procession toward the shrine of the sun goddess. He remembered disapproving of the way she'd styled her shoulder-length hair. Its affront to tradition.

Hours later, Kenshin found himself outside his chamber doors, a strange ache in his right shoulder. Only then did he learn of the attempt made on the emperor's life. He'd lost hold on most of today. His mind, his honor, his truths all betrayed him.

Kenshin knelt among the ruins of the meal and stared into the shadows on the other side of his chamber. He rolled his arm. That same twinge from earlier caught his attention. Reaching inside his *kosode*, he discovered a welt beside his collarbone.

As though he'd shot an arrow.

The sound of tightening sinew emanated from the darkened corner of his room. Immediately Kenshin took to his feet.

"Keep your hands at your sides," a feminine voice rasped at him. "Don't say a word, unless you wish it to be your last."

A small figure—dressed in garments the color of stone—moved from the shadows into a strip of moonlight cast from the open screen nearby.

The girl continued speaking as she moved closer. "I don't understand you, Lord Kenshin. You had a clear shot, and you missed."

Kenshin blinked. He did not know what the intruder was talking about. But he did recognize that voice. It was one of the only things to soothe him of late.

The *maiko* at the teahouse. Yumi.

It took only a moment for him to make the connection.

This girl had tried to kill the emperor.

Kenshin lunged for her, intent on subduing Yumi and calling for his guards. She slid from his grasp with the ease of a wriggling fish. The next instant, she swiped his legs from under him. He struck the floor with a dull thud, the breath knocked from his chest. Yumi pressed her knee on his stomach, then drove the tip of a nocked arrow into his breastbone.

"Try it again, and I will loose this through your heart." Yumi leaned over him, her lovely eyes narrowed. "I don't understand you," she repeated. "Why did you miss your shot? And why would you attack me now? I tried to help you."

"What are you talking about?" Kenshin demanded in a hoarse tone.

The girl's eyes grew wide. "Are you in jest?"

"What?" he ground out. "I do not jest."

Confusion etched lines across her forehead. "You tried to kill the emperor today, Hattori Kenshin."

The Tail of a Snake

———— ✳ ————

Raiden glided down the stone steps toward the two cells housed beneath the main structure of Heian Castle. As soon as he reached the bottom, he heard the retching. Smelled the blood.

The moment he learned the imperial guards had moved the boy they'd caught to a cell in the castle's underbelly, Raiden had begun his trek there.

But Roku had beaten him to it.

The emperor had elected to take on the boy's interrogation, as he had with Takeda Ranmaru. Raiden had cautioned him for this choice even then. Such things were beneath the dignity of a heavenly sovereign. And it had not gone unnoticed by the soldiers. By the samurai who served at Roku's leisure.

Who abided by a strict code of honor.

At the foot of the stone staircase, Raiden came across a

soldier emptying his stomach of its contents. This was not an unseasoned warrior. Age creased his features, and his armor had faded in several places. Yet the sound of his retching continued to echo through the ghostly labyrinth.

Raiden slowed his pace until he neared the two cells. He took position behind his younger brother, who still wore the same fine garments from earlier in the evening, at Raiden's ruined wedding ceremony. Roku's left arm hung from a linen sling. Blood stained the whole of his shoulder. The injury the would-be assassin had inflicted was not a small one. It was only luck that the arrow's path had gone wide.

Perhaps not luck. Perhaps it had all been part of a larger plan. Raiden paused to take note of the empty cell that had contained the son of Takeda Shingen. The traitor had managed to escape in the aftermath of the attempted assassination. This did not strike Raiden as a mere coincidence.

A garbled scream cut through his thoughts. The smell of blood and burning flesh clogged his throat. Raiden coughed, his eyes watering through a haze of oily smoke. When his sight fully readjusted, he turned his gaze toward the prisoner lying across the cell floor. Shock gripped him from the inside, causing his muscles to bunch in his stomach.

"Roku," he whispered in horror.

His younger brother glanced at him, his features calm, save for the frown touching his lips. "Brother, I'll encourage you not to forget whom you are addressing." Dried blood stained his fingers. Marred the hem of his golden robes.

Raiden shook his head. Paused to bow before speaking.

"Please, my sovereign. I implore you. Do not continue with this. Such things are beneath you." He repeated the same words he'd spoken to his younger brother only several days ago.

Though Roku smiled, signs of fury mottled his skin. "Do *not* tell me what to do, brother."

"My sovereign—"

Roku turned in place, his robes swirling through the filth. "Your emperor's blood was spilled today. Our most dangerous prisoner—a threat to my very existence—managed to escape in the chaos he likely orchestrated. It was at *your* request that I kept Lord Ranmaru alive this long. Where is he, Raiden? Find him at once. How dare you concern yourself with anything else!" His reedy voice shook as it reverberated off the rafters.

Frustration coiled in Raiden's throat. He'd specifically asked his younger brother to execute Ranmaru upon their arrival. But it was true he'd changed his position since then . . . at the request of his bride. Another fact that did not escape his notice. With a careful breath, Raiden dipped his head into a low bow. "I apologize, my sovereign. I am here to do as you command."

Roku nodded, then turned toward the soldiers surrounding the prone boy. At least one of them looked sickened, but Raiden was far more concerned with the imperial guard tasked with restraining the boy. This young man appeared as though he were enjoying the sight of such suffering.

Never before in his life had Raiden seen anything so disturbing.

The boy was lying facedown in the packed earth, mud

oozing around him. His body was a mess of blood and carefully flayed flesh. All but unrecognizable. Even the feeble sound that came from his lips seemed subhuman.

Raiden knew there was no way to gain answers or insight from this broken shell of a creature. A part of him wished to learn if his younger brother had thought to properly question the boy before devolving to this madness. As he studied Roku's gleaming eyes and serene smile, Raiden knew the answer without asking.

"Demand that this traitor confess who ordered him to conceal the bow and arrow," Roku said to the soldier holding the boy down. "A boy this size could not have fired a weapon like that from such a distance. He must have been helping someone. If he tells us who it was, I will let him live."

Live? In his current condition, the boy would last until daybreak, at best.

Raiden watched the emperor attempt to lace his hands behind his back as though he were on an evening stroll. The motion pulled at his sling, causing him to cringe. Unmistakable wrath flickered across his features.

"Proceed," Roku said to his soldiers. "Show the traitor the mercy of the imperial city."

The boy no longer had the strength to scream. The faces of the soldiers nearby—save for the one pinning the prisoner to the ground—begged for reprieve. Soldiers well versed in the sight of warfare could no longer stomach these atrocities.

There was no honor in this.

The uncertainty that had taken root in Raiden continued

to flourish amid the darkness. His mother had told him once. Only once. Not long after she learned of his father's death, she'd looked into Raiden's eyes, her gaze searching. He always found it difficult to read his mother's emotions. She refused to show them to anyone. Never fought publicly with a soul. Never said an unkind word, save for the warnings she would offer him about maintaining a close relationship with his younger brother.

But his mother had said something clear and unmistakable to Raiden, in the chaotic morning following his father's death.

"Roku is not fit to rule," she'd said softly. "He is the tail of a snake."

Raiden had recoiled at her words. "He is our emperor. Your words are treasonous, Mother. Never say such things to me again, if you value your life."

She had bowed, both hands held wide as though to convey humility.

"If you are worried he will remove you from court, I know he will not," Raiden had offered as a source of comfort.

"I am not worried for my sake, my son. But I thank you for your concern. You are a true prince among men. I shall try not to trouble you with such matters again." Then his mother had left. When she'd gone, it felt like she'd taken the warmth with her.

She always did that, whenever hatred spewed her way from all corners of the court. His mother would bow. Turn the other cheek. And leach all the warmth from the room.

Raiden had never before understood how she could disregard the injurious sentiments hurled her way, but he thought he could see why now. His mother had done it to set an example for him. To urge him to be better than the spiders at court. And what had Raiden done in response?

He'd cast her aside to serve his emperor.

"My sovereign," Raiden said now. "Please allow me to take charge of questioning this prisoner. You have been wounded, and I worry for your health. As the key to our empire—its beating heart—your safety is paramount. Please permit us to protect you from the traitors in your midst."

Roku considered him for a moment, his head inclined to one side. "How generous of you to make such an offer, brother. After all, it is your wedding night. You have more pleasurable things to attend to."

"I live to serve my sovereign. And no one else." As he bowed again, Raiden let a small object sheathed within the sleeve of his *kosode* fall into his waiting palm.

A moment passed in utter stillness. The only sounds that could be heard were the staggered breaths of those present. The broken rasps of the tortured boy.

"Very well." Roku finally nodded, his eyes flashing. "Report to me if there are any new developments."

Raiden bowed again. Then watched as his younger brother strolled from the room, his soiled finery slithering behind him.

Like the tail of a snake.

"Tighten the bonds on his feet," Raiden ordered the soldier who appeared to enjoy the sight of such savagery.

"Yes, my lord." The soldier stood, jerking the chains tauter.

Raiden knelt beside the broken boy. Leaned forward, until the scent of his singed flesh cloyed in Raiden's throat. He crouched closer. The tang of the boy's metal shackles mixed with the pool of blood and vomit around him, nearly causing Raiden to retch as well.

"You think you can lie to your emperor?" he began, though he felt sickened by the sight. By his participation in it. "You will not lie to me, you filth." Raiden grabbed the back of the boy's hair, and his hand turned slick with sweat and blood. "I'll tell you what happens to fools who betray their heavenly sovereign. Who think to stop the beating heart of our empire." He edged in closer, dropping his voice to a whisper, filling his features with menace. As he moved, he clenched the small metal object tightly in his hand.

"Lunge for me," he breathed beside the prisoner's ear.

"Answer me, you traitor!" Raiden yanked again on the boy's hair.

The boy's eyes widened, until Raiden could see the veins of blood etching through them. Raiden nodded at the same time he loosened his hold. He let his menace rise into the air, as though he meant it. As though it were his truth.

The boy's attempt to lunge for him was feeble. But it was enough.

With a shout, all the soldiers descended on them in a rush.

Raiden let the tiny blade sink between the boy's ribs just beside his heart, then withdrew the knife back into his sleeve. The wound would not kill the boy immediately. But it would end his life sooner.

It was the best Raiden could do. If his brother discovered he had aided this boy by granting him a measure of mercy, Raiden did not know what Roku might do. The boy was strapped down once more. As Raiden stood again, angry shouts and the sounds of fists against broken flesh coiled into the air.

The boy stared up at him, bloody tears falling from his eyes.

Raiden could not breathe.

Roku is not fit to rule. His mother's words circled through his mind, like a tortured song.

A Dark Garden

---✳---

Mariko waited in the bridal bedchamber. She knelt in the corner of the vast space, shrouded in near darkness, until the sounds of pounding feet across wooden floors had died down to a trickle. Her eyes squeezed closed as she held fast to the one thought that kept her tethered to her body:

She'd not heard that the son of Takeda Shingen had been executed.

Ōkami could be safe.

And if he was not?

She would not allow herself to consider anything beyond that. If terrible things were destined to come to pass, it did her no good to worry about it twice. She would worry about it when it came time to worry. There were some who would find this behavior unbecoming of a woman, this ability to detach. But Mariko held it as a strength. Through all the trials that had occurred in the last few weeks, her strengths had guided her. The things she'd considered struggles had offered her solutions. She would not turn her back on what defined her, even if others perceived it as a weakness.

The sliding doors flew open. Darkening the threshold stood the imposing form of Minamoto Raiden, Prince of Wa.

Her new husband.

Dread twisted through her throat at the thought of what was to come. She forced it down in the next breath. Mariko had made this choice. She had decided to wed a boy who represented everything she loathed: her past, the person she had been raised to be, the future dictated by her parents.

She had made this choice, and it was hers alone.

Bracing her hand on the low table nearby, Mariko stood in a soft rustle of silk. She cleared her voice, held her head high. And made her way toward Raiden. As she drew closer, she caught the scent of blood and seared flesh. The unmistakable odor of the castle's cruel underbelly.

Her heart leapt from her chest. She froze mid-step.

Raiden had just come from killing Ōkami.

Mariko saw what would happen next, clear in her mind's eye. She would lunge for him. She would aim for his eyes and throat. She would do as she had done in the forest that first night and drive a hairpin through his eye if need be.

She would fail.

Her ears rang with silent fury. But she kept still. Cold. Detached. Her last remaining strength.

"My brother . . ." Raiden began, his voice hoarse.

Mariko inhaled carefully through her nose. In her desire

to learn Ōkami's fate, she'd nearly forgotten that Minamoto Roku's life had been threatened today. A loyal subject would think of nothing else. "The emperor is well?" Her words sounded like they were carved from ice.

I am not loyal. I am a traitor.

Raiden did not answer immediately. "He is . . . safe."

It did not escape Mariko's notice that he chose a different way to answer. Used different words to convey a similar sentiment.

"May I offer you something to drink, my lord?" Mariko said, trying to force her body to keep still and not betray her flurry of thoughts. "Something to lighten the burden of the day's events?"

"No." Raiden stepped from the shadows into the weak light filtering from the oil lantern hanging above. His features had aged a decade in the matter of a single evening. Her new husband did not pause as he doffed his chest armor. Mariko did not offer to help him. The mere idea of doing something so intimate slithered over her skin like an eel. She thought to call for a servant.

"Takeda Ranmaru escaped during our wedding." Though he watched her sidelong, Raiden spoke as if it were an afterthought. Then proceeded to sigh while struggling with the gauntlet on his left arm.

After a long pause in which her heart lurched into her throat, Mariko moved to help him, some perverse sense of gratitude driving her to take action. She reached for the ties of his gauntlet, and her fingers brushed across his hand.

Embarrassment flooded her cheeks. When Mariko met Raiden's gaze, she was surprised to find his expression had softened.

As though he appreciated her halfhearted attempt to offer comfort.

It felt odd, to be standing beside this boy she barely knew, playing the role of his dutiful wife. Mariko swallowed, quickly bringing to mind the reaction she should have to the news that her captor was once again free.

Raiden continued studying her. "You are unconcerned by the news?"

"My only concern is for your welfare, my lord."

"You lie well, wife."

Her fingers fumbled on the lacing at his shoulder. Since he knew her to be speaking in falsehoods, it was only appropriate for her to accept a measure of blame. "Of course I am concerned for my own well-being, too. It alarms me to know he managed to break free. But am I wrong to assume you would not let something happen to me, now that we have been joined in marriage?"

Raiden did not reply. He maintained his cool appraisal of her features, as though he were trying to focus on the sediments swirling in a muddy ravine.

One side of Mariko's lips curled upward. "I know you do not trust me, my lord. But this is the life we have chosen for ourselves, inasmuch as we were given the right to choose. I do not wish to begin it amid strife. If you believe I helped Lord Ranmaru escape today—though I stood calmly beneath the same pavilion as you, at risk to my own life—then I am already dead in your eyes." She dipped a cloth in a bowl of clean water and brought it to him. No matter how relieved she was to learn that Ōkami was safe, she did not trust her features to remain steady while touching Raiden's face.

He took the cloth and wiped his brow. Then he turned his back to clean his hands. Without a word, Raiden removed the rest of his armor. He stopped short when he saw the pallet as it had been laid out. For their wedding night. After an uncomfortable pause, he looked at her, his features drawn, as though he knew he were on the cusp of making a mistake.

"I'm tired," he said simply.

"Yes." Mariko nodded, relief unfurling through her body. "As am I."

Careful to place his *tantō* beside him, Raiden lay down on the pallet, not bothering to use the silk-tufted blanket provided for them. Mariko waited for a time, then came to kneel at the edge of the pallet, still dressed in her wedding night finery.

She watched Raiden stare at the ceiling above them. At its intricate alcoves and painted silk screens. Every dark eave was interwoven with parts of a story; most were of the conquests made by his family.

Her family now. Though it was likely some of its ranks had tried to kill her, as she'd suspected from the begining. Strange how that seemed to be the least of her worries now. The very question that had driven her to defy her family and disguise her identity. Only to find the truths hidden within.

Mariko waited until Raiden's eyes drifted closed. Beneath his jaw, she caught sight of a muscle twitching, even as he slept. Once he'd fallen asleep, she removed the jeweled pins the servants had placed in her hair and let her tresses tumble to her shoulders. She lay beside him, keeping her body as far away from his as the space would permit.

Mariko chewed on the inside of her cheek, the events of the day winding through her mind. Then Raiden rolled over. He threw an arm around her waist, his fingertips grazing the thin silk at her hip. Mariko froze, the pace of her heart doubling its rhythm. His breaths were long and drawn, as though he were in the throes of deepest sleep. But his body twitched like it was ready at a moment's notice to rise from their pallet, sword in hand.

Mariko eased from beneath his arm, uncomfortable with this unexpected display of intimacy. She slept in a ball at the foot of the pallet, her dreams clouded by images of a dark garden filled with tiny mirrors.

NO ONE'S HERO

---✳---

The smoke curled from the funeral pyre into the twilit sky. Ōkami studied the flames as they danced above Ren's body—all that remained of his friend. The fire crackled and fizzed, filling the air with the scent of burning flesh.

Ōkami leaned against a birch tree along the fringes, disdaining any offer of assistance. It was not that he was too proud. If anything, the misfortunes of his life had proven to him how pointless it was to let pride dictate his actions. No. He was not proud.

He simply wanted to be alone.

It was a strange emotion for him.

After he'd lost his mother as a small child, then witnessed the death of his father only a few years later, one of Ōkami's greatest fears was being left alone. The dreams that tore apart his sleep—that set his teeth on edge—were usually ones in which he was left to fend for himself in cold darkness or blearing sunlight, begging to no one for a cup of water or a bowl of rice.

Ōkami shifted against the tree, and a wave of pain unfurled down his body. Though his demon had worked beneath the moonlight to repair the damage, he was still a shadow of his former self. And he'd left those responsible for it unscathed.

Worse, he'd left Mariko. Alone.

Grimacing, he returned his attention to Ren's funeral pyre.

Under cover of night, the men of the Black Clan had taken them from the clearing to a bamboo forest known as the Ghost's Gambit. Ōkami could not remember how they'd brought him here. He only remembered that he had been unable to relinquish his hold on Ren. He would not leave his friend alone. Anywhere. Even in death. It still stole the breath from his body to know that Ren had died protecting him. Just like Yorishige, that boy who'd reminded him so much of Yoshi.

That child Ōkami had left behind.

Uesama. It had been the last word Ren had spoken in this life.

The smoke from the pyre twisted Ōkami's way. It made his eyes burn, his throat close. He coughed, and moisture collected in his eyelashes. His first reaction was to fight it. Ōkami did not cry, not even when he was sure no one was there to bear witness. He would never allow such weakness to overcome him.

Ren had not deserved to die at so young an age. So uselessly. Perhaps it meant something that he'd died in battle. Died honorably, protecting a friend.

Honor.

Ōkami glared at the fire until his eyes burned once more. Honor was a thing to hate. It drove people to act foolishly, as though they were heroes. As though they were invincible. Ōkami hated heroes more than anything else. As a boy, he'd concluded that heroes cared more about how the world perceived them than they did about those they'd left behind.

Tsuneoki came to stand on the other side of the birch tree. He gave his friend space, though Ōkami knew the gesture to be unlike him. Save for the times he assumed the form of a nightbeast, Tsuneoki was not known for fading quietly into the shadows. Proof of this was in what he'd managed to accomplish in only ten days: the ranks of the Black Clan had swelled to nine times their previous number.

"Would you like for me to send a healer to tend your wounds?" Tsuneoki asked gently.

"Not now."

Tsuneoki waited again. "The loss of Ren—of a friend and brother—is not something that will be easy to forget." His voice turned hoarse. "I'm not sure I ever want to forget it."

Anger sent another spasm of pain shooting through Ōkami's chest. "You should have left me there."

Tsuneoki's morose laughter filled the air. "You would have

liked that. Then you could have died the tragic death you'd always hoped for. Like a hero."

"I am no one's hero." His fists curled at his sides, but Ōkami fought the urge to lash out at his friend. "You're trying to provoke me."

"Is it working?"

"No," he all but snarled back.

"Liar."

Wincing through the smoke, Ōkami looked away. "Why are you doing this?"

"You must feel responsible for what happened."

"If you say so." He raised his shoulders in glib fashion. Another flare of pain nearly caused him to cry out. Ōkami grunted in an effort to conceal it.

"Of course you feel responsible," Tsuneoki repeated.

"I'm not going to humor you with—"

"Stop it. Act like that in your next life." Tsuneoki faced him straight on. "You are not the only one to have lost everything, Takeda Ranmaru. Some of us just choose to do something about it."

A white haze of fury clouded Ōkami's mind. "What makes you think I—"

"I don't have anything more to say to you on the matter." He paused. "I'll send for the healer. And you will listen to what she says." Tsuneoki began walking away, then halted only a few steps from where he'd stood. "I'm happy to see you again, Ōkami. I'm thankful you're safe. When you've given your anger a chance to abate, let a sentry know. There's something I would like to show you."

"Go to hell."

Tsuneoki grinned, his gaze sharp. "Save me the seat beside you."

A measure of solace

Injustice was not a new form of nourishment for her. It had been served every day of Kanako's life. Sometimes it was expected, others it arrived wearing the guise of something less sinister. But always it was there.

Her anger at injustice had become a thing with teeth. Claws. An icy thing that raged between the bones of her chest, howling to be set free.

All her plans had been ruined by Hattori Kenshin's lingering convictions. He was no longer the boy with the pliant mind she'd first selected for this task. His suffering had not made him weaker; it had made him stronger. His fury at the sight of Muramasa Amaya's entrapped form had not been enough for him to take revenge on the emperor. That must have been the reason his shot had gone wide. It could be the only explanation. Hattori Kenshin was known as the Dragon of Kai. A famed warrior—a samurai—of the highest order. It was not possible for him to have missed his mark, not when he'd been granted every opportunity.

Kanako had set everything up perfectly. She'd put her scapegoat—that sniveling child—into position to hide the weapons afterward. Aligned the stars so that no one would see what happened in the shade of the nearby clouds.

Still it had not been enough.

And who had fired that second shot? The one that had nearly struck her son? It had come from a different angle— higher than the first—which meant it had been an entirely different archer. Who would *dare* to threaten Raiden?

Kanako seethed to herself as she wandered through the colorless world of the enchanted *maru*. Her plans had been torn asunder. The injustice of it all continued to writhe beneath her skin, ready to be unleashed.

Then a coolness washed over her. An answer came to mind.

Her failure had been in entrusting others with such important tasks.

She would not fail like this again.

Raiden made his way across the nightingale floors. They squeaked and whistled with every step. Though the sound was irritating, its rhythm was steady, soothing. Consistent. It offered him a strange kind of comfort.

He'd woken in his bridal chamber to find his new wife

asleep at the foot of their pallet, fully dressed. It should have annoyed him.

Instead he'd experienced the strangest tremor by his heart. The girl—his new wife—was most definitely a nuisance. She said less than half of what she thought, and of that half, Raiden was certain only a fifth of it was true. Though she appeared to have been earnestly frightened when the first arrow had struck the emperor, Raiden was not entirely certain of her innocence.

She was a liar. A manipulator.

He should have killed her for it, the moment the doubt first entered his mind. But Raiden had had enough of bloodshed after last night. Enough of it to last a lifetime.

Then—when he was most in need of it—Mariko had simply listened to him. She'd not asked for anything. Simply offered him quiet company. A measure of solace. When he'd been younger, his mother had done that for him. It was the reason Raiden did not feel the need to retaliate against those who shunned him for his birth.

His mother's silent encouragement. The simple fact that she had been there. Often that had been all Raiden had needed as a child. Someone who cared. For a blink of time, he'd seen the same quality in Hattori Mariko. The same quiet strength. Perhaps that was why Raiden had acquiesced to his brother's demands and married her, despite his many reservations.

The girl held tight to her convictions. Once Hattori Mariko had agreed to marry him, Raiden did not sense anything but surety in her. She'd not asked to delay the wedding for any reason—even to ensure her parents' attendance—though Raiden would have understood. Mariko's only requests had been that he allow her to attend a play in the city—to be among the people of Inako—one last time. And that Takeda Ranmaru be executed without any fanfare, in the moments following the ceremony of their marriage. No more torture. Just a clean death.

She had enough of bloodshed as well.

It had moved Raiden that one of her requests was for justice absent malice. He longed for the ability to convince his brother of the merit behind this. His brother's idea of justice made Raiden's flesh crawl as though he'd waded into a pool of maggots.

Though he could not deny that she was a troubling creature, Raiden also admired Mariko for not succumbing to the pressures of court. For not lowering herself to the baser amusements of the nobility, who enjoyed asserting their hierarchy and putting others beneath their feet. When she first arrived, Raiden had questioned those attending her needs, and they divulged that Mariko did not approve of cruel behavior, even though derogatory whispers trailed her every footstep.

She stayed above it, and Raiden admired her for that.

Yet he'd not pressed to consummate their marriage. When given the opportunity, Raiden did not wish to move forward with the act. It did not seem right. Hattori Mariko had said she did not want to begin a life with him amid strife. Her words moved him further. Made him consider the advantage of being in a harmonious marriage. Of having a willing wife. One he could respect for the strength of her convictions.

Locking his gaze upon the tatami mats at his feet, Raiden bowed low, then proceeded toward the low throne upon which his younger brother now sat, an expression of supreme serenity on his face.

In the past, this expression had made Raiden smile.

Today it unnerved him.

He took his place at his brother's side and waited for their meal to be served. His brother sipped his tea from a small cup resting nearby.

"It was a shame the prisoner died before offering any useful information," Roku began.

"Indeed it was."

"I'm assuming you will be continuing with your inquiries."

Raiden bowed. "Of course, my sovereign."

"Do not rest until you learn where the Black Clan has taken Takeda Ranmaru. Until each and every one of them— and all of their family members—are stretched from the ramparts as a warning to those who would dare to challenge me."

Raiden nodded once more.

Roku set down his cup. "Enough of these unseemly matters. Today is your first day as a married man." He smiled at Raiden, as though he were gazing fondly at an errant child. "Tell me, brother . . . was the daughter of Hattori Kano all she swore she would be?"

Raiden had not thought his brother would pursue the

matter in quite so blunt a fashion. That feeling of disquiet coiled up his throat, leaving a bitter taste on his tongue. "Are you asking me to speak with you of my wedding night, my sovereign?"

"I am. It is important that we know whom we can trust, especially if they are to move about in our inner circle. Can we trust Lady Mariko? Was she untouched after living in close quarters with those traitors for several weeks?"

Raiden exhaled. "Would I be so untroubled if she were not?"

"That is not an answer, brother," Roku said. He reached again for his tea. Took another small sip. "You did not lie with her." His tone was pointed. "Perhaps if you are unable to complete the task, I can oblige you on that score."

The disquiet shifted into anger. The kind that simmered in Raiden's stomach. "There is no need for that."

"Then she was a maid?"

"Of course she was," Raiden lied without thinking. He was not sure why he did it. He had never before lied to his brother in such a brazen fashion. But he could not stomach any more of Roku's paranoia. At times, it looked as though the emperor would do anything to ensure loyalty, even destroy the very foundation upon which it was built.

Roku watched his brother's face. Studied it as though it were a stanza from a complicated poem. Then he smiled once more. "I am glad to hear it."

After he returned his brother's grin, Raiden ate his meal in silence, that same roiling feeling ruining his appetite. He missed speaking to his mother. For the second time since his wedding, he wished he had not dismissed her counsel for speaking treasonously about Roku.

He wished he had her voice in his ear at this moment.

He wished she would offer him her advice again.

The first thing Raiden did when he returned to his empty chamber was to remove the bedclothes from his carved *tansu* chest. He unrolled the pallet. Then—with only the slightest of hesitations—he slid his thumb across the blade of his *katana*, creating a shallow cut.

Raiden let his blood drip onto the center of the pallet— proof that Mariko had lost her maidenhead on her wedding night. With this action, he solidified the lie he'd told to his brother to protect his new wife.

Last night, he'd lied to protect the boy.

Today, he'd lied to protect Mariko.

Perhaps that was all Raiden could do. Lie. And protect.

A sea of memories

———— ✳ ————

The last time Ōkami saw his mother's home, he was a boy of no more than five. Thirteen years had passed since that summer. He wondered whether he would recognize it now. Whether the same patch of land produced the same white wildflowers. If the crashing waves still captivated his imagination as they had his mother's. Whether the post on the far-left side of the stable still bore the marks he'd made on it with a wooden sword, the year his father gifted him the toy.

Ōkami rode up to the low stone wall surrounding the outermost border of his mother's domain. He stopped short—his horse rearing—as he took in the sight of the dilapidated barrier. At the sound of galloping hooves at his back, he glanced over his shoulder. The motion caused him to wince, despite his efforts to conceal it. Three nights had passed since Ōkami's arrival at the Black Clan's new camp. In that time, he'd managed to regain most of his strength, but still could not escape the lingering discomfort.

Tsuneoki and Haruki reined in their horses alongside him. They paused to survey the crashing sea in the distance and the rolling stretch of land beyond the dilapidated stone wall.

"Do you feel it?" Ōkami asked, without turning to look at either of his friends.

Haruki nodded. "Did it always feel this way? Like the air is . . . full of spirits?"

"From what I can remember." Ōkami breathed in deeply. The scent of the seawater wafting across the mulberry fields stirred something deep in his memories.

"When Ōkami was a boy, he loved to tell me his mother's home was haunted by ghosts." Tsuneoki steadied his horse as it began to move about, almost as though it had understood its rider.

Ōkami looked at his best friend. He still did not comprehend the reason Tsuneoki had asked him to come here. What he wished to show him. This place dredged up too many things. Images that had long since faded from recollection.

The trio rode past the worn gates, through the sea of swaying grass toward the main compound. Ōkami said little as they traveled past the echoes of his childhood, but he marveled to himself at how effective time was at collecting its due. It troubled him how certain sparks of memory would burn across his vision, only to vanish the next instant. After so many years, he didn't really remember what his mother looked like. He only caught flashes of feeling, ripples of scent, a strong hand clasped tightly to his, even when he tried to yank it away.

His mother had been beautiful, that much he knew. A lover of the sea and all its spoils. A singer and an artist. A woman who'd enjoyed arguing with his father, to their mutual delight. But these things were told to Ōkami when he'd grown older, and it was not unusual for young sons to think their mothers the loveliest of all.

After his wife had been swallowed by a giant wave, Ōkami's father did not speak much about her. For five days and nights, the fishermen in the nearby village tried to find her, but the storm that day had been quick and wild. It had caught her without warning. Now all that remained of his mother were Ōkami's flickers of recollection.

And Ōkami remembered so little.

Her name was Sena. Toyotomi Sena.

As Ōkami dismounted from his horse, he caught sight of fabric scraps lying among the debris. On some of them, he saw the faded remnants of the Toyotomi crest—a sea dragon guarding a trove of diamonds. He stopped beside the entrance to the run-down fortress. Without a word, Ōkami pushed through the splintered gates, their hinges protesting with a rusty whine, their wooden slats warped by the sun. Dried leaves littered the main courtyard. They blew across the moss-covered stone, catching in tiny twists of air.

High above head fluttered a large banner. Even from this distance, Ōkami could see the outline of the Minamoto crest in its center. For an instant, his vision darkened with anger, but Ōkami reached beyond the sentiment, settling for apathy.

It was much easier not to care.

A haunted moan unfolded across the old tile roof. The main edifice had not been constructed as many of the modern strongholds were now built. There were no tiered gables. It possessed a single story. The only form of true protection was the river along the outermost border; a single bridge availed intruders with access to the domain. Back then, these things were thought of as unnecessary. The fallen fortress of the Toyotomi clan had been built when no one thought to challenge their protectors.

Had his father been a protector? Had he truly been a great man who cared about those beneath him? Ōkami had not thought so. For most of his life, he'd believed his father had simply succumbed to a selfish notion of honor. One that idealized his death and held him up as a standard of greatness. But Mariko had offered Ōkami a different perspective. It was not anything she said, but rather all that she done. All she became. Two months ago, Mariko had arrived to their encampment in Jukai forest as a spoiled daughter of a callous daimyō. But she changed. She allowed her mind to be open to other possibilities.

To the chance the things she'd believed all her life might be wrong.

Had Takeda Shingen cared more about those he'd been sworn to protect than his honor? Had he truly been a great man?

Ōkami frowned. No. He was not wrong about his father. Takeda Shingen had wanted to be a hero of legend, not a man of the people. A great man would not have left his only son without answers. His people without hope.

"Why are we here, Tsuneoki?" Ōkami asked. His voice was a low growl. It belied his desire to remain indifferent. He cleared his throat and asked again.

But his friend had already noticed his irritation. "I thought to make this our new stronghold."

"It's a mistake. The emperor will find out." Ōkami spoke without hesitating.

"Of course he will. But the river within this domain flows swiftly and runs deep. A single bridge is the only way to cross it, which should prove difficult for a large army, especially if we rig it to collapse under a certain weight. And I don't expect us to be here long. Either we will prevail or die trying. We've never been equipped for a long siege."

"It's foolish to lead the men here."

Tsuneoki paused. "It's even more foolish to continue hiding them in the forest. You've seen how quickly we've grown. How quickly we continue to grow. A force as large as ours requires adequate space."

Ōkami did not answer as he walked up the steps and into the main residence. Inside were the remnants of many small fires—spots of blackened stone and piles of ash. The domain of the Toyotomi clan was abandoned by Ōkami's family not long after he'd lost his mother. Following the mysterious death of his grandparents, the land was branded as cursed. The few who'd chosen to remain behind burned anything of value, rather than have it be taken by conquerors. This gave Ōkami a measure of comfort. At least the late emperor had not stolen anything of worth from his mother's land. Minamoto Masaru had taken everything from the Takeda family. Even purloined their crest and melded it with his own.

The only thing of value that had been stolen from the Toyotomi clan were its lives. Its beating heart. Somewhere in the darkened corners of the structure—beneath the layers of dried grass and scurrying insects—were most likely the remains of the poor souls who'd fought to defend his mother's land.

What would tie them to it, long after its protectors had left it to ruin?

"If you wish to use this domain as your stronghold, you do not need my permission." Ōkami turned to meet the gaze of his best friend. "You've never needed my permission for anything."

"All the same, I wished to ask."

Ōkami pivoted in place to return to his horse. "It was a waste of time coming here. I thought you were the last person to waste time."

"Ranmaru," Tsuneoki called out.

Ōkami stopped short. Tsuneoki rarely used his given name. And never in the presence of others. "What do you want?"

"You should go to your mother's chambers."

"Why?" His eyes narrowed with suspicion. "To what end?"

"Just go." Tsuneoki kept still as Haruki moved to stand beside him, as though to offer him strength.

Ōkami frowned. Then shrugged.

If he was here, it would not cause him harm to humor his friend.

Redemption

———✳———

Kanako wandered a final time through her garden between worlds. Her fingers floated over the dazzling leaves, the silver of her rings causing their mirrored surfaces to shimmer at the slightest touch.

This would be her last day visiting this place. For almost two decades, this colorless world had provided her with a haven—a place to conceal her true self, even from her son. Today would also mark her final attempt to give Raiden the greatest gift she could offer: the power to rule as heavenly sovereign.

She shook out her hair. Removed the lacquered *zori* and silken *tabi* from her feet, so that she could feel rooted to the earth wherever she stood. Then Kanako raised her hands, the dark sleeves of her kimono fluttering in an enchanted wind. She watched the leaves take flight from their hedges. They encircled Kanako as though she were a black swan, and they her glittering attendants. They began to drift higher until they changed shape, blossoming into the figures of men and women. The ones Kanako had carefully chosen for her flock.

Some would be her bodyguards. Others would provide her with distractions during the coming invasion.

The winged mirrors assumed their human forms, but they did not appear to have control over their minds. They behaved exactly like the mindless creatures Kanako had left behind in the domains east of the imperial city, as a warning.

As a portent of what was to come.

Kanako did not learn much from her lover, Minamoto Masaru. But she learned the inexorable value of fear.

She turned her attention back to the lives she'd collected for her flock. The army she'd amassed in her enchanted world, biding time for the right moment to strike. Some of its ranks were young. Some were elderly. Some were infirmed. Minamoto Roku's imperial soldiers would hesitate before striking them down. And in the heat of battle, to hesitate was to die.

Many more were strong. Young. Warriors bearing the weapons of samurai from the eastern provinces. At the vanguard of this troop stood the tortured figure of Nobutada, Hattori Kano's friend and confidant. His grizzled features twisted with despair as Kanako moved him forward. He lurched as though he were fighting against her control.

Poor fool. Nobutada would be a welcomed sacrifice to a much greater cause.

Death always collected its due.

When Kanako prodded the minds of the soldiers—ordering them to take leave of this place—pain flashed across their features. A pitiful kind of resistance. Honor-bound warriors did not like being led against their will. Unperturbed, Kanako drove them forward in small groups, out into Inako, where they would spread across the city and begin wreaking their havoc. Make it rife for the taking.

Kanako turned to those who remained. Her distractions. They were not to be used now. She would save them for when she planned to overtake the castle, once the city belonged to her son. It would do no good to wrest control of the emperor's stronghold without first securing its borders. She studied her distractions for a moment, particularly captivated by the face of a young boy, who reminded her greatly of Raiden as a child.

The pain in his expression—his silent scream—gave her pause. But only for a moment.

Magic required pain. She, too, had suffered a great deal.

In life, everything worthwhile involved sacrifice.

Kanako waited until most of the castle had fallen asleep. The chaos of the last few days had left its mark everywhere. In corners strewn with colorful banners and broken shards of pottery. In the droves of imperial guards patrolling the castle grounds.

It was good she had sent her flock of warriors beyond

the enchanted *maru*, into the city proper. They would begin seeding their discord in the outermost wards of Inako—the streets least patrolled by imperial soldiers. Then they would make their way toward the golden castle in the city's center. It would not be long before the people bore full witness to their emperor's incompetence. Before they begged for the might of a warrior like Raiden to lead them to safety.

But Kanako knew there were still obstacles to overcome. Unforeseen possibilities. These worries drove her to take precautions. The ring she wore on her right hand had been gifted to her by an especially wicked creature of the wood. An eight-legged demon that had ruled a domain of darkness since the beginning of time. Kanako rarely channeled this spirit. It unsettled her to descend into its form and look upon the world through so many eyes. With such unmitigated hunger.

But this demon would serve her well tonight.

She set the creature's spirit free. The silver of her ring turned to liquid, collecting in a drop at the tip of her finger. As the drop grew to the size of a quail's egg, a spider took shape. Kanako closed her eyes and joined her mind with it. The sounds around her became muffled. But every movement—even the slightest vibration—passed through her body with a jolt. Now her sight was encumbered, as though she gazed upon the world from behind a row of gemstones.

The only scents that interested her were those of blood and fear.

She scuttled quickly down the halls, her tiny form

concealed along the very edges, in the deepest reaches of shadow. Kanako did not need to orient herself, even as this eight-legged creature. She'd dreamed about this night for years.

Several guards were posted outside the dowager empress's bedchamber. Kanako darted past them unnoticed. She paused beside the sleeping form of the empress. Breathed deeply of her blood and its especially sweet perfume. A part of her wanted Genmei to know she was the one responsible. That the dowager empress's last moments in this life were granted at Kanako's leisure. But it was her pride that dictated this wish, and Kanako had learned long ago that pride only served her for the blink of an eye. She'd learned the value of orchestrating disaster from afar.

No, this was not about pride. This was about justice. Justice in the face of unceasing mistreatment. Justice for her son, who'd been an innocent child, suffering for his mother's choices. Justice for Raiden's father—the man Kanako had loved—who'd died betrayed and alone.

Even if Genmei never knew who had brought about her death . . .

Kanako always would.

Born of a Dragon and a Phoenix

---✶---

A part of Ōkami wished to turn back.

As soon as he made his way outside—toward the structure that had housed his mother's private rooms—a haunted wind encircled him, dancing about his shoulders as though it were in celebration.

He breathed deeply of the briny air. Refused to allow his fears to control him. Mariko had said it before in the forest. That fear could either feed her or consume her. She chose to let it be a source of strength.

Ōkami, too, decided to embrace his fear.

The sliding doors before him had fallen to disrepair. He kicked them aside, though he knew the motion would cause him pain. It shot up his leg, reminding him of his own mortality. That he lived by the grace of something beyond him.

Upon his first glimpse inside his mother's chamber, Ōkami narrowed his eyes with irritation. Nothing was there, save an overturned chest coated with cobwebs. Every other corner had been ransacked. The floors were predictably stained with many small scorch marks.

Ōkami started to leave, then thought better of it. Tsuneoki would not have sent him here alone without a reason. Despite his misgivings, he stepped inside. Examined the ceilings. Began pacing the perimeter of the low-ceilinged space. The floorboards squeaked beneath his footsteps; the wood there had turned dangerously soft. Soon the entire structure would fall to ruin. He paused on the remnants of silk drawings. Most of them had been destroyed by vermin and rot.

Ōkami studied the scorch marks at his feet, to see if anything of value had been left behind. Everywhere he stepped, he worried the floor might give way. Then something caught him off guard. Or rather the absence of something. There—in the corner nearest the overturned chest—the floorboards made no protest.

They'd been reinforced from beneath.

Ōkami crouched above them. Placed both hands onto their worn surfaces. Searched the seams until something shifted, clicking open. A hidden compartment, concealed beneath the structure. It was not large. In its depths, Ōkami found a small box of carved acacia wood, meant to survive exposure to the elements. Meant to fend off the intruding damp. On the box's surface was a dragon guarding a trove of diamonds. To one side, a name had been haphazardly etched into a corner, as though by the hand of a child.

Sena.

Ōkami swallowed. Ran his thumb across his mother's name. Then he opened the box. Inside he found four silken pouches. He slid open the ties of the first. An object the size of his palm fell into his hand. It appeared to be some kind of fish scale, its surface iridescent, almost like a pearl. The scale itself was hard. Almost as hard as a rock. Never in his life had Ōkami seen anything like it. When he turned it over, he saw a phrase painted in its center by a shaky hand:

お詫び

Owabi. Deepest apologies.

The next pouch contained a scroll with a waxen seal. Inside it was a poem:

> *A thing of beauty*
> *A love stronger than fear and*
> *Deeper than the sea*

His father's crest was still attached to the worn *washi* paper. Ōkami took a careful breath. It had been years since he'd last seen his father's handwriting. An age since he'd last felt the power of his father's words. The sight of the love poem Takeda Shingen had sent to Toyotomi Sena brought the ghost of a smile to Ōkami's face.

Never once had he considered how his parents' love had come to be.

The third pouch contained two seals wrapped in aging paper. One seal was broken through its center. Split as though it had been trampled beneath a heavy boot. When Ōkami pieced it together, he recognized his mother's family crest. The dragon had been separated from its trove of diamonds. The second seal caused his heart to lurch in his chest. It was a seal bearing his given name.

Takeda Ranmaru.

It had been wrapped carefully in a perfect square of *washi*, surrounded by the official markings of the shōgun. His father had written a short message:

For my son, born of a dragon and a phoenix.

Fight not for greatness, but for goodness.

Ōkami's hands began to shake. It was becoming difficult for him to breathe, as though all the air had been leached from the room. A slew of emotions twisted through him—fury, pain, heartbreak, sadness. Love most of all. He set aside the two seals. With great care, Ōkami opened the last pouch.

A black dagger fell into his hand. A dagger made of a strange rock.

Ōkami had seen a rock like this before. Held it in his hand. It was the kind of dagger he'd used to bind himself with his demon. A thudding ache pulsed through his skull. An ache of understanding. He perused the contents of the box once more. His eyes stopped on the beautiful scale. A scale from a fish larger than any he'd ever seen.

A scale not of this world.

Owabi. Deepest apologies.

Ōkami picked it up. Turned it over in his hand, his thoughts a blur.

His mother had disappeared at sea. They'd never found her body.

Was it possible? Had Toyotomi Sena aligned herself with a demon of the sea? If she had, then where was she? Why had she not come to Ōkami? Why had she not saved his father? Where had she been when they most needed her?

Anger surged through his veins. It washed his sight crimson. In the colors of fire. His father had always said Ōkami was like fire. When he threw the beautiful scale against the wall, it slid to the ground, unbroken. Unscathed.

What was the point in having power if you did not use it to save those you loved?

Fight not for greatness, but for goodness.

Ōkami picked up the fragile piece of *washi*. Reread his father's words to him. A drop of moisture landed beside the script. Then another. His tears flowed freely as Ōkami sat back, staring at the contents of this small wooden box. Things of great value to no one. Things of inestimable value to him. It was the work of a moment. A choice made, and a door pushed open.

It was not up to his mother to save him. Just as it was not up to his father to give him answers. That was not the way of life. Only Ōkami could do what needed to be done. It was time for him to forgive his past. Not forget it. Only a fool would forget such things. But if he could not let go of the demons in his past, how could he ever hope to embrace his greatest fear?

Who he was. Who he'd always been. Who he was meant to be.

In his hands, Takeda Ranmaru held the totality of a life. Of two lives. The beginning and the end of a story. The tale of Sena and Shingen.

But it would not be the end of his parents. Of their family. They'd given their son the gift of great power. Not the kind of power granted by a demon. The kind of power that people laid down their lives to protect.

The power of hope.

the way of the warrior

———✳———

Raiden was torn from his sleep by shouts outside his chamber doors. He wrenched open the papered screens, his blades in his hands.

A servant stared at the ground, his head weighted with sorrow. "Apologies for the hour, my lord. The emperor requests your presence."

"Has he been injured?" Raiden looped his *katana* and *wakizashi* through the cord at his waist.

Fear passing across his features, the servant shook his head. "Please proceed with all haste to the Lotus Pavilion, my lord."

Behind him, Raiden heard Mariko stir. He turned toward her and wordlessly directed her to remain in the room. Then he stepped into the corridors, ordering the guards to stay posted outside. As he walked toward the wing of Heian Castle that housed the dowager empress's chambers, the sounds of quiet sobbing grew louder. Ladies of the court sat huddled together in corners, their faces stained with tears, and their hands shaking in anguish.

Raiden halted in his tracks when he saw his younger brother pacing before the entrance of the dowager empress's bedchamber. The sliding doors had been left wide-open.

It took Raiden only a moment to understand the sight within.

Roku's mother was sprawled across her bedcovers, as though she'd risen from sleep in a panic and collapsed the moment she'd called for help. Her eyes bulged from her skull, the veins around them bloated and purple. White foam ringed her lips.

She'd died in agony. Undoubtedly poisoned.

Dread rising in his veins, Raiden looked at his younger brother. "My sovereign—"

"It's not enough for them to die," Roku began softly, his pacing increasing in intensity with each word he spoke. "I don't simply want to see them writhe in anguish."

Unease bade Raiden to keep silent.

The emperor continued his hushed rant, his brow lined with hatred. "They will watch their mothers, their grand-mothers, their daughters perish first. I will set fire to their homes. Any man, woman, or child in service to them shall burn in the flames." Though Roku spoke of atrocities, his voice did not shake. It did not sound the least bit agitated.

Thus far, the only signs Raiden could see of his brother's fraying emotions were the pacing. The wide-eyed stare. "My sovereign," he started, "perhaps we—"

"Do not say a word to me!" Roku screamed. "Not a single

word!" It ripped from his mouth, echoing into the rafters. The sound startled the ladies of the court, many of whom only cried louder.

"That's enough." Roku turned his rage on them. "Not a single one of you were here to save my mother. I should tear out your throats for it." He grabbed an ornamental vase from its stand and hurled it at the nearest group of terrified young women. A trio of girls who'd long ruled their roost of court-iers. The painted vase shattered in pieces at their feet. "You disgust me," he shouted. "Every last one of you deserves to die! Blood-sucking whores. You come to my city in the guise of guests. Eat my food at your leisure. Sleep safely in my cas-tle. And when you are most needed, all you can do is put on a performance?" Roku's chest heaved as he took a breath. "Get out of my sight!"

The girls bit their tongues, refusing to cry out, their fig-ures huddled against each other. The one nearest to Raiden looked to him for guidance. For mercy.

His features stern, Raiden stepped forward. "Leave this place. All of you. If you value your lives, be gone from this castle at once. Say one word to anyone, and I will have you banished from the city." He towered over them. Though he meant to impart cruelty into his words, his eyes beseeched them to obey without question. To stay safe.

The young women bowed, then fled without a sound.

Raiden turned back to Roku, who glared at nothing, his face twisted in a scowl. "Brother," he entreated again. "Please accept—"

"Where were you tonight?" Roku said, his voice soft once more.

Raiden blinked. Kept silent.

Roku continued. "Were you with your whore?"

Raiden did not move, nor did he change his expression. He remained quiet and still.

"Was your whore with you the whole night?" Roku asked in a perilous whisper. "Or did you help her kill my mother?"

Raiden inhaled through his nose. His brother—his emperor—had just accused him of treachery. There was nothing more to be done or said. His hand twitched of its own volition, as though it ached to grasp a sword.

"Answer me!" Roku demanded.

"My wife and I were in our chambers asleep, my sovereign. There were guards posted outside all night."

"Then who killed my mother?"

Raiden inhaled once more. Then he fell to his knees, his body bowed. In a single smooth motion, he removed the swords from his hip and placed them on the floor before him. His eyes locked on the polished wood floor, Raiden spoke. "My sovereign, my loyalty is to you, until my death. If you believe I have betrayed you in any way—failed you in any way—you have but to ask for my life, and I will gladly give it."

They were the words of a samurai to his sovereign. Ever since Raiden could remember, he'd believed in them. Believed in what they stood for. The honor they imparted. This night, these words rang hollow. Raiden kept his gaze averted. He did not know what his brother might do or say. But Raiden's honor bound him to his creed. It was the way of the warrior. The only way Raiden knew.

Finally Roku spoke. "Stand, brother."

Raiden looked up. Rose to his feet.

Still his brother's features were inscrutable. That was what frightened Raiden most of all. That he no longer knew what his brother thought.

"I appreciate your loyalty," Roku said. "Find Takeda Ranmaru and the Black Clan. Bring them to me, alive. If you fail, I will accept your offer. After that, I will make sure your wife is placed on your funeral pyre to burn alongside you."

A murder of crows burst from the ramparts of Heian Castle as though they were fleeing a stampede. They squawked and swooped down into the city as word of the dowager empress's death flew through the streets of Inako. Whispers of treason trailed in their wake. Of insurrection and unrest.

Then the looting began in the outermost districts.

Strange figures—their motions jerky as though their bodies had been broken and pieced back together—lurched into the winding lanes of the Iwakura ward, moving about as though they saw or cared or felt nothing, like the husk of living humans. They tossed barrels through doors. Broke locks securing valuables. Ignored the shouts of protests.

Some of them even silenced dissenters where they stood. Many of these human husks carried weapons forged by master artisans. Several of them bore the crests of eastern clans loyal to the emperor. Anyone who stood in their way was quickly cut down. As death and devastation raged in the streets, the people of these wards cried out for imperial troops to come to their aid. They rushed toward the city center, abandoning their homes, bringing with them only that which they could carry.

Only to find their paths blocked by lines of silent soldiers.

As word of the mounting unrest carried through Inako—into the homes of the wealthy, closest to the castle gates—the outcry grew. Soon messengers were being dispatched to all corners. Despite the fear and the protests, the looting continued to spread, converging slowly toward the city center. Imperial guards erected barriers preventing entry without expressed permission.

The cries of those left to fend for themselves burgeoned to a roar. Pleas for assistance became shouts of fury. Demands that the emperor open the gates of Heian Castle and offer aid to his people. Protect those in need of it.

As these outcries rose throughout the city, lanterns burst to life. Those still left standing armed and barricaded themselves in their homes, wondering how an enemy force had managed to infiltrate their streets unseen.

In less than two days, Inako was no longer a city of arched bridges and cherry trees. A city of secrets and mystery.

It was a city of death and fear.

overtaken

---✦---

When Kenshin woke, he was naked save for a loincloth. His eyes strained at the morning sunlight.

Morning?

No. Afternoon.

He rolled over on his pallet, knocking over an empty sake bottle. A soft sigh emanated from behind him. When he whipped his head around, his sight locked on a girl of no more than twenty, watching him.

Or rather keeping watch over him.

"Are you finally awake?" she asked. She did not call him "my lord," nor did she offer a hint of obeisance. Her very voice dripped with judgment.

"How long have I been asleep?" He groaned.

The girl was quick to correct him. "You've been lying in a drunken stupor for the better part of two days."

"Who are you?" he said. "And what gives you the right to talk to me like this? Do you know who I am?"

"My name is Kirin. You are in my lady Yumi's home. And I have cleaned the spittle from your chin and washed your stinking body for the past two days." She sniffed. "It doesn't matter who you are, piss is piss."

At this affront, Kenshin sat up with a start, intent on giving Kirin a sound verbal thrashing. Immediately he regretted the motion. An anvil settled on his skull, grinding into his brain. He groaned again and glanced around the room. It was small but tastefully appointed. The furniture in it was of highest quality, and the bedding opulent, if a bit soiled.

A careful appraisal informed Kenshin that he did, in fact, stink. Troubled by the truth of Kirin's words, he decided to overlook her insolence for the time being. "Why was I brought here?"

She laughed softly. "You weren't brought here. You came here, hurling accusations and destroying things like a lovesick fool."

The images swirling through Kenshin's mind came into sharp focus. The last thing he recalled with absolute clarity was this: the *maiko* Yumi revealing that he—Hattori Kenshin, the Dragon of Kai—had been the one responsible for the attempt on the emperor's life. At her words, his thoughts had gone blank. Wrath had barreled up his throat, protests forming on his tongue. And then something had ripped across his vision. A weight had lodged between his eyes, the pain sharp and intense.

It was as though his mind had been split in two.

The pressure on his skull had become unbearable. Like water passing through a crack in a dam. How could he have been the one to commit such an act of treason? How was this possible? It wasn't. It was all a lie. One carefully constructed to distract him from learning how Yumi had snuck into his chamber. What she was doing on the imperial grounds, dressed as a boy, bearing a forbidden weapon.

It had all been too much for him in that moment. Kenshin had fallen to the floor and lost consciousness. He remembered nothing after that.

"Are you ready to return to the castle?" Kirin asked. "Prince Raiden has voiced his concern for you. We sent word with respect to your whereabouts." She paused. "My lady delivered a message to your sister yesterday."

Kenshin shook his head. "I am not going back to the castle. I'm going home."

"I don't think that's possible." The girl crossed her arms, again the portrait of impudence.

"Excuse me?" Kenshin sputtered.

"No one can travel past the outer gates of the city. Not with all the rioting there."

Kenshin pressed his hands to his temples and blinked hard. "I know nothing of what you're saying."

"Right. Because you were so drunk." Kirin nodded. "The districts along the outskirts of the city have been overrun by looters. They appear to be afflicted by a strange plague. The emperor has cordoned off the innermost parts of Inako in order to prevent the unrest from spreading to the castle, so we are safe in Hanami. For now." She sighed. "Believe me, I'd like nothing more than to assist with your departure. I am still amazed that my lady allowed you to remain here, much less in her own home, after the manner in which you treated her."

Kenshin stared blankly at the girl.

"You don't even recall that?" The girl sniffed. "You accused my mistress of treason, in front of five high-ranking advisors to the emperor. I must say, they all found your story quite amusing. They even offered you drinks afterward." Irritation creased her brow. "Until you began throwing things, that is. Now that you are recovered, my lady wishes you safe travels on your way home." She bowed at him smartly. Cheekily.

The gaps in Kenshin's memory struggled to settle, like blurred lines on a hot summer's day. But his mind had failed him on more than one occasion of late. It had left him weak. Vulnerable. He bristled against the idea. Kenshin was a samurai of great renown. Warriors of his ilk knew better than to let their emotions dictate their actions. He would marshal his irritation with this rude maidservant, so that he would not lose the chance to confront her mistress again. He had not forgotten how Yumi had knocked him off his feet with less effort than it took to swat a fly. Only a studied combatant possessed those kind of skills, and the *maiko* would be unlikely to disclose who had trained her. Not without some . . . convincing.

"Is your mistress here now?" Kenshin tried.

Kirin nodded once. "But she has no intention of seeing

you." Another knowing smile. "I'm sure you can understand why."

His legs wobbled from disuse when Kenshin stood. He offered the girl a halfhearted bow. "Please convey my regret to your mistress. My behavior was inexcusable. It shall not happen again."

The maidservant tilted her head in amused disbelief. "I've heard that before." With a snicker, Kirin left his freshly cleaned garments in a pile by his feet.

As Kenshin dressed, he considered how best to confront Yumi. The welt on his shoulder had turned the shade of an eggplant. Though Kenshin did not want to admit it, it frightened him to know that he might have done something else he could not recall. That he could still be acting beyond his own control.

When Kenshin slid open the silk-screened doors, he found Kirin waiting outside with his weapons. She led him to the main gate, making sure never once to leave him alone. With a curt bow, she passed him his swords and led him onto a side street of Hanami, bolting the gate behind him once he'd left.

Kenshin stood outside the stacked stone wall. Considered his next course of action. It was still early in the afternoon. Hanami's tree-lined lanes would not be filled with patrons for many hours.

He made a decision.

If Yumi did not want to see him in her home ever again, he would just have to wait until she came outside.

The sun had just begun its descent when Yumi finally ventured past the gate of her *okiya*. Kenshin watched her from behind the branches of a gingko tree, like an unsavory outlaw picking his next mark. He made no moves as the *maiko* gazed about her, her grey eyes vigilant. The kimono she'd chosen for the outing was simple, her hair styled in a plain fashion. Though she took pains to draw a length of pale silk over her head to conceal her features, her beauty could not be missed. She moved from the side street onto a larger thoroughfare nearby, her *zori* clacking in an easy rhythm.

Kenshin followed her at a distance, pausing now and then to ensure Yumi would not suspect anyone of trailing her. The crowds Kenshin had hoped would aid him in this endeavor were much thinner than he'd expected, as though a spate of bad weather had descended on the city. But the sky above was clear, the setting sun glorious, a balmy wind wafting through the cherry trees. Earlier today, Kirin had warned him of riots in the farthest reaches of the city. Perhaps this was why there were so few people milling about the streets of Hanami. From Kenshin's perspective, he did not sense any signs of a threat close by.

Perhaps the cheeky maidservant had been lying.

Yumi continued moving swiftly toward the main thoroughfare of Hanami. Again Kenshin was surprised by how few people loitered along the route. Many of the little shops were closed. Some had been boarded shut. It struck him as highly unusual, as did the strange air hovering about the space. It felt akin to fear.

This troubling sentiment did not stop men from looking at Yumi with covetous glances. A part of Kenshin disliked the way their eyes followed her every motion. As though her beauty were a thing to be consumed.

Strings of papered lanterns were being lit in front of the most stalwart vendors, the ones determined to go about their business, despite the tinge of malice in the air. Hanami was meant to be a place of excess. On normal afternoons, the wares sold along these lanes offered evidence of this: delicate candy of spun sugar, stalls of vibrant dyes imported from the east, porcelain jars of nightingale cream and finely milled pearl powder.

But many of these vendors had chosen not to open their stalls today.

When Yumi paused at a merchant selling stacks of fine paper, Kenshin ducked into a small shop across the way, specializing in scented oils. One of only three shops welcoming customers along this particular street, out of more than twenty. He'd not been there but a moment when a strange wailing began emanating from outside. Followed by the splintering of wood and the shattering of porcelain. Several lanterns hanging in front of the oil shop started to sway. Kenshin watched two patrons along the road turn around, their eyes going wide, their features gathering with confusion.

Then the wailing turned to screams.

Yumi stepped outside the paper shop just as Kenshin made his way into the street.

Their eyes met.

She did not seem surprised to see him there.

But now was not the time for them to react. Less than a quarter league from where they stood, chaos had begun to take shape. People fled as items were tossed through the air, smashing the wooden stalls on contact. The shapes of those responsible for the destruction were indistinct. Silhouetted by the setting sun. When Kenshin squinted, it looked as though a group of lurching figures was set on destroying everything in sight.

If these were the looters Kirin had mentioned earlier, it was clear they'd managed to break the barriers protecting the innermost portion of the imperial city. But still he did not feel immediate cause for concern. These looters moved about as though they were drunk. And there did not seem to be that many of them.

Why had the imperial troops failed to cut them down where they stood? It did not make sense. A single battalion should have been enough to quash the efforts of these ravagers.

When an elderly man tried to prevent one of the looters from decimating an abandoned stall, a lurching figure whipped out a sword and silenced him without warning or explanation. Angered by the looter's inexplicable cruelty, Kenshin stepped before the man, the setting sun momentarily blinding him, though his right hand grasped the hilt of his *katana*.

"Stand down," Kenshin demanded.

The lurching figure shifted into focus.

What Kenshin saw next caused the blood to drain from his face. The man's features were filthy. Distorted. He looked as though he were caught in a perpetual scream. The outline of a crest was visible on the front of the man's armor, but it was too covered in blood and dirt to discern which noble family he served.

The man—this looter—was a samurai.

And he was obviously not of his right mind.

The crazed warrior barreled toward Kenshin, his eyes filled with terror and his sword angled above his head. When Kenshin moved to disarm him, another mute creature flung herself closer, her bloodied fingers scratching through the air. Kenshin shoved her into a wooden wall, which splintered from the impact. The stench of her fetid breath washed over him, nearly causing him to be sick. Behind her followed a pack of barely human . . . things. Maniacal demons. They said nothing while they destroyed everything in sight. The wizened vendor of the oil stall shoved a rusted blade into the samurai's gut. The creature screamed, blood flowing from his stomach as he writhed on the ground, his strength starting to fade as the light fled his eyes.

So the demons could bleed. They could be injured, which meant some part of them still lived. But they were not whole. Something was fiercely wrong with their minds.

Kenshin had never witnessed mayhem before. He'd only heard of it in passing. This kind of mayhem wasn't like battle.

In battle you knew who to fight. You knew how to win, where to go. What to do. In a battle of honor—a battle between true samurai—there were no innocent bystanders. *Bushidō* did not permit it.

Up until this point, the chaos had unfurled slowly. Now it spiked to a feverish pitch. People ran every which way, their screams rending through the air as the lurching creatures— these poor souls bereft of their own minds—continued obliterating everything in their path. Kenshin flung shattered objects aside and unsheathed his blades. A part of him did not wish to cut down a creature in the throes of madness. He, too, had been guilty of losing his mind more than once in recent memory.

From the corner of his eye, Kenshin saw Yumi struggle with one of them—a man wearing mud-caked armor emblazoned with the crest of the Sugiura clan. The *maiko* ducked the fallen samurai's attempts to silence her, but he appeared to possess inhuman strength. The only weapon she brandished was a small dagger. Against folded steel.

Kenshin dodged a wooden sign as it flew through the air. He came up to Yumi's side just in time to parry a downward blow.

"Get out of here," he demanded to Yumi.

"I don't need your help, Hattori Kenshin."

Kenshin kicked the crazed warrior square in the chest, sending him careening backward into the stall of fine paper. Colorful pages flew everywhere, like leaves caught in a storm. Taking advantage of this distraction, Kenshin grabbed Yumi by the wrist and ran. They flew around one corner, then two, and still Kenshin did not stop. He kept the point of his sword angled downward, ready to engage in combat at any moment.

When he attempted to turn right, Yumi jerked his arm to the left. "This way."

Kenshin did not question her. They continued to fly across the packed earth. The length of silk Yumi had wrapped around her head blew into Kenshin's face, disorienting him.

He did not see her twist around to knock him off his feet until it was too late.

When Kenshin came to, he almost laughed. The knot on his head throbbed. His wrists were bound at his back. He sat in a darkened space that smelled of hay and dried dung. A horse stall from the look of it.

The point of the knife in his back did not surprise him. In truth, Kenshin hoped for precisely this outcome when he first set out to follow Yumi. He'd wanted her to lead him into a trap, so that he could meet face-to-face with the warrior who'd trained her. Kenshin had suspicions as to her teacher's identity.

And now it would finally be revealed.

"You have my attention, Lord Kenshin," a male voice growled from behind him. "What is it you want?"

"You've been busy, Lord Ranmaru," Kenshin shot back. "Especially for a boy who recently escaped the claws of death."

Laughter emanated nearby as a wooden gate slid open.

Yumi crossed toward them, a smile curling up one side of her face.

"Let the fierce Dragon of Kai go," she said. "After all, he did rescue me."

"Then I suppose my thanks are in order," the gruff voice replied.

Kenshin could hear the boy's amusement. The sound infuriated him. After Kenshin had assisted him that night beneath the castle—against his better judgment—this foul boy thought it wise to taunt him?

Insolent swine.

As soon as Kenshin's bonds were cut, he staggered to his feet. Yumi waved her small blade beneath his chin as a warning. His nostrils flaring, the Dragon of Kai whirled around to come face-to-face with . . .

. . . a boy who was not the son of Takeda Shingen.

"Where is Takeda Ranmaru?" Kenshin demanded, looking about. "Where is the leader of the Black Clan?"

The boy standing before him with the broad forehead and toothsome grin crossed his arms. Bowed with a flourish. "I'd like to make a deal with you. I will bring you the leader of the Black Clan." He paused as if in consideration. "In chains, if you like."

"In exchange for what?"

"You will send for your sister. She and I have important matters to discuss."

Kenshin glowered at him. "Who the hell do you—"

"Tell Mariko the nightbeast needs to see her. Now."

unmoored

---✳---

Mariko leapt from the *jinrikisha,* still garbed in her court finery, her feet flying as they raced toward Yumi's *okiya.*

A message had been delivered to Prince Raiden earlier this evening. Hattori Kenshin's condition had worsened following his drunken altercation in Hanami.

The beast of night had overtaken him.

It had been the work of an instant for Mariko to understand the message's hidden meaning. Immediately she'd asked Raiden to allow her to leave the castle so she might tend to her brother's needs, but her new husband had advised against it. Though the imperial troops had managed to keep the districts nearest to the city center free of looters, he did not think it wise to test their bounds. Only this morning, he'd admitted to Mariko that his brother's warriors functioned without direction. Absent the wisdom of a leader at their back.

It appeared nothing could drive the emperor to take action

on behalf of his people. Not even the threat of losing the imperial city. The death of Roku's mother had taken a heavy toll on him. Any protections put in place over the last few days had all been installed at the quiet behest of Raiden. And he would be unlikely to receive praise for it from his brother. Roku was still furious that Raiden had failed to apprehend Takeda Ranmaru. Even more furious that they were now confined to the castle, delaying the possibility of his vengeance even further. Mariko knew—at any instant—that the emperor could fly into an inexplicable rage. Lash out at anyone without reason.

But it was worth the risk of going to Hanami against her husband's advice.

Tsuneoki—the beast of night—was waiting at the teahouse to speak with her.

After Raiden had forbidden her from leaving the castle grounds, Mariko had gone to see his mother. Mariko had relayed the sad tale of Kenshin's recent misfortune, and Kanako had agreed to help her. Indeed she'd almost delighted in the chance to subvert the wishes of her son. With an easy smile, Kanako had led Mariko to an enchanted *maru* and shown her how to enter and exit the castle grounds without being noticed. She'd warned Mariko to return soon. Before Raiden realized his wife had gone missing.

Mariko rapped her knuckles against the gate of Yumi's *okiya*. As soon as her fist touched the wood, Kirin slid open the bolt to allow Mariko entrance.

"Where is he?" she asked the maidservant without preamble. She dropped her voice. "Where is the night-beast?"

Kirin bowed. "Please come with me, my lady."

Mariko removed her *zori*, and they glided through a court-yard lit on all four corners by hanging lanterns fashioned of hammered copper, toward the sliding doors leading to Yumi's personal bedchamber.

The moment she heard his gentle laughter, Mariko raced toward Tsuneoki and threw her arms around his neck. As soon as she'd done so, her face turned hot. She tried to pull away—after all, warriors did not show their emotions in such an exuberant manner—but Tsuneoki laughed again and held her tightly.

"Why did you come to Inako?" she asked him in an urgent whisper. "Every imperial guard in the city will be on the lookout for you. If you are caught, the emperor will—"

"I've heard." Tsuneoki grinned. "He will set fire to all I love and force me to watch as he murders my grandmother, my sister, my aunts, my cousins, anyone I hold dear."

Yumi arched an eyebrow. "Perhaps you should not be so flippant with a threat against my life."

"I've never been flippant with your life." Tsuneoki crossed his arms.

"So you say," Yumi muttered.

Pain crossed Tsuneoki's features. But he said nothing. It was strange for Mariko to witness this exchange. Strange for her to see the elegant *maiko* take on the role of a disgruntled younger sister. A role Mariko knew all too well. Tsuneoki inhaled with care as he considered his sister's expressionless face. Then he sighed and turned back to Mariko.

"Thank you for coming here so quickly," he began. "I need to speak with you about a plan we've devised."

"We?" Mariko glanced about.

"Ōkami and I."

Her pulse took flight. "Is he—"

"Ōkami wanted to come, but his injuries were too severe." When Tsuneoki saw the look on Mariko's face, he squeezed her hand. "Don't trouble yourself. He is on the mend and just as irritating as ever."

Mariko took a step back. "I . . . understand." Disappointment caused her shoulders to sag. She rebelled against it, forcing herself to stand tall. "What matters do you need to discuss with me?"

"Through Yumi's contacts here at the *okiya*, we've established communication with a senior advisor to the emperor. A man who has fond recollections of a time when Takeda Shingen protected the people of Wa. I wish to ask for your help in delivering him a message." Tsuneoki hesitated. "But it could be dangerous, Mariko. I want to warn you. There is no telling how the emperor might react if he learns of your involvement."

Mariko did not need to think twice. "Tell me what you need me to do, and I will do it."

Tsuneoki smiled. "I knew you would." He crooked his lips to one side, as though he were still weighing his next words.

"Is there something else you wished to discuss with me?" Mariko asked.

"Your brother would like to speak to you."

Mariko shook her head. "No. Tell Kenshin I wish him well. But I have no intention of seeing him. Nothing he could do or say would compel me otherwise."

At the harshness of Mariko's pronouncement, Yumi frowned. Tsuneoki's features turned circumspect. He said, "If I may, I think Lord Kenshin is—"

"I am not interested in hearing any excuses for his behavior. I tried to make him understand. And he mistreated me harshly for it. Kenshin believes these things are a matter of honor, and not of what is right. He cannot be trusted with anything I value."

"You are"—Tsnuneoki appeared to search for what to say—"not wrong, Mariko. But after hearing him speak, I do think there is something amiss with him. Something that is not his fault."

Yumi's eyes darkened. "Mariko, I'm afraid some misfortune has fallen upon Kenshin. Your brother does not remember things he's done, and it appears he loses control over his thoughts. I've sent for a healer to speak with him, but he's . . . quite troubled."

"Be that as it may, I no longer want to waste my time persuad him to change his mind. My brother wishes me to be somebody I am not. He's always wished it of me." Mariko's expression turned grim. "If any member of my family ever needs assistance, I will do whatever I can to provide it." She grasped the layers of light silk that made up her kimono. The worst kind of frippery. Fragile and impractical. "But I will not see Kenshin."

Tsuneoki bowed. "I understand," he said softly. "I will convey your wishes to him." With a sidelong glance at his sister, he left.

Yumi regarded Mariko. The sigh that passed the *maiko*'s lips was soul deep. "It was . . . difficult hearing what you said about your brother."

"It was difficult for me to say it." Mariko swallowed. "But it is my truth. Kenshin hurt me. Deeply. He believes in his ridiculous code of honor more than he does anything else."

Yumi nodded. "I've felt the same way about my brother for years. Yet—when I heard how unforgiving you were just now, how final it sounded—it wounded me. Not because I thought you were wrong, but because, for the first time, I thought about what this life must have been like for my brother." A furrow collected above Yumi's brow. "He loved Ōkami for years, you know."

"I know."

Yumi shook her head. "No. Not the love of a friend. More."

It took Mariko a moment to process Yumi's words. When she did, understanding warmed within her. It made sense. In the farthest reaches of memory, Mariko recalled the things

Tsuneoki had said to her about love during their first journey to Inako. About how he had suffered in love.

"I've always known this about Tsuneoki, even when we were children," Yumi said. "I only resented him so much because he chose Ōkami over me. Over and over again, he chose to be free rather than to remain with his family. But it must have been so difficult for my brother. To lose everything and still know there could be so much more you might have to suffer. Things no one else would ever think to suffer." Yumi turned toward the intricate folding screens. "It must have been so lonely for Tsuneoki," she said softly. "Maybe even lonelier than it was for me."

"Yumi—"

"I understand more than you know what it feels like to lose faith in your brother. It is something I struggle with every day of my life, as you've undoubtedly noticed." She reached for Mariko's hands. "You don't have to forgive Kenshin. But try to feel his pain, too. Suffering is never fair to anyone."

"I'm not sure it's possible for me to even begin understanding him." Mariko took a deep breath. "But I promise I will consider it."

"Good." Yumi smiled. "I promise I will try to do the same."

Mariko squeezed their grasped hands. "I should go, before anyone misses me."

"I understand," Yumi said. "Let me find Tsuneoki so that he can pass along the letter he wishes you to deliver."

"Of course." Mariko followed Yumi outside, beneath a small tunnel of wisteria, its pastel blossoms suffusing the air with a musky perfume. Yumi opened another set of sliding doors and led Mariko inside a smaller chamber that smelled of cedar and silk.

"Wait here," Yumi said. "I'll return soon."

"Thank you."

"Of course." The *maiko* floated away like a swan, a knowing smile on her face.

Mariko glanced around the darkened chamber. It was simple and clean. A place in which Yumi displayed many of her most precious kimono, on cedar stands meant to keep wrinkles at bay. These garments were most likely gifts from wealthy men attempting to entice her into choosing them as her benefactor.

Mariko paused at one. Studied the herons as they glided across the golden silk.

"That one is hideous," a voice murmured from behind her. "It reminds me of death."

She turned. "Oh." The word fell from her lips. Immediately she regretted it.

I sound like a fool.

Determined to overcome her misstep, Mariko moved toward Ōkami with the intention of embracing him. But she halted in her tracks. Threaded her hands together. Let her awkwardness and uncertainty win out.

How do I embrace the boy I love after I've willingly married another?

Ōkami smiled as though he could hear her thoughts. Her eyes drank him in as he shifted before her. Most people would not have noticed—for he did an admirable job of concealing it—but Mariko knew his movements still caused him pain.

Even absent any light, it was clear bruises lingered on his face. One eye was still swollen. But as soon as he drew close, Ōkami's features curled upward in a teasing fashion. "After all we've been through together—after all the lectures you've sent my way—don't I deserve more than that?"

"I . . . am not sure what you mean."

His black eyes danced with feeling. "Truly?"

It wasn't an innocent question. Nothing Ōkami ever said was innocent.

Mariko cleared her throat. The happiness she felt at seeing him alive—at seeing him free—made it difficult for her to find the right words. "No. I mean, yes. I mean . . . there is much I would like to say. Much I would like to do." She cleared her throat again.

"Such as?"

"I'd—I'd like to run away with you," she whispered. "Right now. And never turn back."

Ōkami lowered his voice to match hers. "I'd like that as well. Where would we go?"

"To the coast perhaps?"

"On a ship taking us far away from this cursed place."

Mariko frowned. "Of course you would wish to leave." She did not hide her disappointment.

"I did wish it before." Ōkami paused, his expression soft. Searching. "But not anymore."

Surprise flashed across her features. "You would stay in Inako if given the choice? Even after everything you've lost?" Mariko waited for him to vacillate. To equivocate or make a joke, as he usually did. To her shock, Ōkami nodded without hesitation.

"Why?" she asked. "What made you change your mind?"

"My mind hasn't changed. It's only unearthed a truth." He took a careful breath. "The measure of any life is not in greatness. But in goodness."

"And you wish to be good?"

Ōkami's laugh was warm. "For now." His expression sobered. "But I would choose otherwise if you truly wished to leave. I would go anywhere with you."

"And I would go anywhere with you," she replied. "But I must stay. I must return to the castle. Tsuneoki asked me to help him."

"I know." All signs of amusement faded from his features. "I hate that we're sending you back to the castle." Ōkami grimaced. "Back to . . . him."

Mariko inclined her head in consideration. "Raiden is not what I expected. Not good. But not what I expected."

Ōkami stepped closer to her. Close enough to touch. Mariko's entire being ached for him to reach out so that she could feel the warmth of his skin. Breathe the warm stone and wood smoke of his hair. But she knew if she touched him now it would only bring her pain. There was so much for them both to accomplish. So much for them to lose.

A light flared in Ōkami's eyes. "Has he . . ." The muscles in his neck tightened as though anger had stolen his breath. "Has he treated you with respect?"

"Yes."

Ōkami inhaled through his nose. "I am glad to hear it."

"He—" Mariko looked through a fringe of lashes to meet his gaze. "Raiden has been strangely kind to me."

Ōkami's brows shot up. "Though I cannot fathom the possibility, perhaps there's hope for him yet."

"Perhaps." Mariko smiled wistfully into the darkness. "Why does this feel so odd?" she asked. "Why do I feel so . . . at a loss?"

"It feels odd to me because everything I want to say— everything I want to do—seems impossible."

Frustration took hold around her heart. "Is it because I am married?"

"I don't give a damn about you being married."

"Oh," Mariko said again. The feeling in his voice—the way the words rasped from his throat with such conviction— unmoored her. "Is it because I must lie about owing loyalty to the family of Minamoto Roku?"

"You owe no man anything, Mariko."

"Especially not a man such as he." Mariko scowled. "Regardless, I will never be one of those ladies at court who worships a man."

"No matter the man?" Ōkami joked. "Even if he worshipped you?"

"No," Mariko said. "Not even for you."

Ōkami grinned. They fell to silence. Not a searching kind of silence, but a silence filled with many things that could not be said. Things that would only cause them both pain. Dreams that might never come to pass. A part of Mariko wished she could simply run away with Ōkami now. This moment. Turn her back on everyone and everything, to start a new life with the boy she loved.

But the things she'd done—all that she'd fought for and experienced—had proven to her that life was about more than this. More than love. A life absent purpose was not a life Mariko wished to live. Even if she perished while trying to help the Black Clan—even if she lost Ōkami in the process—they both needed to continue this fight.

"I should go," Mariko said. "Tsuneoki still needs to give me the message, and if I am gone too long from court, I will be missed."

Ōkami said nothing. He ran a hand through his unbound hair, and the familiarity of the motion sent a twinge through Mariko's chest. Then he met her gaze once more.

"Thank you for saving me, Mariko."

A tentative grin touched her lips. "Thank you for letting yourself be saved."

"I am glad I was able to see you tonight," he said softly.

Something knifed next to her heart. "As am I." With that,

Mariko gathered the silken folds of her kimono and made her way toward the sliding doors.

It had been such a strange interaction. So unlike the ease of all their times together in the past. Never before had there been so much feeling between them and no way to express it.

No. That's not true.

Mariko turned back. "I love you. Never forget that." With that, she reached for the sliding door.

Ōkami caught her hand. When she met his gaze, he refused to look away. He threaded his fingers through hers. Pulled her close, his eyes gentle, his expression fierce. Then—as if he could not resist—he stroked a thumb along her jaw.

Mariko melted against him. Felt her body mold to his. She'd heard before that foolish people were burned when they toyed with fire. Perhaps Mariko was a fool who did not care about being burned. For just this moment, she wanted to be consumed in this delicious pain. She leaned into his caress. But she didn't dare touch him herself. If she did, Mariko knew there would be no way to let go.

"Will you do something for me?" Ōkami asked.

She looked up. Nodded as one of his hands settled on the side of her face.

"I want to hear you call me by my given name," he said. "Just once."

Mariko's eyes drifted to the exposed skin of his neck. To the horrible brand inked into its side. Then back up to his scarred lips.

Loyalty.

"I love you, Takeda Ranmaru."

Ōkami smiled. Pressed a kiss to her forehead. Then the tip of her nose. Then the underside of her chin. Mariko gasped at how gently he moved.

"Right now, I cannot love you as I want," he whispered against her skin. "So let me worship you for a breath of time."

Mariko closed her eyes. Her hands trembled.

"Tell me to stop, and I will," he said.

"No," Mariko breathed. She felt his fingertips drag along the collar of her kimono. He brushed aside the fabric to reveal the hollow at her throat. When he kissed her there—again so softly—Mariko's fingers turned into fists. In that moment, she could not think of anything she wanted more than to touch him.

He let the back of his hand skim over the layers of fabric gathered at Mariko's waist. Then he knelt at her feet and took hold of her ankle, exposing the skin of her leg. Ōkami pressed another kiss on the inside of her knee.

"Tell me to stop, and I will." His voice slid over her like silk.

Mariko opened her eyes. She knew she should tell him to stop. Knew that she'd already allowed things to progress too far. She had important things to do. Tasks that required her utmost focus. She could not afford this distraction. If she did not leave Hanami soon, Raiden might discover her duplicity.

"No," Mariko said quietly. Clearly. "I don't want you to stop."

Just this once.

Ōkami kissed higher. The feeling of his lips on her thigh sent a frisson of warmth through her body. A delicious shiver curled up her spine.

"Never worship any man, Hattori Mariko." Ōkami steadied her. "But always be worshipped." When he moved again, time slowed to a stutter, then sped forward in a rush.

Mariko closed her eyes and tangled her fingers in his hair. "Yes."

The First to Die

---✳---

The heavenly sovereign of Wa sat on the Chrysanthemum Throne beneath a silken canopy, his eyes bloodshot, his face wan. Even deep within the walls of the Golden Castle, the wails at the gates could still be heard.

The pleas.

The cries for pity.

Yesterday one of the barriers protecting the center of Inako had been breached. In the aftermath, the main thoroughfare of Hanami had been ransacked. Many imperial guards had been sacrificed trying to secure the district. Though they'd been successful, the truth of their predicament had become inescapable to those within the walls of Heian Castle: their city was being rampaged by looters who moved about without signs of feeling, like the walking dead. Some had begun to say they were cursed. That a demon had overtaken them.

The same demon that had plagued the people of the eastern domains for the last few weeks.

And now these creatures were days—perhaps even hours—from storming the castle gates.

"My sovereign," pleaded one of the emperor's most senior advisors—a man who had served the late emperor for the entirety of his reign. "We must do something. I have been forbidden from leaving the castle grounds. The last message I received from my family was two days ago. I do not know if they are safe."

Another advisor to the emperor—one whose daughter had been all but tossed from court the night of the dowager empress's death—continued. "We cannot let the people's pleas go unanswered, my sovereign." His attempts to impart sympathy into his tone were weak at best.

"Then you go out there and help them, Lord Shimazu," Roku said coldly. "They say a plague has ravaged the minds of the looters, and you wish me to add to their ranks by sending my imperial guards into the city?" He stood. "Will you be the one to guard me then? Will you offer your life in exchange for mine?"

Lord Shimazu bowed low, his face draining of color. His pride had undoubtedly been wounded by his daughter's expulsion from court, but he knew better than to continue challenging the emperor.

Raiden watched the scene unfold with a look of supreme detachment. Beneath the surface, unease coiled through his stomach. But there was little he could do. It had been enough for him to persuade Roku to hold an audience with his advisors, who'd been imploring Raiden for the last five days to do something. Anything.

Following the death of his mother, Roku had retreated to his rooms. He'd become even more paranoid, insisting that his food be tested by five people before he would even consider letting it touch his lips. The only times he called for Raiden were the moments he wished to rail at someone.

He'd screamed at Raiden just this morning. "How have you still not learned the location of the Black Clan? Why is Takeda Ranmaru still free to wander the empire?"

True to form, Raiden had said nothing to defend himself. Done nothing. He'd spared the last of his saving grace to organize this audience.

And it was falling apart before his eyes.

"Answer me, Lord Shimazu," Roku demanded. "What would you do if you were emperor? Would you go among the people with your hands outstretched, letting them rip the very clothes from your back? What if I let you go in my stead?" His eyes gleamed, and the hint of madness in their depths turned Raiden's blood cold.

In the far corner—just beyond the series of open screens leading into the throne room—a group of ladies gathered following their afternoon stroll. Mariko and her single courtier—a young woman named Hirata Suke—knelt to one side.

Wishing to put an end to this madness, if even for a

moment, Raiden stood. "Lord Shimazu, how dare you criticize your heavenly sovereign. Be gone from this audience at once, for the next word you speak could be your last."

Lord Shimazu trembled in his silks at Raiden's cruel tone. Nevertheless, he bowed deeply. As he took his leave, the look he sent Raiden was one of unmistakable gratitude.

Raiden kept his expression cool. Composed. Detached. He sat down once more under the watchful gaze of his emperor.

"Don't think I am ignorant to what it is you do, brother," Roku said quietly. "You cannot spare every fool from my justice."

Raiden bowed his head, his eyes locked on the floor. "I live to serve my emperor. Nothing more."

Roku snorted. Then returned his attention to his waiting advisors. "Is there anyone else with guidance they wish to offer their heavenly sovereign?"

The sound of heavy silence descended on the space. Even the ladies of court seated outside ceased with their whispers. It appeared none of those in attendance had the gall to posit a single inquiry.

"My sovereign?" a thin voice rang out from the back of the room. It was followed by the careful shuffle of the eldest advisor to the emperor. He was the grandfather of Mariko's courtier, Hirata Suke. "May I speak?" His back was hunched, his body thin. But his gaze did not waver.

"Lord Hirata." Roku's eyes narrowed. "Please step forward."

With careful steps, Lord Hirata made his way toward the

foot of the Chrysanthemum Throne. "My sovereign, as you know, I have been an advisor on matters of communication throughout the empire for the last thirty years."

Roku waited. His fingers tapped on his bolstered armrests.

"And"—Lord Hirata reached into his shirtsleeve—"I received a most interesting message this morning." He unfolded a piece of *washi* paper.

"What is it?" Roku asked.

No one else present could feel it as keenly as Raiden did, but he sensed—in his bones—the threat lurking beneath Roku's pleasant tone. It almost brought Raiden to his feet. Lord Hirata was an elderly man. One who'd served their father loyally, despite his sadness at the deaths of Takeda Shingen and Asano Naganori. Lord Hirata did not deserve to bear the full brunt of Roku's wrath.

"Would you like for me to read the message, my sovereign?" Lord Hirata asked.

From his periphery, Raiden could see Mariko's courtier shift with unease. He watched Mariko place a hand on Hirata Suke's arm in reassurance.

Roku's voice turned quiet. "No, Lord Hirata. I would not. Simply convey to me the crux of the message."

Lord Hirata paused. Then his features gathered with conviction. "It is a letter from the son of Takeda Shingen."

The entire court took in a breath. The air around Raiden stilled.

Roku laughed as though he were delighted. "And what does the traitor have to say?"

"He offers his condolences on the passing of our heavenly sovereign's parents. Though he suspects you will not believe him, he wishes to reassure you that he had nothing to do with their deaths."

Roku leaned forward, his eyes bright. "Go on."

"And he offers his assistance in helping to quell the . . . unrest within the imperial city."

"His assistance?" Roku eased back, steepling his hands beneath his chin. "How does he suggest going about this?"

"He says that he does not need to come near the castle. That he has no designs on the throne. But he has under his command a force of over a thousand men. If you would disburse an equal number of soldiers—or perhaps rally your vassals from the west—then it might be enough to control the spread of violence. He will begin on the outskirts of Inako. He suggests that you start near the castle. Then the looters can be corralled between both your forces." Lord Hirata took an unsteady step forward. "If you are amenable to his suggestion, he asks that you light the signal fire on the ramparts of Heian Castle."

Roku nodded. "This sounds wholly reasonable, does it not, Lord Hirata?"

Lord Hirata blinked. "I—I am not certain, my sovereign. I only wished to convey his request."

Roku stood.. "It seems entirely reasonable for me to allow a band of assassins and thieves—the ones responsible for my father's murder, my mother's murder—into *my* city, bearing arms, does it not?"

When Lord Hirata looked Raiden's way—seeking a measure of reassurance—Raiden shook his head almost imperceptibly. Implored him to say nothing more.

A shadow crossed the elderly man's face. As though he were supremely disappointed. "It is not up for me to make a judgment, my sovereign." Lord Hirata bowed. "It is only my duty to deliver you this message."

Roku nodded. Another moment passed in heavy silence.

"You will be the first to die today," the emperor said softly.

A gasp emanated from a corner near the entrance of the long room. Mariko's courtier clutched both hands over her mouth. Her brow creasing with concern, Mariko stood suddenly.

Raiden's heart missed a beat.

She should not have stood.

But it was too late. Roku's attention was already caught by Mariko's movements.

"Please, dear sister, step forward," Roku said, his voice eerily pleasant. "I see you have something you wish to say."

"No," Suke gasped. She clutched at Mariko's arm. "My lady—"

Mariko shook her off. Moved into the throne room. Every step she took, Raiden's heart pounded faster. Panic tingled across his skin. He tried to admonish her with a look—to drive her back—but she did not return his gaze. Not once. She paced the entire length of the throne room, her head high, her sight unwavering.

"Please"—Roku gestured for her to move even closer—"share with me your thoughts, as my dear brother's wife."

Mariko bowed low. "Please do not execute Lord Hirata, my sovereign. He is not responsible for sending this letter. He has only delivered a message."

"Ah, how considerate of you," Roku said with a bright smile. "You do not wish an elderly man to perish simply for doing his job."

Mariko bowed again. "Yes, my sovereign."

"So if he is not responsible for delivering this insult, then who is?"

Wisely, Raiden's wife chose to say nothing.

"I find it interesting," Roku said, his reedy voice carrying throughout the space, "how the daughter of Hattori Kano always seems to be part of any conversation involving the son of Takeda Shingen."

Mariko blinked.

Roku snorted. "Brother, it appears your wife has been disloyal to you."

Color flooded Mariko's features. "My sovereign—"

"I always suspected she was in league with Takeda Ranmaru," Roku said, his smile slicing across his skin. "But how mortifying for you to discover her infidelity in such a public manner."

Raiden kept his features flat. He did not even dare to look Mariko's way.

"It seems my brother's wife wishes to offer herself in exchange for Lord Hirata," Roku announced, his eyes gleaming. "Is that the case, you treacherous whore?"

Mariko flinched, but held her chin high. She wet her lips. Swallowed. "Yes, my lord."

"Very well," Roku said. "Put her in chains and have her placed beneath the castle to await my judgment." He turned toward Raiden. "That is—of course—if my brother has no objections."

Raiden sat utterly still. Still enough that he could count the beats of his heart.

He said nothing.

Just like with Lord Hirata, a look of profound sadness passed over Mariko's face.

The entire court watched as imperial soldiers shackled Hattori Mariko and led her from the audience room. When Lord Hirata took a step in her direction as though to stop them, she held up a hand, silencing his efforts.

The stately elder man bowed to her. The ladies of the court watched, their eyes wide, their hair ornaments trembling. Around the room, several advisors to the emperor stole glances at each other, weariness weighing their every motion.

Once Mariko was gone, Roku moved from his throne. Emerged from beneath the silken canopy. He smiled broadly as he gazed about the room, meeting the faces of his most trusted advisors. Those who had served his father—served his family—for generations.

His attention settled on Lord Hirata, who still waited in the same place before the throne, his features vexed. A deep sorrow hovering about the space.

Roku moved toward him. Lord Hirata bowed.

The moment the elderly man stood, Roku slid a small blade across the elderly man's throat.

Lord Hirata's hands covered the wound, blood spurting from between his fingers, a shocked expression on his face. Roku pried his advisor's hands away so that the blood cascaded down the front of Lord Hirata's elegant robe, staining it darkest crimson. When the man fell to his knees, Roku lifted his bloodied hands to his face. Studied the bright color glistening between his fingertips.

A muted scream arose from the end of the audience room. Two ladies of the court fainted. The rest of the advisors took to their feet, their features aghast.

Without a word, Roku returned to his throne.

"You are dismissed," he pronounced.

All the while, Raiden sat rigidly in place, the last of his hope dwindling to nothingness.

my sovereign

———✦———

Raiden could not sleep. No matter where he looked, he saw the image of Lord Hirata's face, mired in sadness. Felt the pain of his failures. And he could not avoid the stark truth:

Mariko was not where she should be.

He glared at the ceiling. It was not his fault. He had not been the one to take a stand against his brother in such a public fashion. Raiden had tried to warn her. He was not culpable for Mariko's stubbornness. The girl was as headstrong as an ox.

But that feeling of wrongness gnawed at Raiden until he could bear it no longer.

The death of Lord Hirata was the final blow to Roku's fragile hold on reality. In the aftermath, the emperor fled the throne room. He'd screamed to all those present, saying if a single one of them stepped forward—thought to challenge him in any way—he would kill each and every one of them. Stain the floors red with their blood.

Now he was nowhere to be found.

Once the moon had reached its apex, Raiden left his chamber to resume the search for his brother. They needed to mend what Roku had broken today, or their family risked losing the support of the nobility. He made his way through the darkness, two of the most trusted members of the *yabusame* at his back. When he did not find Roku anywhere in the emperor's private chambers, he took to searching the Lotus Pavilion, the place where Roku's mother perished.

He found an oil lantern in the center of the dowager empress's floor, its contents still warm.

But no sign of his brother.

A thought entered Raiden's mind. He left the Lotus Pavilion and crossed the nightingale floors toward the entrance of the castle's underbelly. At the top of the stairs, he stopped. Then turned toward the two soldiers in his shadow.

"Stand guard by the dowager empress's chambers," Raiden said under his breath. "If the emperor arrives, watch over him, but do nothing that might upset him. Say nothing. The first chance you get, send word to me."

The two members of the *yabusame* bowed in tandem. One of them looked Raiden squarely in the eye. "My lord?"

Raiden waited.

The soldier continued. "Forgive me for offering my opinion without being asked, but I worry for your safety."

"Do not worry for my safety," Raiden said. "Worry for the safety of your sovereign."

The two soldiers exchanged a look. One whose meaning

could hardly be mistaken.

"Do as you are commanded," Raiden said in a harsh tone.

They hesitated for an instant before they bowed again, taking their leave.

Once they were out of sight, Raiden descended into the bowels of Heian Castle. The stench there had taken on a life of its own. He tried not to dwell on all the images it conjured as he proceeded toward the cells. Toward a place that shaped the worst of his recent nightmares.

His wife calmly sat behind the iron bars, her finery soiled beyond repair. They had not chained her as they had Takeda Ranmaru. Someone had thought to provide her with an evening meal, though Raiden was certain his brother would not be pleased to learn of it. At Mariko's feet sat an untouched bowl of rice and a chipped vessel of water.

Distress tore through Raiden's body like a caged beast fighting to be set free. He could unlock the cell if he wished. He and Roka possessed the only two keys. But that action would be in direct defiance of the emperor. It was enough that Raiden had lied so many times to protect his new wife. Enough that he'd tried to shield her in secret, just as he had with the young courtiers the night of the dowager empress's death. Just as he had with Lord Shimazu earlier today. It was not his fault that Mariko languished in filth, likely awaiting her own death. Her fate was sealed the moment she challenged Roku.

As Raiden took in the sight of her predicament, he attempted to appear dispassionate. In truth, his emotions were far from unaffected. His heart thundered in his chest, and the blood coursed through his veins as though a fire raged beneath his skin.

"My lord," Mariko said in a cool tone.

"Has my brother been here?" Raiden asked. "Has he come to . . . see you?"

Mariko smiled. "No. The emperor has not come to taunt me. Yet."

Raiden almost admonished Mariko for her disrespect. But some part of him rebelled at the notion. Rebelled at its truth. "You are certain?"

"If Roku intended to torment me tonight, I believe he would have made his presence known, my lord. He isn't the type to work in half measures."

She wasn't wrong. Roku did enjoy watching his quarry squirm beneath his stare.

Raiden took a deep breath and immediately regretted it. The stench of burnt flesh was almost unbearable. "Is there something else you wish to eat?" He glanced at the porcelain bowl of untouched food. "Or perhaps to drink?"

"You're trying to help me?" Mariko curved an eyebrow his way. "Now, of all times?"

Raiden frowned. He did not appreciate her censure. "Of course I am."

"Forgive me, my lord, but I think you're trying to help

yourself."

The heat running through Raiden's veins caused his face to flush.

"I don't mind if you're trying to help yourself, Raiden. As long as you also help others," Mariko said softly. "It means some part of you feels guilty. Some part of you knows how wrong this is."

Raiden studied her a moment. Found himself admiring her honesty. "Perhaps I am trying help myself," he admitted.

"Then it's possible I wasn't wrong about you. It's possible the soldiers who led me to this cell were right."

"What are you talking about?"

"They told me to appeal to you for mercy. That you quietly spared those who'd fallen into the path of your brother's rage in recent days. And maybe you would offer me the same consideration."

"I am not merciful, Lady Mariko."

"Not too long ago I would have agreed with you." Mariko paused. "But now I am not so certain."

Raiden bit down on nothing. She was inexorable, that was for certain. "Why did you offer yourself in exchange for a man so near to death?"

"Because if no one cares about what is right or wrong in the seat of our empire—the very seat of our justice—then all we hold dear is lost."

Again, his young bride spoke the truth. It only caused Raiden even more consternation. "You were foolish to challenge Roku."

"And you were foolish to let him rule without question."

Anger spiked through Raiden's core. "I am not responsible for Roku's actions."

"Your passivity gives him leave to act like a monster. If you allow a monster to destroy everything in its path, then you are no better than the monster, Raiden."

Raiden tried to leash his desire to yell at her. His wish to prove her wrong. "I do not need to be lectured by a woman on such important matters."

"Yes, you do. In fact, I think you need to be lectured every day of your life, preferably by a woman." Mariko took a breath. "You are nothing like Roku. I suspect much of that is a result of your mother. The lectures of a woman have made you a far better man than your brother will ever be. They would have made you a far better ruler."

"Your words are treasonous."

"And correct," she said quietly.

"Don't lecture me about being correct, Mariko. You knew that Takeda Ranmaru had sent a message to Roku. I watched you today. The death of Lord Hirata is on your hands."

Mariko blanched. Pain flashed across her features. "He is dead?"

"Yes." Raiden swallowed around the sudden knot in his throat.

"If it helps you, I accept the blame," Mariko said sadly. "I will gladly die for it."

"If you die, it won't be for that. It will be because you were in league with the Black Clan, as Roku always suspected." Another spark of fury rippled through Raiden's chest. "You've been in love with Takeda Ranmaru all along."

"Yes."

"You do not deny it."

"I have no wish to deny it. What purpose would that serve?" Mariko met his gaze. "Now that Ōkami has begun to understand who he truly is—who he might one day become—he will be a fine leader. Just like you would be, too."

The bluntness of her words unseated Raiden. Made him lose focus. "Enough of your poison."

"It is not poison, Raiden. It is the truth." Mariko reached for the chipped vessel of water beside her feet. Then—without warning—she hurled it at the stone wall behind her.

It chipped further. But it did not break.

"Do you know why that silly piece of pottery managed to survive?" Mariko asked.

"Because you did not throw it hard enough."

"No." She sighed. "In order for it to be hard enough to survive, it had to become strong. It had to be stepped on as clay. Shaped beneath the dutiful hand of a potter. And after all that, it had to live through a fire."

Raiden listened to her speak, his gaze piercing.

Mariko continued. "You have lived through fire, Minamoto Raiden. You are stronger than you know. Everyone sees it but you."

"You are mistaken." Even to Raiden's ears, his voice sounded uncertain. But he refused to allow this girl to seed even one more wild notion in his mind. So he spoke his barest truth. "I have no desire to rule this empire."

Her smile curved upward sadly. "Which is exactly why you should."

Raiden was startled from a troubled slumber at daybreak. Outside his chamber stood the two soldiers from the night prior, as well as Lord Shimazu. Their features were tight with worry. Wordlessly, Raiden followed them to the Lotus Pavilion.

Roku was seated on the floor of his mother's chamber, burning pages of used *washi* paper above the flame of an oil lantern. His eyes were bloodshot. His lips were cracked. After Raiden took in the sight, he turned to face the other men.

"We are worried he will set himself aflame, my lord," Lord Shimazu said in a barely audible tone.

Roku muttered something to himself. But he did not break away from his task.

After a moment of consideration, Raiden spoke. "Bring pails of water. Keep them just outside the chamber. Stand watch over him." With that, he drew the doors partially closed.

As Raiden began walking from the Lotus Pavilion, a voice at his back halted him in his tracks.

"What do we do about the looters, my lord?" Lord Shimazu wrung his hands, distress forming creases around his mouth.

"We are no longer able to bring supplies into the city. Soon the creatures will be at the very gates of the castle. We can no longer afford to be idle."

Raiden stared at Lord Shimazu. It should not be his decision. It was not his responsibility. But if he left everything to his brother, the entire city would fall to ruin. There were not many options left to them. If they'd only sent word for their vassals from the east to rally toward them, perhaps something could be done about the situation. But now?

It seemed their most distasteful choice had become Raiden's only option. The force Takeda Ranmaru commanded remained on the outskirts of the city, awaiting a signal fire along the ramparts of Heian Castle.

If Raiden did this and worked alongside the son of Takeda Shingen to restore order to Inako, Roku might kill him. He'd never before considered it possible. But his brother was not the same boy who'd hidden sweets in his sleeve and participated in archery drills with Raiden, even when he'd been too small to wield a bow.

Those days had passed. And if Raiden ever wished for there to be more—for his city to survive this scourge—it was time for him to worry less about what might happen to him and focus more on the people wailing at the gates.

His people.

"Lord Shimazu, I want you to gather two of your most trusted samurai," Raiden directed. "Tell them to meet me on the ramparts of Heian Castle."

"Then you intend to—"

"Do as you are told, Lord Shimazu. I will listen to any question—any grievance you have—later today."

Lord Shimazu bowed low. "My sovereign."

Raiden frowned. "I am not your sovereign, Lord Shimazu. It is treason for you to suggest otherwise."

"Of course." Lord Shimazu bowed again. "I spoke in error. My deepest apologies."

But Raiden could not ignore the relief that passed across Lord Shimazu's features.

The same relief he felt in his soul.

Kanako floated in her sleep, fending off her exhaustion. She'd been far too tired to venture from her chambers today, though she wished to seek out Raiden. She made inquiries as to his whereabouts—even sent her swallow to trail after him—but her son was too occupied trying to protect the ransacked imperial city. The same city Kanako had filled this morning with her remaining "distractions." The poor souls—the innocent, the elderly, the infirm—that would serve to unbridle Roku's imperial soldiers. Cause them to lose focus.

They were so close. Kanako was so close to achieving her goals.

Earlier today, she had asked her little swallow—her tiniest spy—to flutter around the castle, eavesdropping as it always had, even for Masaru. It returned to tell her that Roku had murdered his most senior advisor in cold blood. The nobility was on the cusp of rebelling against him.

And Raiden was fast becoming a source of strength for all of them.

Unbridled joy took hold of Kanako's heart, even as she struggled to deny the toll of her efforts. All else was proceeding according to plan. The many bands of looters she'd sent into Inako continued wreaking their havoc. The distractions were already creating even more sources of discord within the imperial ranks.

But Kanako still struggled to regain her strength. These tasks were far more taxing than she'd thought they would be. Her food sat beside her untouched. But it did not matter. Soon her son would have all that she'd dreamed for him. She only needed to continue her efforts a short while longer.

Never mind that it might cause irrevocable damage to her health.

Never mind that she struggled to control the last band of looters she'd sent into Hanami.

Everything worthwhile in life came with a sacrifice.

And Death always collected its due.

Bitter Relief

✳

I fear the only way to stop them is to kill them all," Tsuneoki said, his face smeared with blood and soot.

"You can't kill them all," Yumi argued. "They are not of their right minds." While she spoke, she tucked her daggers into their sheaths. "The best we can do is hope to immobilize them."

"I don't think their right minds matter as long as they continue murdering indiscriminately," Ōkami said. "But Yumi is right. Some of them are elderly. I saw at least five of these desperate creatures who could be no more than ten years of age. Children." His expression turned grim. "We cannot kill them."

"Of course not," Haruki said as he struck the soot from his *kosode*. It swelled around him like a dark cloud, but he did not seem troubled by it. As a metalsmith, he often worked around burning things.

Smoke from the fires in the Iwakura ward continued billowing all around them, blocking out the light of the sun. Many people had fled the city. The vassals Minamoto Raiden had requested from the east were dispatched two days ago, but most of them had yet to arrive. And the maddened creatures set on destroying the imperial city appeared to be endless in quantity. It was impossible to know where they came from. Where they meant to go next.

Or how to stop them.

Despite these many hindrances, the men marching beneath the banner of the Black Clan—four diamonds inspired by the crest of the Toyotomi clan—managed to secure the Iwakura ward and another smaller ward beside it. They barricaded the streets with broken furniture and started strategic fires to prevent the creatures from encroaching once more on the fortified space.

Ōkami mopped the sweat from his brow. Soon the men would need to rally and reassemble. There was far more work to be done.

"We will move along to the next ward in two hours," Ōkami directed. "Tell the men not posted along the barricades to rest. Take in some nourishment. It will be a long night."

"My lord," Yumi said with a bow. She swung into the saddle of a waiting stallion and dug her heels into its side.

"If I'd only known enough to put a stop to this," Tsuneoki said in a rueful tone as he watched his sister gallop away. "She deserves better than a bloody battlefield."

"Who are you to decide what she deserves?" Ōkami eyed him sidelong. "If you'd tried to stop her, you would have failed. And it would have been glorious to behold."

Haruki laughed softly.

Before Tsuneoki could retort, a rider emerged from the rising smoke, racing toward them at full speed. Shock flared through Ōkami when he recognized the insignia emblazoned on the samurai's armor. Hattori Kenshin did not wait for his horse to stop before dismounting. "Prince Raiden requests an audience with you." His chest heaved as he spoke. "The fighting around the castle has gotten worse. We need your help."

Ōkami pushed through the fleeing crowds, trying his best to keep his horse calm. Panic had driven the wealthiest members of the city to throw items of value in carts, wheelbarrows. There was no thought to their movements. Only terror.

It was a risk, coming here. Ōkami saw the look on Tsuneoki's face when Hattori Kenshin had asked.

If he rode to meet the son of Minamoto Masaru, death would be sure to follow. The last time a member of the Minamoto clan had met with the head of the Takeda clan, Ōkami's father was bound in chains and ordered to take his own life.

But there had been many opportunities in the last few days for Ōkami to shy away from his responsibilities. He refused to allow his fear of Prince Raiden's fury to take control of him.

Especially when the son of Minamoto Masaru had much to fear as well.

When Ōkami arrived at the post nearest to the castle—an odd settlement of makeshift tents with weapons strewn about in haphazard piles—he was surprised further by Hattori Kenshin's behavior. His awkward deference. Once Ōkami had dismounted, Kenshin bowed quickly, granting Ōkami the immediate position of authority. Only days before, the Dragon of Kai had taunted him from his cell. Then offered him the means to free himself. Perhaps this was how Minamoto Raiden intended to lure Ōkami to his demise. By sending along someone he thought Ōkami might trust.

Kenshin paused just outside the largest tent, the canvas flaps at the entrance fluttering in a sooty breeze.

"You will need to leave your blades here, Lord Takeda," Kenshin said.

"No," Ōkami replied without the slightest hesitation. "I will not."

Kenshin sighed. "Mariko said you—"

"Is Mariko here?" Ōkami wrapped a hand around the hilt of his *katana*.

Kenshin shook his head, a worrisome look passing across his features. "No. She is not." He narrowed his eyes. "It is one of the reasons I have requested your blades."

The Dragon of Kai was deliberately concealing something from Ōkami, which raised his suspicions even further.

"Where is Mariko?"

"Prince Raiden will tell you."

"You are not accompanying me?"

"I have a task to which I must attend," Kenshin said. He frowned, then dipped his head in a bow. "I will ask once more for you to relinquish your weapons."

"And I will refuse a final time."

Kenshin sighed, then pushed open the flap of the tent. After the Dragon of Kai had departed, Ōkami stepped into a round room filled with the smell of iron and ash.

The prince hovered over a map in its center, marking through territory and listening to a frazzled runner offer updates. As soon as the flap fell, Raiden glanced up at Ōkami. It was difficult for Ōkami to miss the flash of emotion that passed across Raiden's features. Difficult to identify its source. A knot pulled tightly in Ōkami's chest. A fear he did not wish to dwell upon. His memories were awash with the pain of their last encounter. It was a strange feeling for Ōkami. To hate someone with such fire and know all at once that his death would bring Ōkami no solace. That—in order for them to survive— his hatred would need to become a thing of the past.

Perhaps this was what the son of Minamoto Masaru wrestled with in his own heart, too.

"You requested my presence," Ōkami said to Raiden. He did not bow. His right hand remained on the hilt of his *katana*. A fact which did not go unnoticed by the prince.

"My runners tell me you've successfully secured the Iwakura ward," Raiden began without preamble.

"We have," Ōkami said. The sound of Raiden's voice caused the rage to simmer beneath his skin. The memories were still too sharp.

But Ōkami would not flinch. Nor would he succumb.

Raiden stared at him. For a moment, he seemed to falter. As though he, too, was at a loss for how to behave in Ōkami's presence. "Do you have any suggestions for how we can bring about the same outcome in the rest of the city?" the prince asked. "What directives did you pass along to your men? I've tried to move about in a grid pattern, but as soon as I gain a foothold in one, I lose it in another."

Ōkami inhaled slowly to allow the ghost of his pain to break free. "We barricaded the main streets. Took the furniture from any homes there and piled them up until they were twice as high as a warrior. The people of the Iwakura ward assisted us."

"How did you rally them to help you?"

"We asked." Ōkami almost smiled. "Well, Tsuneoki asked. The people there would follow him anywhere."

A flicker of irritation passed across the prince's features. "I've heard the same said about you."

Ōkami did not respond.

Lines of consternation formed above Raiden's brow. He looked down at the map of the city spread on the table before him. "I don't know that we can ask our people to help," he admitted quietly. "We've failed them in so many ways."

Ōkami considered the prince for a time. Despite the

image Prince Raiden wished to convey—one of unwavering strength—it was interesting to witness him struggle in so open a fashion. Ōkami would not have expected the prince to divulge any weaknesses before him.

"Begin with the nobility," Ōkami said. "Ask them to set the example of helping to secure the streets. Demand that they rally under your watch instead of only fighting to preserve the things they value."

Raiden nodded. "It's a good idea."

"It is not mine alone." Ōkami paused. "It helps to have friends at my back."

"I envy you your friends, Lord Ranmaruo."

Ōkami's eyes narrowed at the edges. As though the use of his given name had rekindled his anger. "Where is your wife?"

Raiden looked away. As though he were steeling himself.

Alarm flared through Ōkami. "Where is Mariko?"

"After she helped deliver your message, Roku ordered her to be placed beneath the castle."

It took Ōkami a moment to process this truth. Then— without warning—his rage overtook him. He unsheathed his *katana* with a rasp. "Why have you not set her free?"

Raiden looked at the blade brandished before him. A sadness tugged at his lips. "Because I was afraid of what my brother would to do me. What he might do to her."

"Be afraid of what I might do to you instead."

"You would not be wrong to seek vengeance." Raiden

winced. "My family has wronged yours in many ways." He took a deep breath, then bowed. "One day, I hope to ask for your forgiveness."

Ōkami clutched the hilt of his *katana* as confusion swarmed through his veins. "Forgiveness is not a thing granted. It is a thing earned." It was a phrase his father often used.

Its truth appeared to resonate with Raiden. He crouched before the table and removed an item concealed in its shadow. When he pulled back a length of muslin, the edge of an ivory and gold *samegawa* came into view.

"This belongs to you," Raiden said. He held up the sword, offering it to Ōkami with a curt bow.

Ōkami sheathed the blade he'd brandished in a threat only a moment before. Then he wrapped a hand around the hilt of his father's sword. The Fūrinkazan seemed to warm at his touch. The next instant, Raiden reached into his sleeve and removed an iron ring containing several keys.

"Follow me," Raiden said. "It is time we right another wrong."

Raiden unlocked Mariko's cell, his mind awash with thoughts. His recent exchange with Takeda Ranmaru had caused him a great deal of discomfort. It did not sit well with him to admit his faults. But their exchange also gave him a glimpse of what could be. A future in which Raiden relied upon the opinions of others. Saw the strength in consultation.

This feeling of possibility had begun with Mariko. It formed in the wake of her many admonitions. And he allowed his brother to imprison her. Threaten her.

He was not a husband to her. Much less a friend.

After the bars swung open, Mariko rose to her feet. Shock etched across her features.

Raiden could well understand her surprise.

Before her stood the boy she married. Next to him waited the man she loved.

It should have angered Raiden to know these things. Instead he felt a sense of calm. Of rightness, even in the face of so much uncertainty.

Mariko stood still. Takeda Ranmaru moved toward her, catching her in an embrace. Taking her hand in his. Making it clear to Raiden that he would not accept even a hint of challenge by her husband.

"We must hurry," Raiden said. "We will need to find my mother. Mariko must go into hiding at once, before Roku discovers she is gone."

As Mariko passed by him, she stopped. Turned to look up at his face.

"Thank you, Raiden."

He nodded. Then they raced through the labyrinth and made their way up the stairs. Though Raiden knew better than to let his guard down for even an instant, he had not been expecting it. That was why he did not realize what had happened until it was too late.

The dagger lodged itself deep within Raiden's breastplate, its tip sinking into his skin with precision. It stopped Raiden mid-step, his legs faltering. But he did not fall immediately. A figure hurled itself from the darkness. The mad screech that followed turned Raiden's blood to ice.

His brother. Roku.

"Raiden!" Mariko yelled.

Immediately Takeda Ranmaru tore the Fūrinkazan from his scabbard. Its blade glowed white. Roku grabbed the hilt of the dagger buried in Raiden's chest, trying to tear it free. When it refused to dislodge, he shoved Raiden at Lord Ranmaru, who immediate drew his weapon back so as not to injure Raiden.

The distraction gave Roku all the time he needed.

He turned on Mariko and attacked her.

In the next instant, Mariko grabbed the front of Roku's stained robe. He lunged for her throat, their bodies careening to the stone floor. Mariko used the momentum to propel them further, their bodies rolling as they struggled for control.

They did not slow down as they moved toward the stairs.

The daughter of Hattori Kano intended to throw their bodies into the underbelly of the castle. Takeda Ranmaru realized the truth in the same instant as Raiden.

He caught Mariko by the arm, yanking her back.

Raiden limped toward his brother, whose body had rolled to a halt a hairsbreadth from the top of the stairs.

"Traitor," Roku seethed. Blood dripped from his cracked lips. His chest moved in shallow breaths. "You think this is the end?" He coughed. "I will kill you, and I will watch your mother burn. Your whore wife will die alongside her. I will return to the city and take what is rightfully—"

Raiden kicked him down the stairs.

It was not a quick death. The heavenly sovereign of Wa did not go quietly. His screams echoed into the rafters, reverberating off the stones. The memory of his brother's cries would undoubtedly haunt Raiden for many years to come.

But when the Emperor of Wa stilled at the bottom of the stairs, it was not sadness that tore at Raiden's throat.

It was the bitter taste of relief.

Death's Due

Kanako's little sparrow delivered the news to her in the moon pavilion. It had spied on Raiden when her son had met with the son of Takeda Shingen. It watched when they descended into the bowels of Heian Castle and emerged not long after with Hattori Mariko in tow. It passed along the message that Raiden had been wounded, but would live.

It informed Kanako that Minamoto Roku was no more.

Finally. The ox had put an end to the reign of the rat.

Her lips parched and her throat dry, Kanako listened. She struggled to sit up. Called for help. Called for someone—anyone—to bear witness to her triumph. But it had taken nearly all her strength to move from her chambers to the moon pavilion.

No one heard her feeble cries. No one came to her aid. Why would they?

She'd arrived to Inako alone, many years ago. Disdained any advice or help. Permitted herself to be shunned at court, all in service to a great goal.

Now her son would become emperor.

It was time for Kanako to put an end to the looters and the distractions. Their purpose had been served. Kanako pulled her thoughts into a tight ball deep in her stomach, intent on opening her mind and releasing these souls from their bonds.

But she did not have the strength.

Again she called for help.

Again no one responded.

Kanako wished Raiden were here. A slow panic wrapped around her like a snake's deadly vise. She could not control the people she'd unleashed on the city. She was too weak. Her powers had fled.

"Help me," she said once more. Her cheek fell to the polished wood floor, its surface cool against her skin.

"My lady?" a muffled voice broke through Kanako's thoughts.

Two sets of footsteps rumbled across the floor. The first person—a young woman—knelt beside her.

"My lady Kanako?" the girl said.

Kanako looked up. Even through the haze surrounding her vision, she recognized the girl. She was the sister of Asano Tsuneoki. Yumi. The same girl Kanako had sworn to enact vengeance on for her brother's misdeeds that night at Akechi fortress.

403

Strange how far away that seemed in this moment. How ridiculous the idea of revenge felt in such a moment of triumph.

The second set of footsteps halted beside her. Heavier. Decidely male. Hope warmed through her chest. Perhaps her son had finally found her. Now they could rejoice together.

"Lady Kanako."

She recognized that voice. It was not the one she most wanted to hear.

Hattori Kenshin.

"I am no lady," Kanako said. She forced open her eyes. Forced herself to look up at the young man and young woman crouched above her. Her past and her future, perhaps in a different life. "My name is Oda Kanako. I am the illegitimate daughter of a fisherwoman and a *daimyō*. I was destined for greatness." Kanako closed her eyes. "And this is how I will achieve it." She pressed her hand to the floor of the moon pavilion, rooting herself to its magic.

With the last of her strength, she let the spider take shape from the silver of her ring. The demon swallowed her vision, her thoughts a muddle of blood and fear.

Through it all, she clung to an image of her son. An image of the boy Kanako knew would one day be a great man A sense of peace unfurled within her

But everything came with a price.

Kanako sent the spider toward her broken body. Let death collect its due.

All around the city of Inako, the lurching creatures halted. Collapsed where they stood. They did not move, though they still possessed the faintest of pulses. Soon they began to awaken, their memories lost, and their bodies aching from the pain of their ordeal.

As order began to be restored, the screams of before became cries of gratitude.

Inside the castle grounds—just beyond the moon pavilion—a young girl emerged from a colorless world. Half her face was scarred.

On her chest was the image of a handprint.

Epilogue

※

Mariko wandered by the burbling stream, her heart content. She'd just attended the city's celebration honoring their new emperor. A part of her still marveled at the turn of events. That she would feel such joy in her heart to know that Prince Raiden had ascended the Chrysanthemum Throne. It would be a story she told to those around her for years to come. Perhaps even shared with her children one day.

The time she'd been the wife of the emperor.

As she smiled to herself. Raiden would be a great emperor if he remained on this path.

Mariko felt a presence behind her. She turned in place, the silk of her elegant kimono shifting in the afternoon sun.

"Lord Ranmaru." She smiled brightly. "Our new shōgun."

Ōkami returned the gesture, but it did not touch his eyes. "You sent for me, my lady." He bowed.

"I did."

"It is an honor to be of service to our new empress."

Mariko laughed. "Let me know when you see her. I hope Raiden finds a strong match. One who tests his patience as much as he tests hers."

"What?" Confusion marred Ōkami's brow.

"I am not the empress of Wa, Takeda Ranmaru."

His eyes narrowed. "What did Raiden—"

"The *emperor*," she corrected, "informed me that since our wedding ceremony was interrupted before it was finalized, he had consulted with his advisors. Our marriage never took place." She grinned. "I am an unwed woman, whose reputation is forever tarnished by his rejection."

Ōkami stood there. Disbelief flashed across his features. Then suspicion.

"Did you send for me so that I would—"

"No. I'm going to do it," Mariko interrupted. "Lord Ranmaru, traitor and thief, will you marry a fallen woman with no chance of redemption in the eyes of our court?"

Ōkami laughed before he swept Mariko into his arms. "Yes," he whispered in her ear. The feeling of warmth as his breath passed over her skin sent a thrill up Mariko's spine.

"And will you swear never to interfere when I experiment with strange chemicals at all hours of the night?"

"Of course." Ōkami framed her face between his hands. "Upon who else would I rely for exploding gourds and crystals that burn brighter than flame?"

Mariko smiled up at him, her hands covering his. "And will you be happy if she wishes to do whatever suits her in that moment, even if it causes you fear?"

"I would expect nothing else." Ōkami pressed a kiss to her forehead. "Ours is a love stronger than fear and deeper than the sea," he said softly.

Then he kissed her. The touch of his lips ignited something inside her chest. It burned through her with a delicious pain. Made her feel alive as she'd never felt before.

There was music all around her. Mariko listened. Breathed deeply. The water flowing at her feet. A blue sky basking above.

This was what it meant to be truly free. To be herself and no one else.

To be loved as she was.

Glossary

Akuma—an evil spirit from folklore

amazura—a sweet syrup

anate—the command for "fire," as in "to fire an arrow"

ashigaru—foot soldiers

Bansenshukai—the ancient manual on the shinobi no mono, or the art of the ninja

bō—staff

boro—patchwork fabric worn by maidservants and peasants

bushidō—the way of the warrior

-chan—a diminutive and expression of endearment, as in Chiyo-chan

chūgi—loyalty; one of the tenets of bushidō

daifuku—a confection of glutinous rice stuffed with bean paste

daimyō—a feudal lord who is typically a vassal of the shōgun; the equivalent of an English earl

dō—chest armour

Fūrinkazan—a sword of light, associated with the Takeda clan; it is inscribed with the phrases As swift as the wind. As silent as the forest. As fierce as the fire. As unshakable as the mountain.

geiko—geisha

gi—integrity; one of the tenets of bushidō

Go—game

hachimaki—headband

hakama—traditional clothing of pleated trousers over a kimono top

haori—type of coat

honshō—true

ichi-go, ichi-e—one lifetime, one meeting; i.e., "live in the moment," "for this time only"

jin—benevolence; one of the tenets of bushidō

jinmaku—camp enclosure

jubokko—vampiric tree

kaburaya—a whistling arrow

kagemusha—a shadow warrior; man behind the scenes

kanabō—a spiked club or truncheon

kata—set combinations of movements for martial arts practice

katana—type of sword

koku—a unit of measurement, typically associated in feudal times with land

kosode—simple robe worn by both sexes

kunai—type of dagger

maiko—apprentice geiko

makoto—honesty; one of the tenets of bushidō

maru—castle bailey

meiyo—honor; one of the tenets of bushidō

naginata—bladed weapon on a long shaft

norimono—litter, vehicle; palanquin

obi—wide sash

okaa—mother

ponzu—sauce containing citrus, vinegar, and soy

rei—respect; one of the tenets of bushidō

rōnin—masterless samurai

ryō—gold currency

-sama—a term of respect, a little more formal than -san, as in
    Mariko-sama

samurai—a member of the military caste, typically in service to a
    liege lord or daimyō

-san—a term of respect, as in Akira-san

saya—scabbard

sensei—teacher

seppuku—ritual suicide

shamisen—stringed instrument

shinobi no mono—the art of the ninja

shodo—calligraphy

shōgun—military leader

sumimasen—I'm sorry, please, thank you

tabi—split-toed socks

tantō—blade shorter than the wakizashi

tatami—a woven mat traditionally made of rice straw

tatsumura—a rare type of silk gauze, used to fashion priceless kimono

tsuba—hand guard of a sword

uba—nursemaid

umeshu—plum wine

wakasama—young lord

wakizashi—blade similar to but shorter than the katana; samurai traditionally wear both blades at once

washi—a type of paper commonly made using fibers from the bark of the gampi tree

yabusame—mounted archers

yōkai—forest demon

yoroihitatare—armored robe

yūki—courage; one of the tenets of bushidō

yuzu—a small citrus fruit with a tart flavor similar to a pomelo

zori—type of sandals

YOUR GUIDE TO RENÉE AHDIEH:

EXPERIENCE
RENÉE AHDIEH'S
NEWEST SERIES

Sneak Peek on Next Page

STILL CRAVING
MORE
RENÉE AHDIEH?

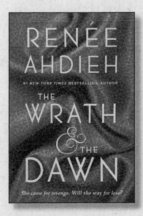

Excerpt on Page 423

———◇◇◇◇———

New Orleans is a city ruled by the dead.

I remember the moment I first heard someone say this. The old man meant to frighten me. He said there was a time when coffins sprang from the ground following a heavy rain, the dead flooding the city streets. He claimed to know of a Créole woman on Rue Dauphine who could commune with spirits from the afterlife.

I believe in magic. In a city rife with illusionists, it's impossible to doubt its existence. But I didn't believe this man. *Be faithful,* he warned. *For the faithless are alone in death, blind and terrified.*

I feigned shock at his words. In truth, I found him amusing. He was the sort to scare errant young souls with stories of a shadowy creature lurking in darkened alcoves. But I was also intrigued, for I possess an errant young soul of my own. From childhood, I hid it beneath pressed garments and polished words, but it persisted in plaguing me. It called to me like a Siren, driving me to dash all pretense against the rocks and surrender to my true nature.

It drove me to where I am now. But I am not ungrateful.

For it brought to bear two of my deepest truths: I will always possess an errant young soul, no matter my age.

And I will always be the shadowy creature in darkened alcoves, waiting . . .

For you, my love. For you.

NOT WHAT IT SEEMED

———⟡———

The *Aramis* was supposed to arrive at first light, like it did in Celine's dreams.

She would wake beneath a sunlit sky, the brine of the ocean winding through her nose, the city looming bright on the horizon.

Filled with promise. And absolution.

Instead the brass bell on the bow of the *Aramis* tolled in the twilight hour, the time of day her friend Pippa called "the gloaming." It was—in Celine's mind—a very British thing to say.

She'd begun collecting these phrases not long after she'd met Pippa four weeks ago, when the *Aramis* had docked for two days in Liverpool. Her favorite so far was "not bloody likely." Celine didn't know why they mattered to her at the time. Perhaps it was because she thought Very British Things would serve her better in America than the Very French Things she was apt to say.

The moment Celine heard the bell clang, she made her way portside, Pippa's light footsteps trailing in her wake. Inky tendrils of darkness fanned out across the sky, a ghostly mist shrouding the Crescent City. The air thickened as the two girls listened to the *Aramis* sluice through the waters of the Mississippi, drawing closer to New Orleans. Farther from the lives they'd left behind.

Pippa sniffed and rubbed her nose. In that instant, she looked younger than her sixteen years. "For all the stories, it's not as pretty as I thought it would be."

"It's exactly what I thought it would be," Celine said in a reassuring tone.

"Don't lie." Pippa glanced at her sidelong. "It won't make me feel better."

A smile curled up Celine's face. "Maybe I'm lying for me as much as I'm lying for you."

"In any case, lying is a sin."

"So is being obnoxious."

"That's not in the Bible."

"But it should be."

Pippa coughed, trying to mask her amusement. "You're terrible. The sisters at the Ursuline convent won't know what to do with you."

"They'll do the same thing they do with every unmarried girl who disembarks in New Orleans, carrying with her all her worldly possessions: they'll find me a husband." Celine refrained from frowning. This had been her choice. The best of the worst.

"If you strike them as ungodly, they'll match you with the ugliest fool in Christendom. Definitely someone with a bulbous nose and a paunch."

"Better an ugly man than a boring one. And a paunch means he eats well, so . . ." Celine canted her head to one side.

"Really, Celine." Pippa laughed, her Yorkshire accent weaving through the words like fine Chantilly lace. "You're the most incorrigible French girl I've ever met."

Celine smiled at her friend. "I'd wager you haven't met many French girls."

"At least not ones who speak English as well as you do. As if you were born to it."

"My father thought it was important for me to learn." Celine lifted one shoulder, as though this were the whole of it, instead of barely half. At the mention of her father—a staid Frenchman who'd studied linguistics at Oxford—a shadow threatened to descend. A sadness with a weight Celine could not yet bear. She fixed a wry grin on her face.

Pippa crossed her arms as though she were hugging herself. Worry gathered beneath the fringe of blond on her forehead as the two girls continued studying the city in the distance. Every young woman on board had heard the whispered accounts. At sea, the myths they'd shared over cups of gritty, bitter coffee had taken on lives of their own. They'd blended with the stories of the Old World to form richer, darker tales. New Orleans was haunted. Cursed by pirates. Prowled by scalawags. A last refuge for those who believed in magic and mysticism. Why, there was even talk of women possessing as much power and influence as that of any man.

Celine had laughed at this. As she'd dared to hope. Perhaps New Orleans was not what it seemed at first glance. Fittingly, neither was she.

And if anything could be said about the young travelers

aboard the *Aramis*, it was that the possibility of magic like this—a world like this—had become a vital thing. Especially for those who wished to shed the specter of their pasts. To become something better and brighter.

And especially for those who wanted to escape.

Pippa and Celine watched as they drew closer to the unknown. To their futures.

"I'm frightened," Pippa said softly.

Celine did not respond. Night had seeped through the water, like a dark stain across organza. A scraggly sailor balanced along a wooden beam with all the grace of an aerialist while lighting a lamp on the ship's prow. As if in response, tongues of fire leapt to life across the water, rendering the city in even more ghoulishly green tones.

The bell of the *Aramis* pealed once more, telling those along the port how far the ship had left to travel. Other passengers made their way from below deck, coming to stand alongside Celine and Pippa, muttering in Portuguese and Spanish, English and French, German and Dutch. Young women who'd taken leaps of faith and left their homelands for new opportunities. Their words melted into a soft cacophony of sound that would—under normal circumstances—soothe Celine.

Not anymore.

Ever since that fateful night amid the silks in the atelier, Celine had longed for comfortable silence. It had been weeks since she'd felt safe in the presence of others. Safe with the riot of her own thoughts. The closest she'd ever come to wading through calmer waters had been in the presence of Pippa.

When the ship drew near enough to dock, Pippa took sudden hold of Celine's wrist, as though to steel herself. Celine gasped. Flinched at the unexpected touch. Like a spray of blood had shot across her face, the salt of it staining her lips.

"Celine?" Pippa asked, her blue eyes wide. "What's wrong?"

Breathing through her nose to steady her pulse, Celine wrapped both hands around Pippa's cold fingers. "I'm frightened, too."

TURN THE PAGE
FOR AN EXCERPT OF

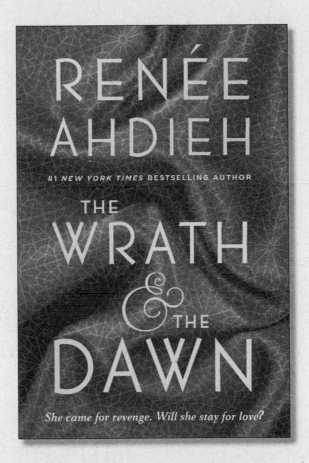

RENÉE
AHDIEH

#1 *NEW YORK TIMES* BESTSELLING AUTHOR

THE
WRATH
&
THE
DAWN

She came for revenge. Will she stay for love?

MEDITATIONS
ON GOSSAMER AND GOLD

THEY WERE NOT GENTLE. AND WHY SHOULD THEY BE?
After all, they did not expect her to live past the next morning.

The hands that tugged ivory combs through Shahrzad's waist-length hair and scrubbed sandalwood paste on her bronze arms did so with a brutal kind of detachment.

Shahrzad watched one young servant girl dust her bare shoulders with flakes of gold that caught the light from the setting sun.

A breeze gusted along the gossamer curtains lining the walls of the chamber. The sweet scent of citrus blossoms wafted through the carved wooden screens leading to the terrace, whispering of a freedom now beyond reach.

This was my choice. Remember Shiva.

"I don't wear necklaces," Shahrzad said when another girl began to fasten a jewel-encrusted behemoth around her throat.

"It is a gift from the caliph. You must wear it, my lady."

Shahrzad stared down at the slight girl in amused disbelief. "And if I don't? Will he kill me?"

"Please, my lady, I—"

Shahrzad sighed. "I suppose now is not the time to make this point."

"Yes, my lady."

"My name is Shahrzad."

"I know, my lady." The girl glanced away in discomfort before turning to assist with Shahrzad's gilded mantle. As the two young women eased the weighty garment onto her glittering shoulders, Shahrzad studied the finished product in the mirror before her.

Her midnight tresses gleamed like polished obsidian, and her hazel eyes were edged in alternating strokes of black kohl and liquid gold. At the center of her brow hung a teardrop ruby the size of her thumb; its mate dangled from a thin chain around her bare waist, grazing the silk sash of her trowsers. The mantle itself was pale damask and threaded with silver and gold in an intricate pattern that grew ever chaotic as it flared by her feet.

I look like a gilded peacock.

"Do they all look this ridiculous?" Shahrzad asked.

Again, the two young women averted their gazes with unease.

I'm sure Shiva didn't look this ridiculous . . .

Shahrzad's expression hardened.

Shiva would have looked beautiful. Beautiful and strong.

Her fingernails dug into her palms; tiny crescents of steely resolve.

At the sound of a quiet knock at the door, three heads turned— their collective breaths bated.

In spite of her newfound mettle, Shahrzad's heart began to pound.

"May I come in?" The soft voice of her father broke through the silence, pleading and laced in tacit apology.

Shahrzad exhaled slowly . . . carefully.

"Baba, what are you doing here?" Her words were patient, yet wary.

Jahandar al-Khayzuran shuffled into the chamber. His beard and temples were streaked with grey, and the myriad colors in his hazel eyes shimmered and shifted like the sea in the midst of a storm.

In his hand was a single budding rose, its center leached of color, and the tips of its petals tinged a beautiful, blushing mauve.

"Where is Irsa?" Shahrzad asked, alarm seeping into her tone.

Her father smiled sadly. "She is at home. I did not allow her to come with me, though she fought and raged until the last possible moment."

At least in this he has not ignored my wishes.

"You should be with her. She needs you tonight. Please do this for me, Baba? Do as we discussed?" She reached out and took his free hand, squeezing tightly, beseeching him in her grip to follow the plans she had laid out in the days before.

"I—I can't, my child." Jahandar lowered his head, a sob rising in his chest, his thin shoulders trembling with grief. "Shahrzad—"

"Be strong. For Irsa. I promise you, everything will be fine." Shahrzad raised her palm to his weathered face and brushed away the smattering of tears from his cheek.

"I cannot. The thought that this may be your last sunset—"

"It will not be the last. I will see tomorrow's sunset. This I swear to you."

Jahandar nodded, his misery nowhere close to mollified. He held out the rose in his hand. "The last from my garden; it has not yet bloomed fully, but I wanted to give you one remembrance of home."

She smiled as she reached for it, the love between them far past mere gratitude, but he stopped her. When she realized the reason, she began to protest.

"No. At least in this, I might do something for you," he muttered, almost to himself. He stared at the rose, his brow furrowed and his mouth drawn. One servant girl coughed in her fist while the other looked to the floor.

Shahrzad waited patiently. Knowingly.

The rose started to unfurl. Its petals twisted open, prodded to life by an invisible hand. As it expanded, a delicious perfume filled the space between them, sweet and perfect for an instant . . . but soon, it became overpowering. Cloying. The edges of the flower changed from a brilliant, deep pink to a shadowy rust in the blink of an eye.

And then the flower began to wither and die.

Dismayed, Jahandar watched its dried petals wilt to the white marble at their feet.

"I—I'm sorry, Shahrzad," he cried.

"It doesn't matter. I will never forget how beautiful it was for that moment, Baba." She wrapped her arms around his neck and pulled him close. By his ear, in a voice so low only he could hear, she said, "Go to Tariq, as you promised. Take Irsa and go."

He nodded, his eyes shimmering once more. "I love you, my child."

"And I love you. I will keep my promises. All of them."

Overcome, Jahandar blinked down at his elder daughter in silence.

This time, the knock at the door demanded attention rather than requested it.

Shahrzad's forehead whipped back in its direction, the bloodred ruby swinging in tandem. She squared her shoulders and lifted her pointed chin.

Jahandar stood to the side, covering his face with his hands, as his daughter marched forward.

"I'm sorry—so very sorry," she whispered to him before striding across the threshold to follow the contingent of guards leading the processional. Jahandar slid to his knees and sobbed as Shahrzad turned the corner and disappeared.

With her father's grief resounding through the halls, Shahrzad's feet refused to carry her but a few steps down the cavernous corridors of the palace. She halted, her knees shaking beneath the thin silk of her voluminous *sirwal* trowsers.

"My lady?" one of the guards prompted in a bored tone.

"He can wait," Shahrzad gasped.

The guards exchanged glances.

Her own tears threatening to blaze a telltale trail down her cheeks, Shahrzad pressed a hand to her chest. Unwittingly, her fingertips brushed the edge of the thick gold necklace clasped around her throat, festooned with gems of outlandish size and untold variety. It felt heavy . . . stifling. Like a bejeweled fetter. She allowed her fingers to wrap around the offending instrument, thinking for a moment to rip it from her body.

The rage was comforting. A friendly reminder.

Shiva.

Her dearest friend. Her closest confidante.

She curled her toes within their sandals of braided bullion and threw back her shoulders once more. Without a word, she resumed her march.

Again, the guards looked to one another for an instant.

When they reached the massive double doors leading into the throne room, Shahrzad realized her heart was racing at twice its normal speed. The doors swung open with a distended groan, and she focused on her target, ignoring all else around her.

At the very end of the immense space stood Khalid Ibn al-Rashid, the Caliph of Khorasan.

The King of Kings.

The monster from my nightmares.

With every step she took, Shahrzad felt the hate rise in her blood, along with the clarity of purpose. She stared at him, her eyes never wavering. His proud carriage stood out amongst the men in his retinue, and details began to emerge the closer she drew to his side.

He was tall and trim, with the build of a young man proficient in warfare. His dark hair was straight and styled in a manner suggesting a desire for order in all things.

As she strode onto the dais, she looked up at him, refusing to balk, even in the face of her king.

His thick eyebrows raised a fraction. They framed eyes so pale a shade of brown they appeared amber in certain flashes of light, like those of a tiger. His profile was an artist's study in angles, and he remained motionless as he returned her watchful scrutiny.

A face that cut; a gaze that pierced.

He reached a hand out to her.

Just as she extended her palm to grasp it, she remembered to bow.

The wrath seethed below the surface, bringing a flush to her cheeks.

When she met his eyes again, he blinked once.

"Wife." He nodded.

"My king."

I will live to see tomorrow's sunset. Make no mistake. I swear I will live to see as many sunsets as it takes.

And I will kill you.

With my own hands.

acknowledgments

Debts of gratitude are interesting things. Sometimes I think they can never be truly paid. But I want everyone included here to know: If ever you wish to hurl sense into the wind and write a book, I will be there to support all your harebrained schemes and clean up every single one of the notecards you leave strewn about like writerly petals.

To my agent, Barbara Poelle: Thank you for answering all my questions, never hesitating to charge into the fray, and offering me the kind of guidance that extends far beyond books. I'm grateful beyond words for you.

To my editor, Stacey Barney: I have such respect for you and your brilliant insight and your beautiful laughter. Thank you for being my champion and never hesitating to challenge me. My books are what they are because of you.

To my Penguin team: None of this is possible without you. A special note of thanks to my publicist, Marisa Russell, for always supporting me and being such a tremendous advocate. Shout-outs to Carmela Iaria, Venessa Carson, Doni Kay, Christina Colangelo, Kara Brammer, Theresa Evangelista, Elyse Marshall, Shanta Newlin, Erin Berger, Colleen Conway, Allan Winebarger, Kaitlin Kneafsey, Felicia Frazer, Lindsay Boggs, Emily Romero, Caitlin Whalen, Jocelyn Schmidt, Felicity Vallence, Elora Sullivan, and Bri Lockhart.

Thank you to all the readers, librarians, bloggers, and book lovers from all corners of the globe for all your enthusiasm and support. Book people are the best people.

To Joy Callaway, Ricki Schultz, Sarah Henning, JJ, Roshani Chokshi, Carrie Ryan, Marie Rutkoski, Sarah Nicole Lemon, Emily Pan, Sona Charaipotra, Marie Lu, Dhonielle Clayton, and Brendan Reichs: Thank you for being the kind of friends who always participate in group texts. Without you, no plans would be made. Ever.

To Sabaa: There are no words left to convey how lucky I feel to call you friend. Also, I just sent you a text. Are you still awake?

To Elaine: Seventeen years strong. Thank you for wiping away every tear, staying up to eat the leftovers with me, and always laughing at my dumb jokes. My life is better and brighter because of you.

To Erica: Let's not count the years. But thank you for being my sister. It's one of the best gifts I've ever been given. Also, thank you for Chris. He's another amazing gift, but don't tell him I said that. He won't read this, so it can be our secret.

To Ian and my new sister Izzy: I'm so glad to share a family with you both.

To Omid, Julie, Navid, Jinda, Evelyn, Isabelle, Andrew, Ella, and Lily: I am so grateful for all of you. Thank you so much for coming to all the signings, waiting in line, and buying a book you already have just so you can tell someone else about it. Also, Lily: Your email brightened my day.

To all four of my parents: Thank you for your unceasing love and guidance.

And to Vic: You are better than magic.

Photo credit: Crystal Stokes

RENÉE AHDIEH is a graduate of the University of North Carolina at Chapel Hill. In her spare time, she likes to dance salsa and collect shoes. She is passionate about all kinds of curry, rescue dogs, and college basketball. The first few years of her life were spent in a high-rise in South Korea; consequently, Renée enjoys having her head in the clouds. She lives in Charlotte, North Carolina, with her husband and their tiny overlord of a dog. She is the author of *The Beautiful*, *Flame in the Mist*, and *Smoke in the Sun* as well as the #1 *New York Times* bestselling *The Wrath & the Dawn* and its sequel, *The Rose & the Dagger*.

You can visit Renée Ahdieh at
reneeahdieh.com